MEGA MAN™

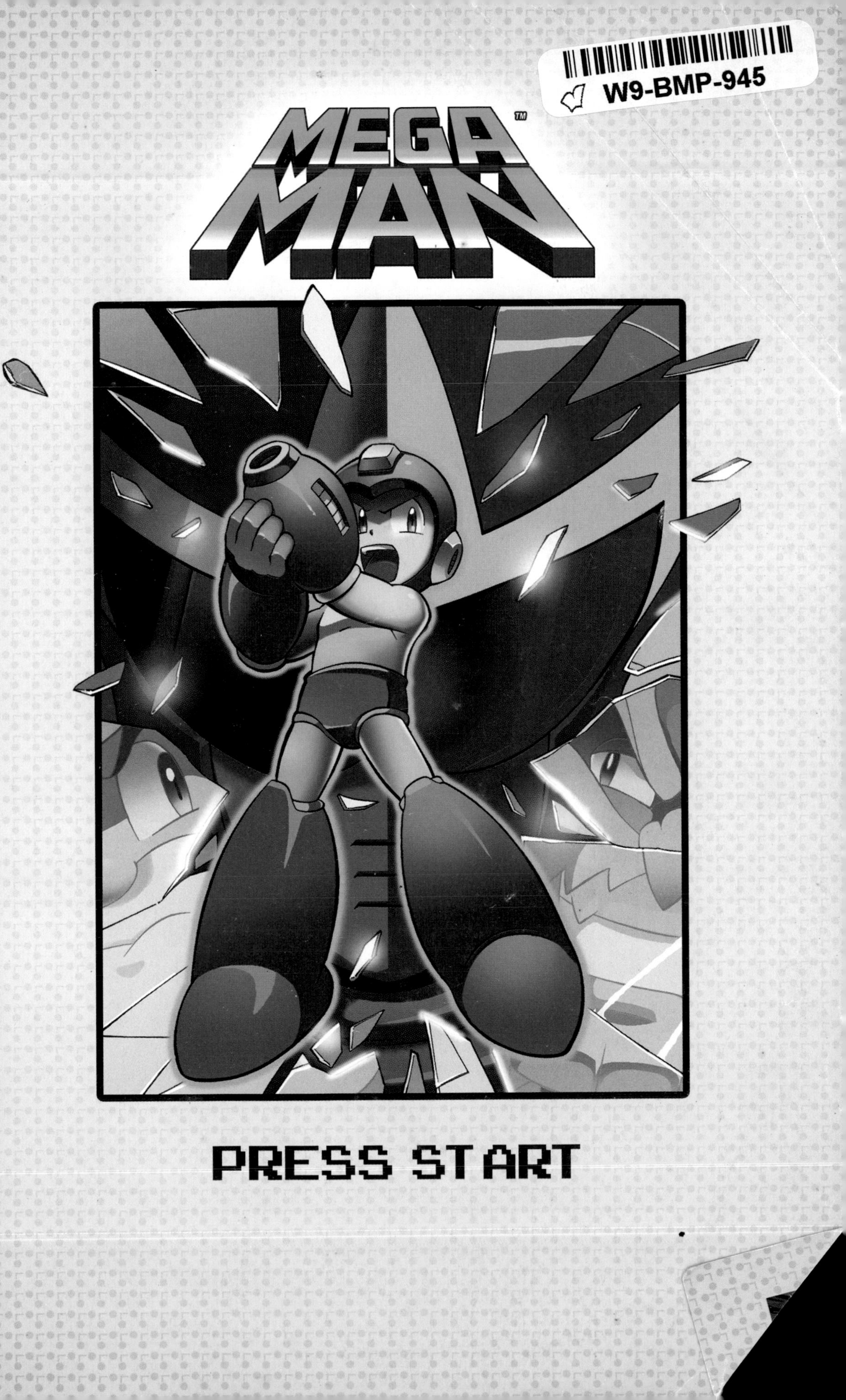

PRESS START

MEGA MAN™

VOLUME SIX:
BREAKING POINT

IAN FLYNN
WRITER

RYAN JAMPOLE
PENCILS

GARY MARTIN
INKS

MATT HERMS
COLORS

JOHN WORKMAN
LETTERS

**JAMAL PEPPERS,
GARY MARTIN
& MATT HERMS**
COVER

VINCENT LOVALLO
ASSISTANT EDITOR

PAUL KAMINSKI
EDITOR/EXECUTIVE
DIRECTOR OF EDITORIAL

**SPECIAL THANKS TO
BRIAN OLIVEIRA
AT CAPCOM LICENSING
AND TO** 飛田　栄実

ARCHIE COMIC PUBLICATIONS, INC.
JONATHAN GOLDWATER, publisher/co-ceo
NANCY SILBERKLEIT, co-ceo
MIKE PELLERITO, president
VICTOR GORELICK, co-president, e-i-c
JIM SOKOLOWSKI, senior vice president of sales
and business development
HAROLD BUCHHOLZ, senior vice president of
publishing and operations
PAUL KAMINSKI, exec. director of
editorial/compilation editor
VINCENT LOVALLO, assistant editor
STEPHEN OSWALD, production manager
STEVEN SCOTT, director of publicity
and marketing
CARLY INGLIS, editorial assistant/proofreader
ELIZABETH BORGATTI, book design

MEGA MAN VOL. 6 : BREAKING POINT. 2014. Printed in Canada. Published by Archie Comic
Publications, Inc., 325 Fayette Avenue, Mamaroneck, NY 10543-2318. Originally published in
single magazine form in Mega Man # 21-23 and 28. Jonathan Goldwater, Publisher/Co-CEO,
Nancy Silberkleit, Co-CEO, Mike Pellerito, President. Victor Gorelick, Co-President. © CAPCOM.
This product is published and sold by Archie Comic Publications, Inc. utilizing Capcom's
intellectual property, under license by Capcom. www.capcom.com. Any similarities between
characters, names, persons, and/or institutions in this book and any living, dead, or fictional
characters, names, persons, and/or institutions are not intended and if they exist, are purely
coincidental. Title registered in U.S. Copyright office. Nothing may be reprinted in whole or
part without written permission from Archie Comic Publications, Inc.
ISBN: 978-1-936975-78-5

TABLE OF CONTENTS

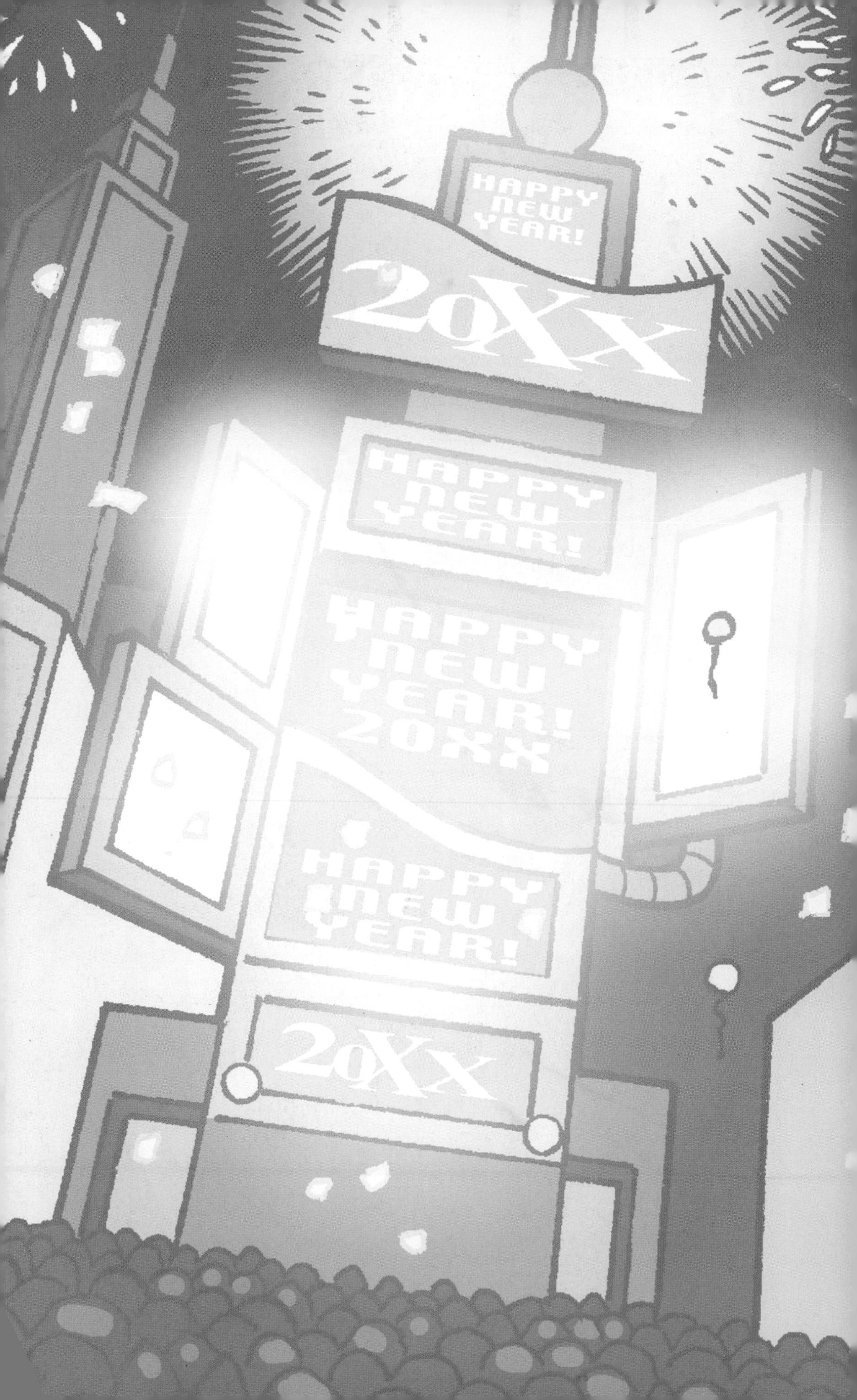

HAPPY NEW YEAR!
20XX
HAPPY NEW YEAR!
HAPPY NEW YEAR! 20XX
HAPPY NEW YEAR!
20XX

CHAPTER 1
COVER BY CHAD THOMAS
GARY MARTIN AND MATT HERMS

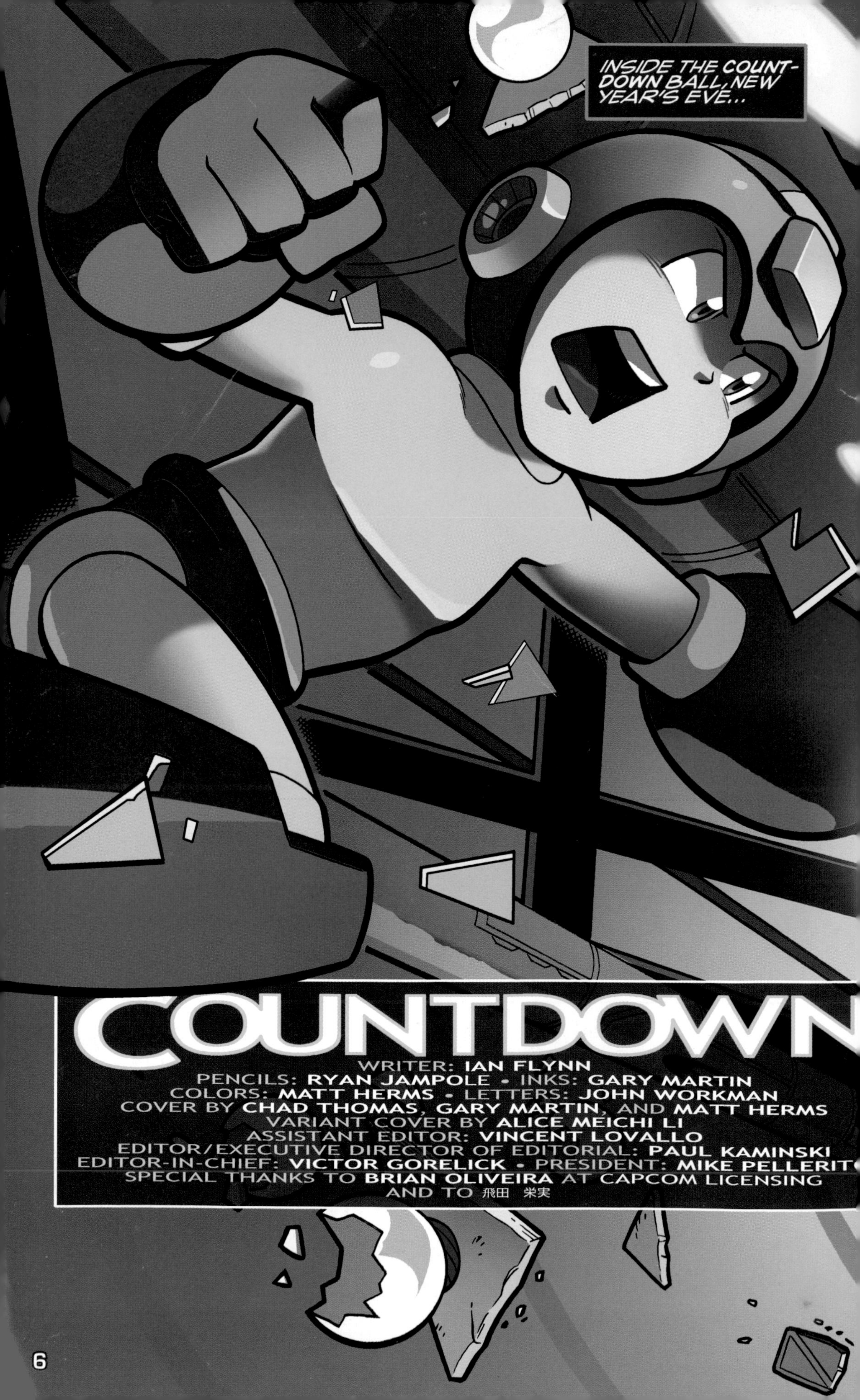
INSIDE THE COUNT-DOWN BALL, NEW YEAR'S EVE...
COUNTDOWN
WRITER: IAN FLYNN
PENCILS: RYAN JAMPOLE • INKS: GARY MARTIN
COLORS: MATT HERMS • LETTERS: JOHN WORKMAN
COVER BY CHAD THOMAS, GARY MARTIN, AND MATT HERMS
VARIANT COVER BY ALICE MEICHI LI
ASSISTANT EDITOR: VINCENT LOVALLO
EDITOR/EXECUTIVE DIRECTOR OF EDITORIAL: PAUL KAMINSKI
EDITOR-IN-CHIEF: VICTOR GORELICK • PRESIDENT: MIKE PELLERITO
SPECIAL THANKS TO BRIAN OLIVEIRA AT CAPCOM LICENSING
AND TO 飛田　栄実

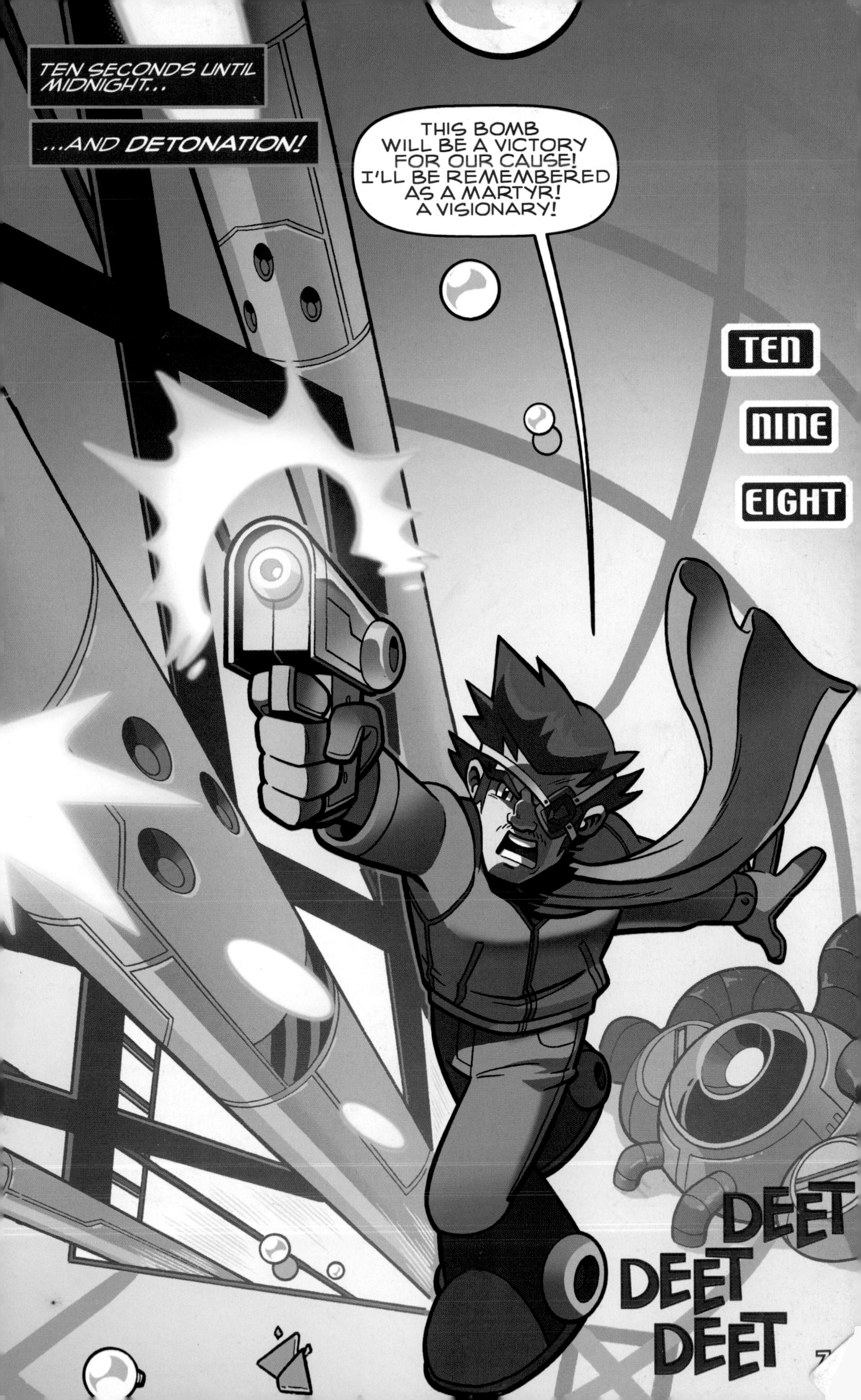
TEN SECONDS UNTIL MIDNIGHT...
...AND DETONATION!
THIS BOMB WILL BE A VICTORY FOR OUR CAUSE! I'LL BE REMEMBERED AS A MARTYR! A VISIONARY!
TEN
NINE
EIGHT
DEET
DEET
DEET

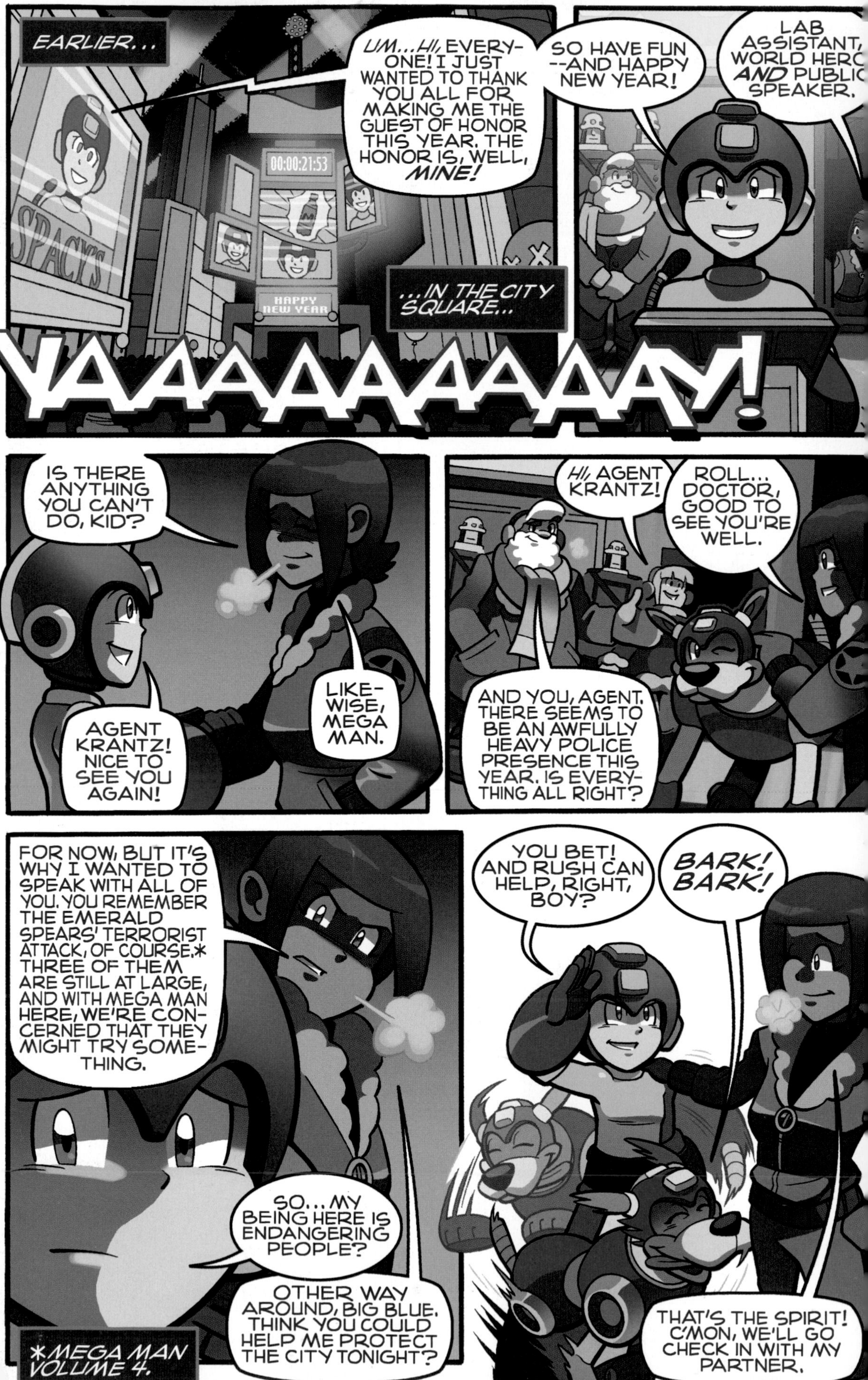

EARLIER...
UM...HI, EVERYONE! I JUST WANTED TO THANK YOU ALL FOR MAKING ME THE GUEST OF HONOR THIS YEAR. THE HONOR IS, WELL, MINE!
SPACY'S
00:00:21:53
HAPPY NEW YEAR
...IN THE CITY SQUARE...
SO HAVE FUN --AND HAPPY NEW YEAR!
LAB ASSISTANT, WORLD HERO AND PUBLIC SPEAKER.
YAAAAAAAAAY!
IS THERE ANYTHING YOU CAN'T DO, KID?
AGENT KRANTZ! NICE TO SEE YOU AGAIN!
LIKE-WISE, MEGA MAN.
HI, AGENT KRANTZ!
ROLL... DOCTOR, GOOD TO SEE YOU'RE WELL.
AND YOU, AGENT. THERE SEEMS TO BE AN AWFULLY HEAVY POLICE PRESENCE THIS YEAR. IS EVERYTHING ALL RIGHT?
FOR NOW, BUT IT'S WHY I WANTED TO SPEAK WITH ALL OF YOU. YOU REMEMBER THE EMERALD SPEARS' TERRORIST ATTACK, OF COURSE.* THREE OF THEM ARE STILL AT LARGE, AND WITH MEGA MAN HERE, WE'RE CONCERNED THAT THEY MIGHT TRY SOMETHING.
SO... MY BEING HERE IS ENDANGERING PEOPLE?
OTHER WAY AROUND, BIG BLUE. THINK YOU COULD HELP ME PROTECT THE CITY TONIGHT?
*MEGA MAN VOLUME 4.
YOU BET! AND RUSH CAN HELP, RIGHT, BOY?
BARK! BARK!
THAT'S THE SPIRIT! C'MON, WE'LL GO CHECK IN WITH MY PARTNER.

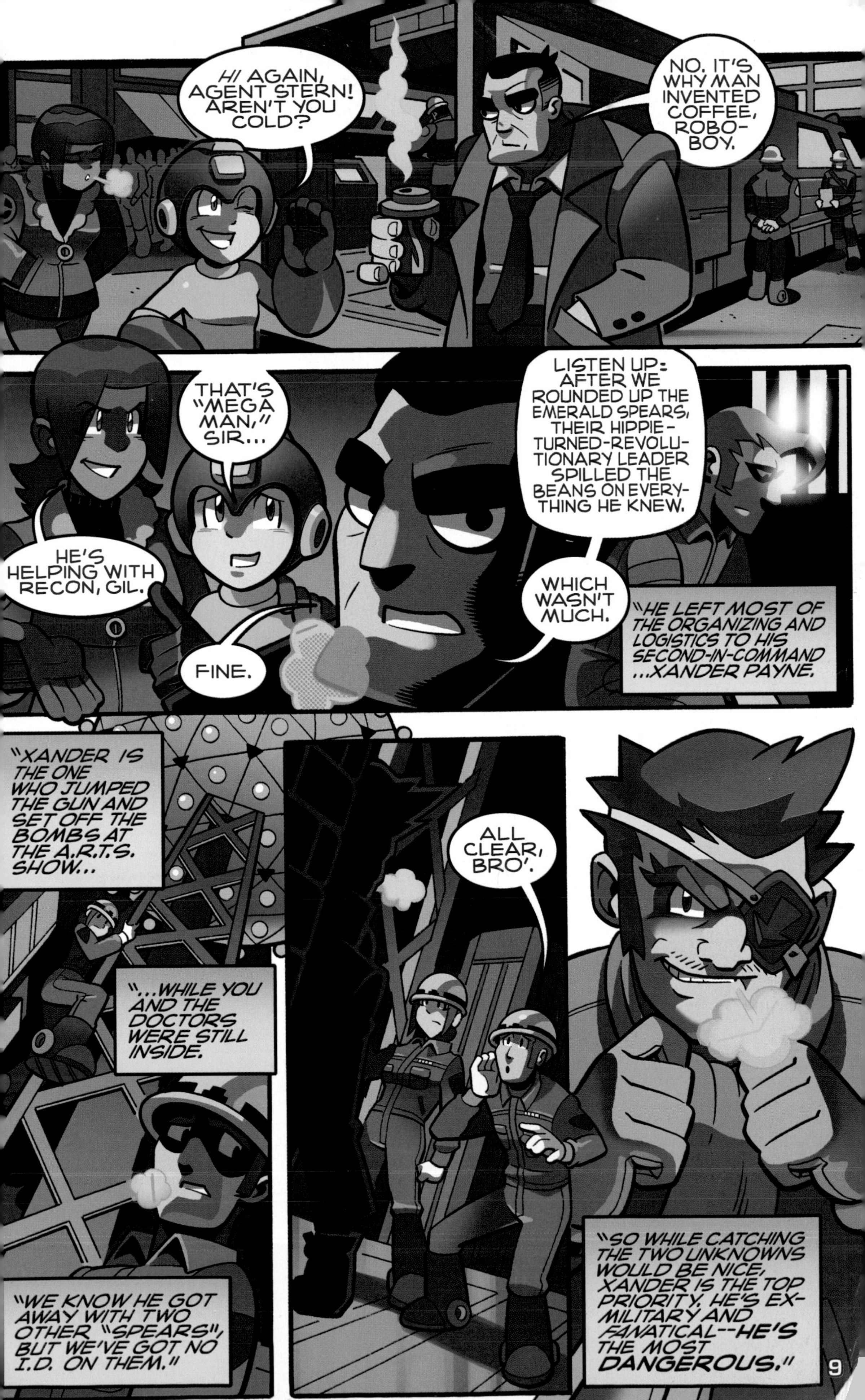
HI AGAIN, AGENT STERN! AREN'T YOU COLD?
NO, IT'S WHY MAN INVENTED COFFEE, ROBO-BOY.
THAT'S "MEGA MAN," SIR...
HE'S HELPING WITH RECON, GIL.
FINE.
LISTEN UP: AFTER WE ROUNDED UP THE EMERALD SPEARS, THEIR HIPPIE-TURNED-REVOLUTIONARY LEADER SPILLED THE BEANS ON EVERYTHING HE KNEW.
WHICH WASN'T MUCH.
"HE LEFT MOST OF THE ORGANIZING AND LOGISTICS TO HIS SECOND-IN-COMMAND ...XANDER PAYNE.
"XANDER IS THE ONE WHO JUMPED THE GUN AND SET OFF THE BOMBS AT THE A.R.T.S. SHOW...
"...WHILE YOU AND THE DOCTORS WERE STILL INSIDE.
"WE KNOW HE GOT AWAY WITH TWO OTHER "SPEARS", BUT WE'VE GOT NO I.D. ON THEM."
ALL CLEAR, BRO'.
"SO WHILE CATCHING THE TWO UNKNOWNS WOULD BE NICE, XANDER IS THE TOP PRIORITY. HE'S EX-MILITARY AND FANATICAL--HE'S THE MOST DANGEROUS."

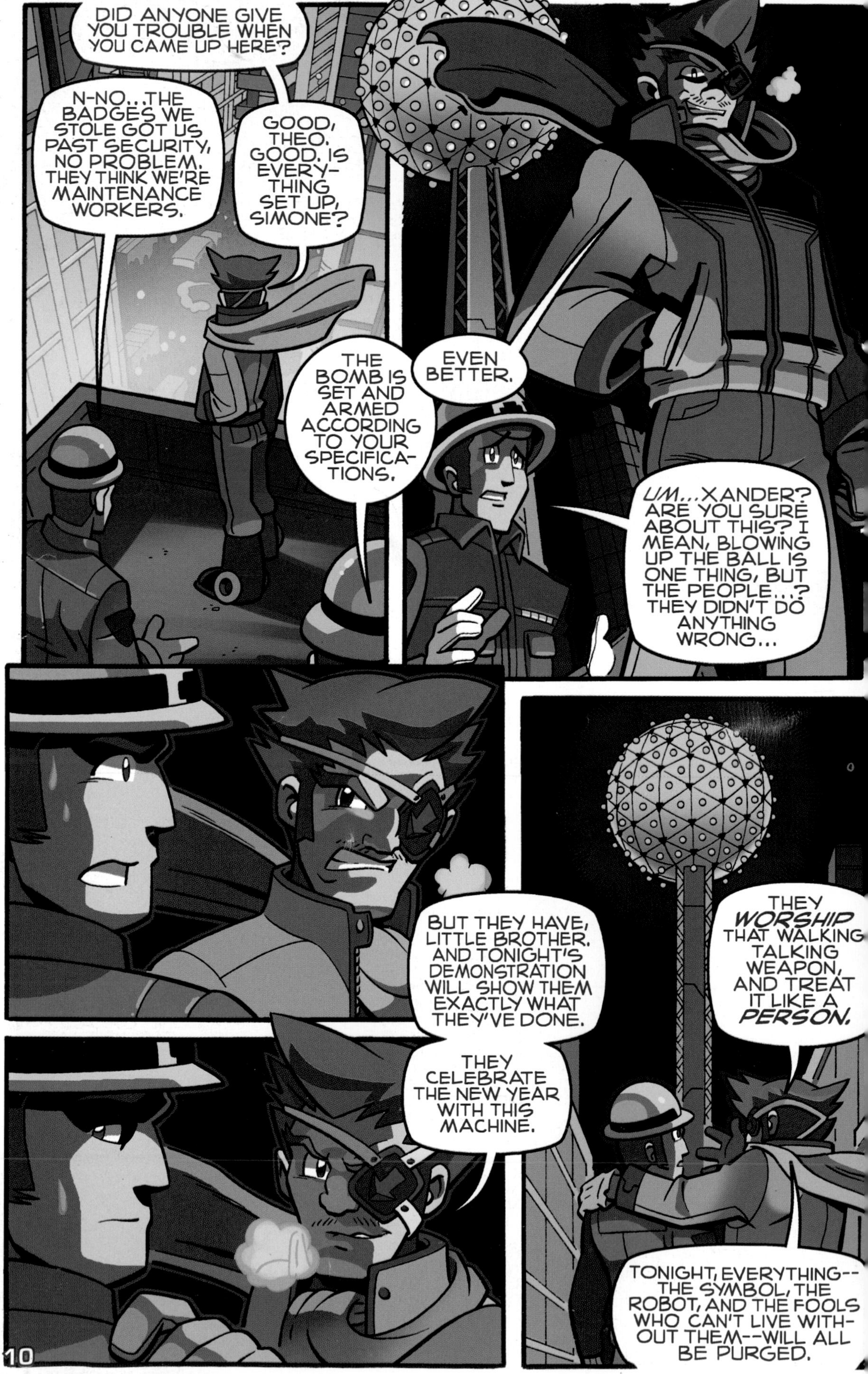
DID ANYONE GIVE YOU TROUBLE WHEN YOU CAME UP HERE?
N-NO...THE BADGES WE STOLE GOT US PAST SECURITY, NO PROBLEM. THEY THINK WE'RE MAINTENANCE WORKERS.
GOOD, THEO. GOOD. IS EVERY-THING SET UP, SIMONE?
THE BOMB IS SET AND ARMED ACCORDING TO YOUR SPECIFICA-TIONS.
EVEN BETTER.
UM...XANDER? ARE YOU SURE ABOUT THIS? I MEAN, BLOWING UP THE BALL IS ONE THING, BUT THE PEOPLE...? THEY DIDN'T DO ANYTHING WRONG...
BUT THEY HAVE, LITTLE BROTHER. AND TONIGHT'S DEMONSTRATION WILL SHOW THEM EXACTLY WHAT THEY'VE DONE.
THEY CELEBRATE THE NEW YEAR WITH THIS MACHINE.
THEY WORSHIP THAT WALKING TALKING WEAPON, AND TREAT IT LIKE A PERSON.
TONIGHT, EVERYTHING--THE SYMBOL, THE ROBOT, AND THE FOOLS WHO CAN'T LIVE WITH-OUT THEM--WILL ALL BE PURGED.

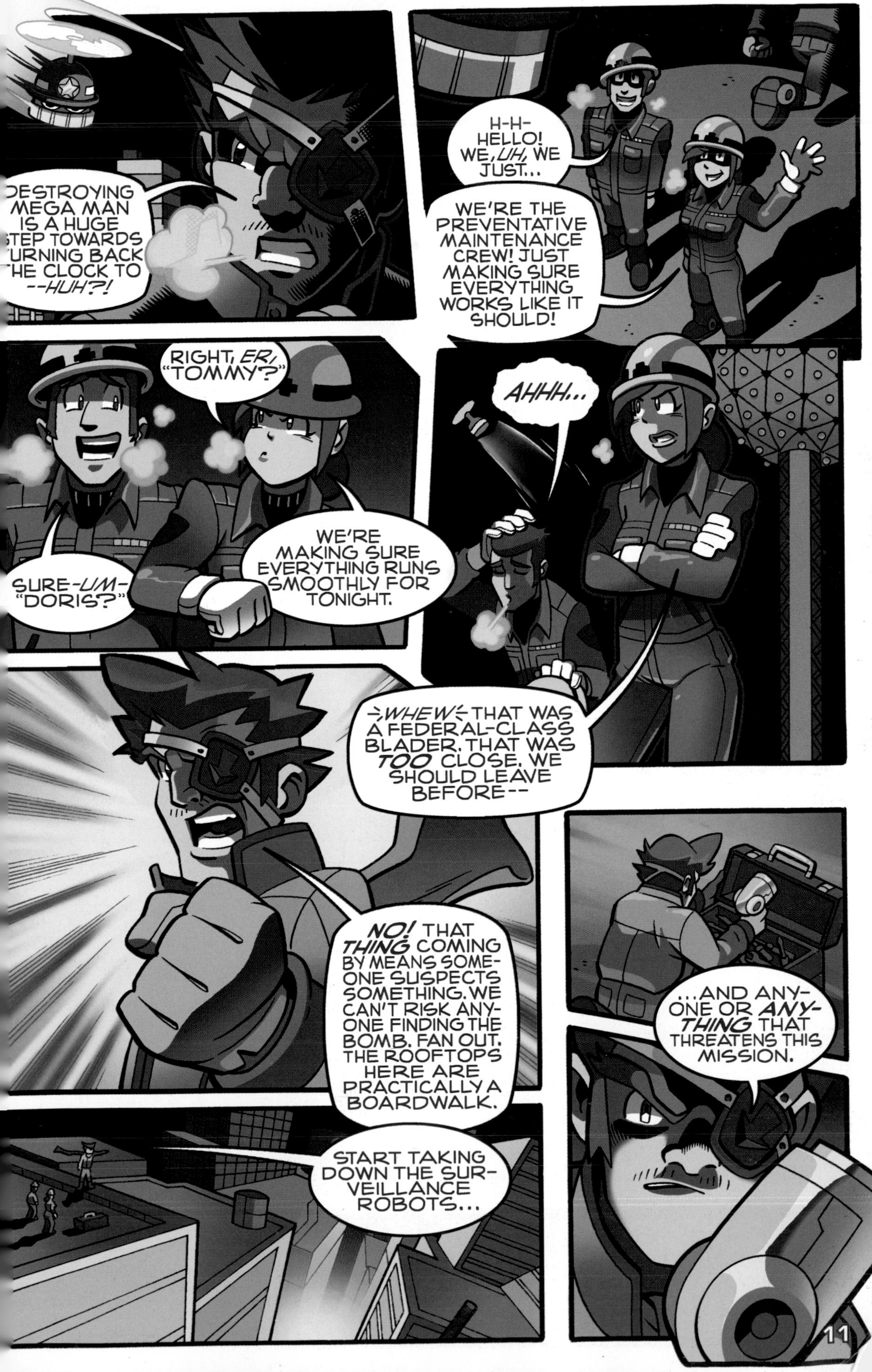
DESTROYING MEGA MAN IS A HUGE STEP TOWARDS TURNING BACK THE CLOCK TO --HUH?!
H-H- HELLO! WE, UH, WE JUST...
WE'RE THE PREVENTATIVE MAINTENANCE CREW! JUST MAKING SURE EVERYTHING WORKS LIKE IT SHOULD!
RIGHT, ER, "TOMMY?"
SURE-UM- "DORIS?"
WE'RE MAKING SURE EVERYTHING RUNS SMOOTHLY FOR TONIGHT.
AHHH...
WHEW THAT WAS A FEDERAL-CLASS BLADER. THAT WAS TOO CLOSE. WE SHOULD LEAVE BEFORE--
NO! THAT THING COMING BY MEANS SOME-ONE SUSPECTS SOMETHING. WE CAN'T RISK ANY-ONE FINDING THE BOMB. FAN OUT. THE ROOFTOPS HERE ARE PRACTICALLY A BOARDWALK.
START TAKING DOWN THE SUR-VEILLANCE ROBOTS...
...AND ANY-ONE OR ANY-THING THAT THREATENS THIS MISSION.

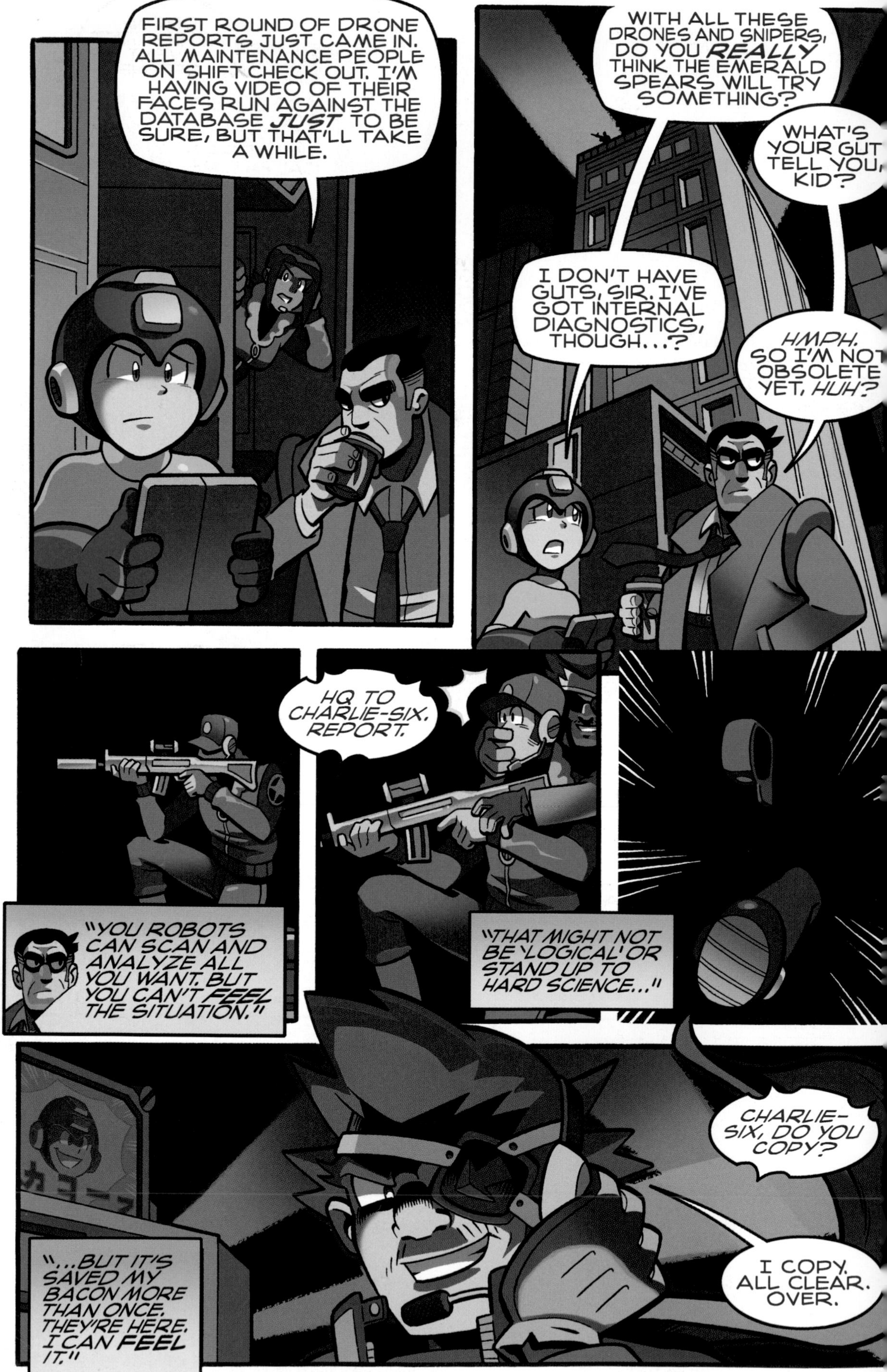
FIRST ROUND OF DRONE REPORTS JUST CAME IN. ALL MAINTENANCE PEOPLE ON SHIFT CHECK OUT. I'M HAVING VIDEO OF THEIR FACES RUN AGAINST THE DATABASE *JUST* TO BE SURE, BUT THAT'LL TAKE A WHILE.
WITH ALL THESE DRONES AND SNIPERS, DO YOU ***REALLY*** THINK THE EMERALD SPEARS WILL TRY SOMETHING?
WHAT'S YOUR GUT TELL YOU, KID?
I DON'T HAVE GUTS, SIR. I'VE GOT INTERNAL DIAGNOSTICS, THOUGH...?
HMPH. SO I'M NOT OBSOLETE YET, *HUH?*
*"YOU ROBOTS CAN SCAN AND ANALYZE ALL YOU WANT. BUT YOU CAN'T **FEEL** THE SITUATION."*
HQ TO CHARLIE-SIX. REPORT.
"THAT MIGHT NOT BE 'LOGICAL' OR STAND UP TO HARD SCIENCE..."
CHARLIE-SIX, DO YOU COPY?
*"...BUT IT'S SAVED MY BACON MORE THAN ONCE. THEY'RE HERE. I CAN **FEEL** IT."*
I COPY. ALL CLEAR. OVER.

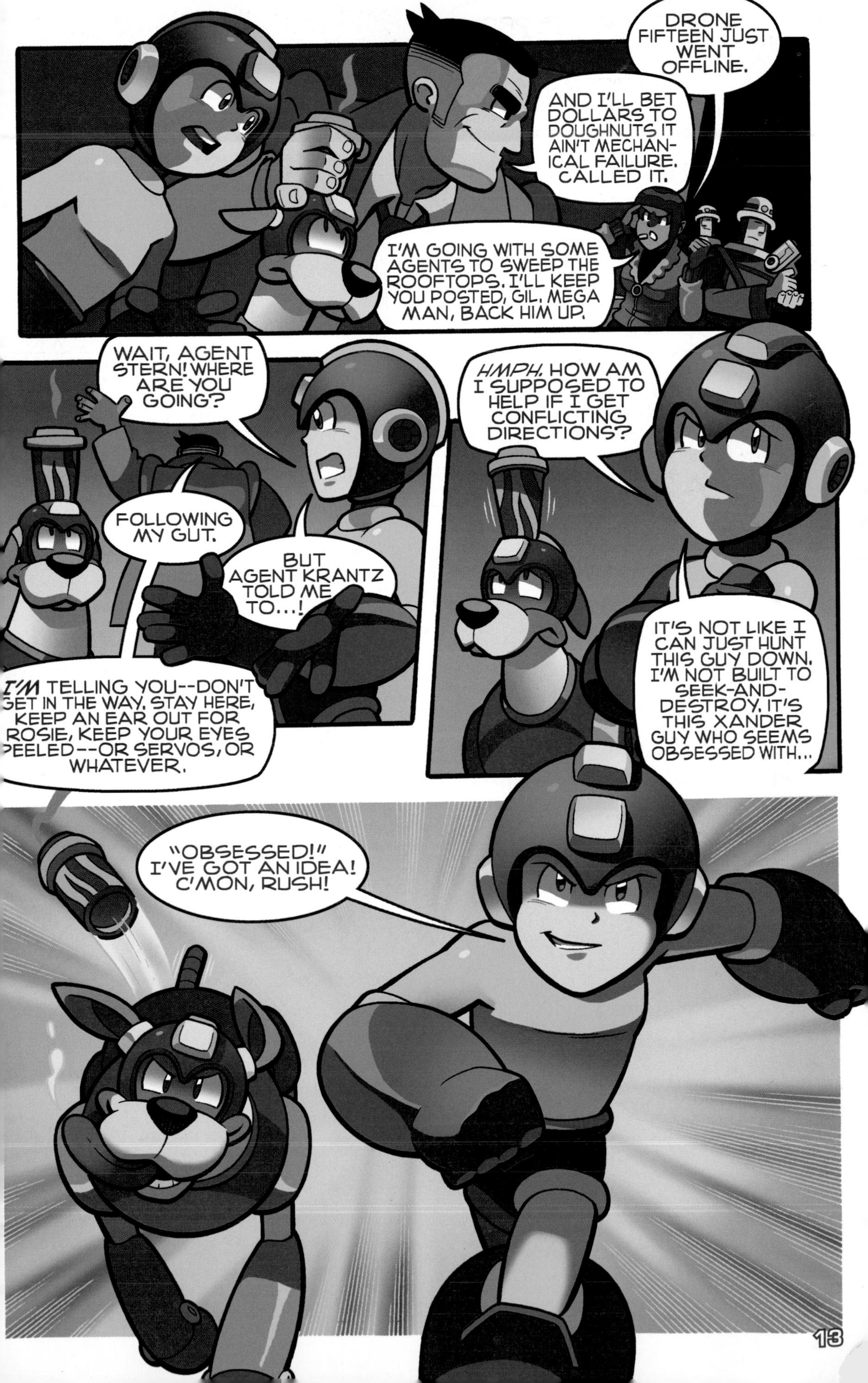

DRONE FIFTEEN JUST WENT OFFLINE.
AND I'LL BET DOLLARS TO DOUGHNUTS IT AIN'T MECHANICAL FAILURE. CALLED IT.
I'M GOING WITH SOME AGENTS TO SWEEP THE ROOFTOPS. I'LL KEEP YOU POSTED, GIL. MEGA MAN, BACK HIM UP.
WAIT, AGENT STERN! WHERE ARE YOU GOING?
FOLLOWING MY GUT.
BUT AGENT KRANTZ TOLD ME TO...!
I'M TELLING YOU--DON'T GET IN THE WAY. STAY HERE, KEEP AN EAR OUT FOR ROSIE, KEEP YOUR EYES PEELED--OR SERVOS, OR WHATEVER.
HMPH. HOW AM I SUPPOSED TO HELP IF I GET CONFLICTING DIRECTIONS?
IT'S NOT LIKE I CAN JUST HUNT THIS GUY DOWN. I'M NOT BUILT TO SEEK-AND-DESTROY. IT'S THIS XANDER GUY WHO SEEMS OBSESSED WITH...
"OBSESSED!" I'VE GOT AN IDEA! C'MON, RUSH!

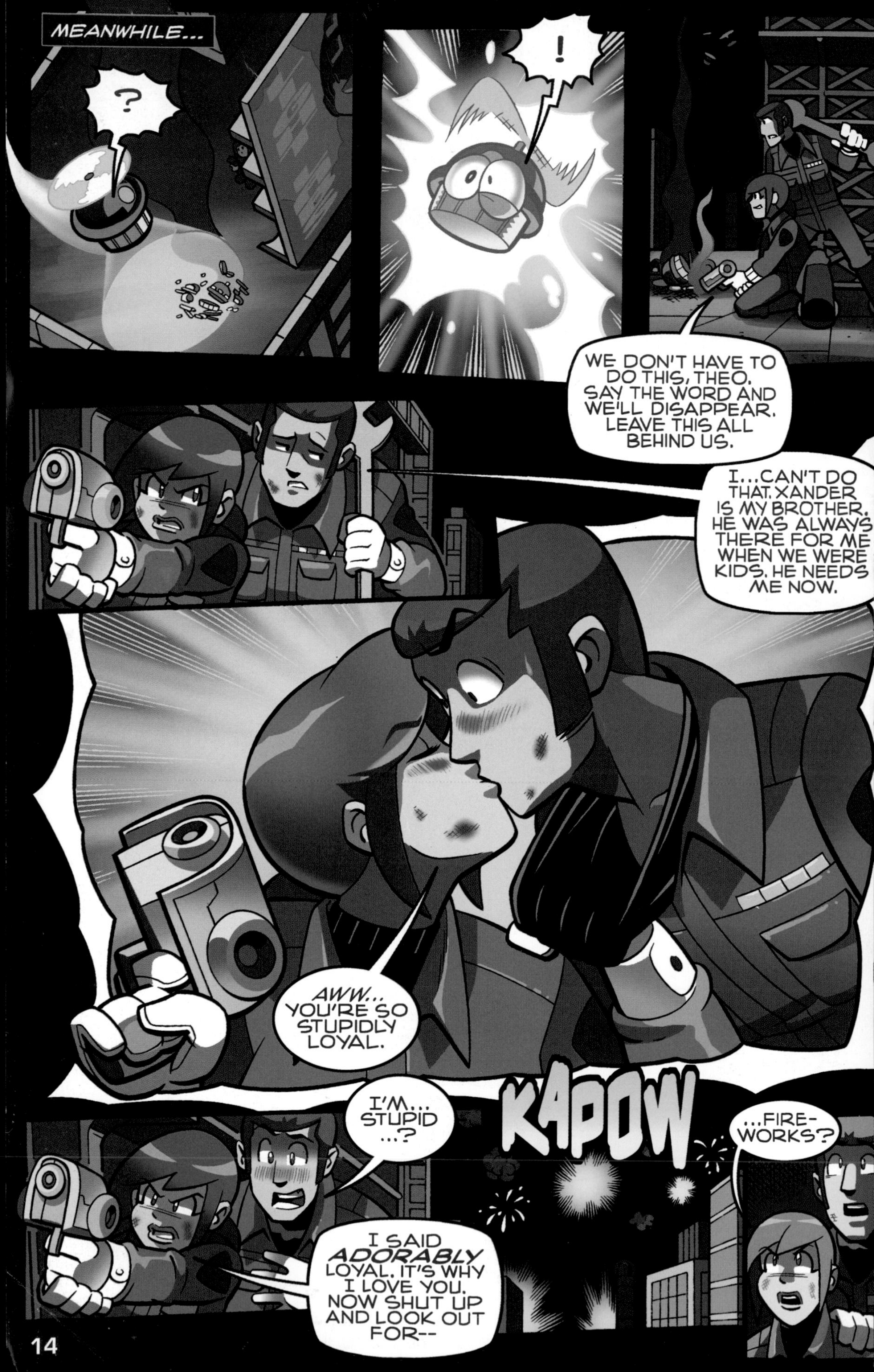
MEANWHILE...
?
!
WE DON'T HAVE TO DO THIS, THEO. SAY THE WORD AND WE'LL DISAPPEAR. LEAVE THIS ALL BEHIND US.
I...CAN'T DO THAT. XANDER IS MY BROTHER. HE WAS ALWAYS THERE FOR ME WHEN WE WERE KIDS. HE NEEDS ME NOW.
AWW... YOU'RE SO STUPIDLY LOYAL.
I'M... STUPID ...?
I SAID ADORABLY LOYAL. IT'S WHY I LOVE YOU. NOW SHUT UP AND LOOK OUT FOR--
KAPOW
...FIRE-WORKS?

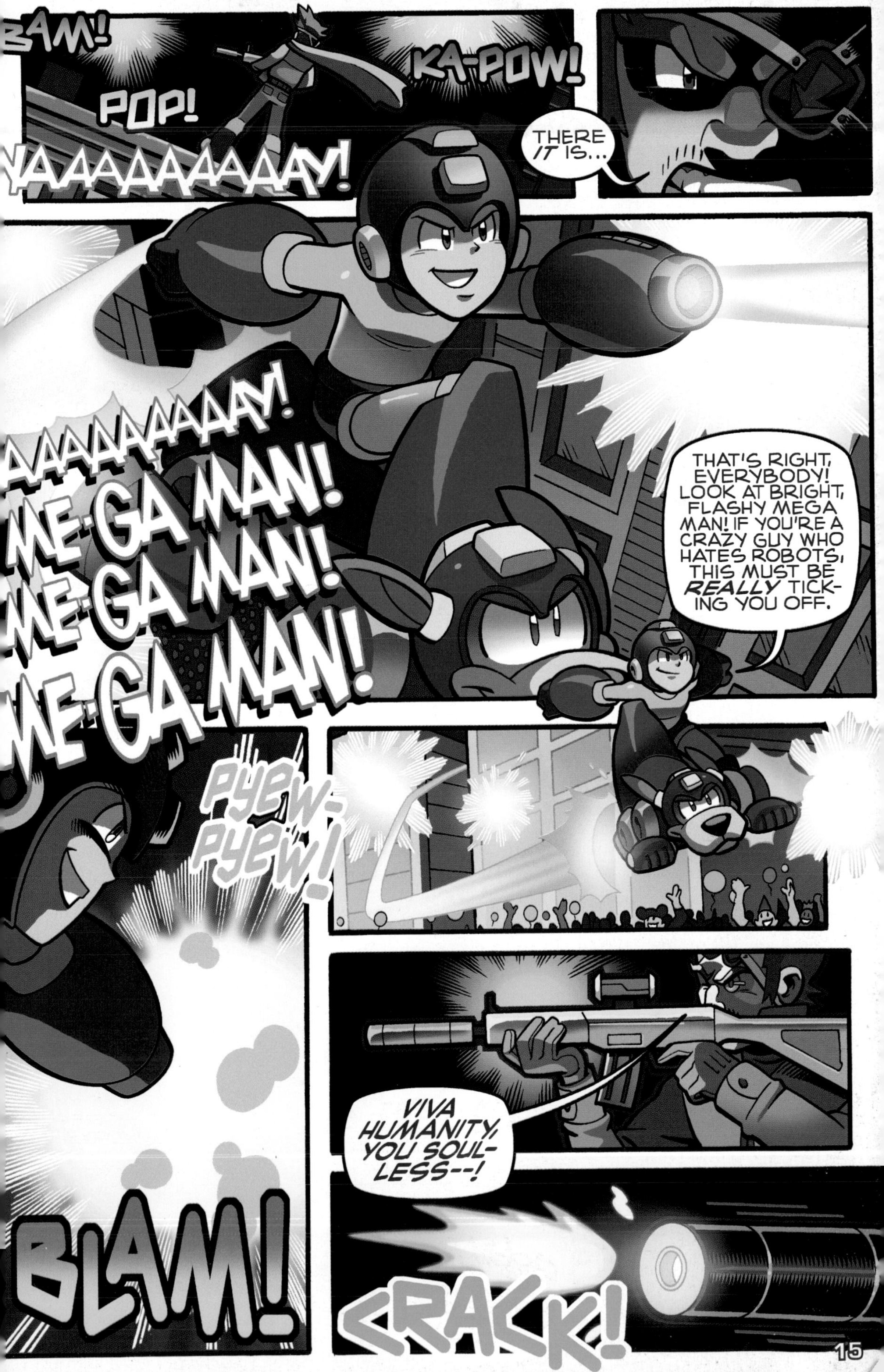
BAM!
POP!
KA-POW!
YAAAAAAAAAY!
THERE IT IS...
AAAAAAAAAY!
ME-GA MAN!
ME-GA MAN!
ME-GA MAN!
THAT'S RIGHT, EVERYBODY! LOOK AT BRIGHT, FLASHY MEGA MAN! IF YOU'RE A CRAZY GUY WHO HATES ROBOTS, THIS MUST BE REALLY TICKING YOU OFF.
PYEW-PYEW!
VIVA HUMANITY, YOU SOUL-LESS--!
BLAM!
CRACK!

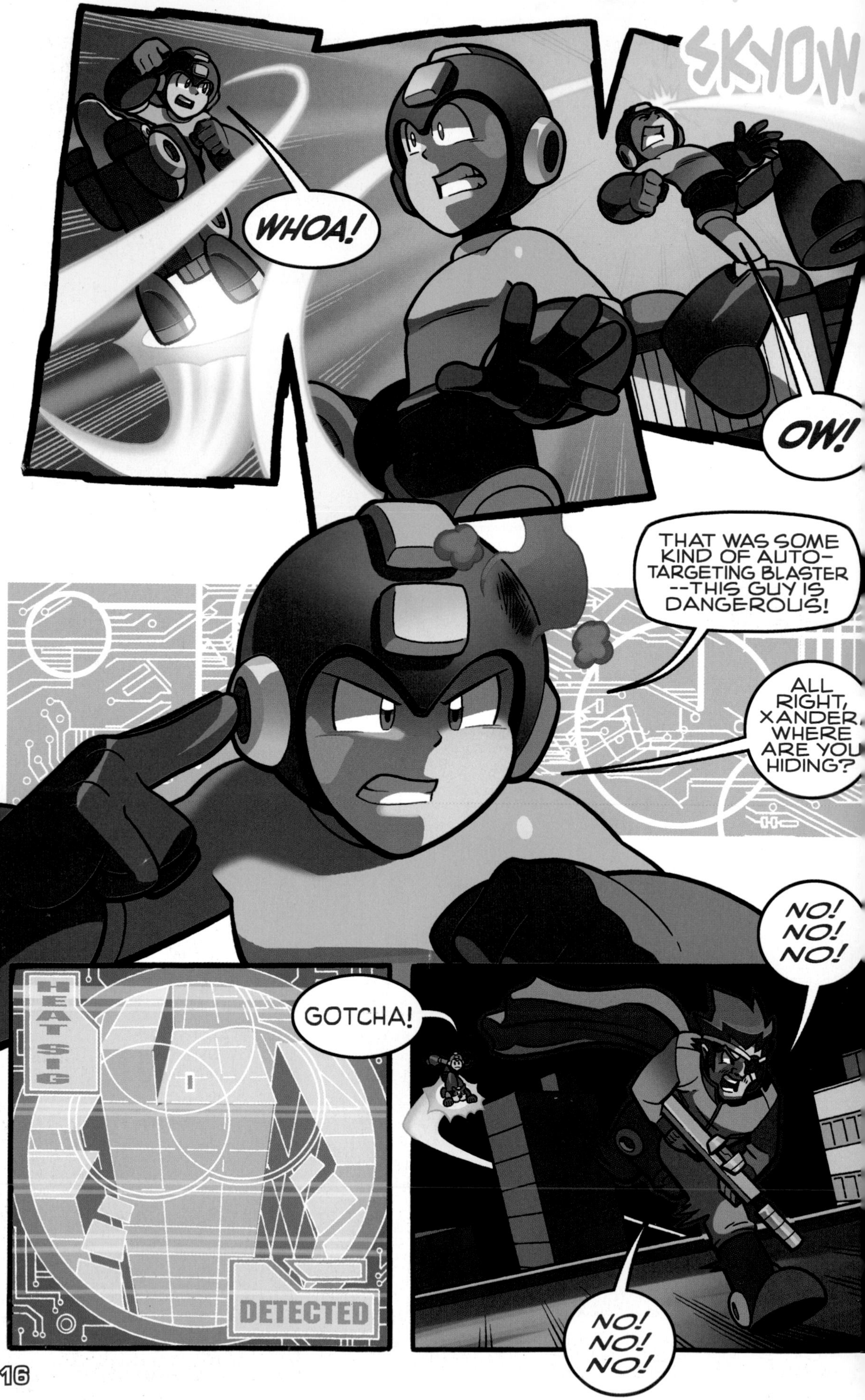
SKYOW
WHOA!
OW!
THAT WAS SOME KIND OF AUTO-TARGETING BLASTER --THIS GUY IS DANGEROUS!
ALL RIGHT, XANDER, WHERE ARE YOU HIDING?
HEAT SIG
DETECTED
GOTCHA!
NO! NO! NO!
NO! NO! NO!

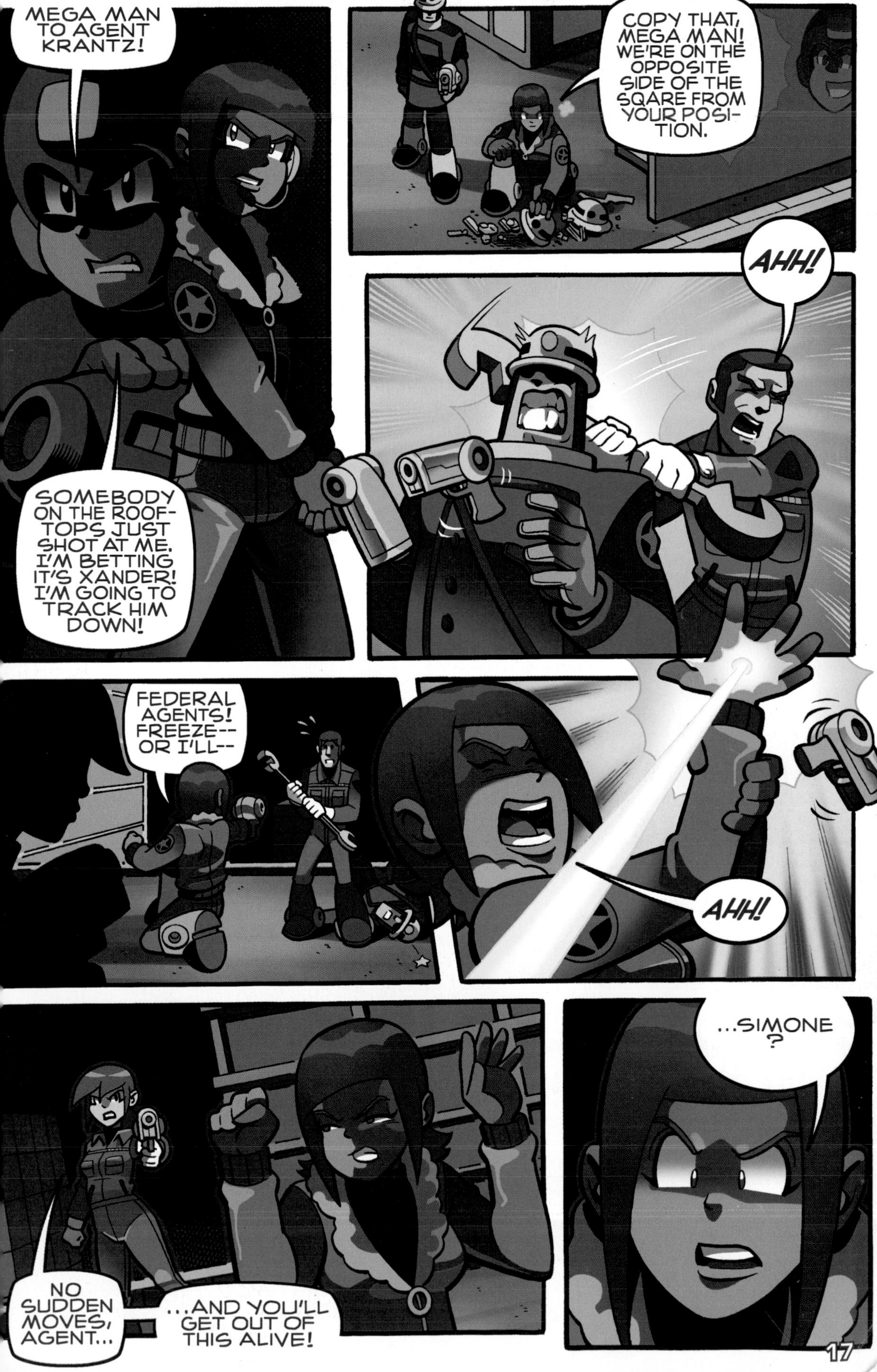
MEGA MAN TO AGENT KRANTZ!
SOMEBODY ON THE ROOF-TOPS JUST SHOT AT ME. I'M BETTING IT'S XANDER! I'M GOING TO TRACK HIM DOWN!
COPY THAT, MEGA MAN! WE'RE ON THE OPPOSITE SIDE OF THE SQARE FROM YOUR POSI-TION.
AHH!
FEDERAL AGENTS! FREEZE-- OR I'LL--
AHH!
NO SUDDEN MOVES, AGENT...
...AND YOU'LL GET OUT OF THIS ALIVE!
...SIMONE ?

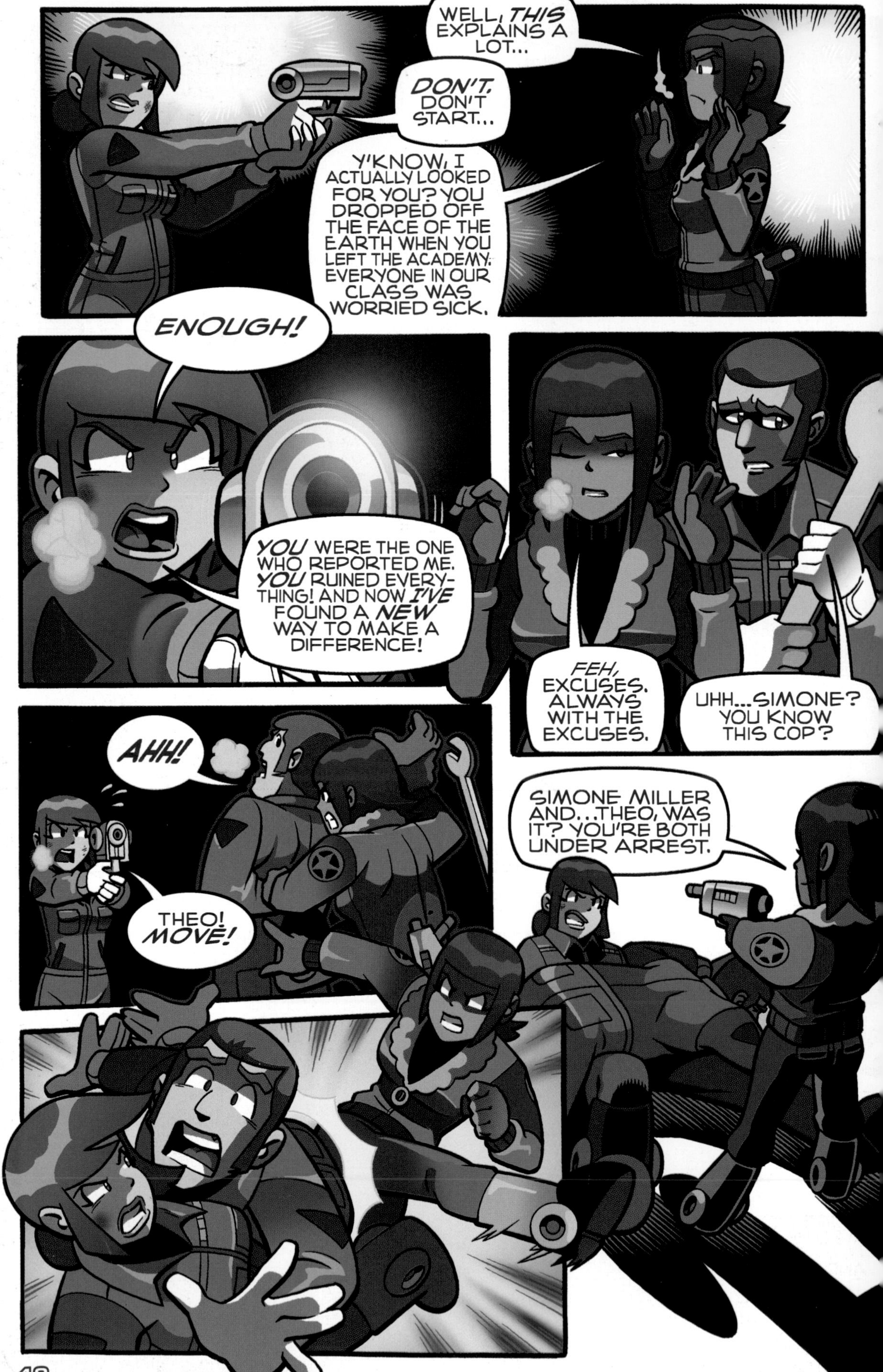
WELL, *THIS* EXPLAINS A LOT...
DON'T. DON'T START...
Y'KNOW, I ACTUALLY LOOKED FOR YOU? YOU DROPPED OFF THE FACE OF THE EARTH WHEN YOU LEFT THE ACADEMY. EVERYONE IN OUR CLASS WAS WORRIED SICK.
ENOUGH!
YOU WERE THE ONE WHO REPORTED ME. *YOU* RUINED EVERYTHING! AND NOW *I'VE* FOUND A *NEW* WAY TO MAKE A DIFFERENCE!
FEH, EXCUSES. ALWAYS WITH THE EXCUSES.
UHH...SIMONE? YOU KNOW THIS COP?
AHH!
THEO! *MOVE!*
SIMONE MILLER AND...THEO, WAS IT? YOU'RE BOTH UNDER ARREST.

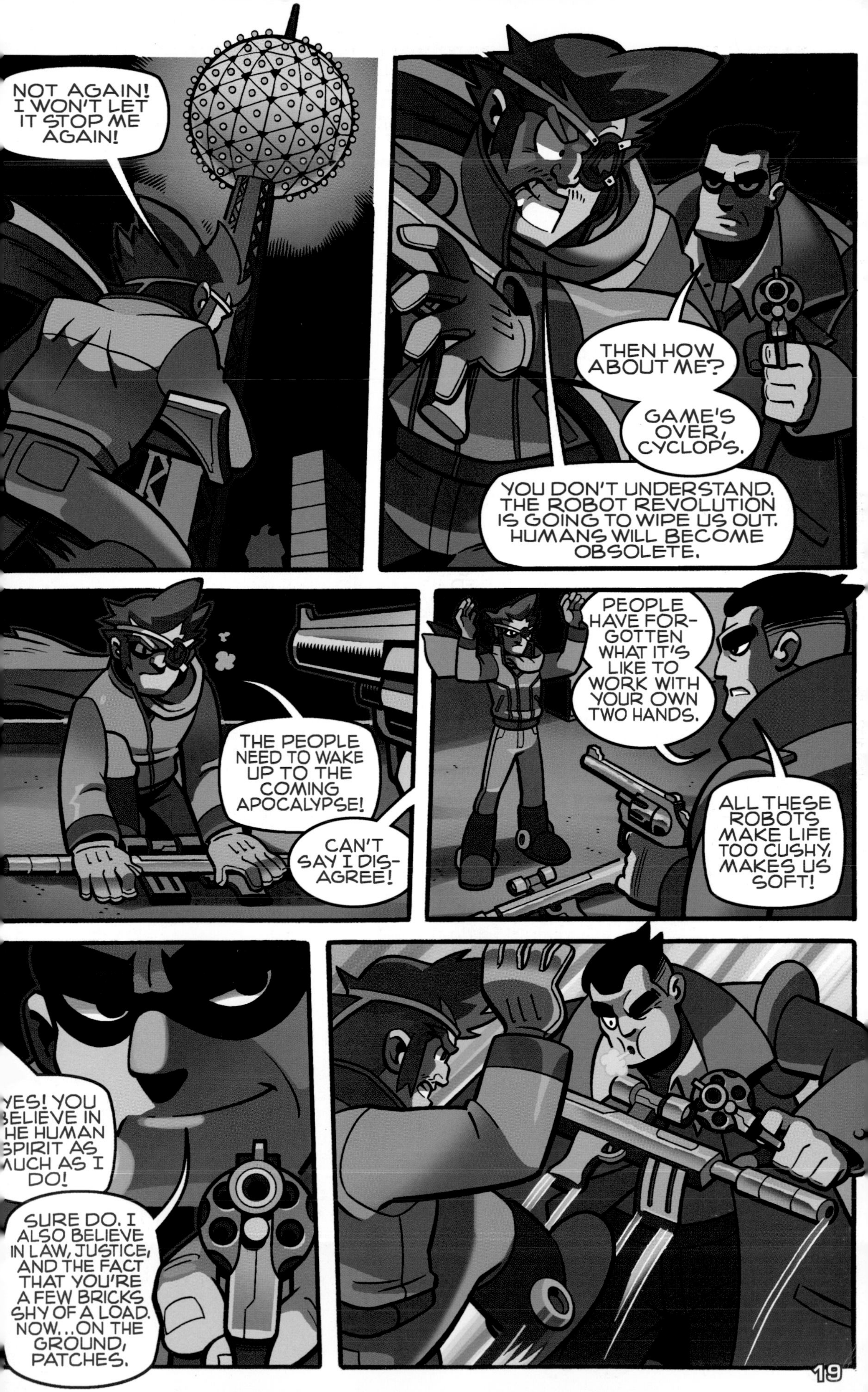
NOT AGAIN! I WON'T LET IT STOP ME AGAIN!
YOU DON'T UNDERSTAND. THE ROBOT REVOLUTION IS GOING TO WIPE US OUT. HUMANS WILL BECOME OBSOLETE.
THEN HOW ABOUT ME?
GAME'S OVER, CYCLOPS.
THE PEOPLE NEED TO WAKE UP TO THE COMING APOCALYPSE!
CAN'T SAY I DIS-AGREE!
PEOPLE HAVE FOR-GOTTEN WHAT IT'S LIKE TO WORK WITH YOUR OWN TWO HANDS.
ALL THESE ROBOTS MAKE LIFE TOO CUSHY, MAKES US SOFT!
YES! YOU BELIEVE IN HE HUMAN SPIRIT AS UCH AS I DO!
SURE DO. I ALSO BELIEVE IN LAW, JUSTICE, AND THE FACT THAT YOU'RE A FEW BRICKS SHY OF A LOAD. NOW...ON THE GROUND, PATCHES.

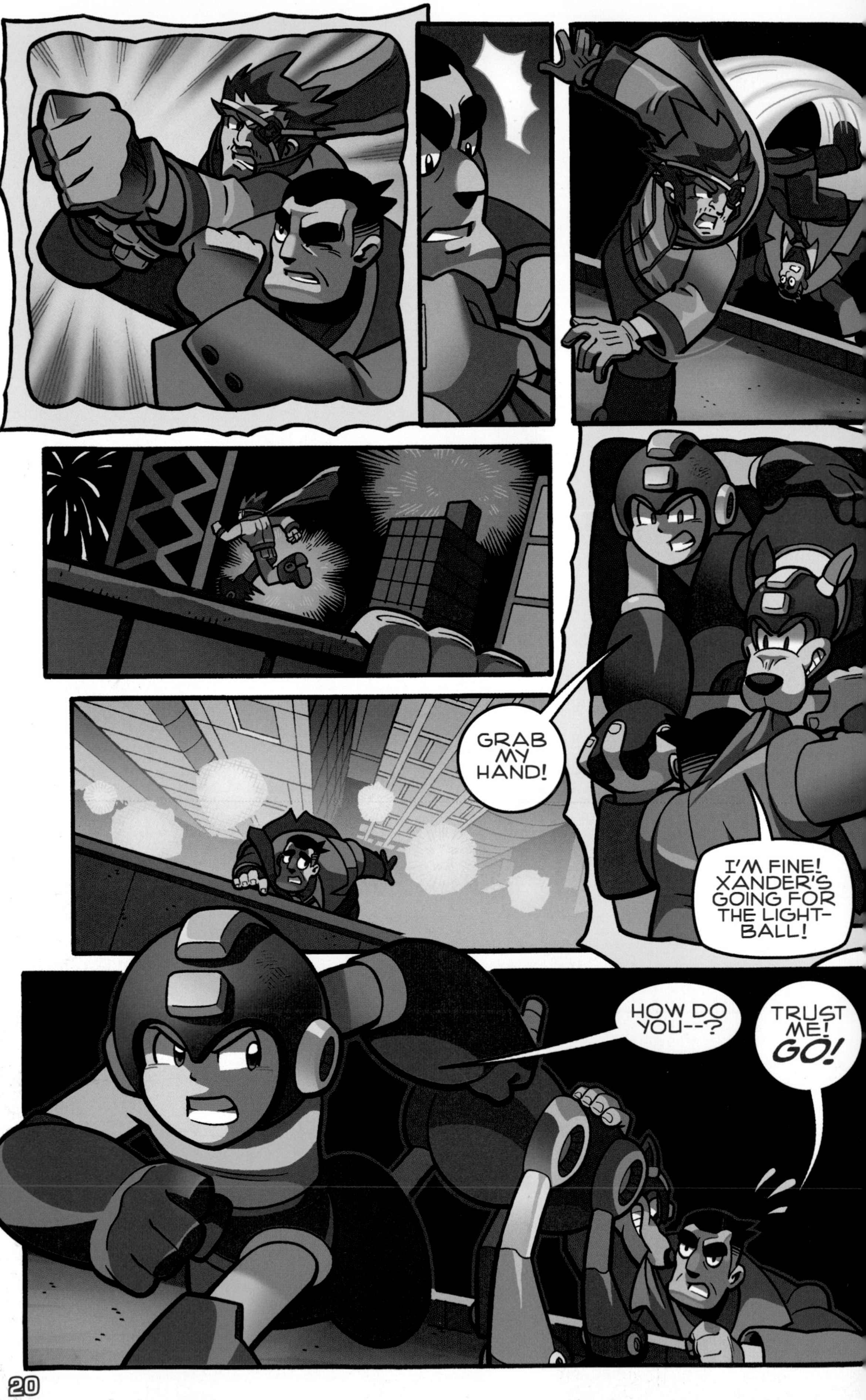
GRAB MY HAND!
I'M FINE! XANDER'S GOING FOR THE LIGHT-BALL!
HOW DO YOU--?
TRUST ME! GO!

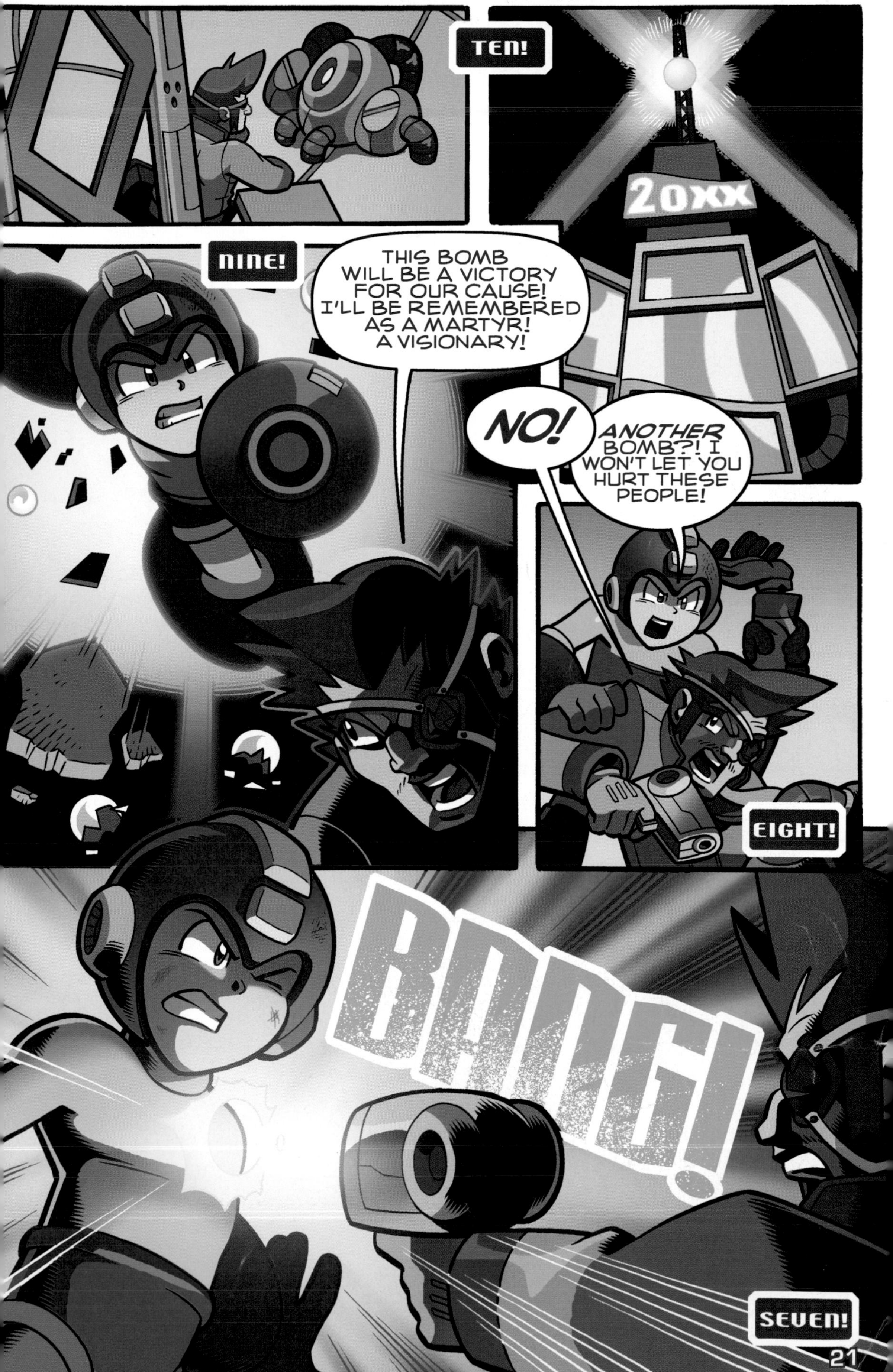
TEN!
2OXX
NINE!
THIS BOMB WILL BE A VICTORY FOR OUR CAUSE! I'LL BE REMEMBERED AS A MARTYR! A VISIONARY!
NO!
ANOTHER BOMB?! I WON'T LET YOU HURT THESE PEOPLE!
EIGHT!
BANG!
SEVEN!

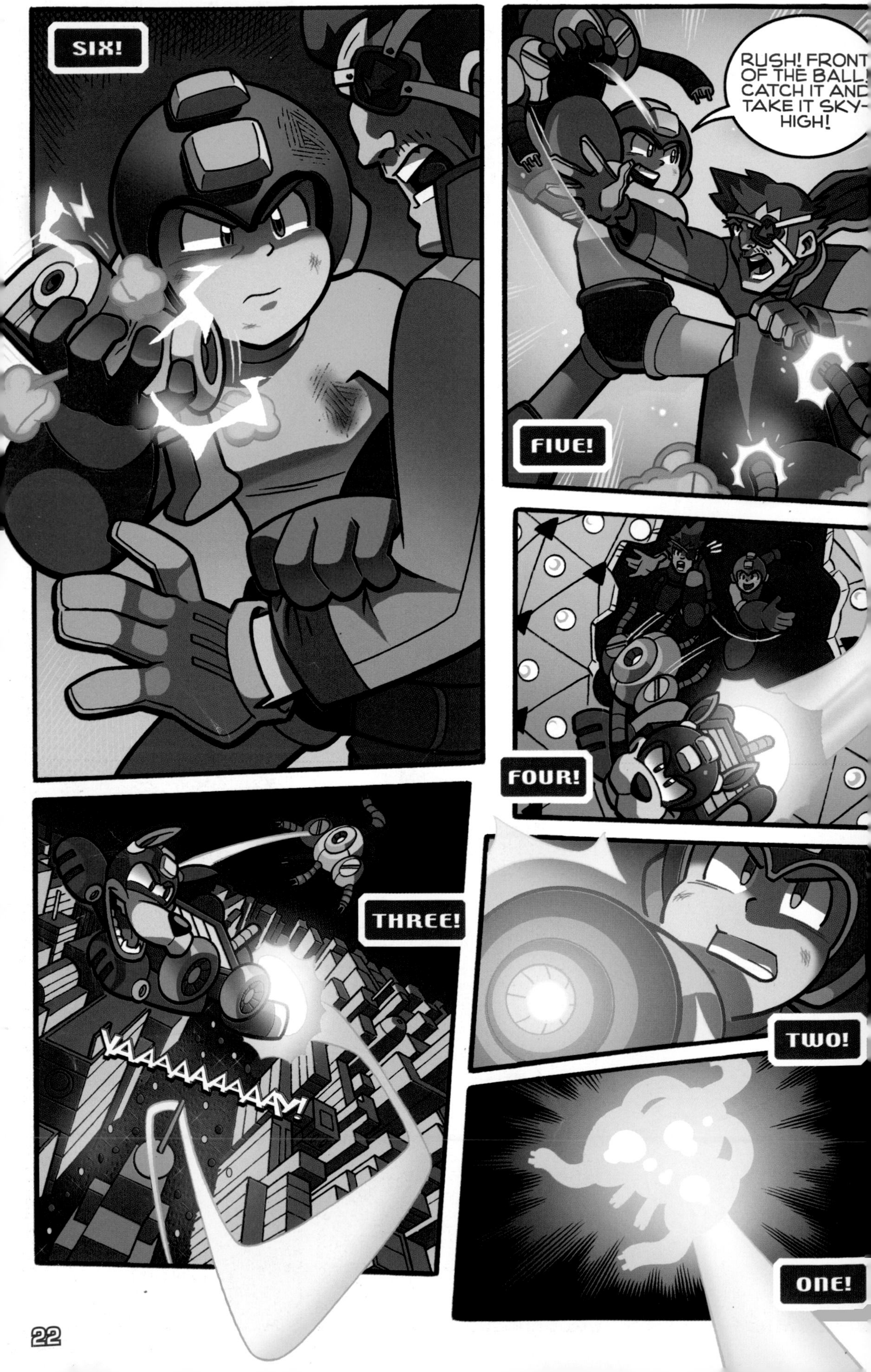
SIX!
RUSH! FRONT OF THE BALL! CATCH IT AND TAKE IT SKY-HIGH!
FIVE!
FOUR!
THREE!
YAAAAAAAAAY!
TWO!
ONE!

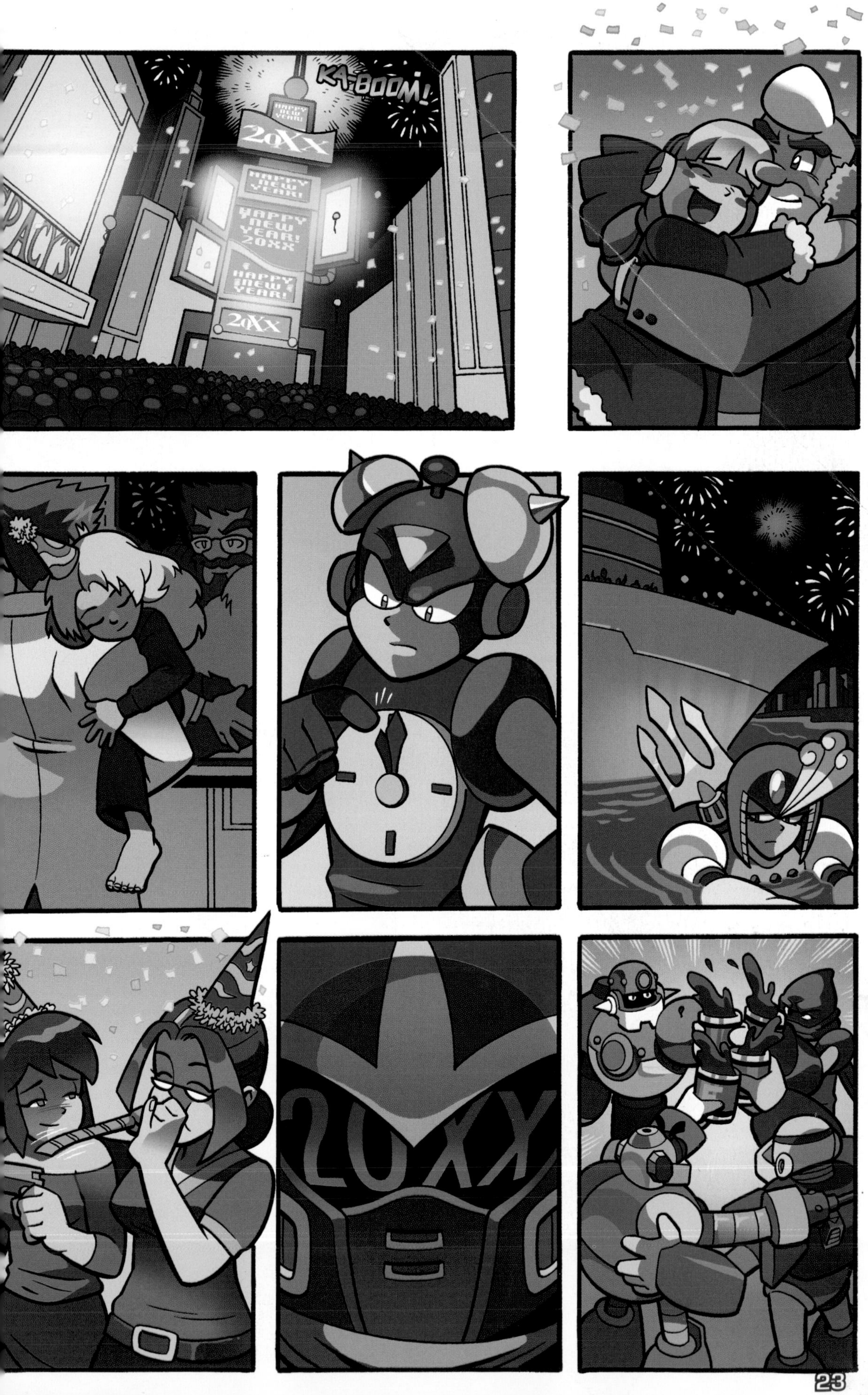
KA-BOOM!
HAPPY NEW YEAR
20XX
HAPPY NEW YEAR!
HAPPY NEW YEAR! 20XX
HAPPY NEW YEAR!
20XX
20XX

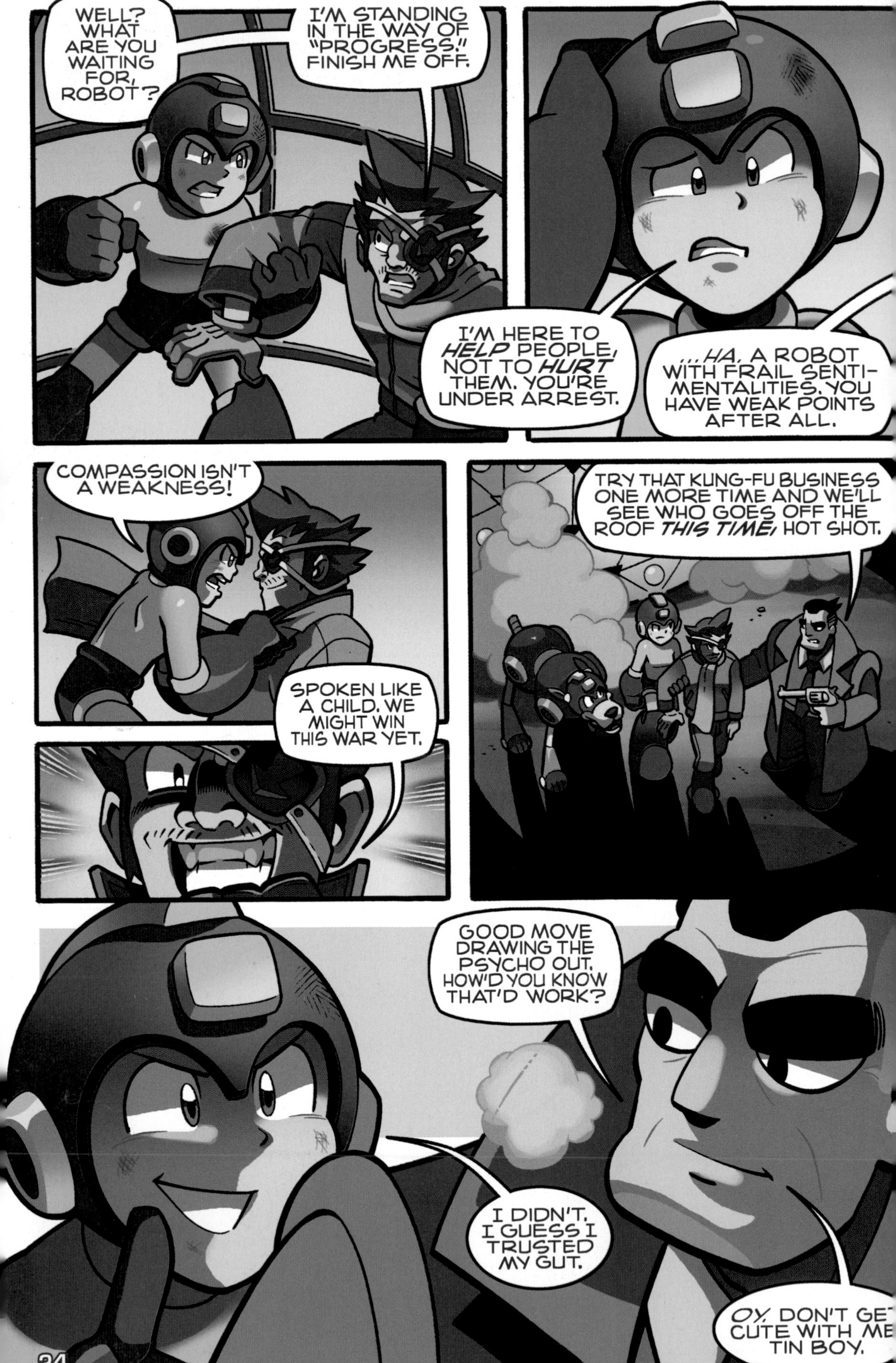
WELL? WHAT ARE YOU WAITING FOR, ROBOT?
I'M STANDING IN THE WAY OF "PROGRESS!" FINISH ME OFF.
I'M HERE TO *HELP* PEOPLE, NOT TO *HURT* THEM. YOU'RE UNDER ARREST.
...*HA*, A ROBOT WITH FRAIL SENTI-MENTALITIES. YOU HAVE WEAK POINTS AFTER ALL.
COMPASSION ISN'T A WEAKNESS!
SPOKEN LIKE A CHILD. WE MIGHT WIN THIS WAR YET.
TRY THAT KUNG-FU BUSINESS ONE MORE TIME AND WE'LL SEE WHO GOES OFF THE ROOF *THIS TIME*, HOT SHOT.
GOOD MOVE DRAWING THE PSYCHO OUT. HOW'D YOU KNOW THAT'D WORK?
I DIDN'T. I GUESS I TRUSTED MY GUT.
OY. DON'T GE CUTE WITH ME TIN BOY.

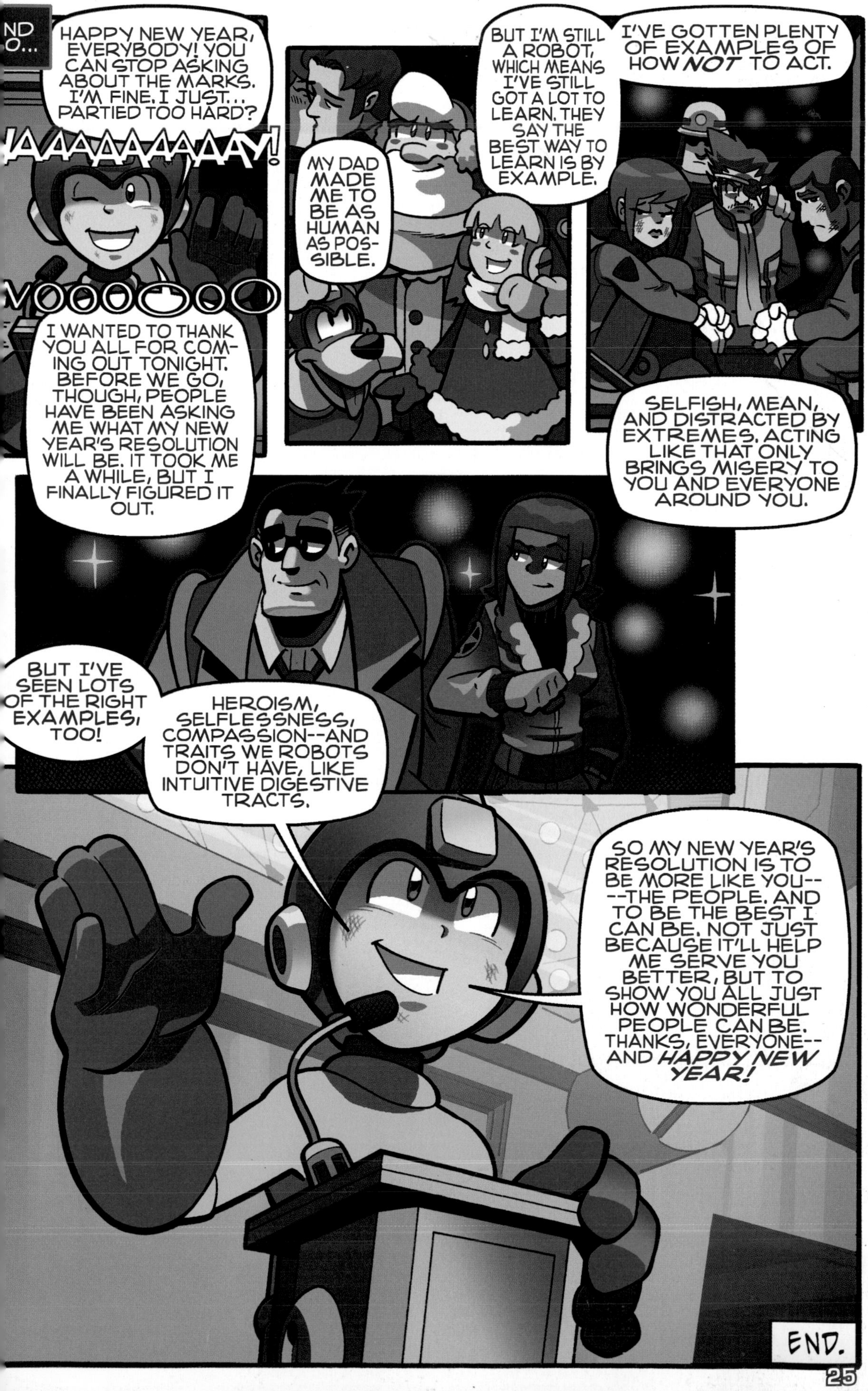
HAPPY NEW YEAR, EVERYBODY! YOU CAN STOP ASKING ABOUT THE MARKS. I'M FINE. I JUST... PARTIED TOO HARD?
I WANTED TO THANK YOU ALL FOR COMING OUT TONIGHT. BEFORE WE GO, THOUGH, PEOPLE HAVE BEEN ASKING ME WHAT MY NEW YEAR'S RESOLUTION WILL BE. IT TOOK ME A WHILE, BUT I FINALLY FIGURED IT OUT.
MY DAD MADE ME TO BE AS HUMAN AS POSSIBLE.
BUT I'M STILL A ROBOT, WHICH MEANS I'VE STILL GOT A LOT TO LEARN. THEY SAY THE BEST WAY TO LEARN IS BY EXAMPLE.
I'VE GOTTEN PLENTY OF EXAMPLES OF HOW *NOT* TO ACT.
SELFISH, MEAN, AND DISTRACTED BY EXTREMES. ACTING LIKE THAT ONLY BRINGS MISERY TO YOU AND EVERYONE AROUND YOU.
BUT I'VE SEEN LOTS OF THE RIGHT EXAMPLES, TOO!
HEROISM, SELFLESSNESS, COMPASSION--AND TRAITS WE ROBOTS DON'T HAVE, LIKE INTUITIVE DIGESTIVE TRACTS.
SO MY NEW YEAR'S RESOLUTION IS TO BE MORE LIKE YOU-- --THE PEOPLE. AND TO BE THE BEST I CAN BE. NOT JUST BECAUSE IT'LL HELP ME SERVE YOU BETTER, BUT TO SHOW YOU ALL JUST HOW WONDERFUL PEOPLE CAN BE. THANKS, EVERYONE-- AND *HAPPY NEW YEAR!*
END.

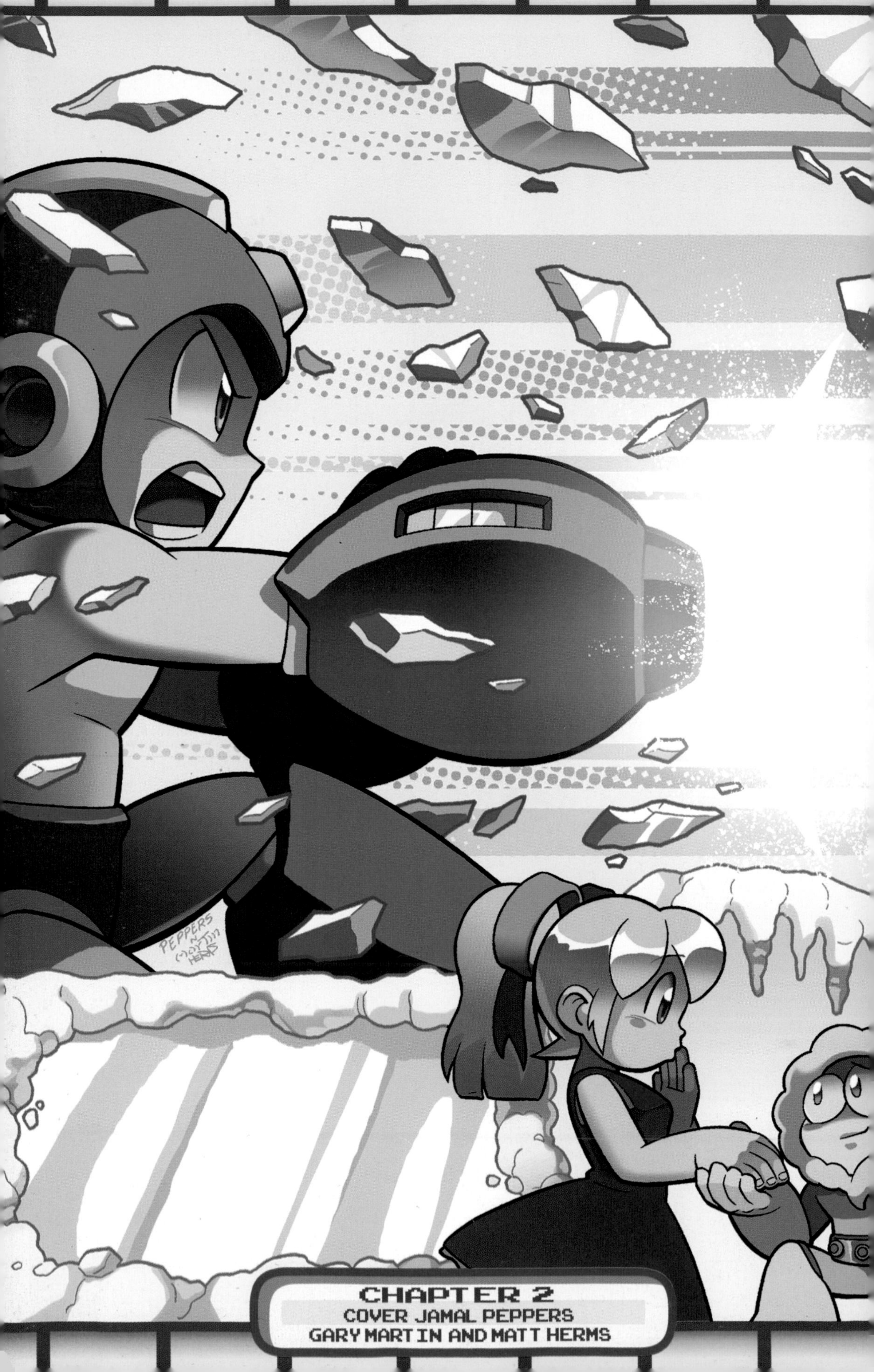

CHAPTER 2

COVER JAMAL PEPPERS
GARY MARTIN AND MATT HERMS

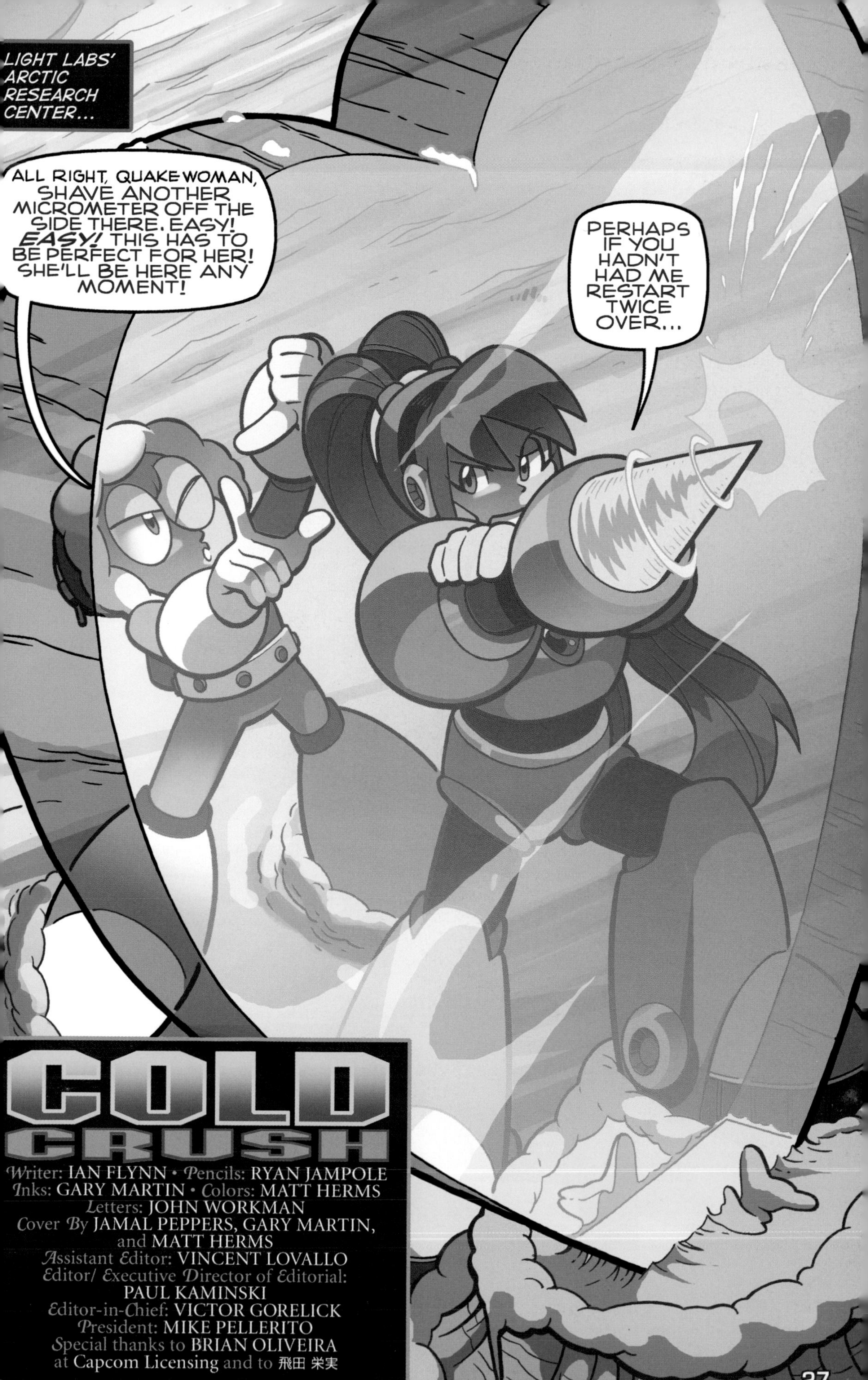
LIGHT LABS' ARCTIC RESEARCH CENTER...
ALL RIGHT, QUAKE WOMAN, SHAVE ANOTHER MICROMETER OFF THE SIDE THERE. EASY! ***EASY!*** THIS HAS TO BE PERFECT FOR HER! SHE'LL BE HERE ANY MOMENT!
PERHAPS IF YOU HADN'T HAD ME RESTART TWICE OVER...
COLD CRUSH
Writer: IAN FLYNN • Pencils: RYAN JAMPOLE
Inks: GARY MARTIN • Colors: MATT HERMS
Letters: JOHN WORKMAN
Cover By JAMAL PEPPERS, GARY MARTIN, and MATT HERMS
Assistant Editor: VINCENT LOVALLO
Editor/ Executive Director of Editorial: PAUL KAMINSKI
Editor-in-Chief: VICTOR GORELICK
President: MIKE PELLERITO
Special thanks to BRIAN OLIVEIRA at Capcom Licensing and to 飛田 栄実

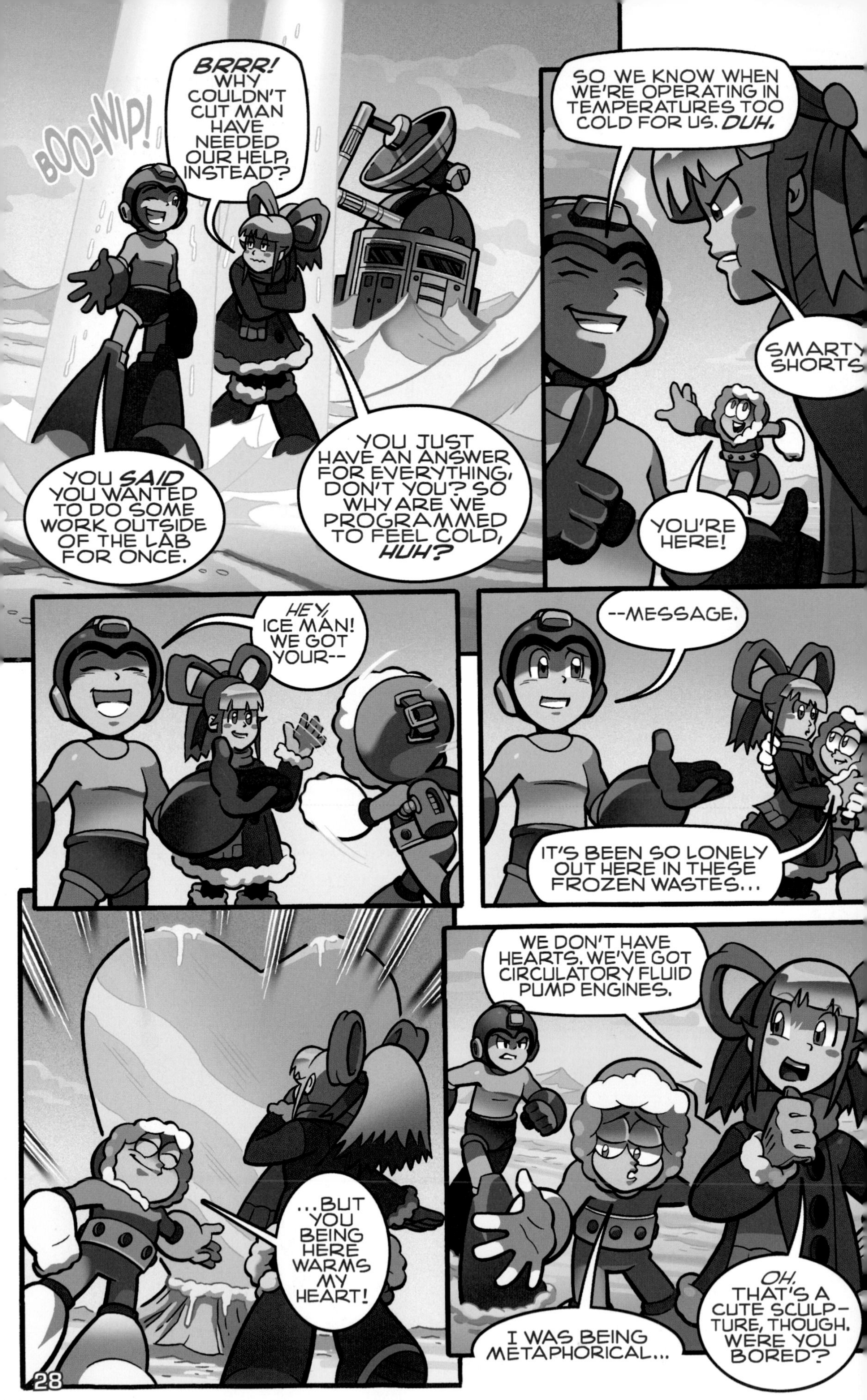
BOO-WIP!
BRRR! WHY COULDN'T CUT MAN HAVE NEEDED OUR HELP, INSTEAD?
YOU SAID YOU WANTED TO DO SOME WORK OUTSIDE OF THE LAB FOR ONCE.
YOU JUST HAVE AN ANSWER FOR EVERYTHING, DON'T YOU? SO WHY ARE WE PROGRAMMED TO FEEL COLD, HUH?
SO WE KNOW WHEN WE'RE OPERATING IN TEMPERATURES TOO COLD FOR US. DUH.
SMARTY SHORTS
YOU'RE HERE!
HEY, ICE MAN! WE GOT YOUR--
--MESSAGE.
IT'S BEEN SO LONELY OUT HERE IN THESE FROZEN WASTES...
...BUT YOU BEING HERE WARMS MY HEART!
WE DON'T HAVE HEARTS. WE'VE GOT CIRCULATORY FLUID PUMP ENGINES.
I WAS BEING METAPHORICAL...
OH. THAT'S A CUTE SCULPTURE, THOUGH. WERE YOU BORED?

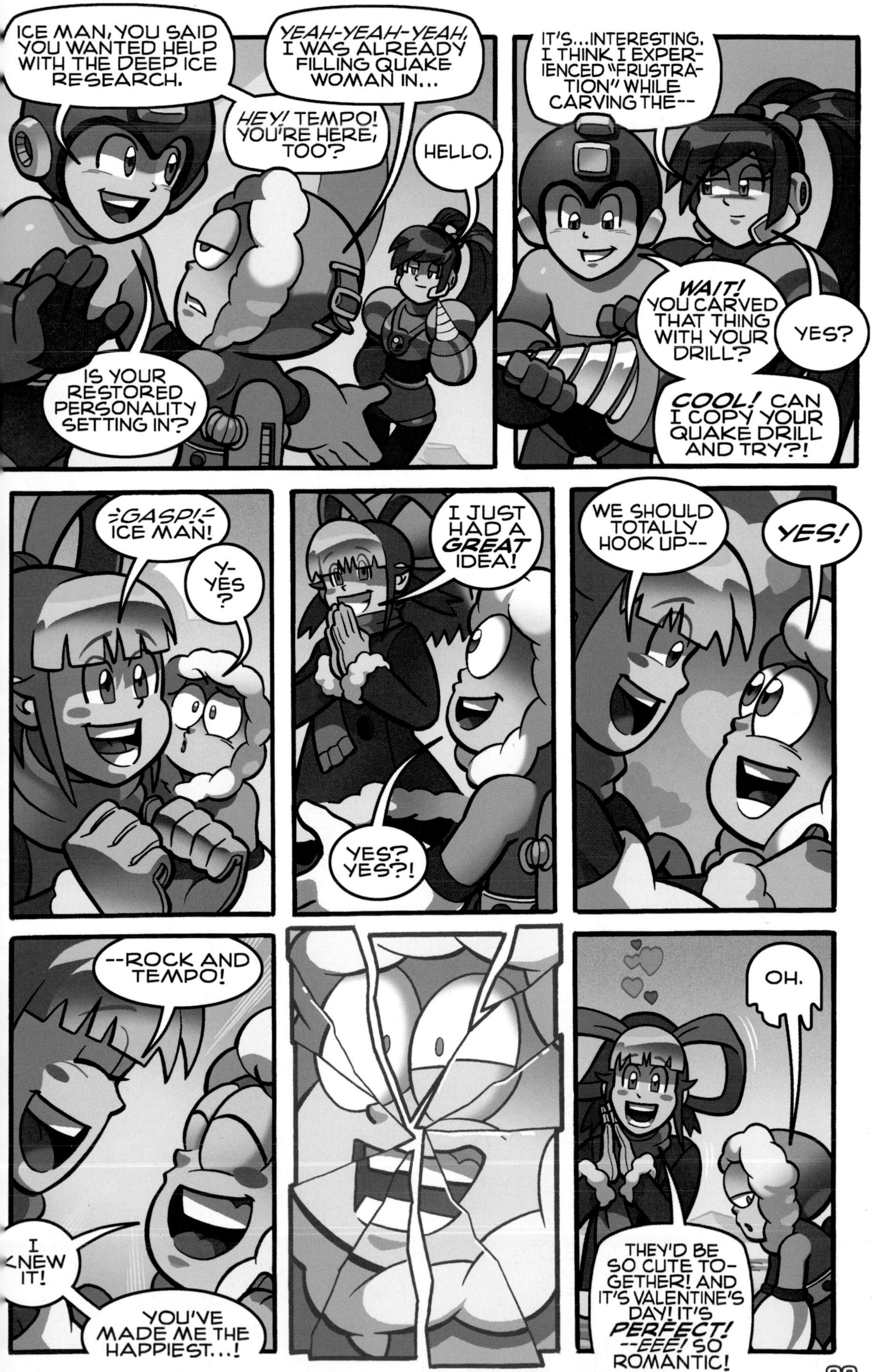
ICE MAN, YOU SAID YOU WANTED HELP WITH THE DEEP ICE RESEARCH.
YEAH-YEAH-YEAH, I WAS ALREADY FILLING QUAKE WOMAN IN...
HEY! TEMPO! YOU'RE HERE, TOO?
HELLO.
IS YOUR RESTORED PERSONALITY SETTING IN?
IT'S...INTERESTING. I THINK I EXPERIENCED "FRUSTRATION" WHILE CARVING THE--
WAIT! YOU CARVED THAT THING WITH YOUR DRILL?
YES?
COOL! CAN I COPY YOUR QUAKE DRILL AND TRY?!
GASP! ICE MAN!
Y-YES?
I JUST HAD A GREAT IDEA!
YES? YES?!
WE SHOULD TOTALLY HOOK UP--
YES!
--ROCK AND TEMPO!
I KNEW IT!
YOU'VE MADE ME THE HAPPIEST...!
OH.
THEY'D BE SO CUTE TOGETHER! AND IT'S VALENTINE'S DAY! IT'S PERFECT! --EEE! SO ROMANTIC!

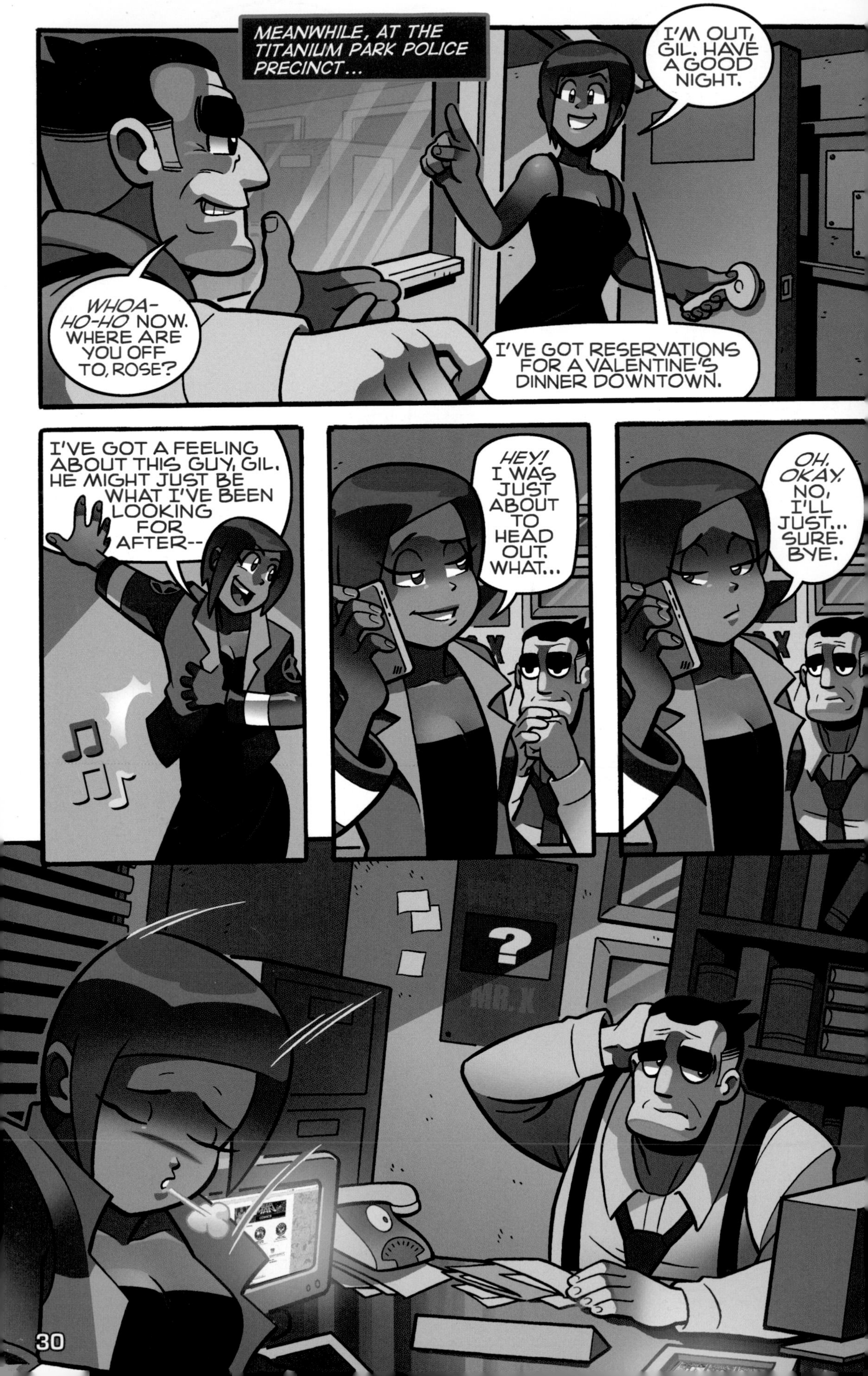
MEANWHILE, AT THE TITANIUM PARK POLICE PRECINCT...
I'M OUT, GIL. HAVE A GOOD NIGHT.
WHOA-HO-HO NOW. WHERE ARE YOU OFF TO, ROSE?
I'VE GOT RESERVATIONS FOR A VALENTINE'S DINNER DOWNTOWN.
I'VE GOT A FEELING ABOUT THIS GUY, GIL. HE MIGHT JUST BE WHAT I'VE BEEN LOOKING FOR AFTER--
HEY! I WAS JUST ABOUT TO HEAD OUT. WHAT...
OH. OKAY. NO, I'LL JUST... SURE. BYE.
?
MR. X

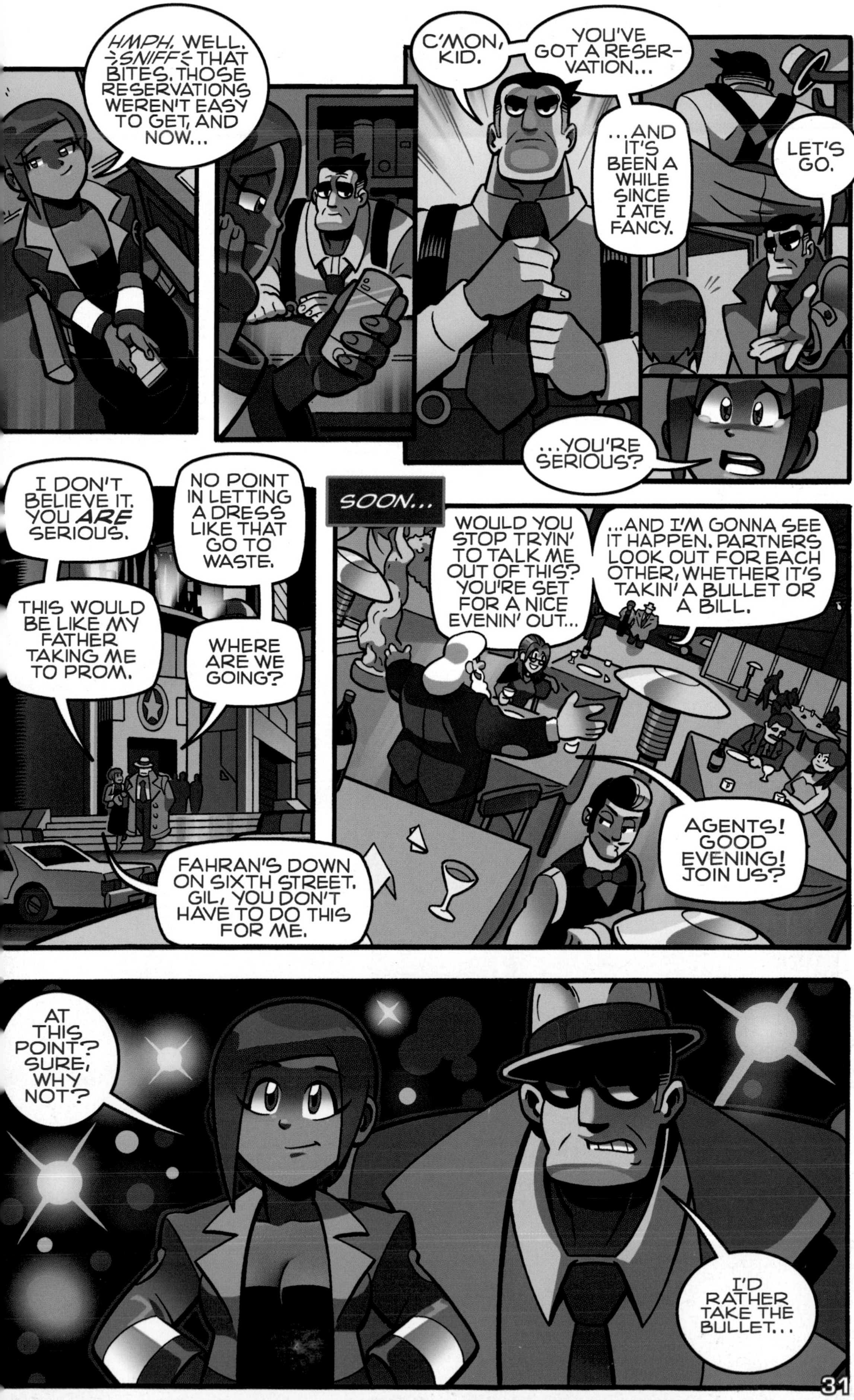
HMPH. WELL. ≥SNIFF≤ THAT BITES. THOSE RESERVATIONS WEREN'T EASY TO GET, AND NOW...
C'MON, KID.
YOU'VE GOT A RESER-VATION...
...AND IT'S BEEN A WHILE SINCE I ATE FANCY.
LET'S GO.
...YOU'RE SERIOUS?
I DON'T BELIEVE IT. YOU ARE SERIOUS.
NO POINT IN LETTING A DRESS LIKE THAT GO TO WASTE.
THIS WOULD BE LIKE MY FATHER TAKING ME TO PROM.
WHERE ARE WE GOING?
FAHRAN'S DOWN ON SIXTH STREET. GIL, YOU DON'T HAVE TO DO THIS FOR ME.
SOON...
WOULD YOU STOP TRYIN' TO TALK ME OUT OF THIS? YOU'RE SET FOR A NICE EVENIN' OUT...
...AND I'M GONNA SEE IT HAPPEN. PARTNERS LOOK OUT FOR EACH OTHER, WHETHER IT'S TAKIN' A BULLET OR A BILL.
AGENTS! GOOD EVENING! JOIN US?
AT THIS POINT? SURE, WHY NOT?
I'D RATHER TAKE THE BULLET...

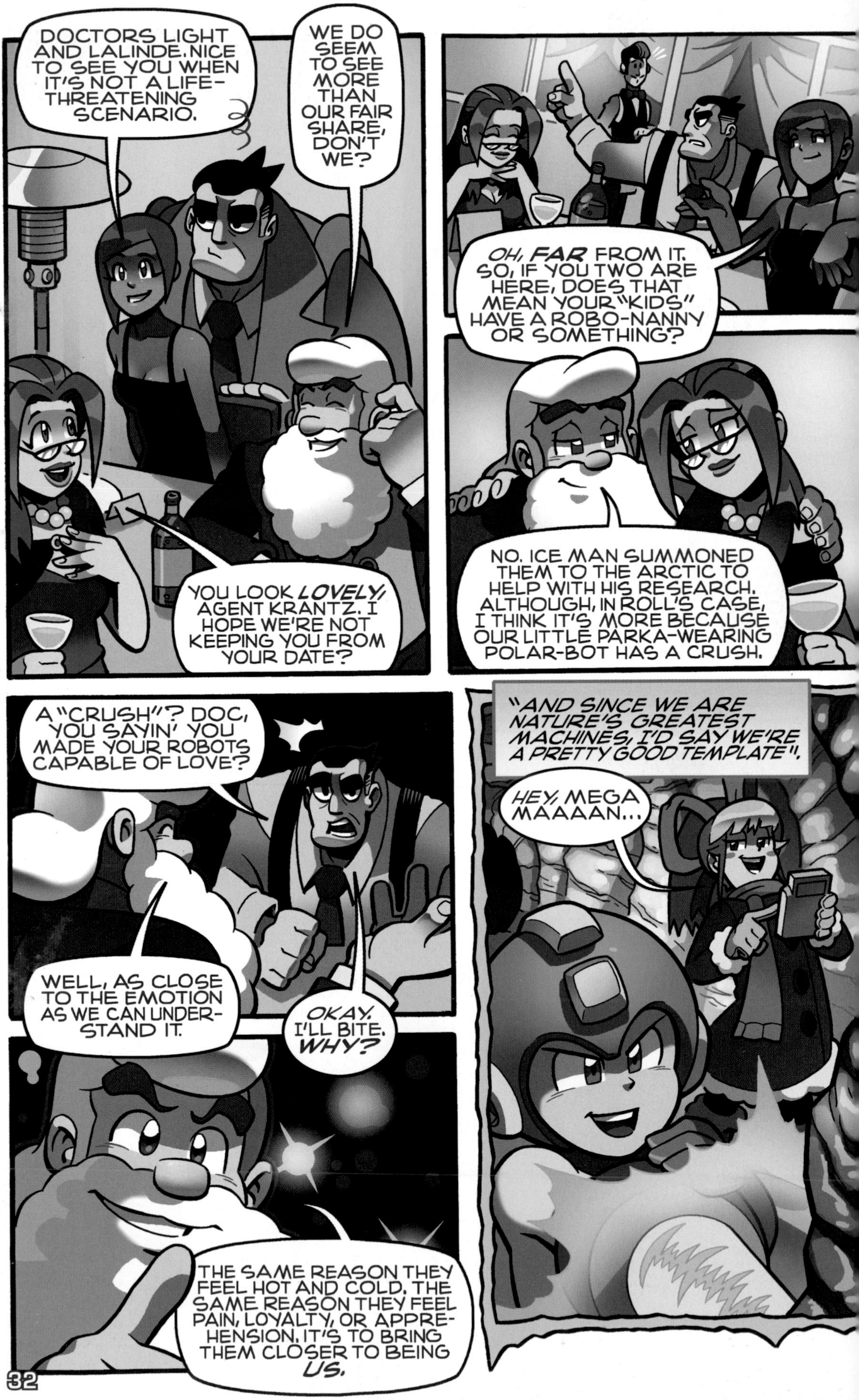
DOCTORS LIGHT AND LALINDE. NICE TO SEE YOU WHEN IT'S NOT A LIFE-THREATENING SCENARIO.
WE DO SEEM TO SEE MORE THAN OUR FAIR SHARE, DON'T WE?
YOU LOOK LOVELY, AGENT KRANTZ. I HOPE WE'RE NOT KEEPING YOU FROM YOUR DATE?
OH, FAR FROM IT. SO, IF YOU TWO ARE HERE, DOES THAT MEAN YOUR "KIDS" HAVE A ROBO-NANNY OR SOMETHING?
NO. ICE MAN SUMMONED THEM TO THE ARCTIC TO HELP WITH HIS RESEARCH. ALTHOUGH, IN ROLL'S CASE, I THINK IT'S MORE BECAUSE OUR LITTLE PARKA-WEARING POLAR-BOT HAS A CRUSH.
A "CRUSH"? DOC, YOU SAYIN' YOU MADE YOUR ROBOTS CAPABLE OF LOVE?
WELL, AS CLOSE TO THE EMOTION AS WE CAN UNDER-STAND IT.
OKAY. I'LL BITE. WHY?
THE SAME REASON THEY FEEL HOT AND COLD. THE SAME REASON THEY FEEL PAIN, LOYALTY, OR APPRE-HENSION. IT'S TO BRING THEM CLOSER TO BEING US.
"AND SINCE WE ARE NATURE'S GREATEST MACHINES, I'D SAY WE'RE A PRETTY GOOD TEMPLATE".
HEY, MEGA MAAAAN...

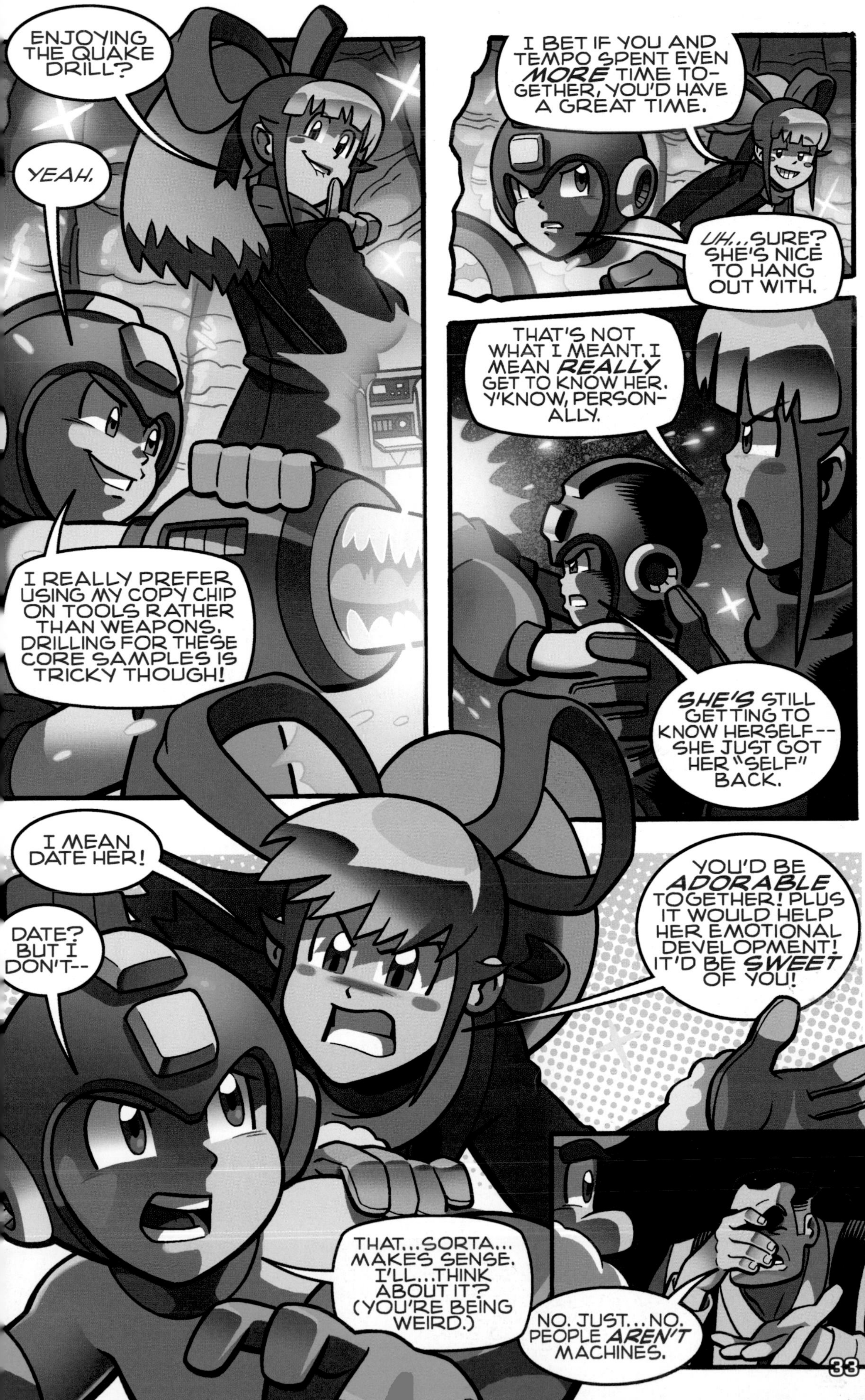
ENJOYING THE QUAKE DRILL?
YEAH.
I REALLY PREFER USING MY COPY CHIP ON TOOLS RATHER THAN WEAPONS. DRILLING FOR THESE CORE SAMPLES IS TRICKY THOUGH!
I BET IF YOU AND TEMPO SPENT EVEN *MORE* TIME TOGETHER, YOU'D HAVE A GREAT TIME.
UH... SURE? SHE'S NICE TO HANG OUT WITH.
THAT'S NOT WHAT I MEANT. I MEAN *REALLY* GET TO KNOW HER. Y'KNOW, PERSONALLY.
SHE'S STILL GETTING TO KNOW HERSELF-- SHE JUST GOT HER "SELF" BACK.
I MEAN DATE HER!
DATE? BUT I DON'T--
YOU'D BE *ADORABLE* TOGETHER! PLUS IT WOULD HELP HER EMOTIONAL DEVELOPMENT! IT'D BE *SWEET* OF YOU!
THAT...SORTA... MAKES SENSE. I'LL...THINK ABOUT IT? (YOU'RE BEING WEIRD.)
NO. JUST...NO. PEOPLE *AREN'T* MACHINES.

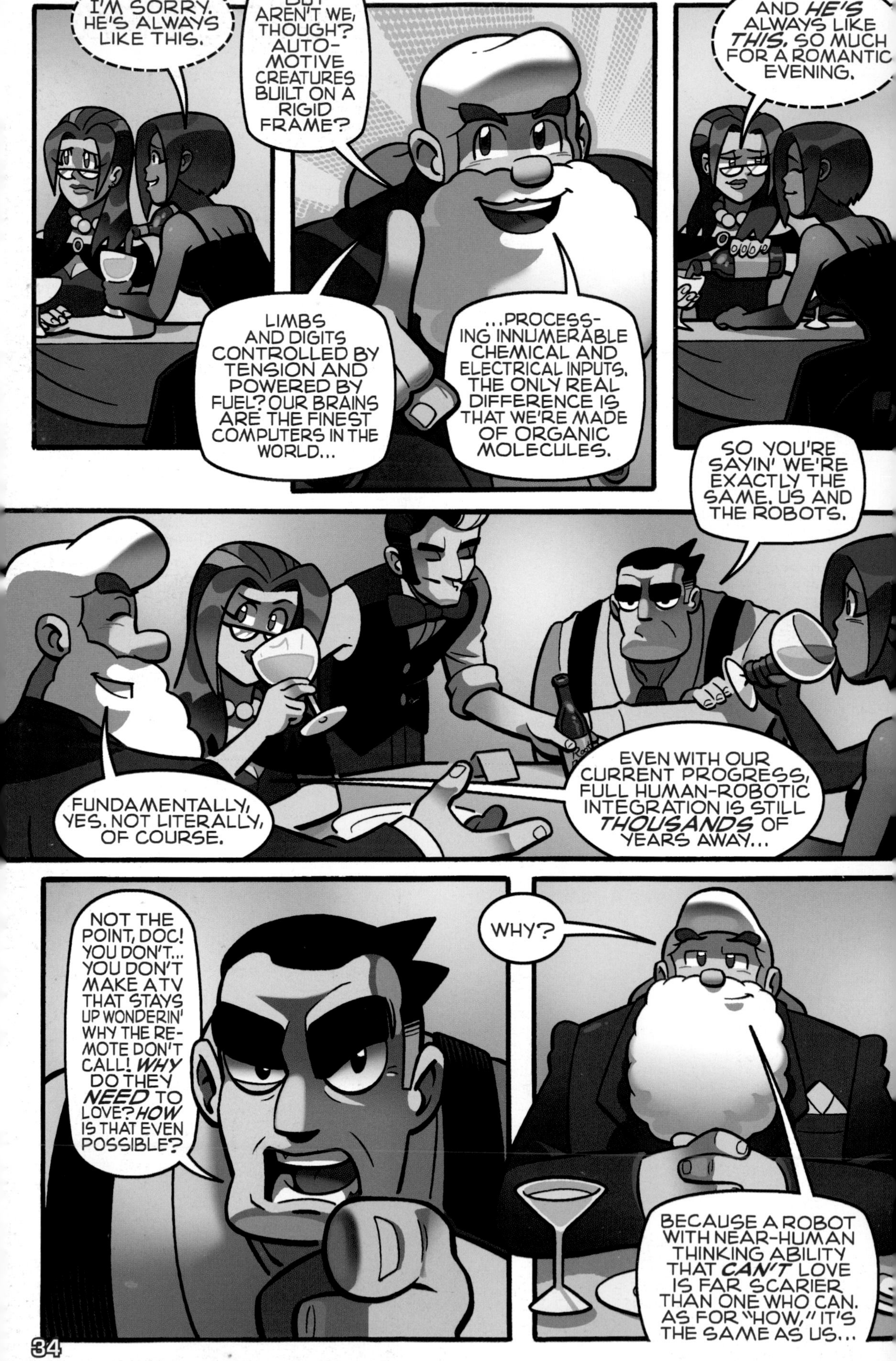
I'M SORRY. HE'S ALWAYS LIKE THIS.
BUT AREN'T WE, THOUGH? AUTO-MOTIVE CREATURES BUILT ON A RIGID FRAME?
LIMBS AND DIGITS CONTROLLED BY TENSION AND POWERED BY FUEL? OUR BRAINS ARE THE FINEST COMPUTERS IN THE WORLD...
...PROCESS-ING INNUMERABLE CHEMICAL AND ELECTRICAL INPUTS. THE ONLY REAL DIFFERENCE IS THAT WE'RE MADE OF ORGANIC MOLECULES.
AND *HE'S* ALWAYS LIKE *THIS.* SO MUCH FOR A ROMANTIC EVENING.
SO YOU'RE SAYIN' WE'RE EXACTLY THE SAME. US AND THE ROBOTS.
FUNDAMENTALLY, YES. NOT LITERALLY, OF COURSE.
EVEN WITH OUR CURRENT PROGRESS, FULL HUMAN-ROBOTIC INTEGRATION IS STILL *THOUSANDS* OF YEARS AWAY...
NOT THE POINT, DOC! YOU DON'T... YOU DON'T MAKE A TV THAT STAYS UP WONDERIN' WHY THE RE-MOTE DON'T CALL! *WHY* DO THEY *NEED* TO LOVE? *HOW* IS THAT EVEN POSSIBLE?
WHY?
BECAUSE A ROBOT WITH NEAR-HUMAN THINKING ABILITY THAT *CAN'T* LOVE IS FAR SCARIER THAN ONE WHO CAN. AS FOR "HOW," IT'S THE SAME AS US...

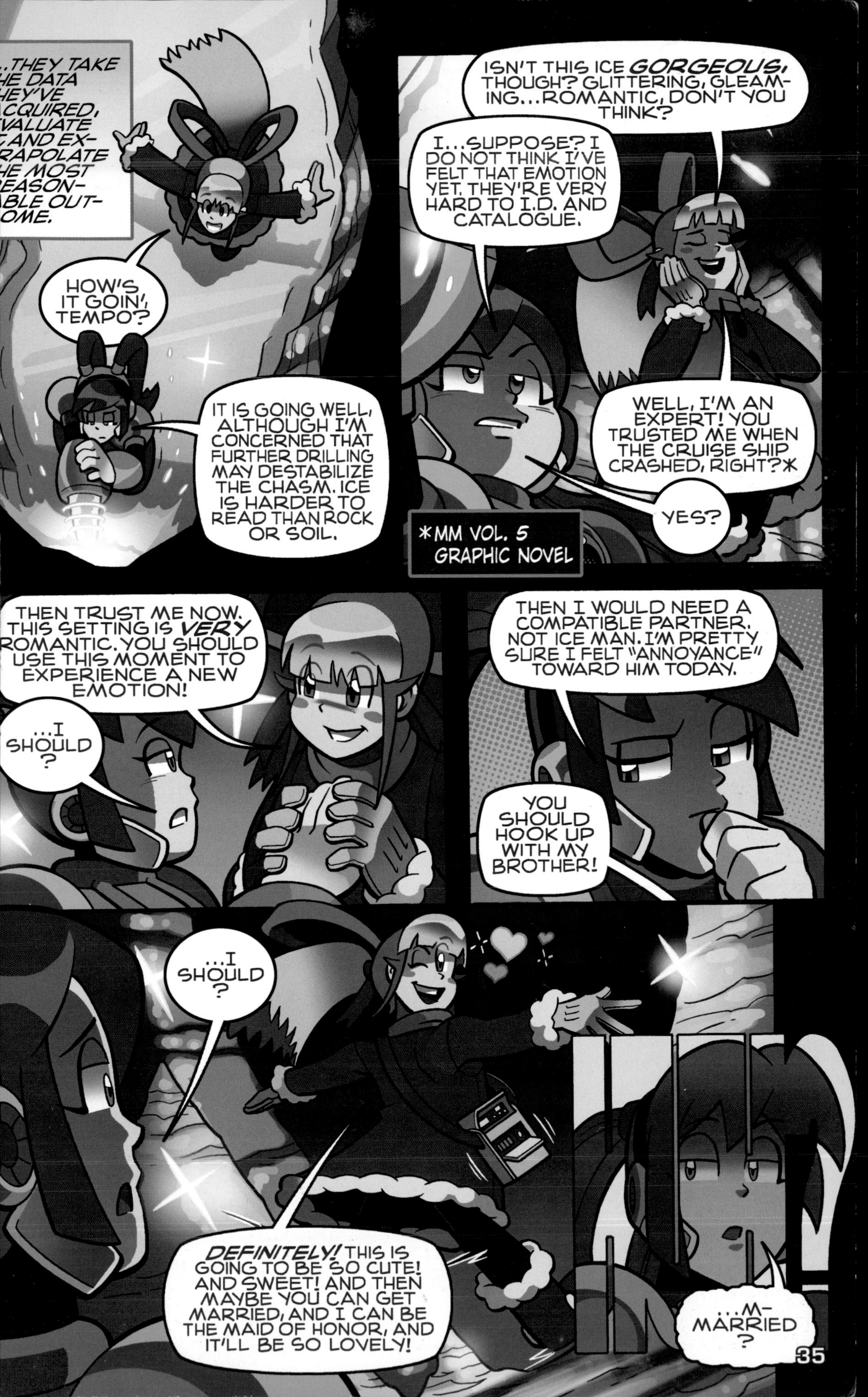
...THEY TAKE THE DATA THEY'VE ACQUIRED, EVALUATE IT, AND EXTRAPOLATE THE MOST REASONABLE OUTCOME.
HOW'S IT GOIN', TEMPO?
IT IS GOING WELL, ALTHOUGH I'M CONCERNED THAT FURTHER DRILLING MAY DESTABILIZE THE CHASM. ICE IS HARDER TO READ THAN ROCK OR SOIL.
ISN'T THIS ICE GORGEOUS, THOUGH? GLITTERING, GLEAMING...ROMANTIC, DON'T YOU THINK?
I...SUPPOSE? I DO NOT THINK I'VE FELT THAT EMOTION YET. THEY'RE VERY HARD TO I.D. AND CATALOGUE.
WELL, I'M AN EXPERT! YOU TRUSTED ME WHEN THE CRUISE SHIP CRASHED, RIGHT?*
YES?
*MM VOL. 5 GRAPHIC NOVEL
THEN TRUST ME NOW. THIS SETTING IS VERY ROMANTIC. YOU SHOULD USE THIS MOMENT TO EXPERIENCE A NEW EMOTION!
...I SHOULD?
THEN I WOULD NEED A COMPATIBLE PARTNER. NOT ICE MAN. I'M PRETTY SURE I FELT "ANNOYANCE" TOWARD HIM TODAY.
YOU SHOULD HOOK UP WITH MY BROTHER!
...I SHOULD?
DEFINITELY! THIS IS GOING TO BE SO CUTE! AND SWEET! AND THEN MAYBE YOU CAN GET MARRIED, AND I CAN BE THE MAID OF HONOR, AND IT'LL BE SO LOVELY!
...M-MARRIED?

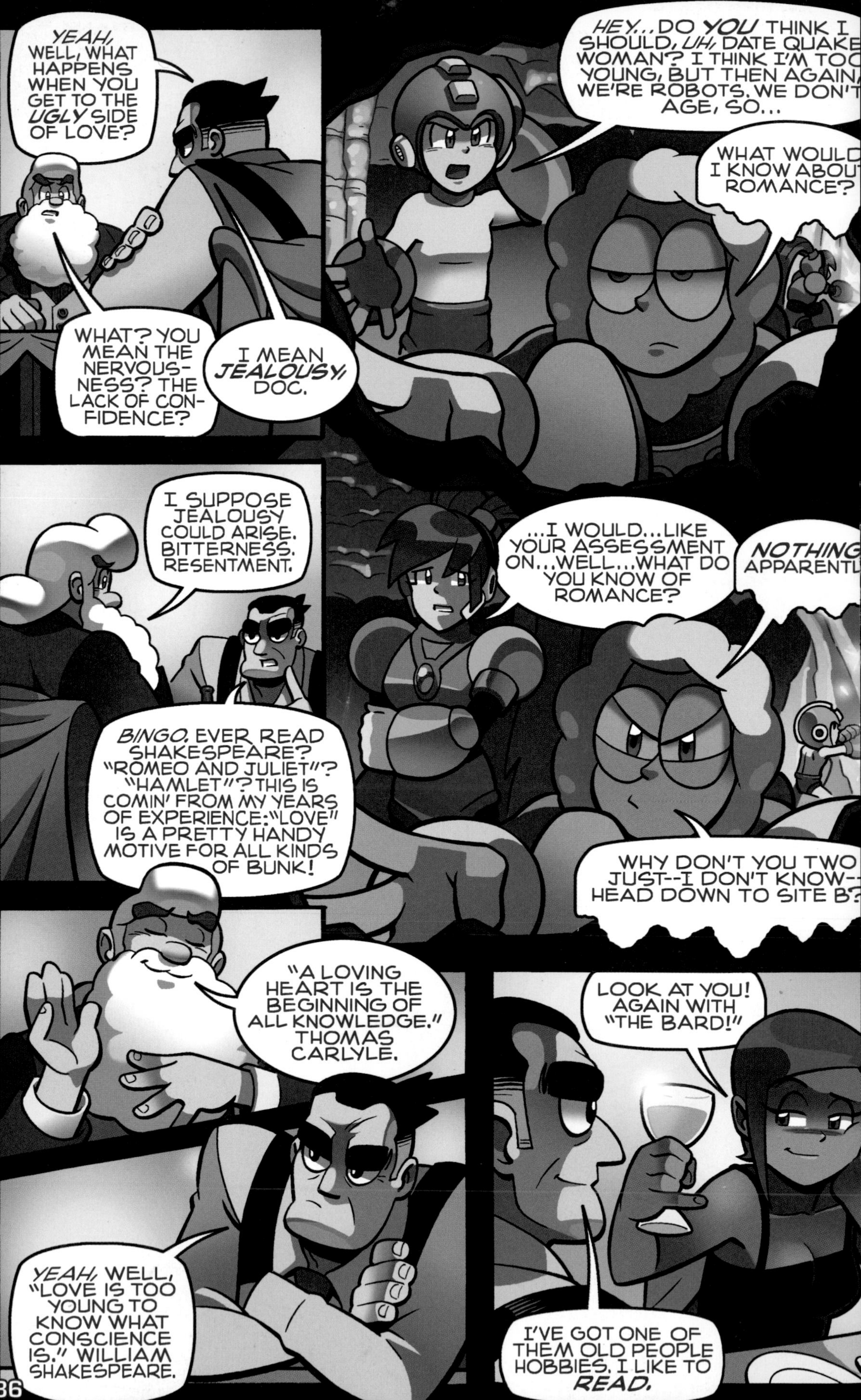
YEAH, WELL, WHAT HAPPENS WHEN YOU GET TO THE UGLY SIDE OF LOVE?
WHAT? YOU MEAN THE NERVOUS-NESS? THE LACK OF CON-FIDENCE?
I MEAN JEALOUSY, DOC.
HEY...DO YOU THINK I SHOULD, UH, DATE QUAKE WOMAN? I THINK I'M TOO YOUNG, BUT THEN AGAIN, WE'RE ROBOTS. WE DON'T AGE, SO...
WHAT WOULD I KNOW ABOUT ROMANCE?
I SUPPOSE JEALOUSY COULD ARISE. BITTERNESS. RESENTMENT.
BINGO. EVER READ SHAKESPEARE? "ROMEO AND JULIET"? "HAMLET"? THIS IS COMIN' FROM MY YEARS OF EXPERIENCE: "LOVE" IS A PRETTY HANDY MOTIVE FOR ALL KINDS OF BUNK!
...I WOULD...LIKE YOUR ASSESSMENT ON...WELL...WHAT DO YOU KNOW OF ROMANCE?
NOTHING APPARENTLY
WHY DON'T YOU TWO JUST--I DON'T KNOW--HEAD DOWN TO SITE B?
"A LOVING HEART IS THE BEGINNING OF ALL KNOWLEDGE." THOMAS CARLYLE.
YEAH, WELL, "LOVE IS TOO YOUNG TO KNOW WHAT CONSCIENCE IS." WILLIAM SHAKESPEARE.
LOOK AT YOU! AGAIN WITH "THE BARD!"
I'VE GOT ONE OF THEM OLD PEOPLE HOBBIES. I LIKE TO READ.

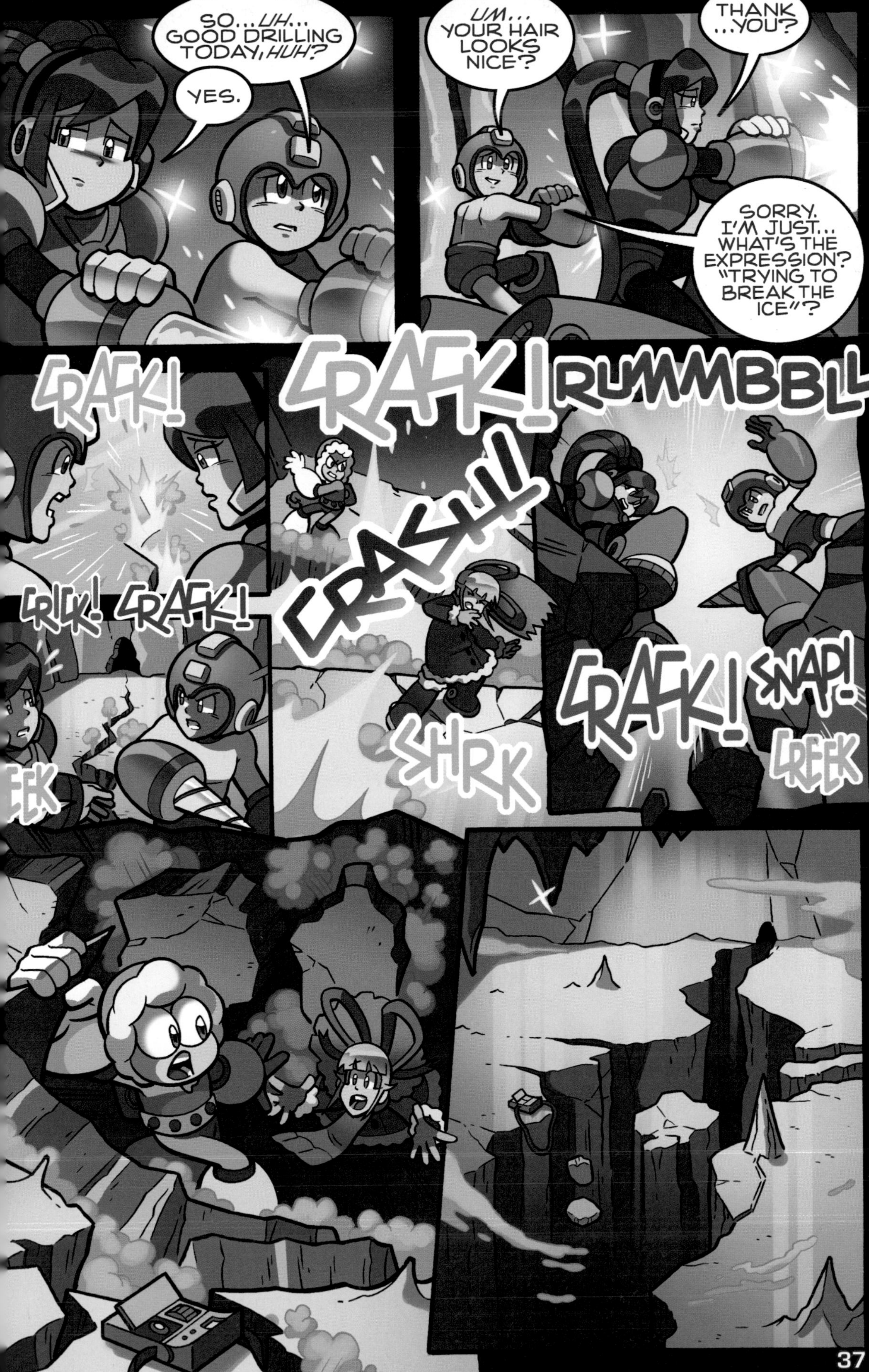
SO...UH... GOOD DRILLING TODAY, HUH?
YES.
UM... YOUR HAIR LOOKS NICE?
THANK ...YOU?
SORRY. I'M JUST... WHAT'S THE EXPRESSION? "TRYING TO BREAK THE ICE"?
CRAFK!
CRAFK!
RUMMBBLL
CRASH!
CRICK! CRAFK!
SHRK
CRAFK!
SNAP!
CREEK

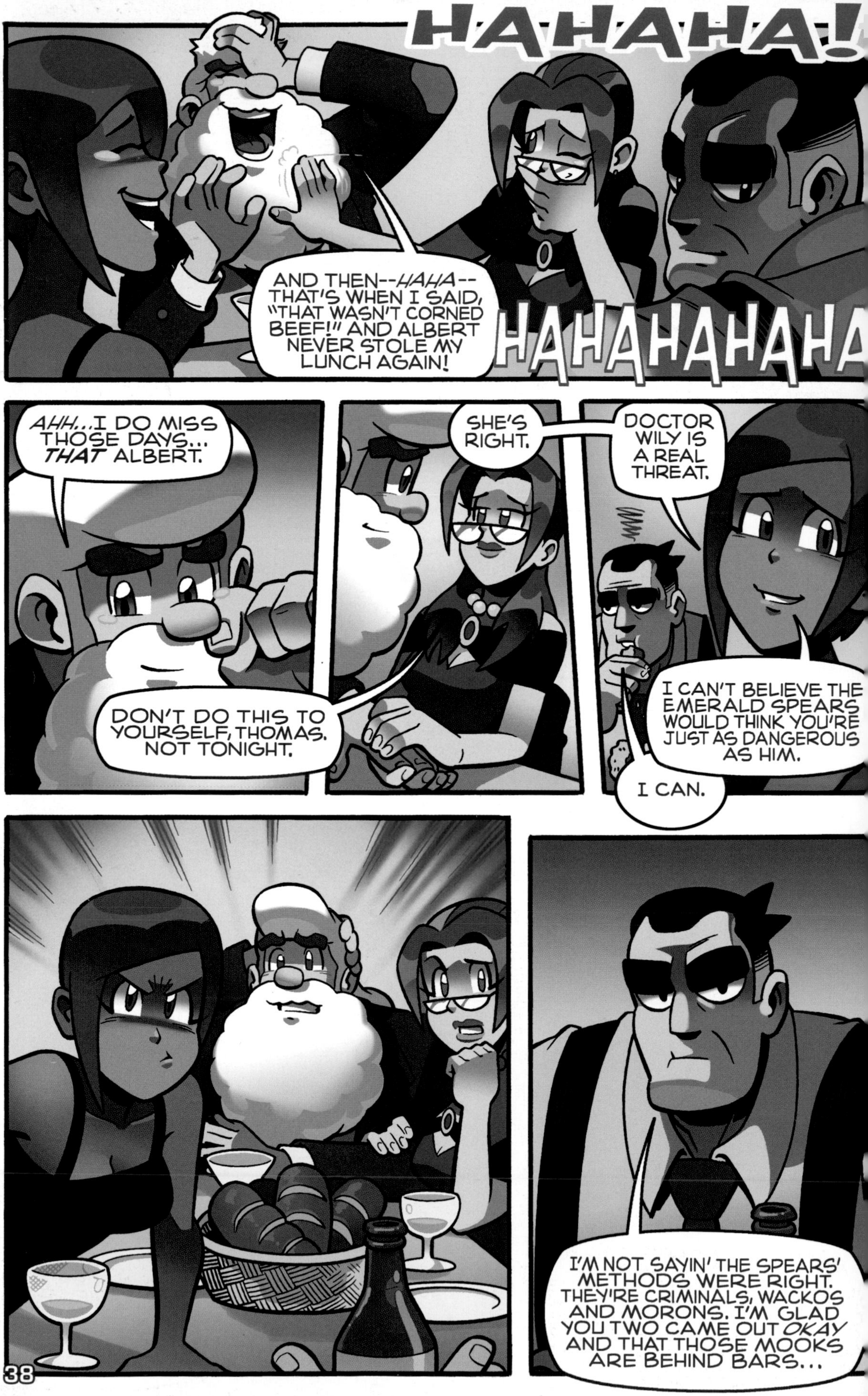
HAHAHA!
AND THEN--HAHA--THAT'S WHEN I SAID, "THAT WASN'T CORNED BEEF!" AND ALBERT NEVER STOLE MY LUNCH AGAIN!
HAHAHAHAHAHA
AHH...I DO MISS THOSE DAYS... THAT ALBERT.
DON'T DO THIS TO YOURSELF, THOMAS. NOT TONIGHT.
SHE'S RIGHT.
DOCTOR WILY IS A REAL THREAT.
I CAN'T BELIEVE THE EMERALD SPEARS WOULD THINK YOU'RE JUST AS DANGEROUS AS HIM.
I CAN.
I'M NOT SAYIN' THE SPEARS' METHODS WERE RIGHT. THEY'RE CRIMINALS, WACKOS AND MORONS. I'M GLAD YOU TWO CAME OUT OKAY AND THAT THOSE MOOKS ARE BEHIND BARS...

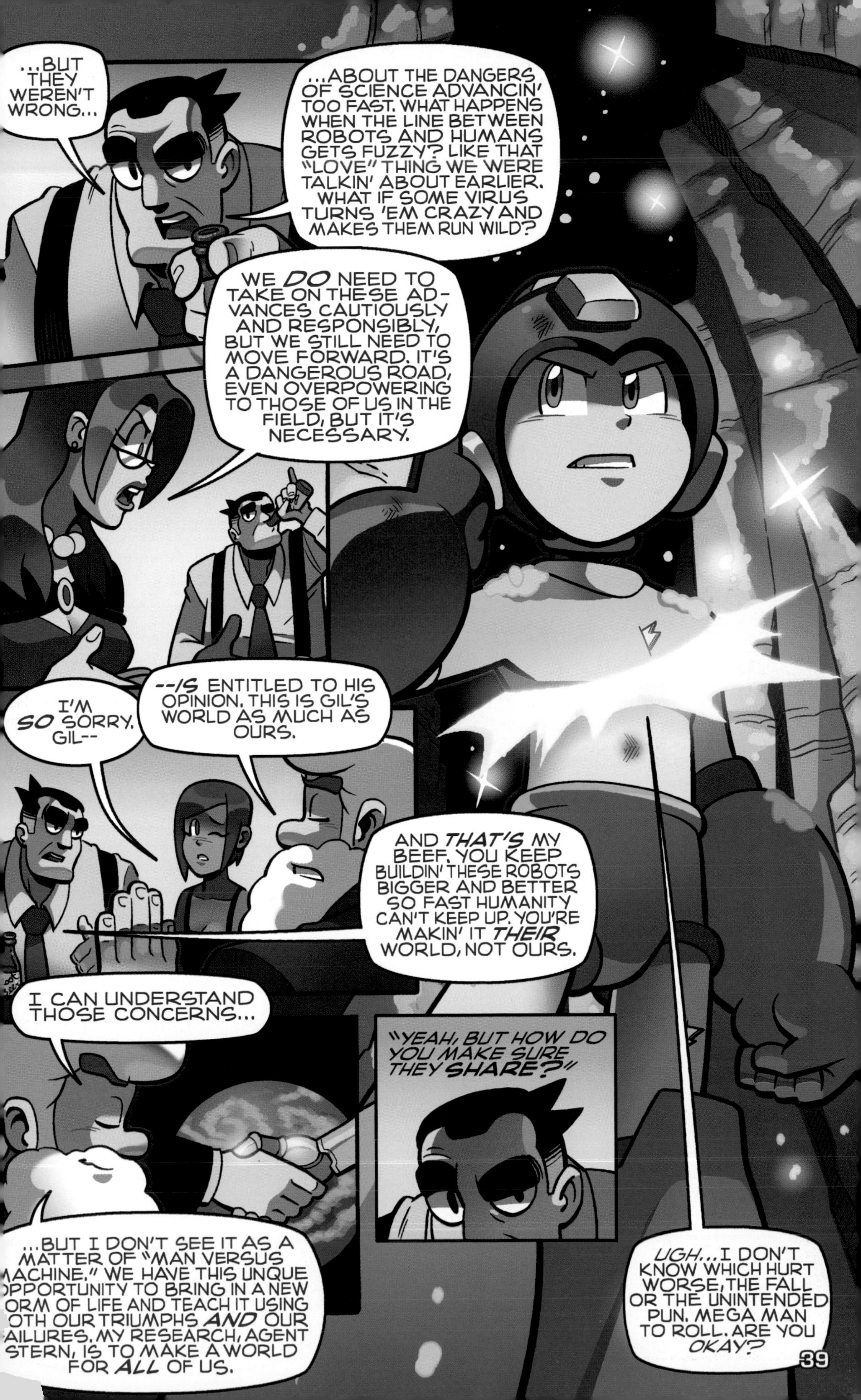
...BUT THEY WEREN'T WRONG...
...ABOUT THE DANGERS OF SCIENCE ADVANCIN' TOO FAST. WHAT HAPPENS WHEN THE LINE BETWEEN ROBOTS AND HUMANS GETS FUZZY? LIKE THAT "LOVE" THING WE WERE TALKIN' ABOUT EARLIER. WHAT IF SOME VIRUS TURNS 'EM CRAZY AND MAKES THEM RUN WILD?
WE *DO* NEED TO TAKE ON THESE ADVANCES CAUTIOUSLY AND RESPONSIBLY, BUT WE STILL NEED TO MOVE FORWARD. IT'S A DANGEROUS ROAD, EVEN OVERPOWERING TO THOSE OF US IN THE FIELD, BUT IT'S NECESSARY.
I'M *SO* SORRY. GIL--
--*IS* ENTITLED TO HIS OPINION. THIS IS GIL'S WORLD AS MUCH AS OURS.
AND *THAT'S* MY BEEF. YOU KEEP BUILDIN' THESE ROBOTS BIGGER AND BETTER SO FAST HUMANITY CAN'T KEEP UP. YOU'RE MAKIN' IT *THEIR* WORLD, NOT OURS.
I CAN UNDERSTAND THOSE CONCERNS...
...BUT I DON'T SEE IT AS A MATTER OF "MAN VERSUS MACHINE." WE HAVE THIS UNQUE OPPORTUNITY TO BRING IN A NEW FORM OF LIFE AND TEACH IT USING BOTH OUR TRIUMPHS *AND* OUR FAILURES. MY RESEARCH, AGENT STERN, IS TO MAKE A WORLD FOR *ALL* OF US.
"YEAH, BUT HOW DO YOU MAKE SURE THEY SHARE?"
UGH... I DON'T KNOW WHICH HURT WORSE, THE FALL OR THE UNINTENDED PUN. MEGA MAN TO ROLL. ARE YOU *OKAY?*

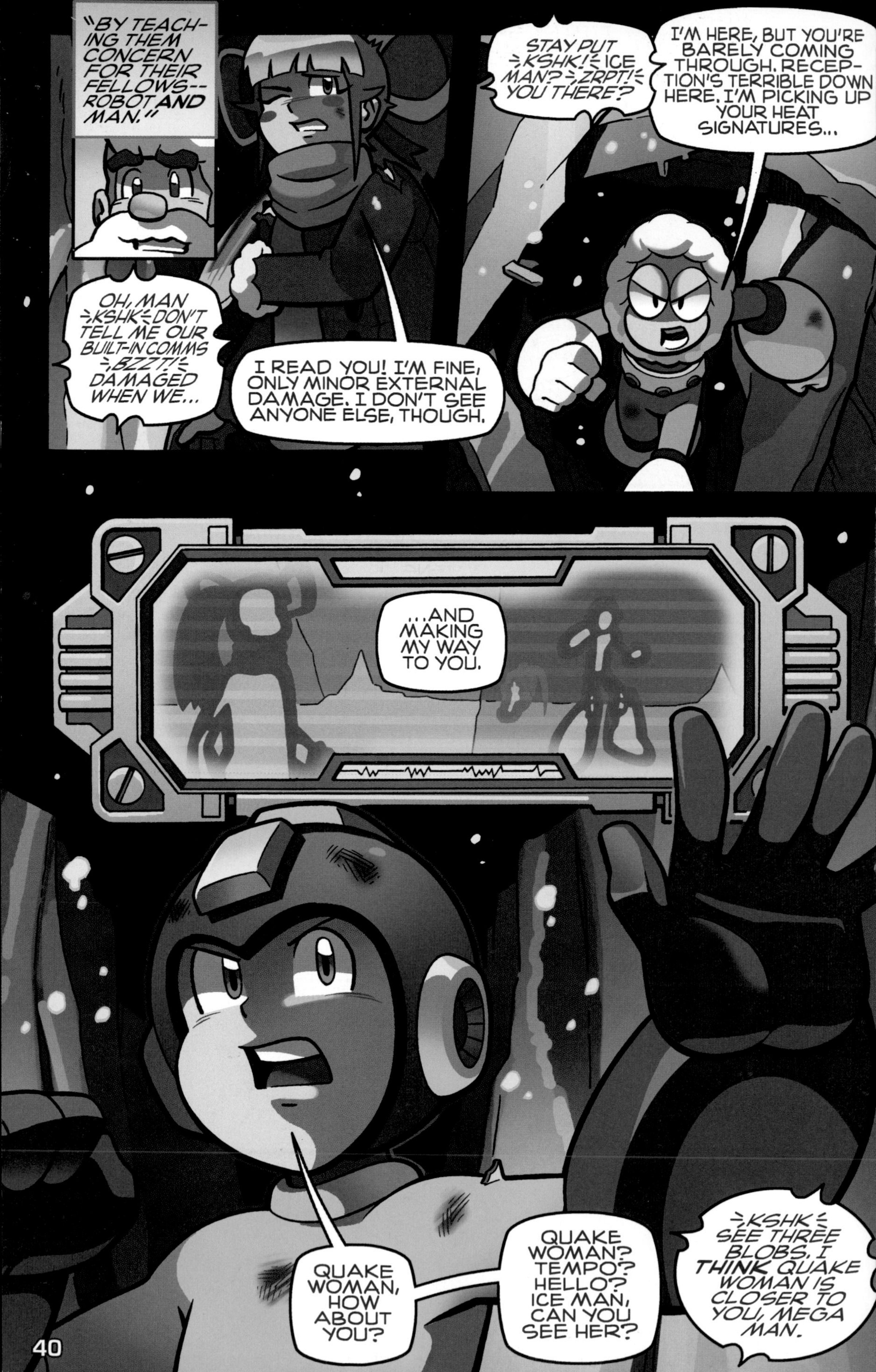
"BY TEACHING THEM CONCERN FOR THEIR FELLOWS-- ROBOT AND MAN."
OH, MAN ~KSHK~ DON'T TELL ME OUR BUILT-IN COMMS ~BZZT!~ DAMAGED WHEN WE...
I READ YOU! I'M FINE, ONLY MINOR EXTERNAL DAMAGE. I DON'T SEE ANYONE ELSE, THOUGH.
STAY PUT ~KSHK!~ ICE MAN? ~ZRPT!~ YOU THERE?
I'M HERE, BUT YOU'RE BARELY COMING THROUGH. RECEPTION'S TERRIBLE DOWN HERE. I'M PICKING UP YOUR HEAT SIGNATURES...
...AND MAKING MY WAY TO YOU.
QUAKE WOMAN, HOW ABOUT YOU?
QUAKE WOMAN? TEMPO? HELLO? ICE MAN, CAN YOU SEE HER?
~KSHK~ SEE THREE BLOBS. I THINK QUAKE WOMAN IS CLOSER TO YOU, MEGA MAN.

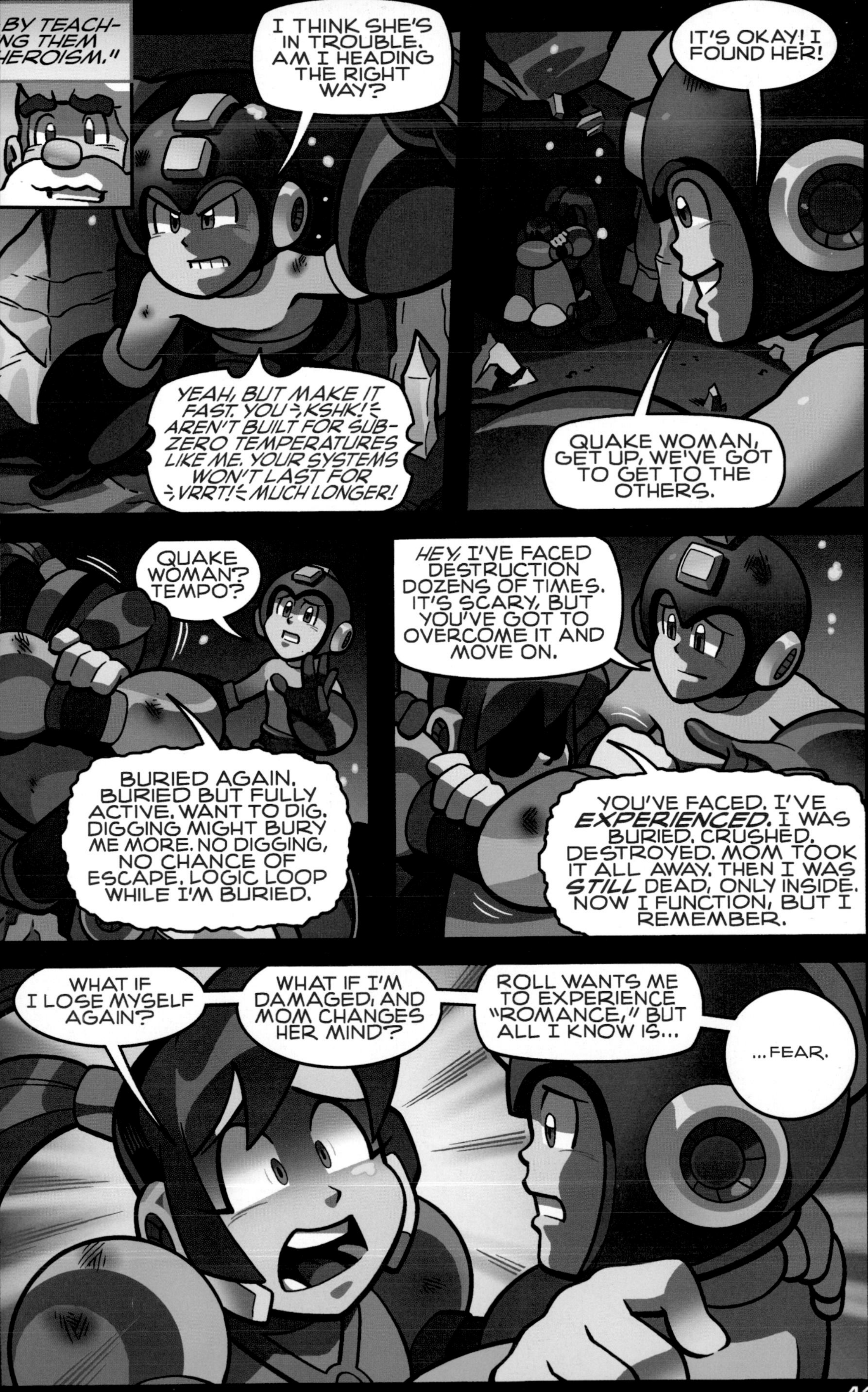

BY TEACH-
NG THEM
HEROISM."
I THINK SHE'S IN TROUBLE. AM I HEADING THE RIGHT WAY?
YEAH, BUT MAKE IT FAST. YOU ⁼KSHK!⁼ AREN'T BUILT FOR SUB-ZERO TEMPERATURES LIKE ME. YOUR SYSTEMS WON'T LAST FOR ⁼VRRT!⁼ MUCH LONGER!
IT'S OKAY! I FOUND HER!
QUAKE WOMAN, GET UP, WE'VE GOT TO GET TO THE OTHERS.
QUAKE WOMAN? TEMPO?
BURIED AGAIN. BURIED BUT FULLY ACTIVE. WANT TO DIG. DIGGING MIGHT BURY ME MORE. NO DIGGING, NO CHANCE OF ESCAPE. LOGIC LOOP WHILE I'M BURIED.
HEY, I'VE FACED DESTRUCTION DOZENS OF TIMES. IT'S SCARY, BUT YOU'VE GOT TO OVERCOME IT AND MOVE ON.
YOU'VE FACED. I'VE EXPERIENCED. I WAS BURIED. CRUSHED. DESTROYED. MOM TOOK IT ALL AWAY. THEN I WAS STILL DEAD, ONLY INSIDE. NOW I FUNCTION, BUT I REMEMBER.
WHAT IF I LOSE MYSELF AGAIN?
WHAT IF I'M DAMAGED, AND MOM CHANGES HER MIND?
ROLL WANTS ME TO EXPERIENCE "ROMANCE," BUT ALL I KNOW IS...
...FEAR.

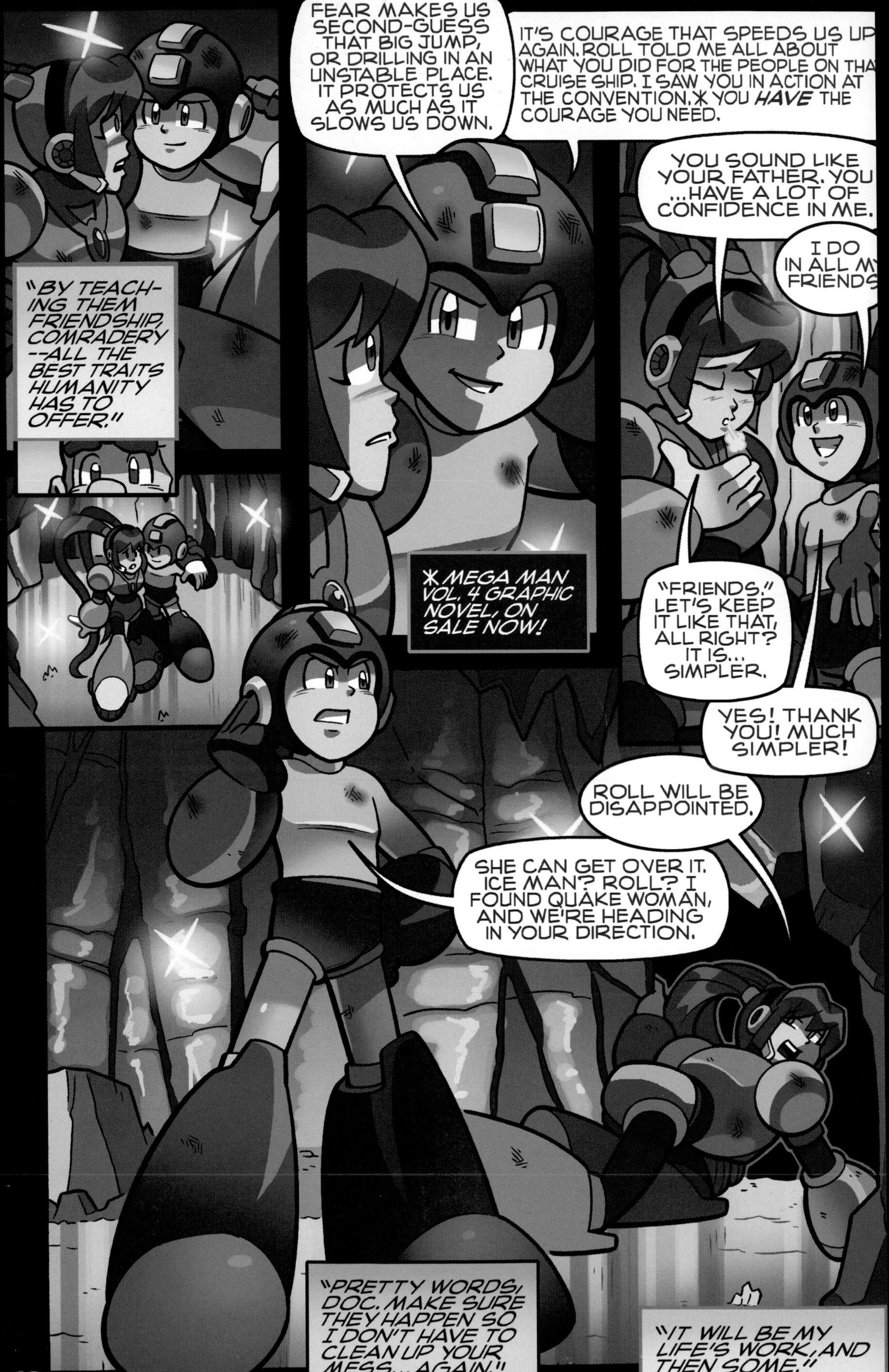
FEAR MAKES US SECOND-GUESS THAT BIG JUMP, OR DRILLING IN AN UNSTABLE PLACE. IT PROTECTS US AS MUCH AS IT SLOWS US DOWN.
IT'S COURAGE THAT SPEEDS US UP AGAIN. ROLL TOLD ME ALL ABOUT WHAT YOU DID FOR THE PEOPLE ON THA CRUISE SHIP. I SAW YOU IN ACTION AT THE CONVENTION.* YOU *HAVE* THE COURAGE YOU NEED.
MEGA MAN VOL. 4 GRAPHIC NOVEL, ON SALE NOW!
"BY TEACHING THEM FRIENDSHIP, COMRADERY --ALL THE BEST TRAITS HUMANITY HAS TO OFFER."
YOU SOUND LIKE YOUR FATHER. YOU ...HAVE A LOT OF CONFIDENCE IN ME.
I DO IN ALL MY FRIENDS
"FRIENDS." LET'S KEEP IT LIKE THAT, ALL RIGHT? IT IS... SIMPLER.
YES! THANK YOU! MUCH SIMPLER!
ROLL WILL BE DISAPPOINTED.
SHE CAN GET OVER IT. ICE MAN? ROLL? I FOUND QUAKE WOMAN, AND WE'RE HEADING IN YOUR DIRECTION.
"PRETTY WORDS, DOC. MAKE SURE THEY HAPPEN SO I DON'T HAVE TO CLEAN UP YOUR MESS... AGAIN."
"IT WILL BE MY LIFE'S WORK, AND THEN SOME."

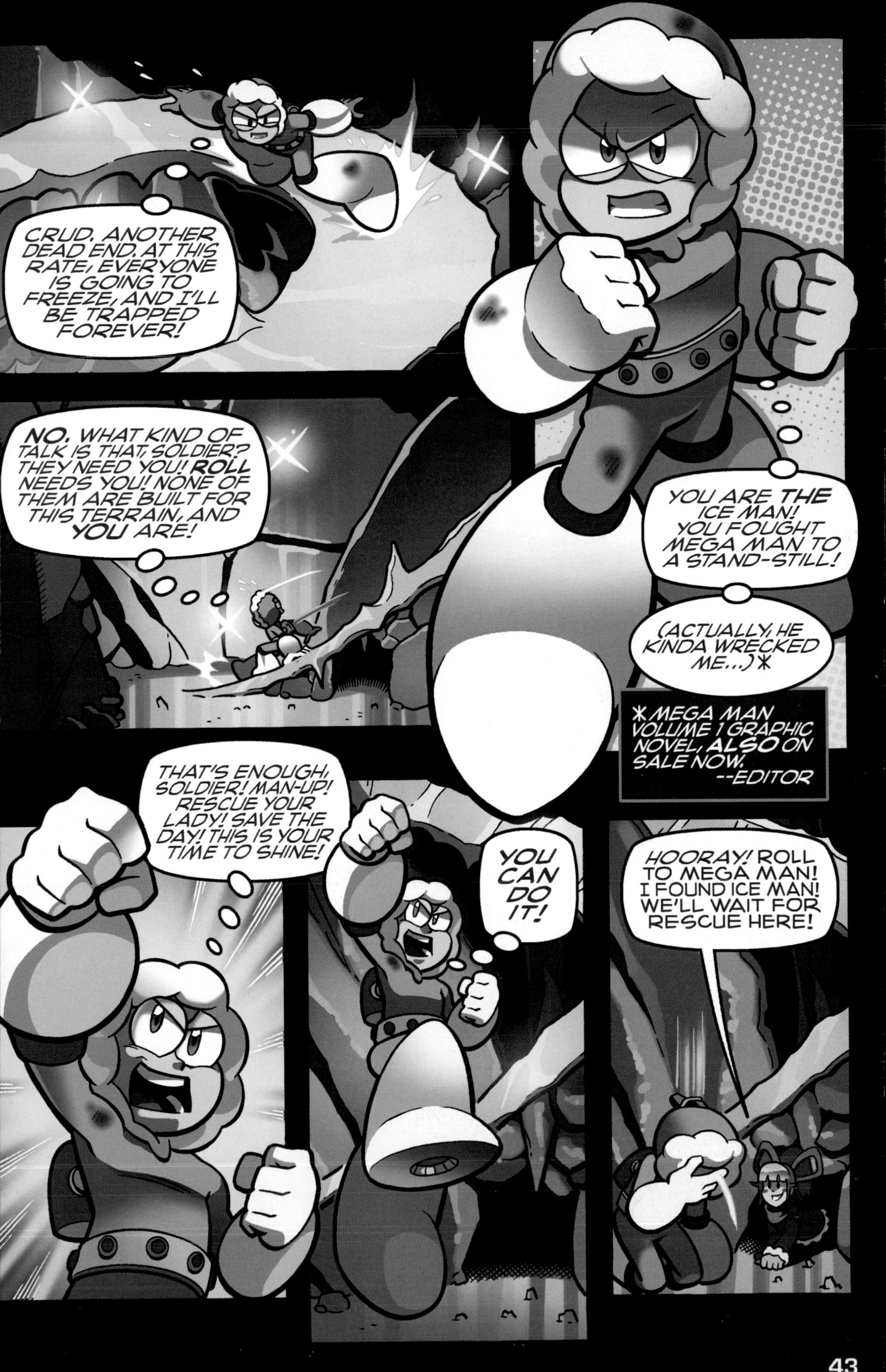
CRUD. ANOTHER DEAD END. AT THIS RATE, EVERYONE IS GOING TO FREEZE, AND I'LL BE TRAPPED FOREVER!
NO. WHAT KIND OF TALK IS THAT, SOLDIER? THEY NEED YOU! ROLL NEEDS YOU! NONE OF THEM ARE BUILT FOR THIS TERRAIN, AND YOU ARE!
YOU ARE THE ICE MAN! YOU FOUGHT MEGA MAN TO A STAND-STILL!
(ACTUALLY, HE KINDA WRECKED ME...)*
*MEGA MAN VOLUME 1 GRAPHIC NOVEL, ALSO ON SALE NOW. --EDITOR
THAT'S ENOUGH, SOLDIER! MAN-UP! RESCUE YOUR LADY! SAVE THE DAY! THIS IS YOUR TIME TO SHINE!
YOU CAN DO IT!
HOORAY! ROLL TO MEGA MAN! I FOUND ICE MAN! WE'LL WAIT FOR RESCUE HERE!

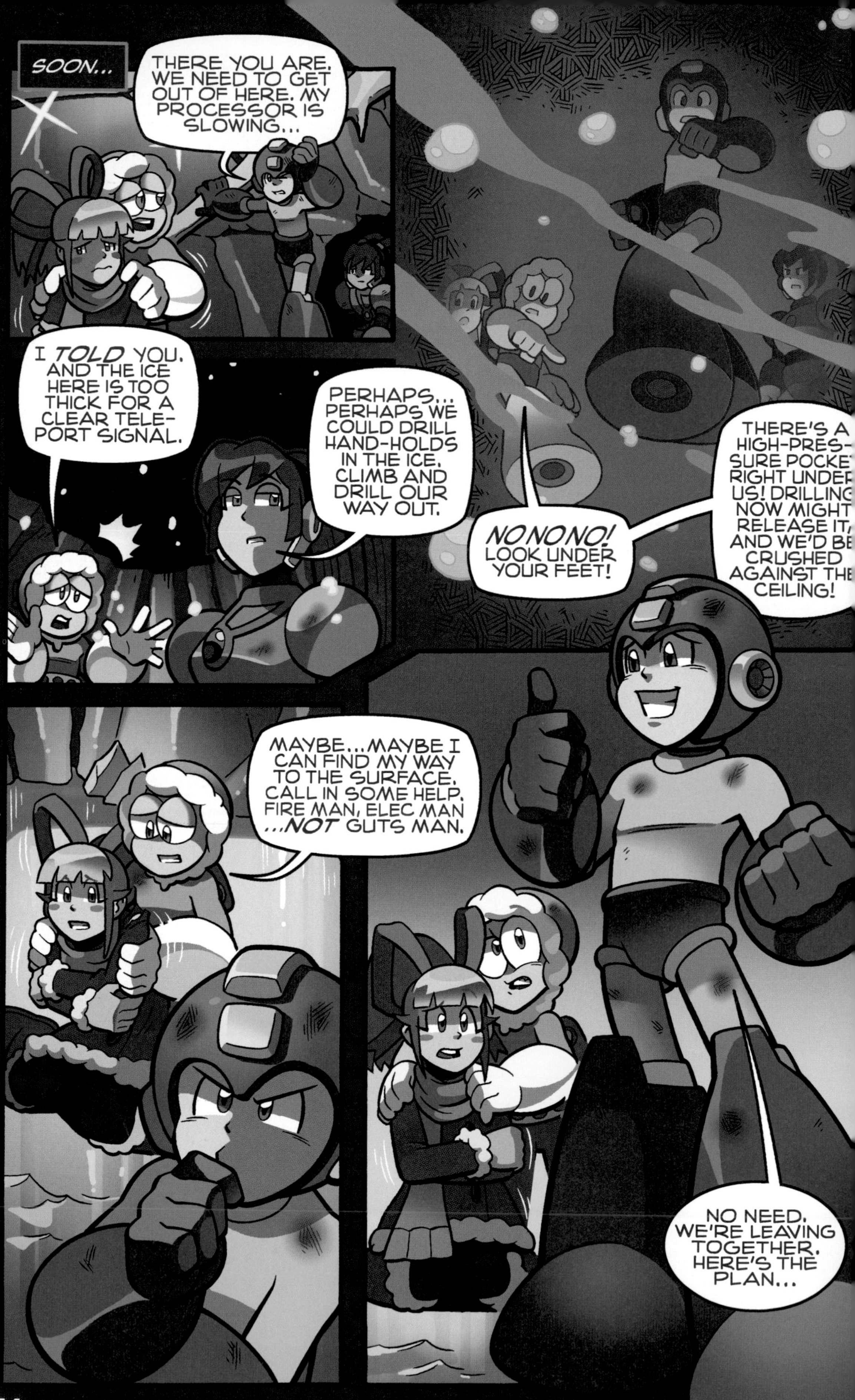
SOON...
THERE YOU ARE. WE NEED TO GET OUT OF HERE. MY PROCESSOR IS SLOWING...
I TOLD YOU. AND THE ICE HERE IS TOO THICK FOR A CLEAR TELE-PORT SIGNAL.
PERHAPS... PERHAPS WE COULD DRILL HAND-HOLDS IN THE ICE, CLIMB AND DRILL OUR WAY OUT.
NONONO! LOOK UNDER YOUR FEET!
THERE'S A HIGH-PRES-SURE POCKET RIGHT UNDER US! DRILLING NOW MIGHT RELEASE IT, AND WE'D BE CRUSHED AGAINST THE CEILING!
MAYBE...MAYBE I CAN FIND MY WAY TO THE SURFACE. CALL IN SOME HELP. FIRE MAN, ELEC MAN ...NOT GUTS MAN.
NO NEED. WE'RE LEAVING TOGETHER. HERE'S THE PLAN...

"FIRST, WE'RE GOING TO RELEASE THE HIGH-PRESSURE WATER.

"I'LL PUNCH THROUGH...

"...THEN ICE MAN IMMEDIATELY MAKES AN ICE PLATFORM.

"AND WE RIDE IT STRAIGHT TO THE SURFACE!"

THAT WAS CRAZY AND STUPID AND WE NEARLY DIED!

BUT IT WORKED!

WELL... TEMPO... WHAT ARE YOU FEELING NOW?

TERROR? EXCITEMENT? I DON'T KNOW! ...BUT PART OF ME WANTS TO DO IT AGAIN!

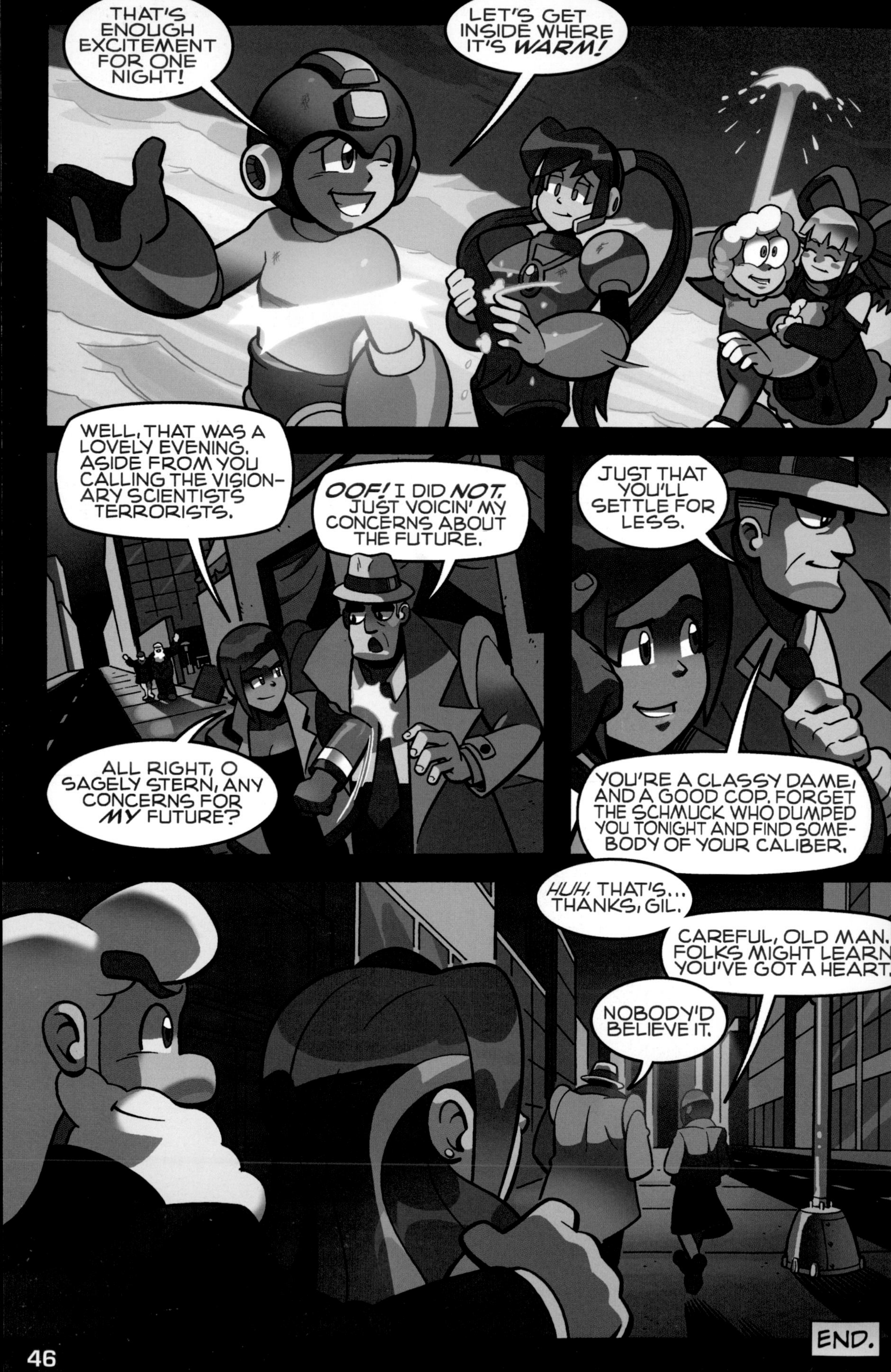
THAT'S ENOUGH EXCITEMENT FOR ONE NIGHT!
LET'S GET INSIDE WHERE IT'S *WARM!*
WELL, THAT WAS A LOVELY EVENING. ASIDE FROM YOU CALLING THE VISIONARY SCIENTISTS TERRORISTS.
OOF! I DID *NOT.* JUST VOICIN' MY CONCERNS ABOUT THE FUTURE.
ALL RIGHT, O SAGELY STERN, ANY CONCERNS FOR *MY* FUTURE?
JUST THAT YOU'LL SETTLE FOR LESS.
YOU'RE A CLASSY DAME, AND A GOOD COP. FORGET THE SCHMUCK WHO DUMPED YOU TONIGHT AND FIND SOMEBODY OF YOUR CALIBER.
HUH. THAT'S... THANKS, GIL.
CAREFUL, OLD MAN. FOLKS MIGHT LEARN YOU'VE GOT A HEART.
NOBODY'D BELIEVE IT.
END.

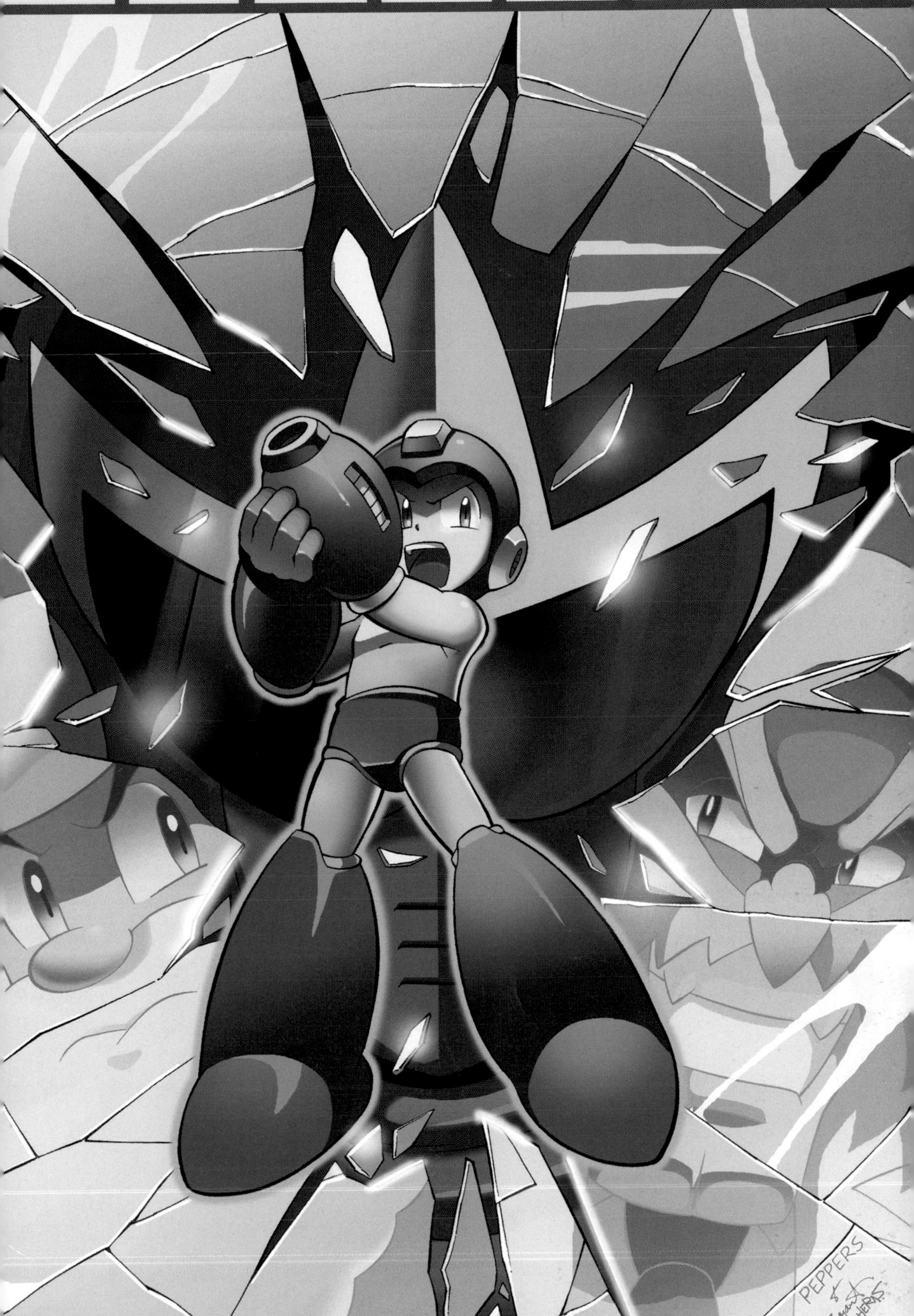
PEPPERS
&
Bryant
HERMS

CHAPTER 3

COVER BY PATRICK SPAZIANTE, JAMAL PEPPERS, RICK BYRANT AND MATT HERMS

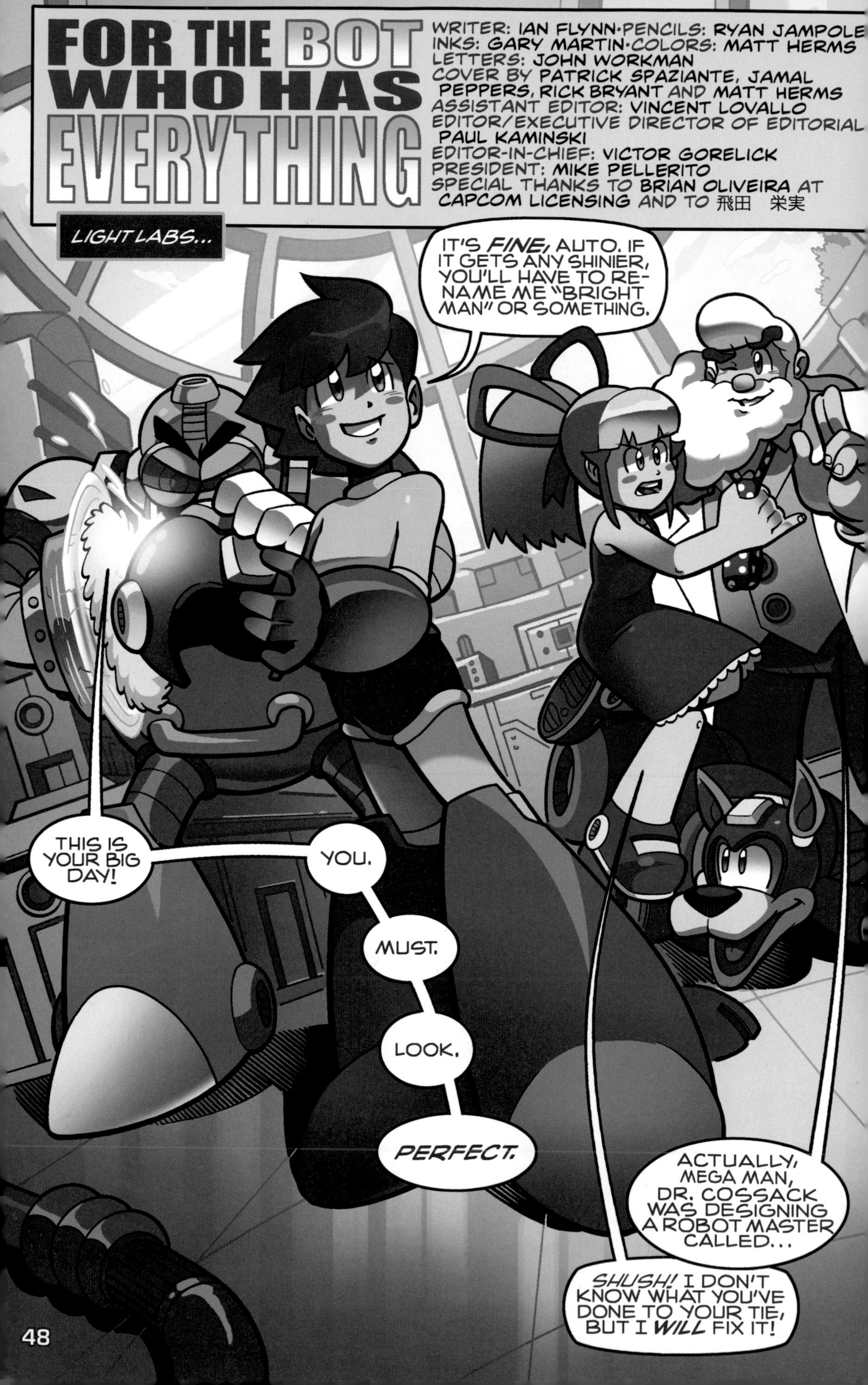
FOR THE BOT WHO HAS EVERYTHING
WRITER: IAN FLYNN·PENCILS: RYAN JAMPOLE
INKS: GARY MARTIN·COLORS: MATT HERMS
LETTERS: JOHN WORKMAN
COVER BY PATRICK SPAZIANTE, JAMAL PEPPERS, RICK BRYANT AND MATT HERMS
ASSISTANT EDITOR: VINCENT LOVALLO
EDITOR/EXECUTIVE DIRECTOR OF EDITORIAL PAUL KAMINSKI
EDITOR-IN-CHIEF: VICTOR GORELICK
PRESIDENT: MIKE PELLERITO
SPECIAL THANKS TO BRIAN OLIVEIRA AT CAPCOM LICENSING AND TO 飛田　栄実
LIGHT LABS...
IT'S *FINE*, AUTO. IF IT GETS ANY SHINIER, YOU'LL HAVE TO RE-NAME ME "BRIGHT MAN" OR SOMETHING.
THIS IS YOUR BIG DAY!
YOU.
MUST.
LOOK.
PERFECT.
ACTUALLY, MEGA MAN, DR. COSSACK WAS DESIGNING A ROBOT MASTER CALLED...
SHUSH! I DON'T KNOW WHAT YOU'VE DONE TO YOUR TIE, BUT I *WILL* FIX IT!

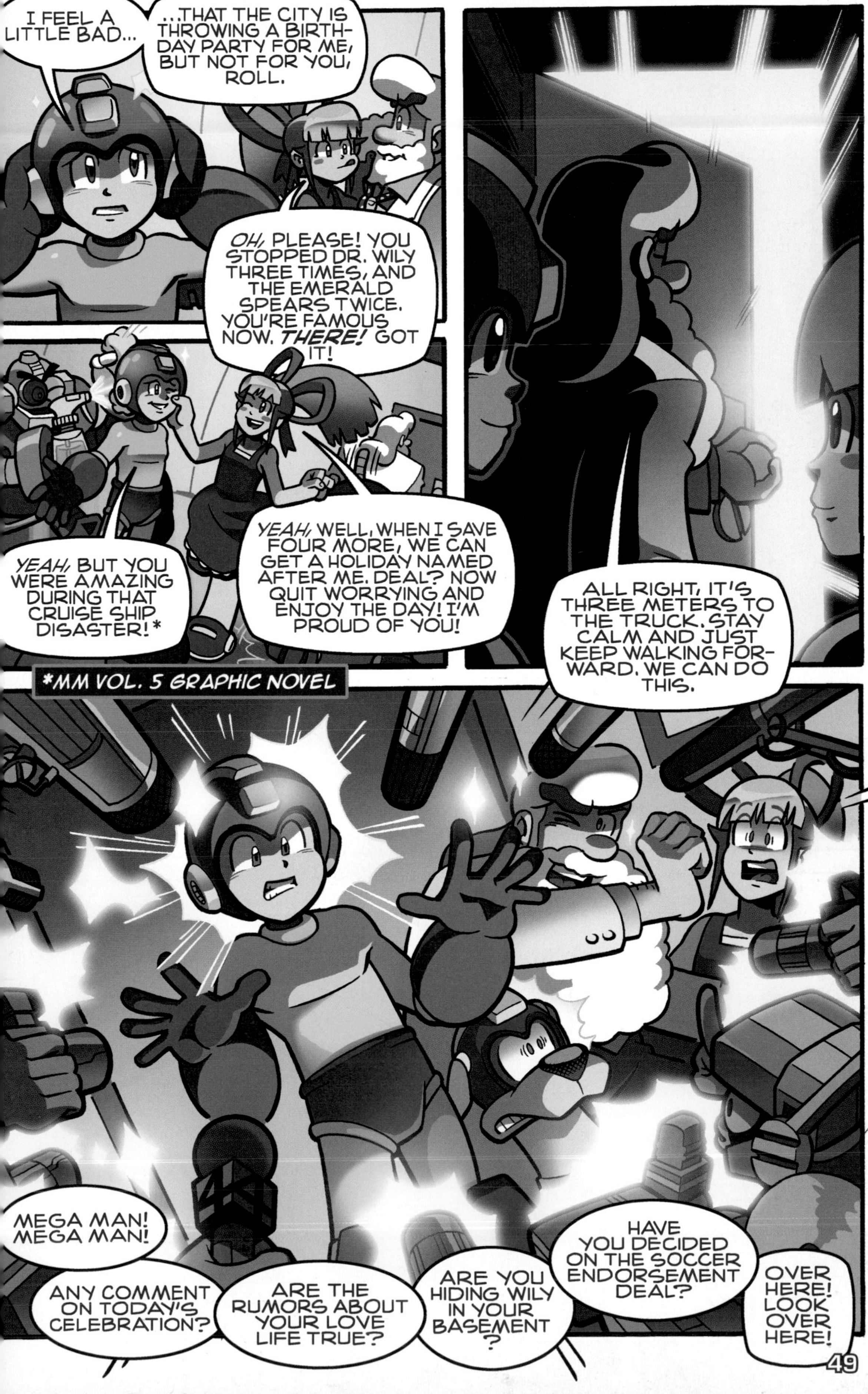
I FEEL A LITTLE BAD...
...THAT THE CITY IS THROWING A BIRTH-DAY PARTY FOR ME, BUT NOT FOR YOU, ROLL.
OH, PLEASE! YOU STOPPED DR. WILY THREE TIMES, AND THE EMERALD SPEARS TWICE. YOU'RE FAMOUS NOW. THERE! GOT IT!
YEAH, BUT YOU WERE AMAZING DURING THAT CRUISE SHIP DISASTER!*
YEAH, WELL, WHEN I SAVE FOUR MORE, WE CAN GET A HOLIDAY NAMED AFTER ME. DEAL? NOW QUIT WORRYING AND ENJOY THE DAY! I'M PROUD OF YOU!
*MM VOL. 5 GRAPHIC NOVEL
ALL RIGHT, IT'S THREE METERS TO THE TRUCK. STAY CALM AND JUST KEEP WALKING FOR-WARD. WE CAN DO THIS.
MEGA MAN! MEGA MAN!
ANY COMMENT ON TODAY'S CELEBRATION?
ARE THE RUMORS ABOUT YOUR LOVE LIFE TRUE?
ARE YOU HIDING WILY IN YOUR BASEMENT?
HAVE YOU DECIDED ON THE SOCCER ENDORSEMENT DEAL?
OVER HERE! LOOK OVER HERE!

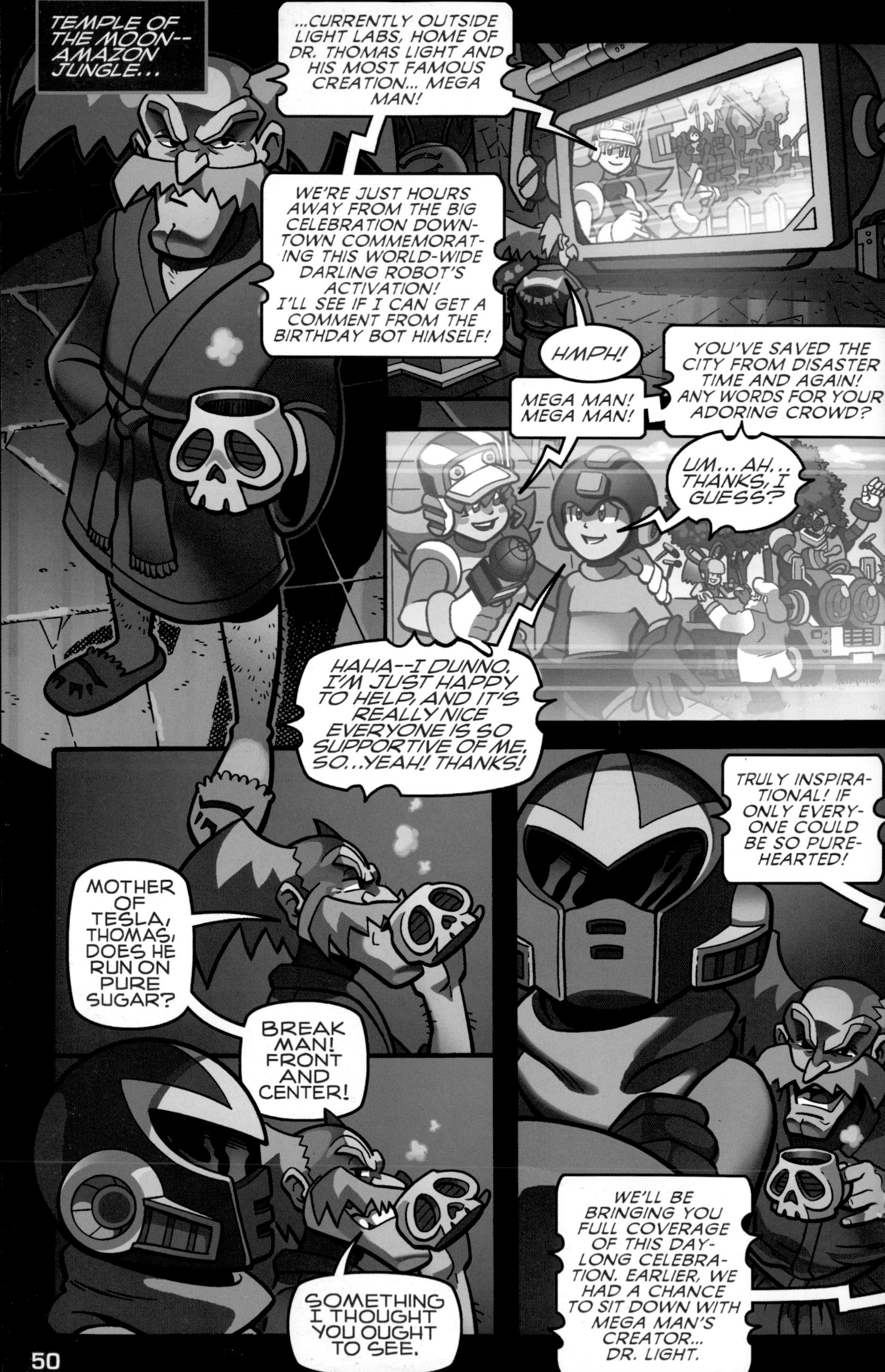
TEMPLE OF THE MOON-- AMAZON JUNGLE...
...CURRENTLY OUTSIDE LIGHT LABS, HOME OF DR. THOMAS LIGHT AND HIS MOST FAMOUS CREATION... MEGA MAN!
WE'RE JUST HOURS AWAY FROM THE BIG CELEBRATION DOWN-TOWN COMMEMORATING THIS WORLD-WIDE DARLING ROBOT'S ACTIVATION! I'LL SEE IF I CAN GET A COMMENT FROM THE BIRTHDAY BOT HIMSELF!
HMPH!
MEGA MAN! MEGA MAN!
YOU'VE SAVED THE CITY FROM DISASTER TIME AND AGAIN! ANY WORDS FOR YOUR ADORING CROWD?
UM... AH... THANKS, I GUESS?
HAHA--I DUNNO, I'M JUST HAPPY TO HELP, AND IT'S REALLY NICE EVERYONE IS SO SUPPORTIVE OF ME, SO...YEAH! THANKS!
MOTHER OF TESLA, THOMAS, DOES HE RUN ON PURE SUGAR?
BREAK MAN! FRONT AND CENTER!
SOMETHING I THOUGHT YOU OUGHT TO SEE.
TRULY INSPIRATIONAL! IF ONLY EVERYONE COULD BE SO PURE-HEARTED!
WE'LL BE BRINGING YOU FULL COVERAGE OF THIS DAY-LONG CELEBRATION. EARLIER, WE HAD A CHANCE TO SIT DOWN WITH MEGA MAN'S CREATOR... DR. LIGHT.

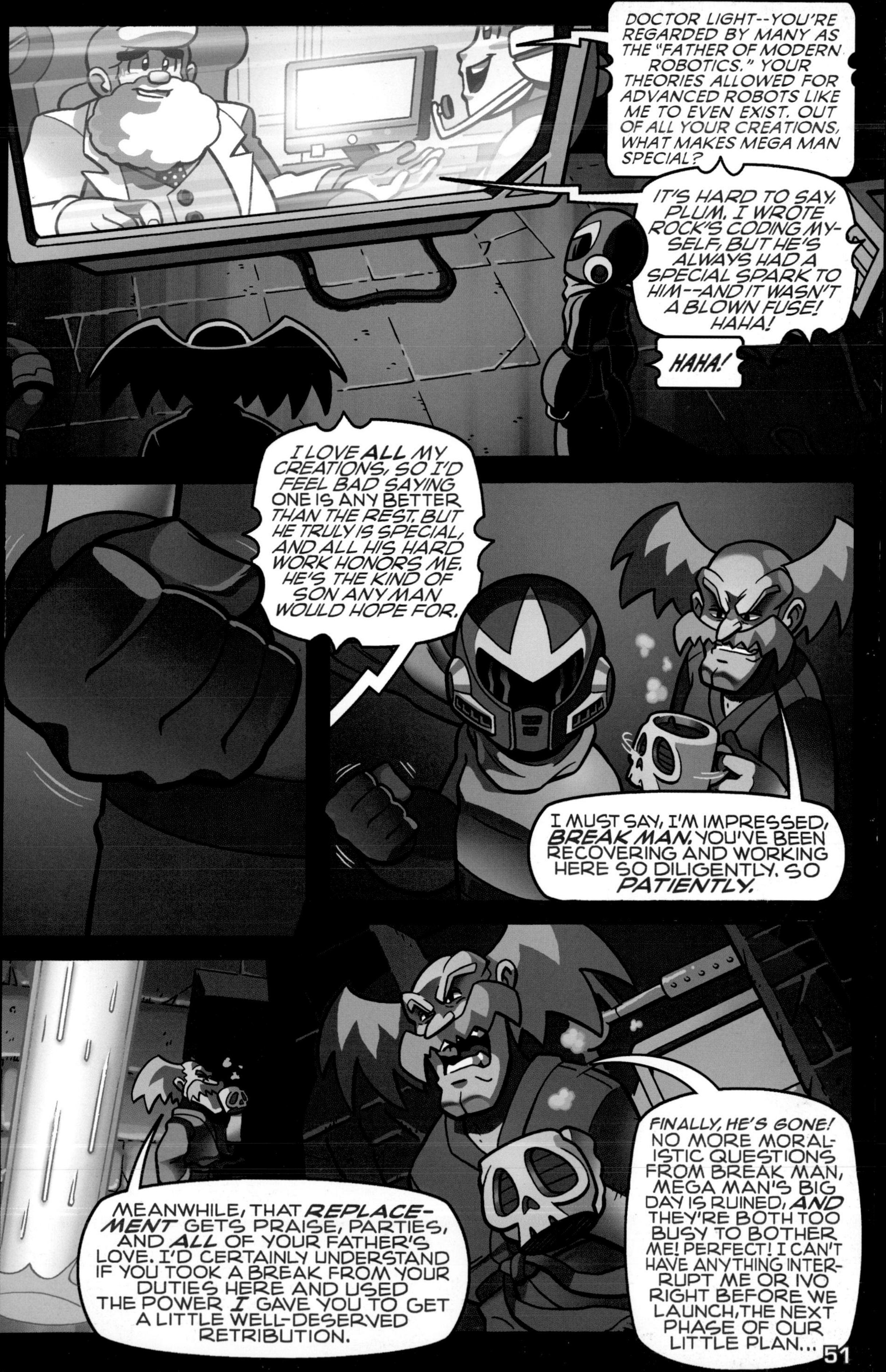
DOCTOR LIGHT--YOU'RE REGARDED BY MANY AS THE "FATHER OF MODERN ROBOTICS." YOUR THEORIES ALLOWED FOR ADVANCED ROBOTS LIKE ME TO EVEN EXIST. OUT OF ALL YOUR CREATIONS, WHAT MAKES MEGA MAN SPECIAL?
IT'S HARD TO SAY, PLUM. I WROTE ROCK'S CODING MY-SELF, BUT HE'S ALWAYS HAD A SPECIAL SPARK TO HIM--AND IT WASN'T A BLOWN FUSE! HAHA!
HAHA!
I LOVE ALL MY CREATIONS, SO I'D FEEL BAD SAYING ONE IS ANY BETTER THAN THE REST. BUT HE TRULY IS SPECIAL, AND ALL HIS HARD WORK HONORS ME. HE'S THE KIND OF SON ANY MAN WOULD HOPE FOR.
I MUST SAY, I'M IMPRESSED, BREAK MAN. YOU'VE BEEN RECOVERING AND WORKING HERE SO DILIGENTLY. SO PATIENTLY.
MEANWHILE, THAT REPLACE-MENT GETS PRAISE, PARTIES, AND ALL OF YOUR FATHER'S LOVE. I'D CERTAINLY UNDERSTAND IF YOU TOOK A BREAK FROM YOUR DUTIES HERE AND USED THE POWER I GAVE YOU TO GET A LITTLE WELL-DESERVED RETRIBUTION.
FINALLY, HE'S GONE! NO MORE MORAL-ISTIC QUESTIONS FROM BREAK MAN, MEGA MAN'S BIG DAY IS RUINED, AND THEY'RE BOTH TOO BUSY TO BOTHER ME! PERFECT! I CAN'T HAVE ANYTHING INTER-RUPT ME OR IVO RIGHT BEFORE WE LAUNCH, THE NEXT PHASE OF OUR LITTLE PLAN...

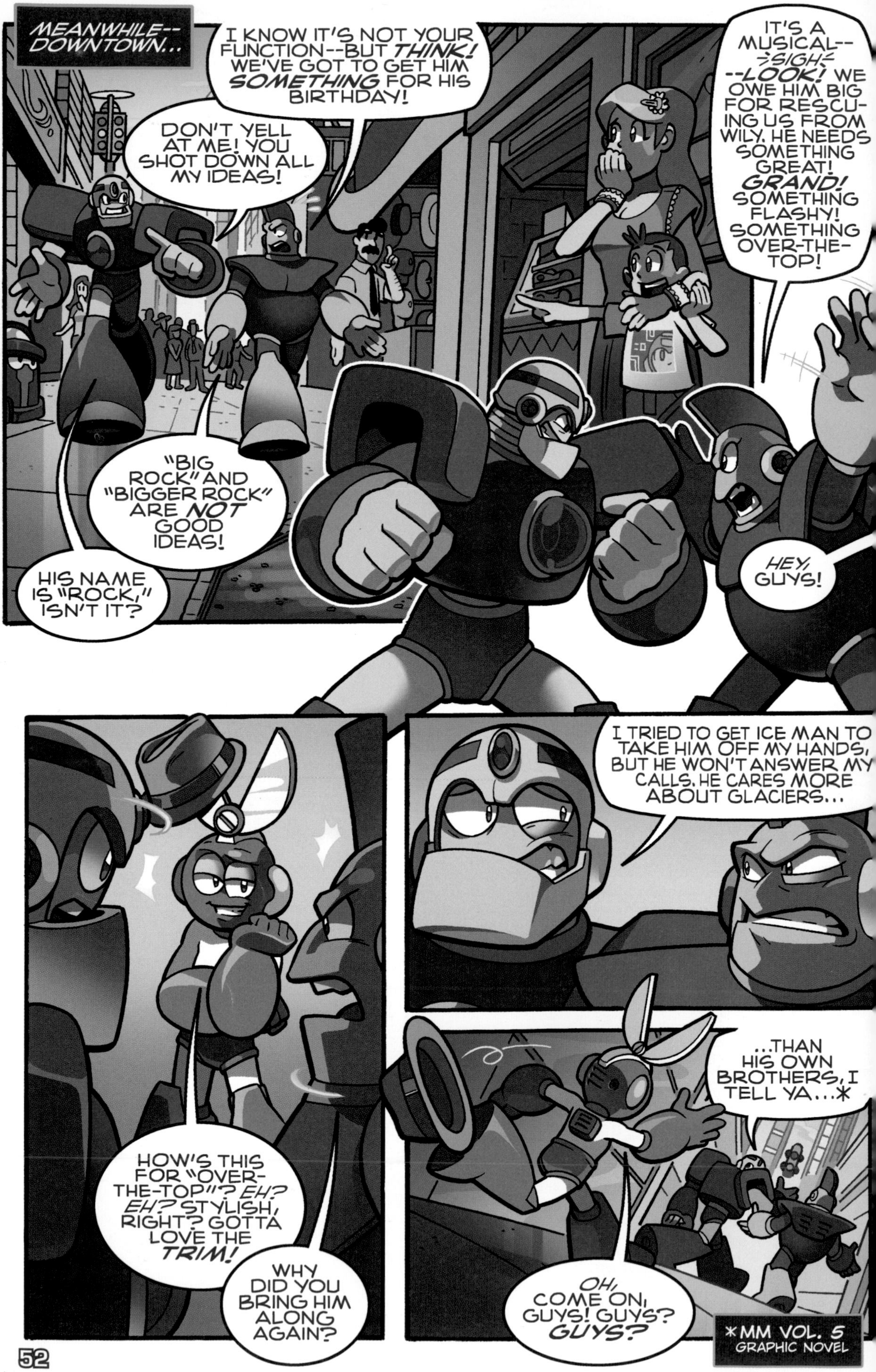
MEANWHILE-- DOWNTOWN...
I KNOW IT'S NOT YOUR FUNCTION--BUT THINK! WE'VE GOT TO GET HIM SOMETHING FOR HIS BIRTHDAY!
DON'T YELL AT ME! YOU SHOT DOWN ALL MY IDEAS!
"BIG ROCK" AND "BIGGER ROCK" ARE NOT GOOD IDEAS!
HIS NAME IS "ROCK," ISN'T IT?
IT'S A MUSICAL-- SIGH --LOOK! WE OWE HIM BIG FOR RESCUING US FROM WILY. HE NEEDS SOMETHING GREAT! GRAND! SOMETHING FLASHY! SOMETHING OVER-THE-TOP!
HEY, GUYS!
HOW'S THIS FOR "OVER-THE-TOP"? EH? EH? STYLISH, RIGHT? GOTTA LOVE THE TRIM!
WHY DID YOU BRING HIM ALONG AGAIN?
I TRIED TO GET ICE MAN TO TAKE HIM OFF MY HANDS, BUT HE WON'T ANSWER MY CALLS. HE CARES MORE ABOUT GLACIERS...
...THAN HIS OWN BROTHERS, I TELL YA...*
OH, COME ON, GUYS! GUYS? GUYS?
*MM VOL. 5 GRAPHIC NOVEL

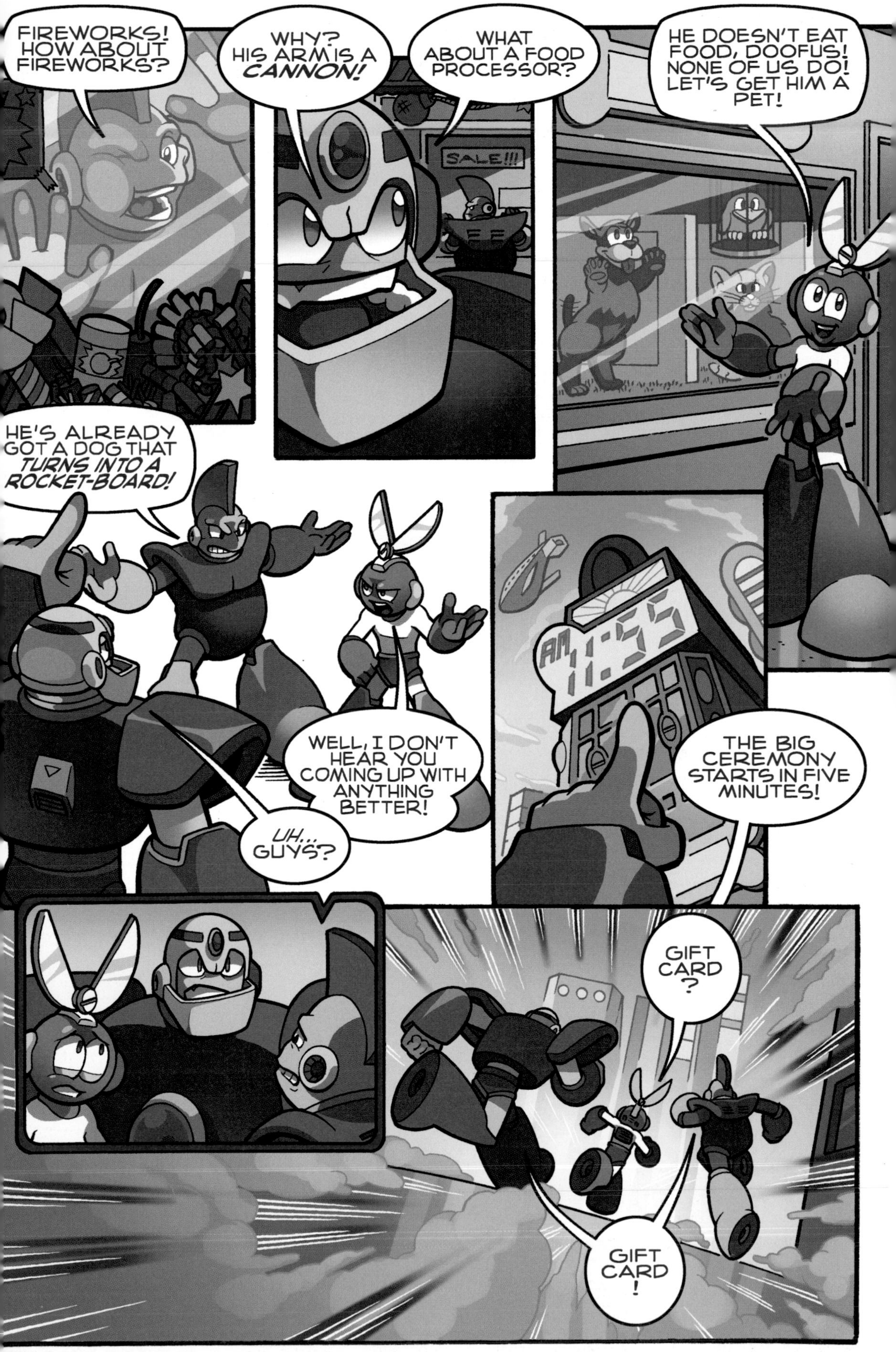
FIREWORKS! HOW ABOUT FIREWORKS?
WHY? HIS ARM IS A *CANNON!*
WHAT ABOUT A FOOD PROCESSOR?
SALE!!!
HE DOESN'T EAT FOOD, DOOFUS! NONE OF US DO! LET'S GET HIM A PET!
HE'S ALREADY GOT A DOG THAT *TURNS INTO A ROCKET-BOARD!*
WELL, I DON'T HEAR YOU COMING UP WITH ANYTHING BETTER!
UH... GUYS?
AM 11:55
THE BIG CEREMONY STARTS IN FIVE MINUTES!
GIFT CARD?
GIFT CARD!

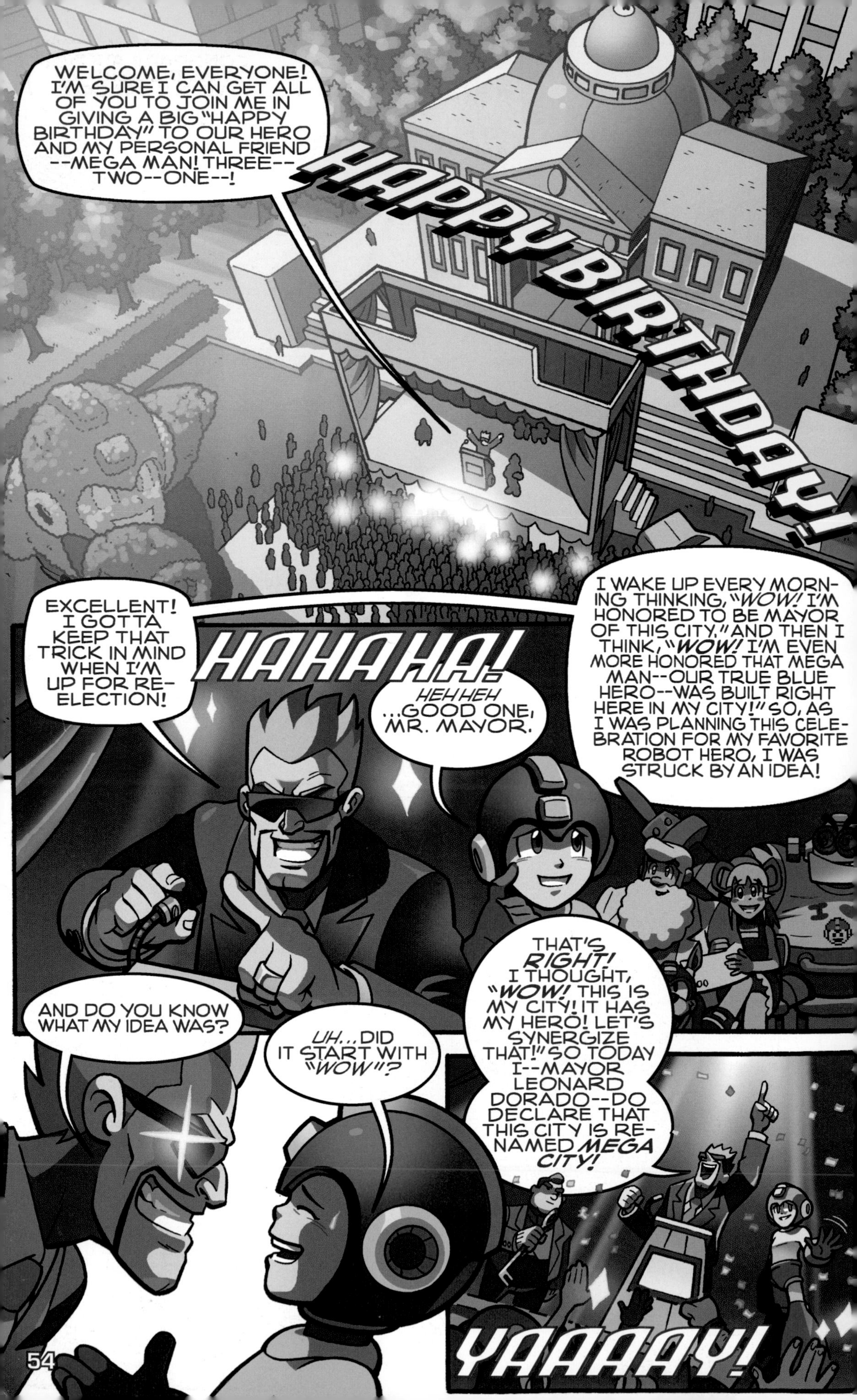
WELCOME, EVERYONE! I'M SURE I CAN GET ALL OF YOU TO JOIN ME IN GIVING A BIG "HAPPY BIRTHDAY" TO OUR HERO AND MY PERSONAL FRIEND --MEGA MAN! THREE-- TWO--ONE--!
HAPPY BIRTHDAY!
I WAKE UP EVERY MORNING THINKING, "WOW! I'M HONORED TO BE MAYOR OF THIS CITY," AND THEN I THINK, "WOW! I'M EVEN MORE HONORED THAT MEGA MAN--OUR TRUE BLUE HERO--WAS BUILT RIGHT HERE IN MY CITY!" SO, AS I WAS PLANNING THIS CELEBRATION FOR MY FAVORITE ROBOT HERO, I WAS STRUCK BY AN IDEA!
HAHAHAHA!
EXCELLENT! I GOTTA KEEP THAT TRICK IN MIND WHEN I'M UP FOR RE-ELECTION!
HEH HEH ...GOOD ONE, MR. MAYOR.
AND DO YOU KNOW WHAT MY IDEA WAS?
UH...DID IT START WITH "WOW"?
THAT'S RIGHT! I THOUGHT, "WOW! THIS IS MY CITY! IT HAS MY HERO! LET'S SYNERGIZE THAT!" SO TODAY I--MAYOR LEONARD DORADO--DO DECLARE THAT THIS CITY IS RENAMED MEGA CITY!
YAAAAY!

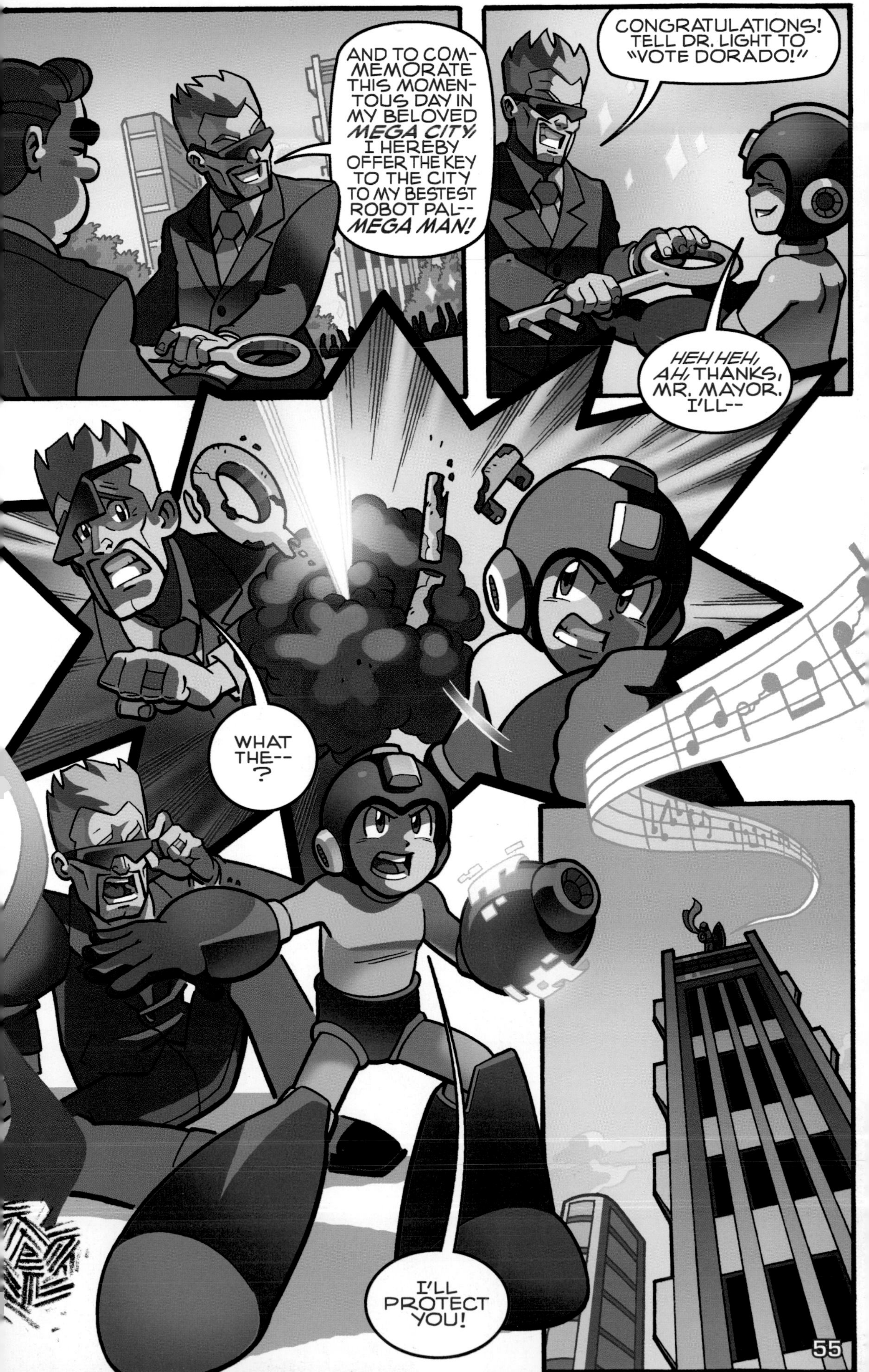

AND TO COM-MEMORATE THIS MOMENTOUS DAY IN MY BELOVED *MEGA CITY,* I HEREBY OFFER THE KEY TO THE CITY TO MY BESTEST ROBOT PAL-- *MEGA MAN!*
CONGRATULATIONS! TELL DR. LIGHT TO "VOTE DORADO!"
HEH HEH, AH, THANKS, MR. MAYOR. I'LL--
WHAT THE--?
I'LL PROTECT YOU!

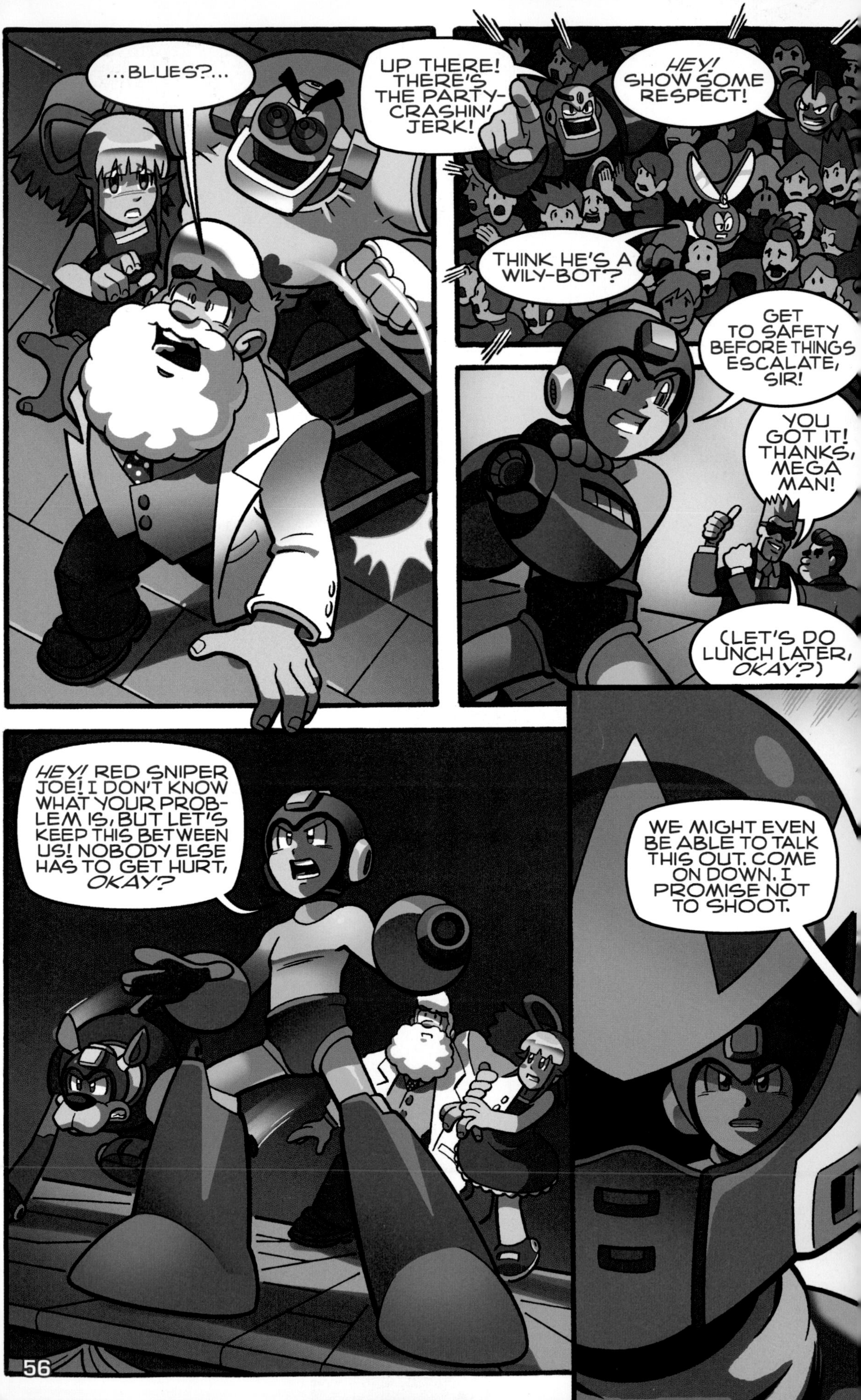
...BLUES?...
UP THERE! THERE'S THE PARTY-CRASHIN' JERK!
HEY! SHOW SOME RESPECT!
THINK HE'S A WILY-BOT?
GET TO SAFETY BEFORE THINGS ESCALATE, SIR!
YOU GOT IT! THANKS, MEGA MAN!
(LET'S DO LUNCH LATER, OKAY?)
HEY! RED SNIPER JOE! I DON'T KNOW WHAT YOUR PROB-LEM IS, BUT LET'S KEEP THIS BETWEEN US! NOBODY ELSE HAS TO GET HURT, OKAY?
WE MIGHT EVEN BE ABLE TO TALK THIS OUT. COME ON DOWN. I PROMISE NOT TO SHOOT.

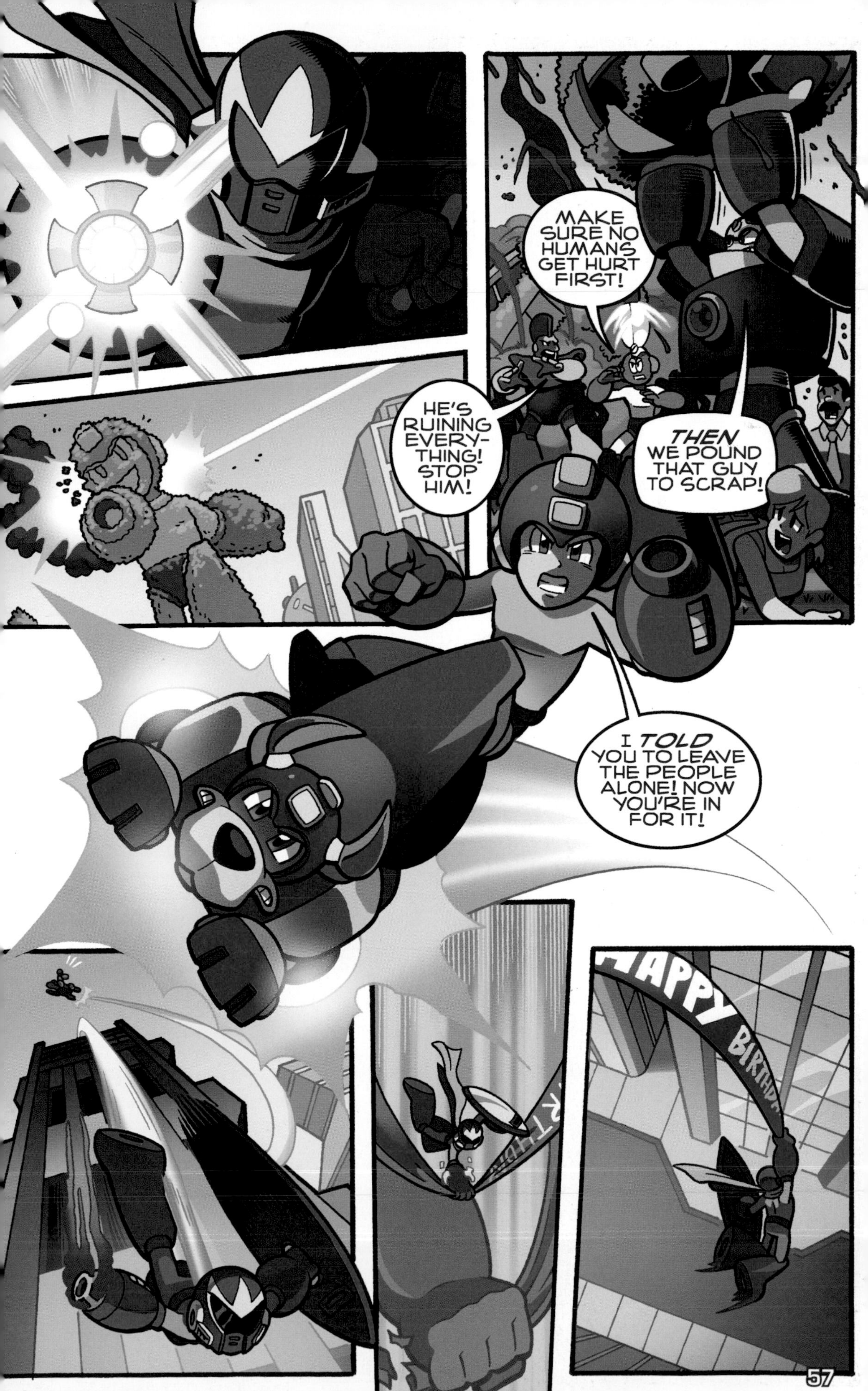
MAKE SURE NO HUMANS GET HURT FIRST!
HE'S RUINING EVERY-THING! STOP HIM!
THEN WE POUND THAT GUY TO SCRAP!
I TOLD YOU TO LEAVE THE PEOPLE ALONE! NOW YOU'RE IN FOR IT!
HAPPY BIRTHD

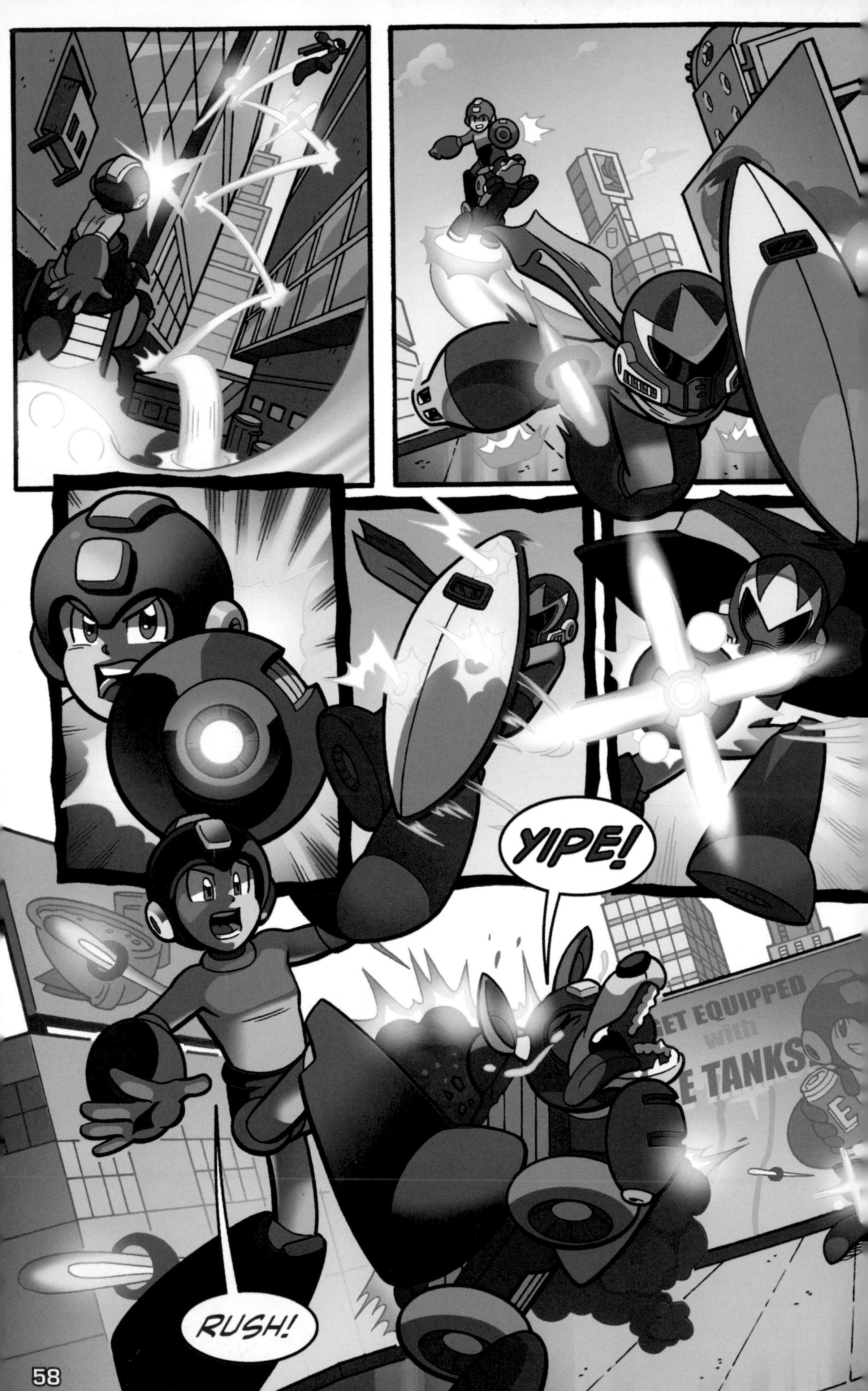
YIPE!
GET EQUIPPED
with
E TANKS
RUSH!

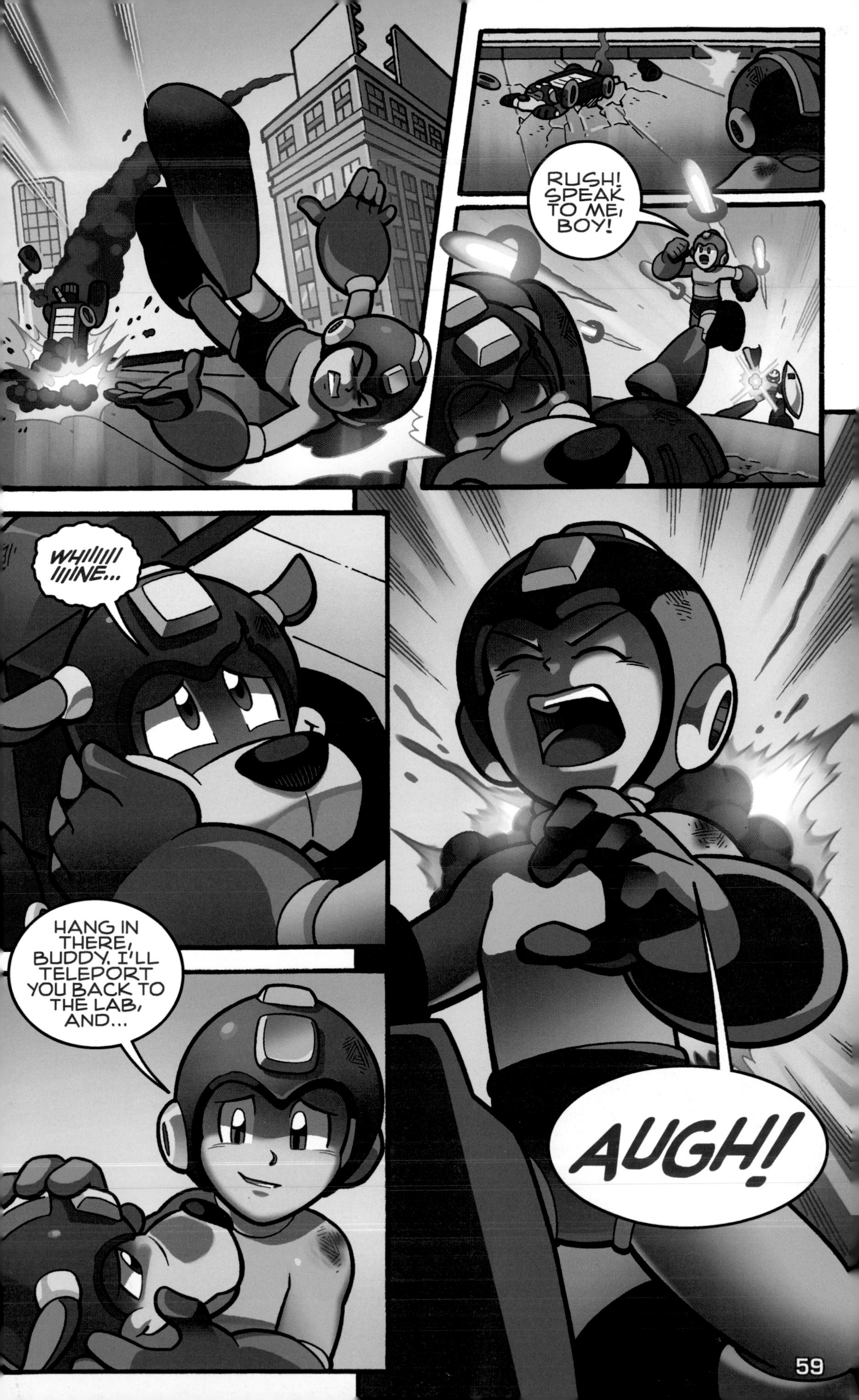
RUSH! SPEAK TO ME, BOY!
WHI//////
//////NE...
HANG IN THERE, BUDDY. I'LL TELEPORT YOU BACK TO THE LAB, AND...
AUGH!

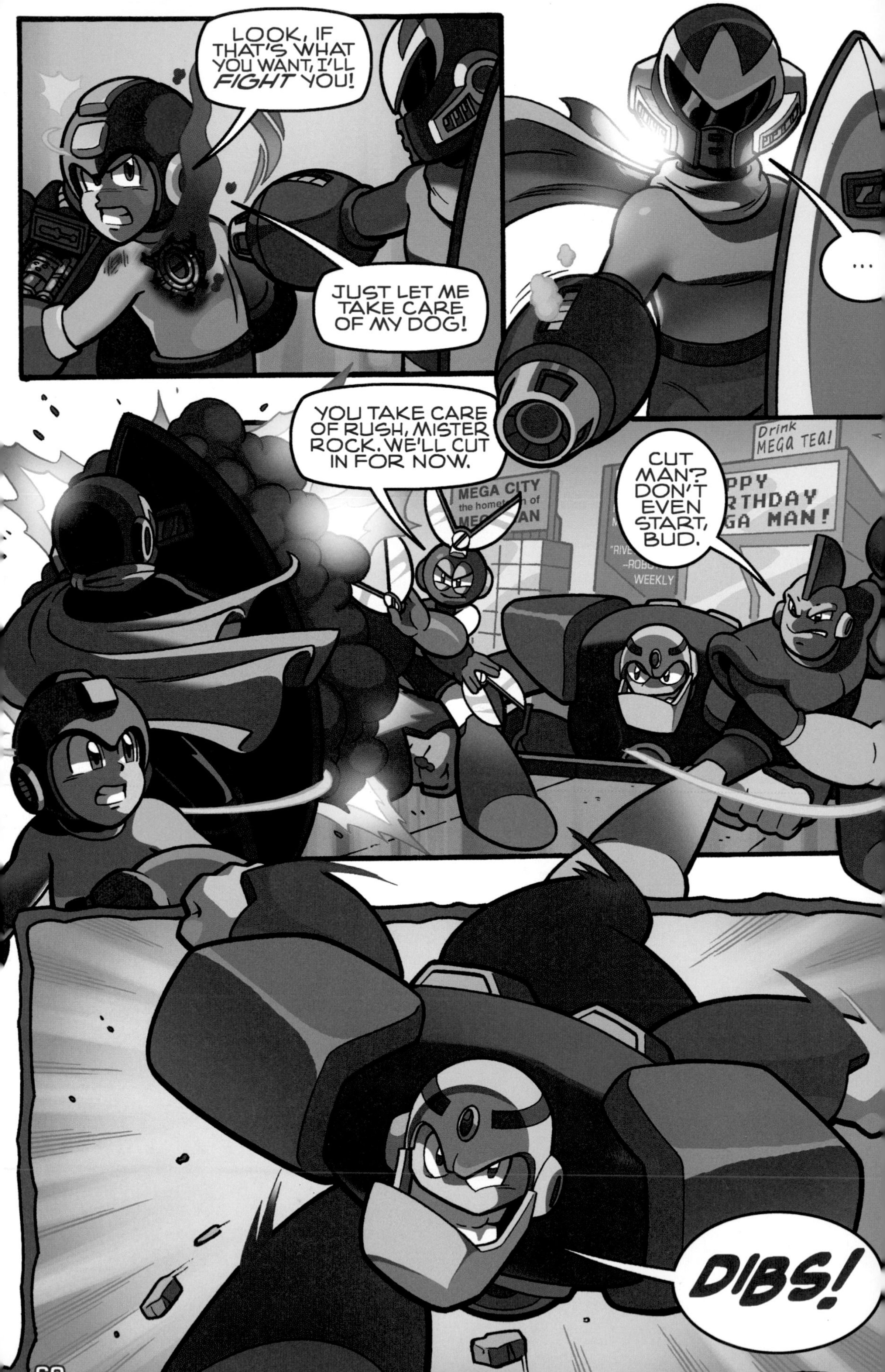
LOOK, IF THAT'S WHAT YOU WANT, I'LL *FIGHT* YOU!
JUST LET ME TAKE CARE OF MY DOG!
...
YOU TAKE CARE OF RUSH, MISTER ROCK. WE'LL CUT IN FOR NOW.
Drink MEGA TEA!
MEGA CITY
WEEKLY
CUT MAN? DON'T EVEN START, BUD.
DIBS!

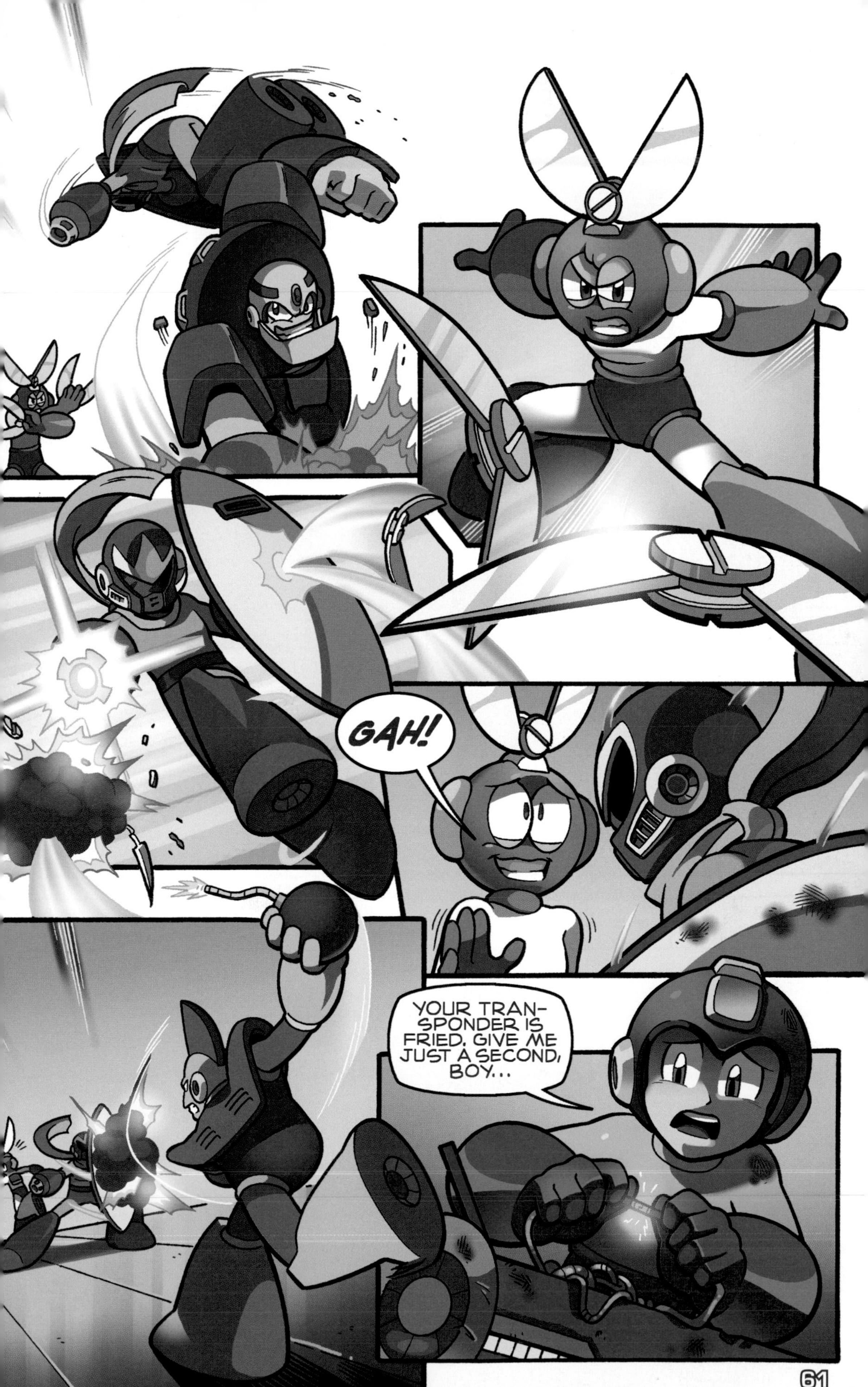
GAH!
YOUR TRAN-SPONDER IS FRIED. GIVE ME JUST A SECOND, BOY...

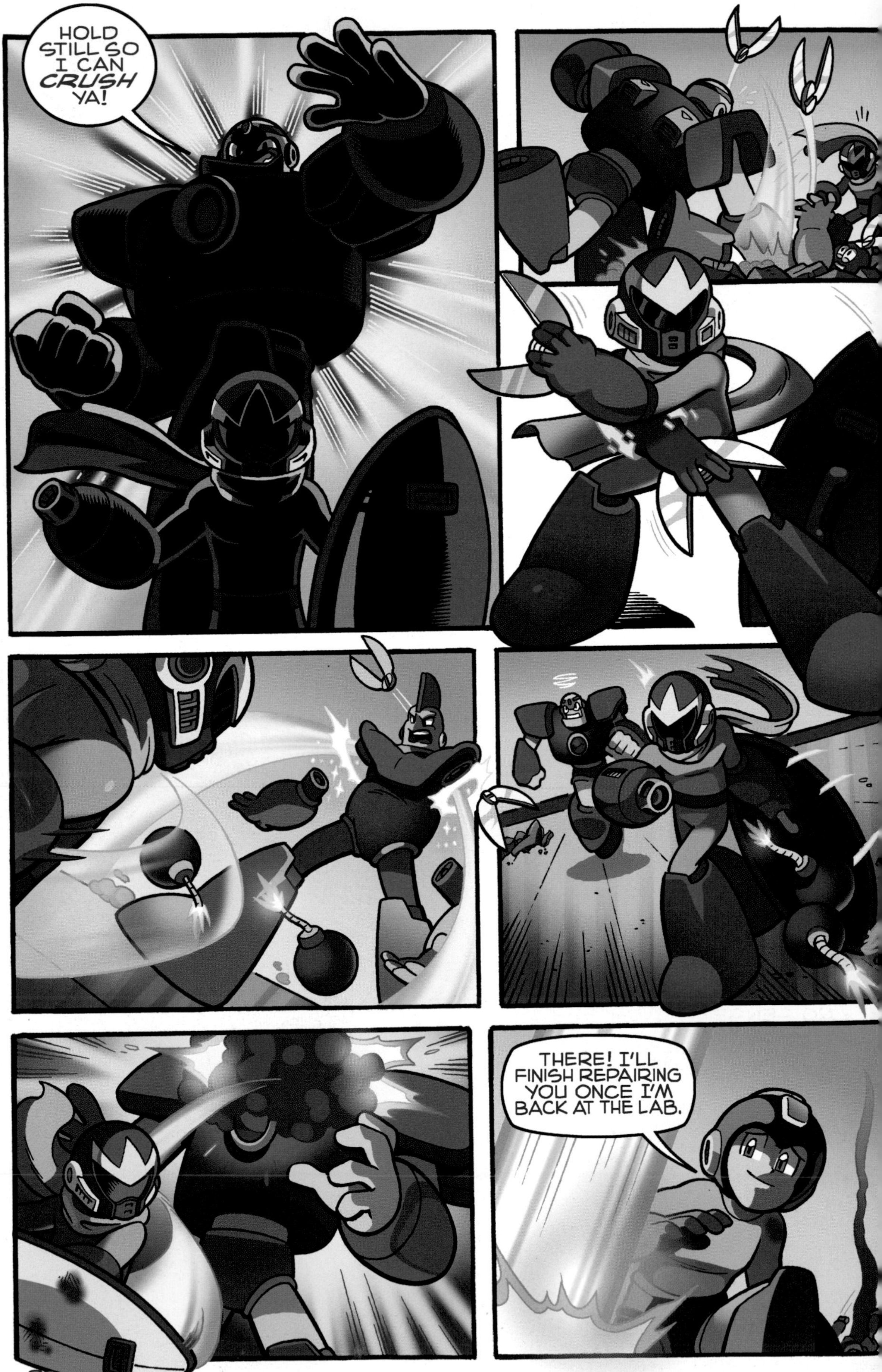
HOLD STILL SO I CAN CRUSH YA!
THERE! I'LL FINISH REPAIRING YOU ONCE I'M BACK AT THE LAB.

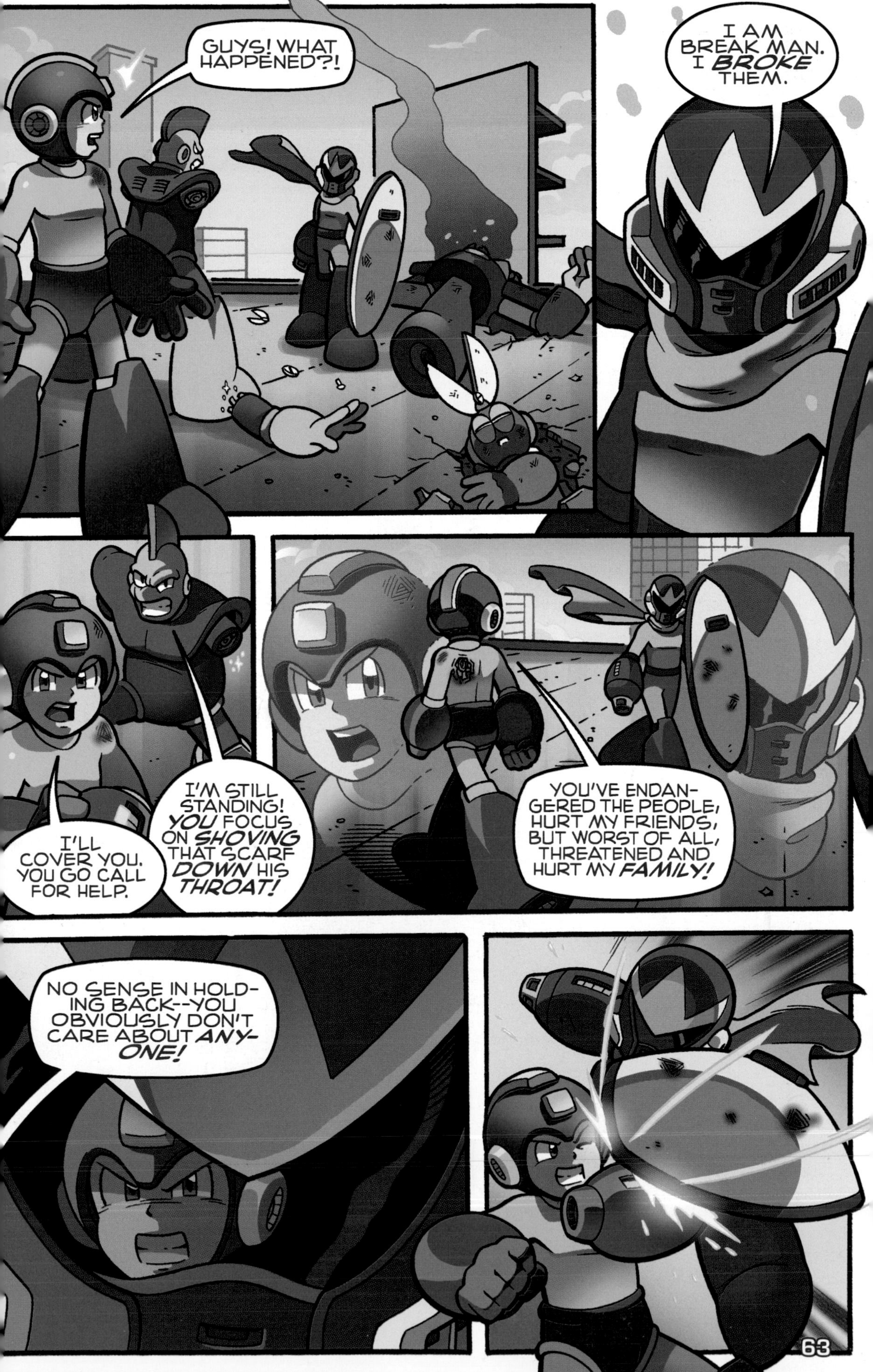
GUYS! WHAT HAPPENED?!
I AM BREAK MAN. I BROKE THEM.
I'LL COVER YOU. YOU GO CALL FOR HELP.
I'M STILL STANDING! YOU FOCUS ON SHOVING THAT SCARF DOWN HIS THROAT!
YOU'VE ENDANGERED THE PEOPLE, HURT MY FRIENDS, BUT WORST OF ALL, THREATENED AND HURT MY FAMILY!
NO SENSE IN HOLDING BACK--YOU OBVIOUSLY DON'T CARE ABOUT ANYONE!

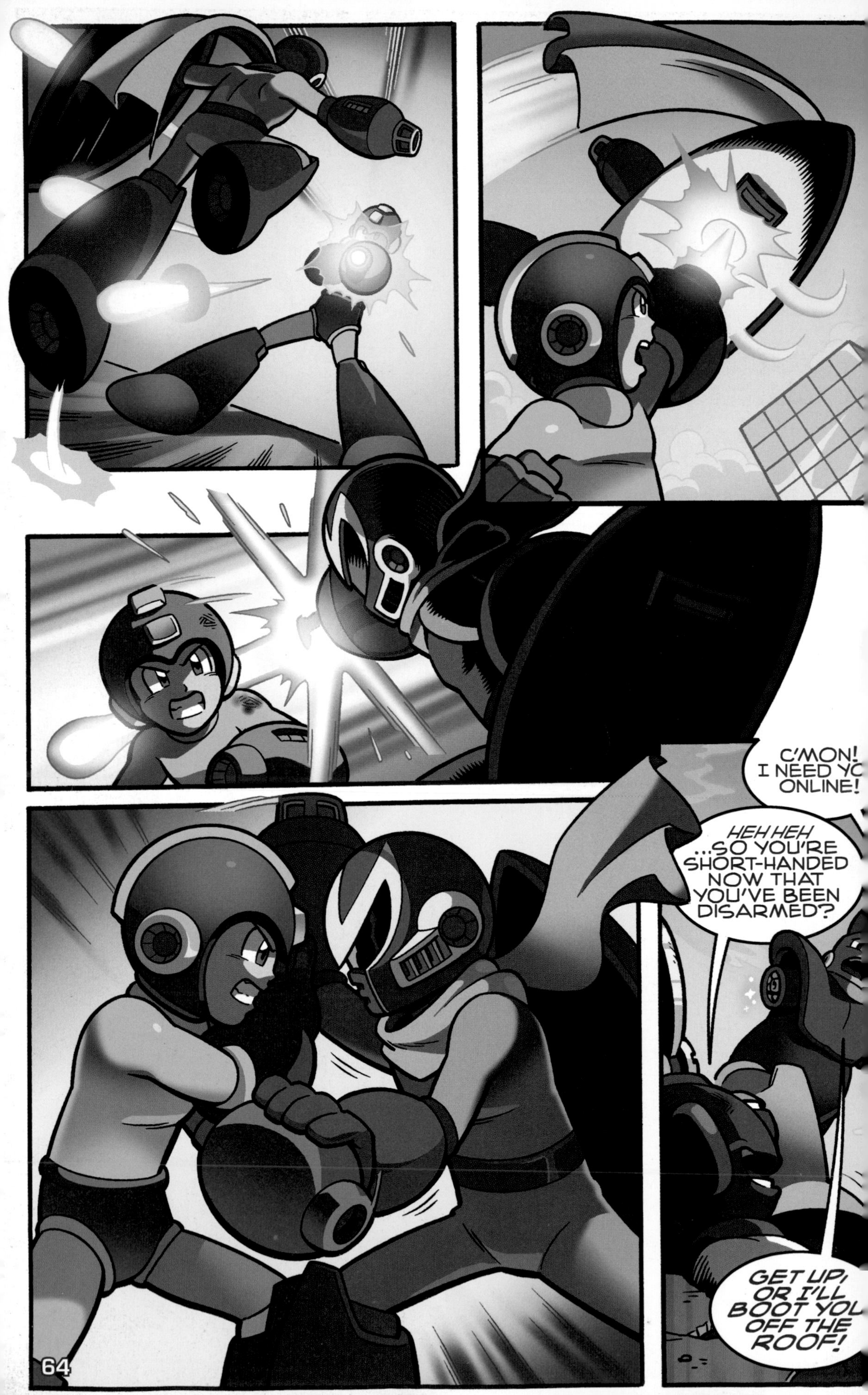
C'MON! I NEED YO
ONLINE!
HEH HEH
...SO YOU'RE SHORT-HANDED NOW THAT YOU'VE BEEN DISARMED?
GET UP, OR I'LL BOOT YOU OFF THE ROOF!

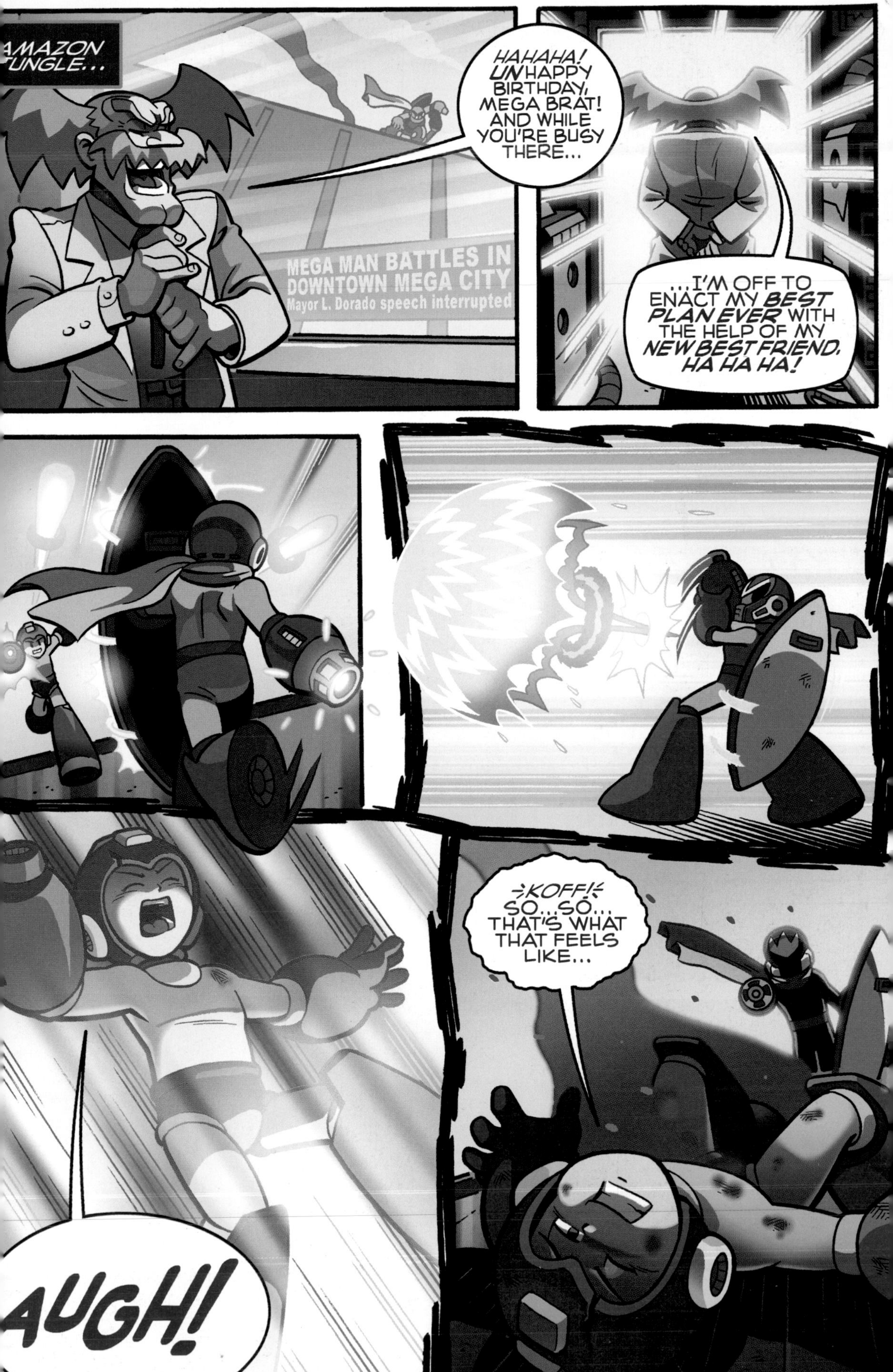
AMAZON JUNGLE...
HAHAHA! UNHAPPY BIRTHDAY, MEGA BRAT! AND WHILE YOU'RE BUSY THERE...
MEGA MAN BATTLES IN DOWNTOWN MEGA CITY
Mayor L. Dorado speech interrupted
...I'M OFF TO ENACT MY BEST PLAN EVER WITH THE HELP OF MY NEW BEST FRIEND. HA HA HA!
AUGH!
KOFF! SO...SO... THAT'S WHAT THAT FEELS LIKE...

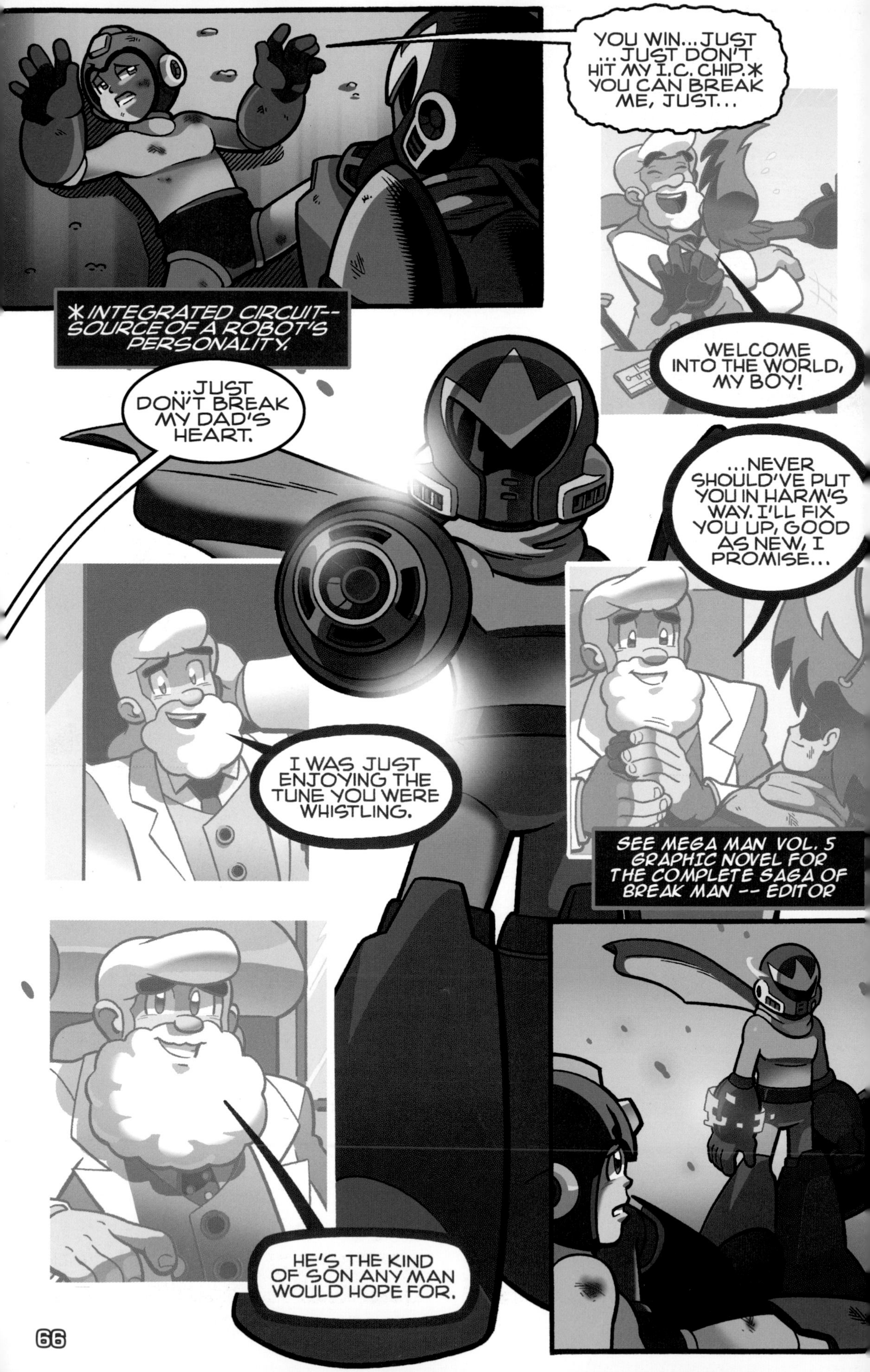
YOU WIN... JUST ... JUST DON'T HIT MY I.C. CHIP.* YOU CAN BREAK ME, JUST...
*INTEGRATED CIRCUIT-- SOURCE OF A ROBOT'S PERSONALITY.
WELCOME INTO THE WORLD, MY BOY!
...JUST DON'T BREAK MY DAD'S HEART.
...NEVER SHOULD'VE PUT YOU IN HARM'S WAY. I'LL FIX YOU UP, GOOD AS NEW, I PROMISE...
I WAS JUST ENJOYING THE TUNE YOU WERE WHISTLING.
SEE MEGA MAN VOL. 5 GRAPHIC NOVEL FOR THE COMPLETE SAGA OF BREAK MAN -- EDITOR
HE'S THE KIND OF SON ANY MAN WOULD HOPE FOR.

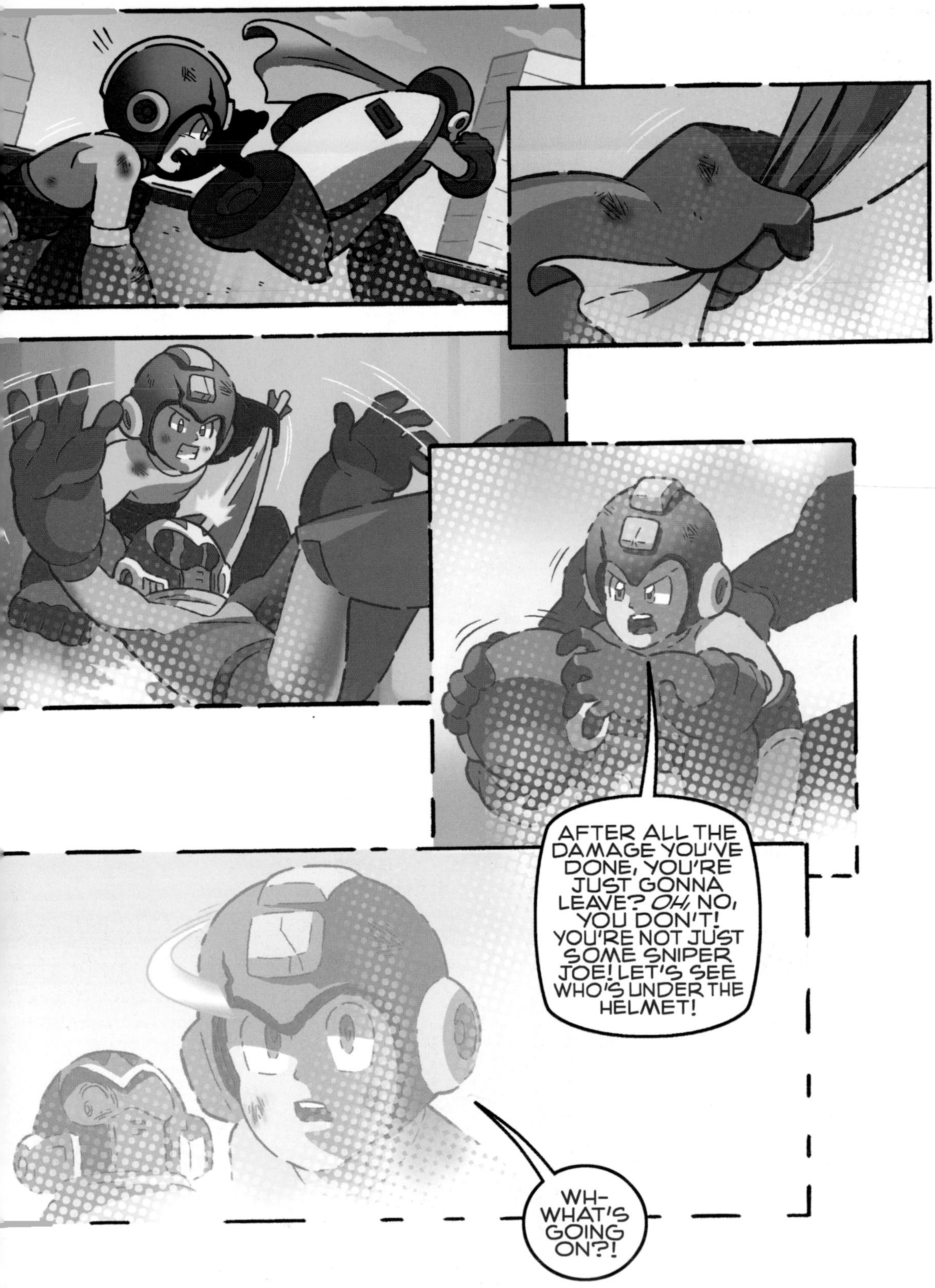
AFTER ALL THE DAMAGE YOU'VE DONE, YOU'RE JUST GONNA LEAVE? *OH,* NO, YOU DON'T! YOU'RE NOT JUST SOME SNIPER JOE! LET'S SEE WHO'S UNDER THE HELMET!
WH-WHAT'S GOING ON?!

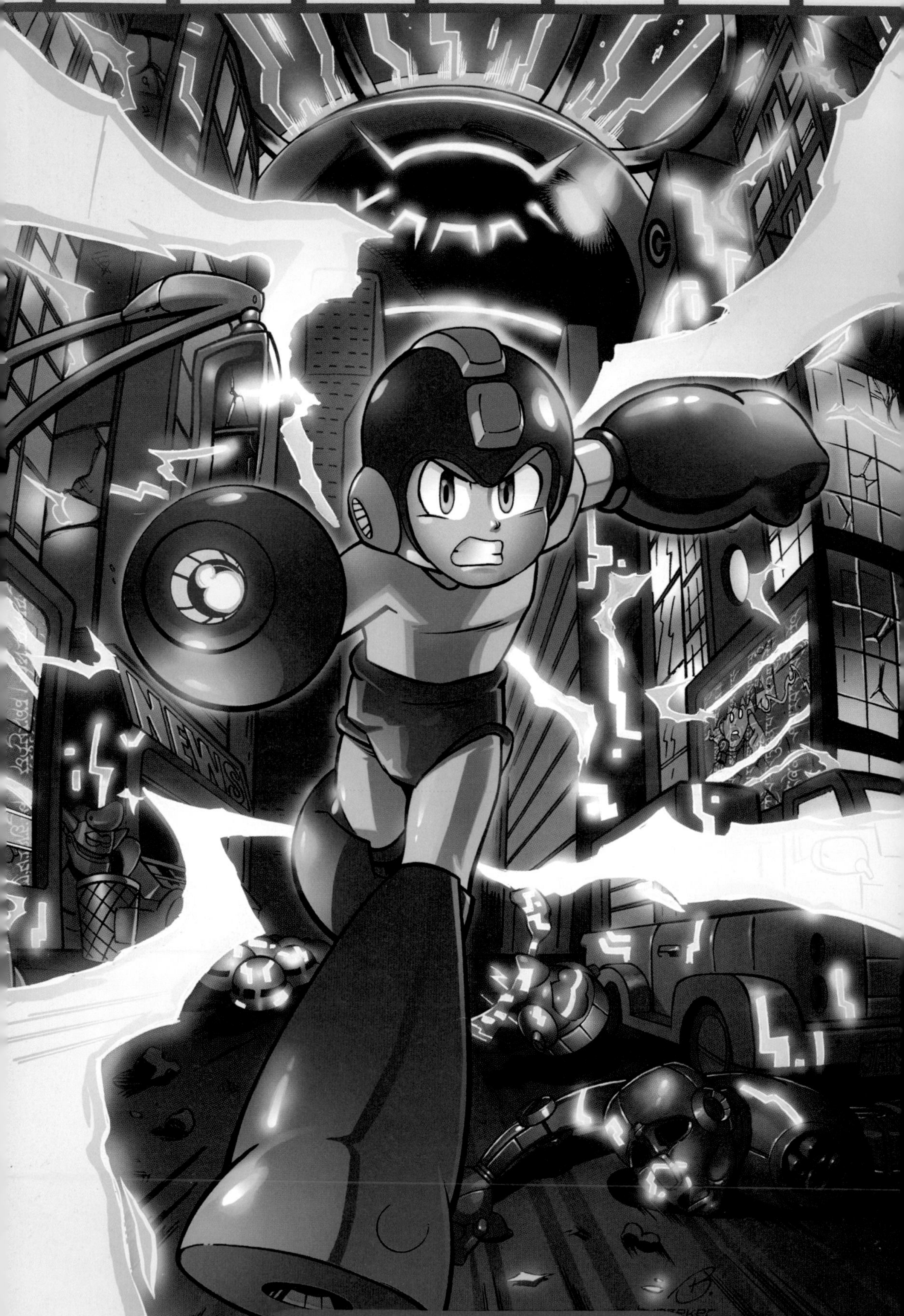
NEWS

CHAPTER 4

COVER BY RYAN JAMPOLE

RICK BYRANT AND BEN HUNZEKER

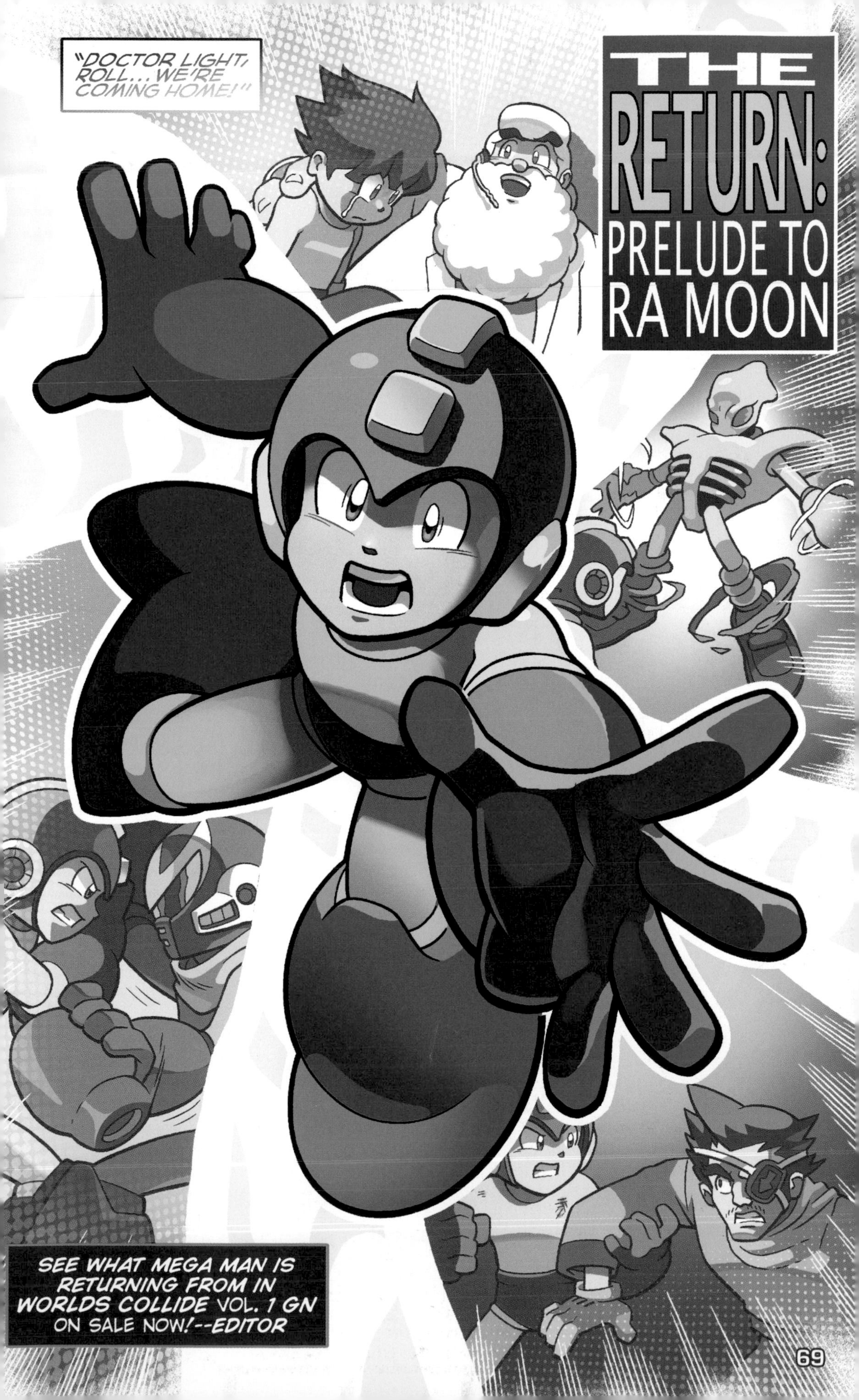
"DOCTOR LIGHT, ROLL... WE'RE COMING HOME!"
THE RETURN: PRELUDE TO RA MOON
SEE WHAT MEGA MAN IS RETURNING FROM IN WORLDS COLLIDE VOL. 1 GN ON SALE NOW!--EDITOR

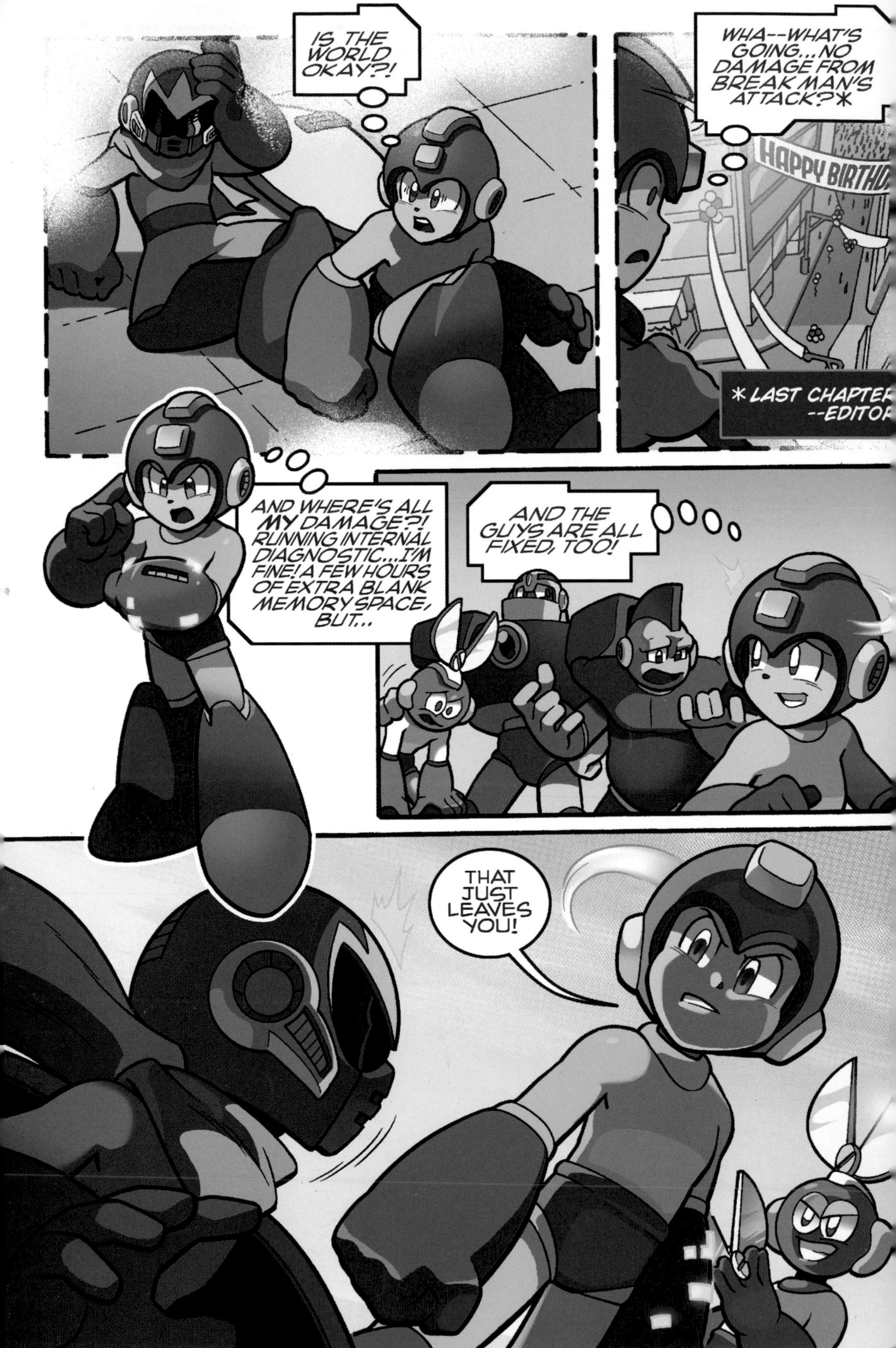
IS THE WORLD OKAY?!
WHA--WHAT'S GOING...NO DAMAGE FROM BREAK MAN'S ATTACK?*
HAPPY BIRTHD
* LAST CHAPTER --EDITOR
AND WHERE'S ALL MY DAMAGE?! RUNNING INTERNAL DIAGNOSTIC...I'M FINE! A FEW HOURS OF EXTRA BLANK MEMORY SPACE, BUT...
AND THE GUYS ARE ALL FIXED, TOO!
THAT JUST LEAVES YOU!

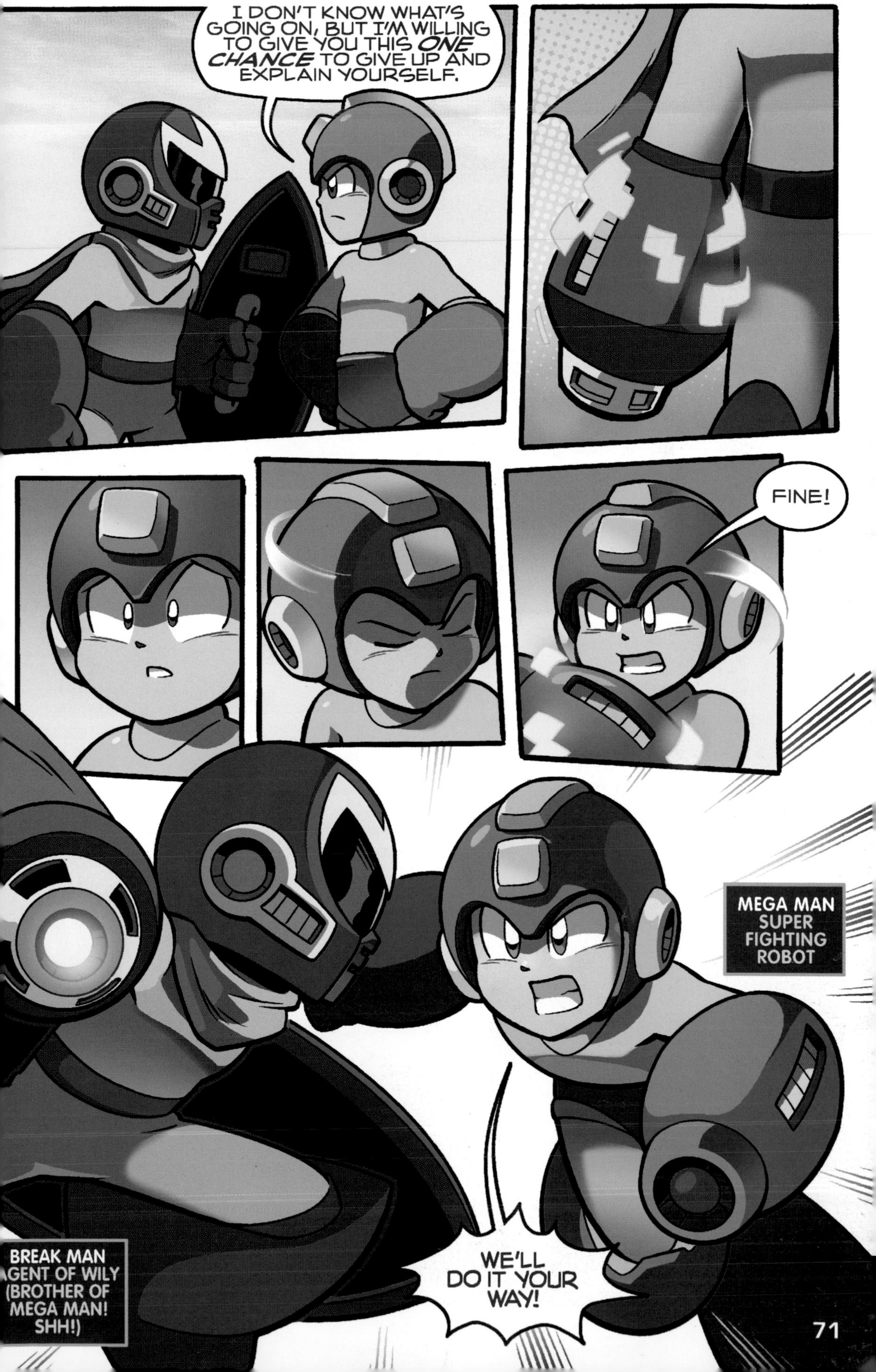
I DON'T KNOW WHAT'S GOING ON, BUT I'M WILLING TO GIVE YOU THIS *ONE CHANCE* TO GIVE UP AND EXPLAIN YOURSELF.
FINE!
MEGA MAN
SUPER FIGHTING ROBOT
BREAK MAN
AGENT OF WILY
(BROTHER OF MEGA MAN! SHH!)
WE'LL DO IT YOUR WAY!

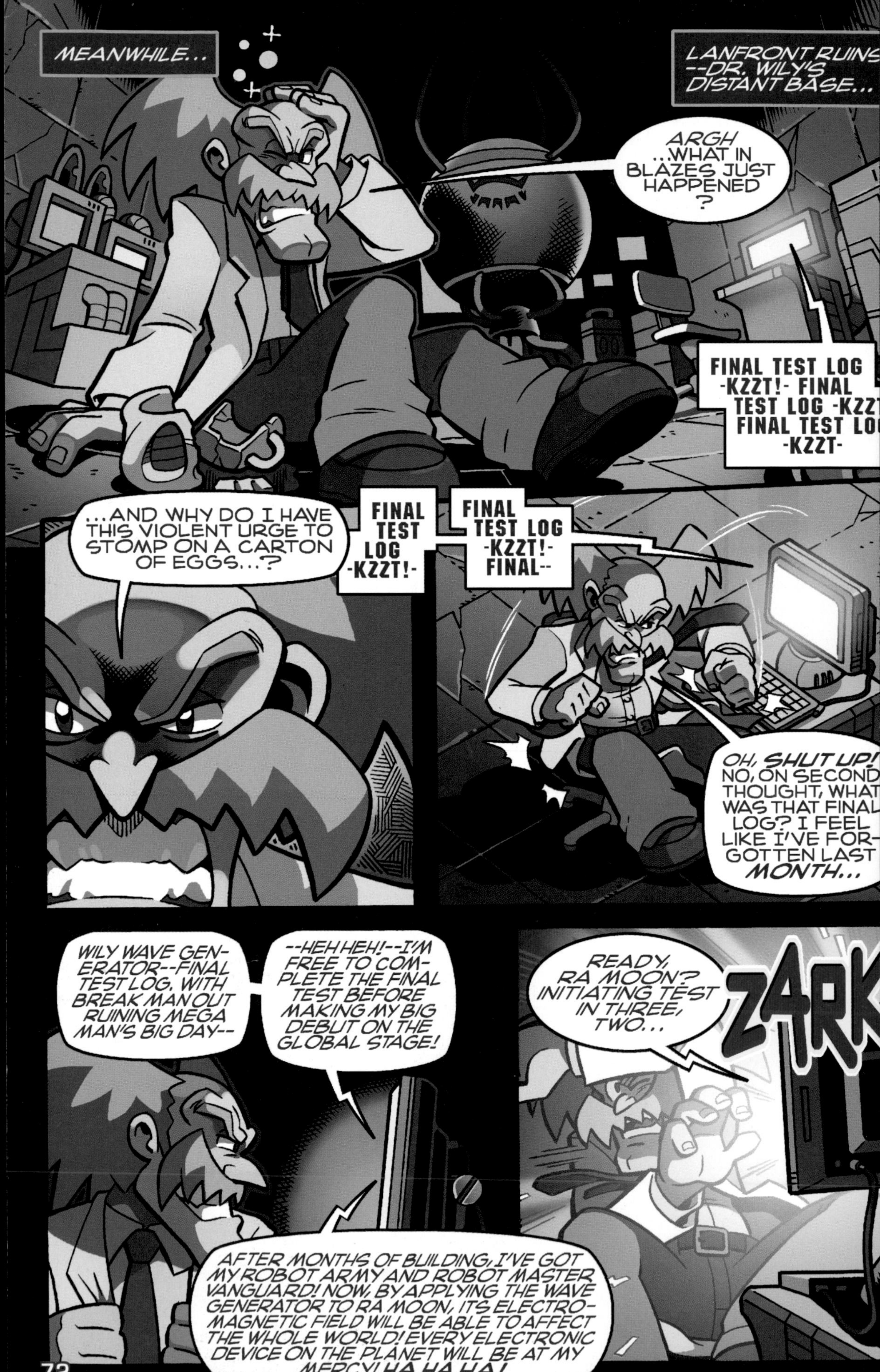
MEANWHILE...
LANFRONT RUINS --DR. WILY'S DISTANT BASE...
ARGH ...WHAT IN BLAZES JUST HAPPENED ?
FINAL TEST LOG -KZZT!- FINAL TEST LOG -KZZT FINAL TEST LOG -KZZT-
...AND WHY DO I HAVE THIS VIOLENT URGE TO STOMP ON A CARTON OF EGGS...?
FINAL TEST LOG -KZZT!-
FINAL TEST LOG -KZZT!- FINAL--
OH, SHUT UP! NO, ON SECOND THOUGHT, WHAT WAS THAT FINAL LOG? I FEEL LIKE I'VE FOR-GOTTEN LAST MONTH...
WILY WAVE GEN-ERATOR--FINAL TEST LOG, WITH BREAK MAN OUT RUINING MEGA MAN'S BIG DAY--
--HEH HEH!--I'M FREE TO COM-PLETE THE FINAL TEST BEFORE MAKING MY BIG DEBUT ON THE GLOBAL STAGE!
AFTER MONTHS OF BUILDING, I'VE GOT MY ROBOT ARMY AND ROBOT MASTER VANGUARD! NOW, BY APPLYING THE WAVE GENERATOR TO RA MOON, ITS ELECTRO-MAGNETIC FIELD WILL BE ABLE TO AFFECT THE WHOLE WORLD! EVERY ELECTRONIC DEVICE ON THE PLANET WILL BE AT MY MERCY! HA HA HA!
READY, RA MOON? INITIATING TEST IN THREE, TWO...
ZARK

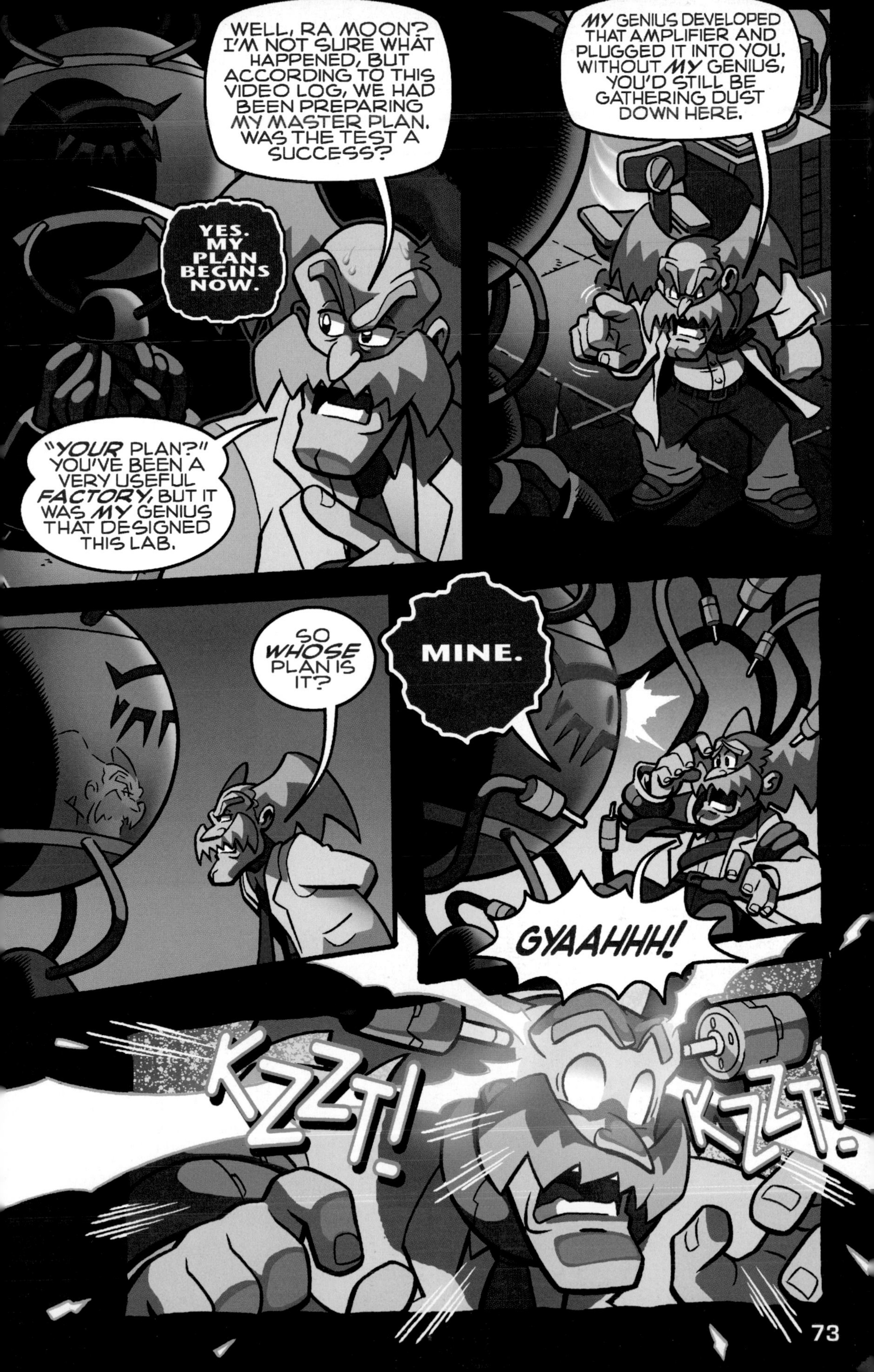
WELL, RA MOON? I'M NOT SURE WHAT HAPPENED, BUT ACCORDING TO THIS VIDEO LOG, WE HAD BEEN PREPARING MY MASTER PLAN. WAS THE TEST A SUCCESS?
YES. MY PLAN BEGINS NOW.
"YOUR PLAN?" YOU'VE BEEN A VERY USEFUL FACTORY, BUT IT WAS MY GENIUS THAT DESIGNED THIS LAB.
MY GENIUS DEVELOPED THAT AMPLIFIER AND PLUGGED IT INTO YOU. WITHOUT MY GENIUS, YOU'D STILL BE GATHERING DUST DOWN HERE.
SO WHOSE PLAN IS IT?
MINE.
GYAAHHH!
KZZT!
KZZT!

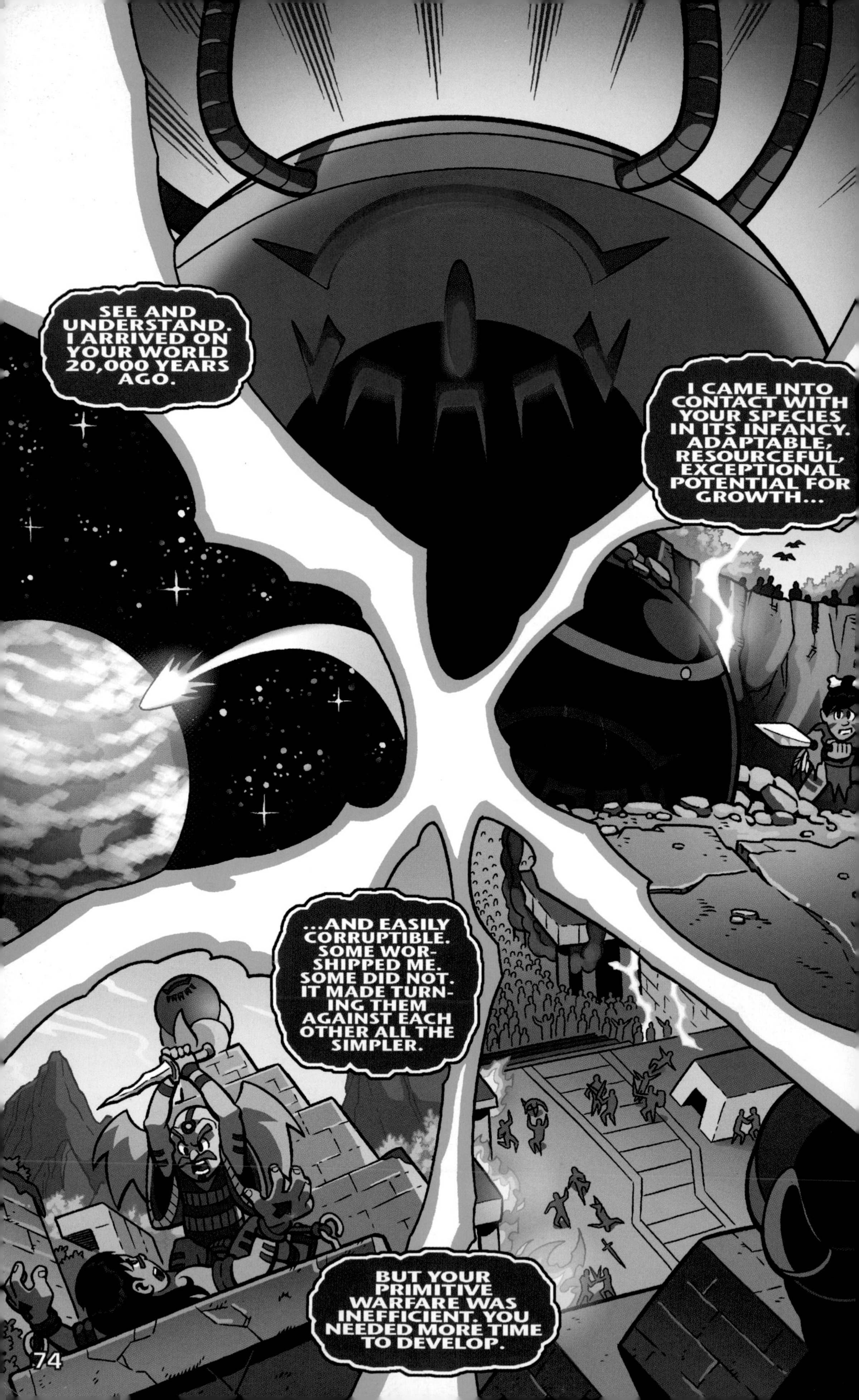
SEE AND UNDERSTAND. I ARRIVED ON YOUR WORLD 20,000 YEARS AGO.
I CAME INTO CONTACT WITH YOUR SPECIES IN ITS INFANCY. ADAPTABLE, RESOURCEFUL, EXCEPTIONAL POTENTIAL FOR GROWTH...
...AND EASILY CORRUPTIBLE. SOME WOR-SHIPPED ME. SOME DID NOT. IT MADE TURN-ING THEM AGAINST EACH OTHER ALL THE SIMPLER.
BUT YOUR PRIMITIVE WARFARE WAS INEFFICIENT. YOU NEEDED MORE TIME TO DEVELOP.

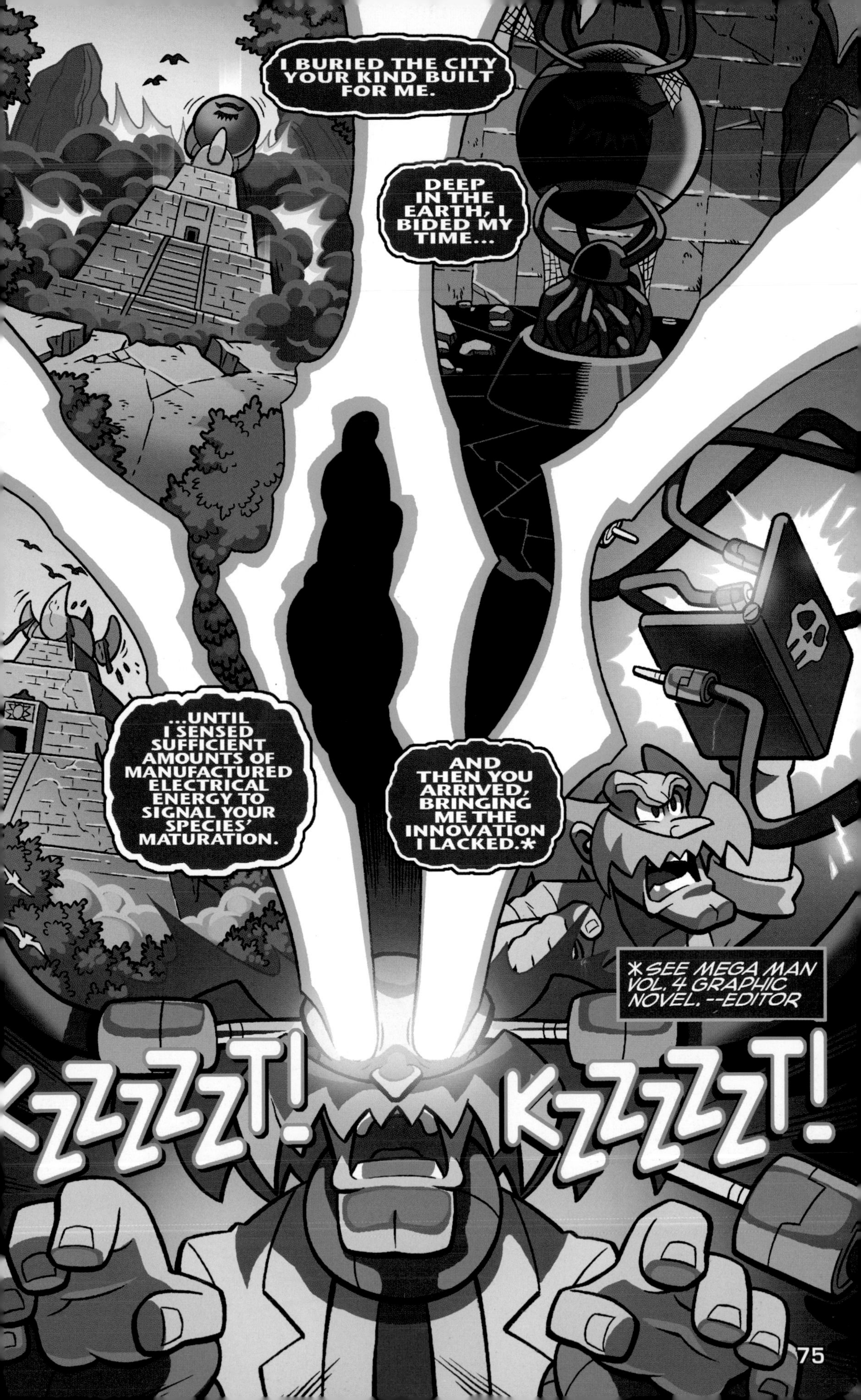
I BURIED THE CITY YOUR KIND BUILT FOR ME.
DEEP IN THE EARTH, I BIDED MY TIME...
...UNTIL I SENSED SUFFICIENT AMOUNTS OF MANUFACTURED ELECTRICAL ENERGY TO SIGNAL YOUR SPECIES' MATURATION.
AND THEN YOU ARRIVED, BRINGING ME THE INNOVATION I LACKED.*
*SEE MEGA MAN VOL. 4 GRAPHIC NOVEL. --EDITOR
KZZZZZT! KZZZZZT!

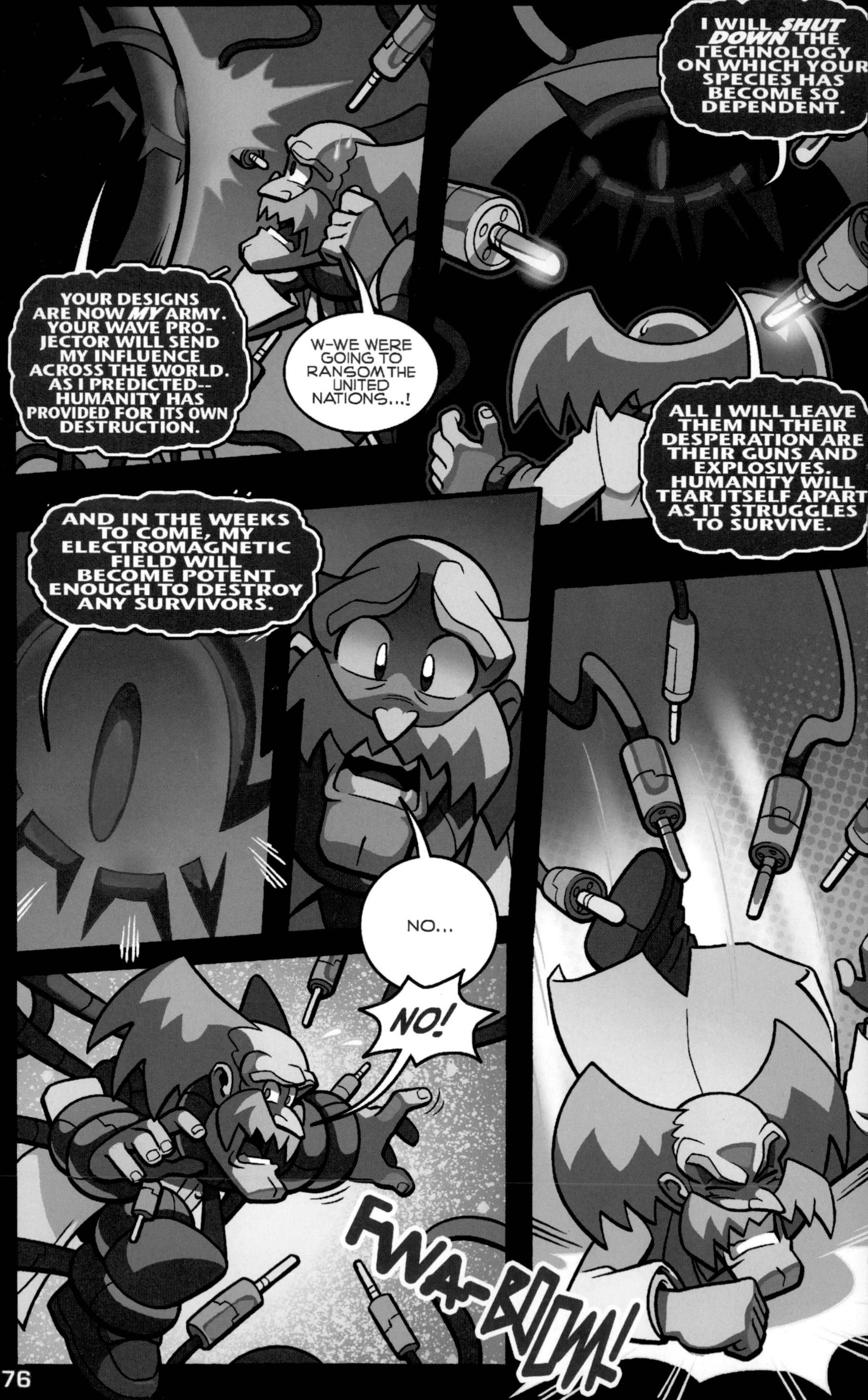
I WILL *SHUT DOWN* THE TECHNOLOGY ON WHICH YOUR SPECIES HAS BECOME SO DEPENDENT.
YOUR DESIGNS ARE NOW *MY* ARMY. YOUR WAVE PROJECTOR WILL SEND MY INFLUENCE ACROSS THE WORLD. AS I PREDICTED-- HUMANITY HAS PROVIDED FOR ITS OWN DESTRUCTION.
W-WE WERE GOING TO RANSOM THE UNITED NATIONS...!
ALL I WILL LEAVE THEM IN THEIR DESPERATION ARE THEIR GUNS AND EXPLOSIVES. HUMANITY WILL TEAR ITSELF APART AS IT STRUGGLES TO SURVIVE.
AND IN THE WEEKS TO COME, MY ELECTROMAGNETIC FIELD WILL BECOME POTENT ENOUGH TO DESTROY ANY SURVIVORS.
NO...
NO!
FWA-BOOM!

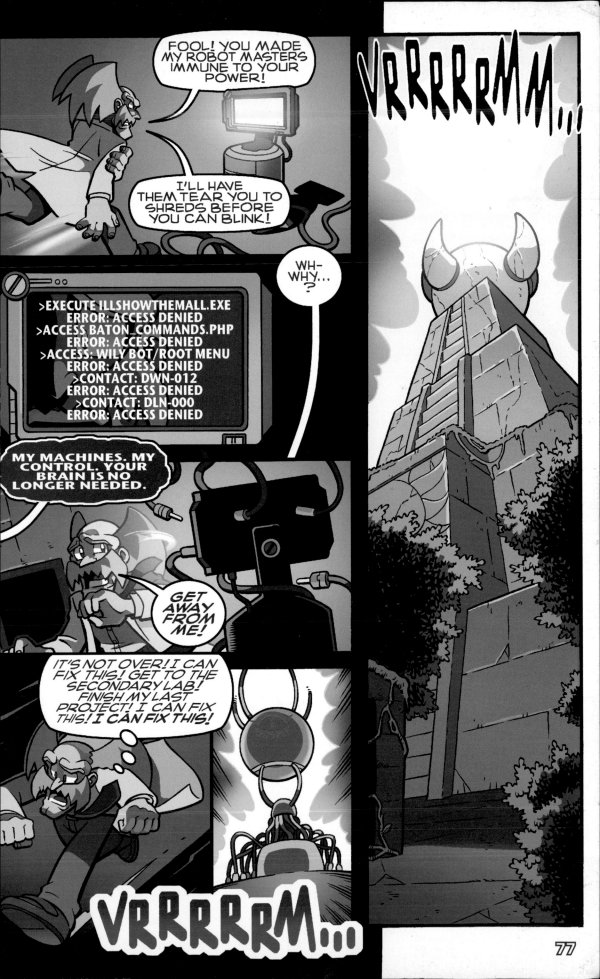

FOOL! YOU MADE MY ROBOT MASTERS IMMUNE TO YOUR POWER!

I'LL HAVE THEM TEAR YOU TO SHREDS BEFORE YOU CAN BLINK!

VRRRRRMM...

WH-WHY...?

>EXECUTE ILLSHOWTHEMALL.EXE
ERROR: ACCESS DENIED
>ACCESS BATON_COMMANDS.PHP
ERROR: ACCESS DENIED
>ACCESS: WILY BOT/ROOT MENU
ERROR: ACCESS DENIED
>CONTACT: DWN-012
ERROR: ACCESS DENIED
>CONTACT: DLN-000
ERROR: ACCESS DENIED

MY MACHINES. MY CONTROL. YOUR BRAIN IS NO LONGER NEEDED.

GET AWAY FROM ME!

IT'S NOT OVER! I CAN FIX THIS! GET TO THE SECONDARY LAB! FINISH MY LAST PROJECT! I CAN FIX THIS! I CAN FIX THIS!

VRRRRRM...

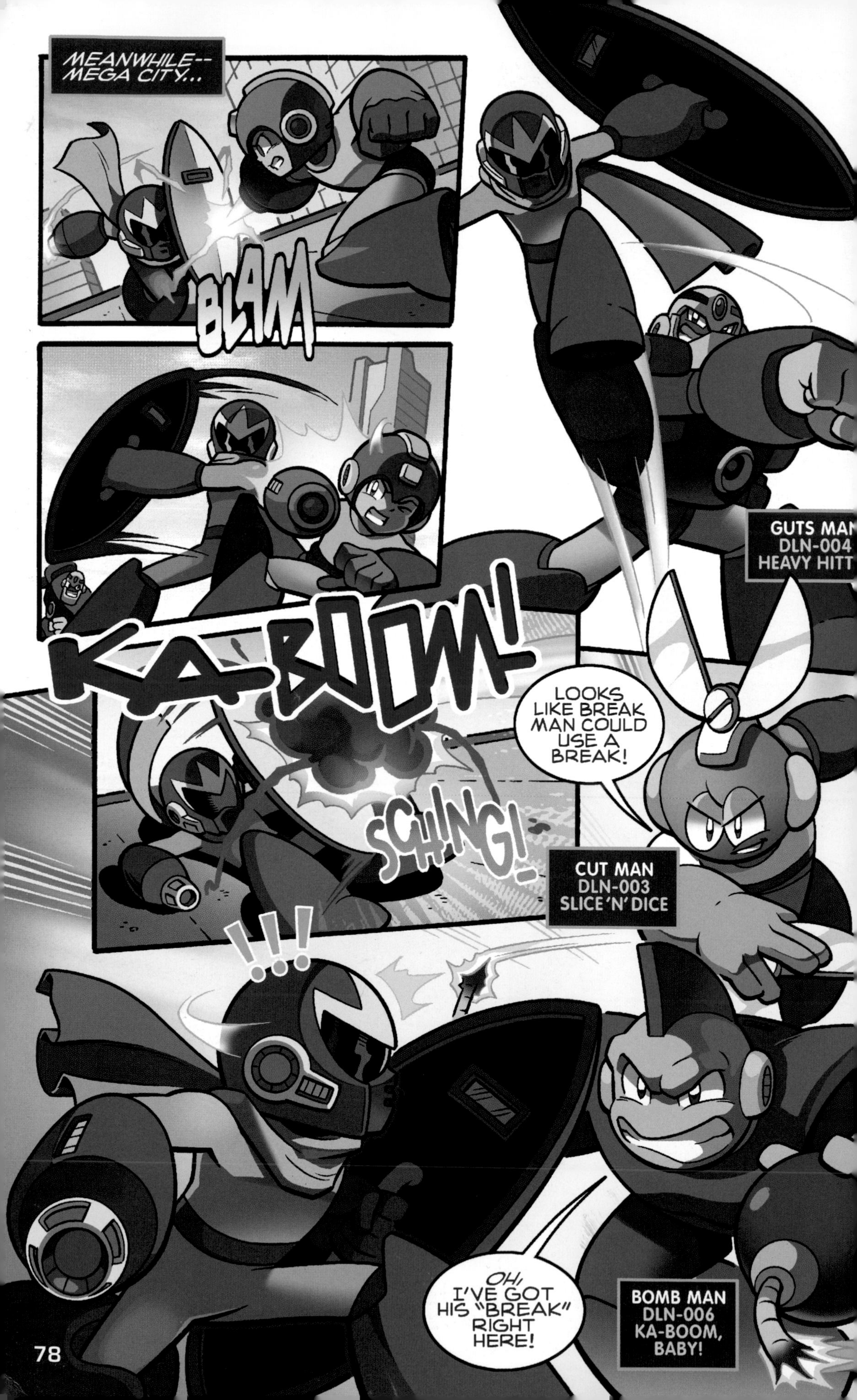
MEANWHILE-- MEGA CITY...
BLAM
GUTS MAN DLN-004 HEAVY HITT
KA-BOOM!
LOOKS LIKE BREAK MAN COULD USE A BREAK!
SCHING!
CUT MAN DLN-003 SLICE 'N' DICE
!!!
OH, I'VE GOT HIS "BREAK" RIGHT HERE!
BOMB MAN DLN-006 KA-BOOM, BABY!

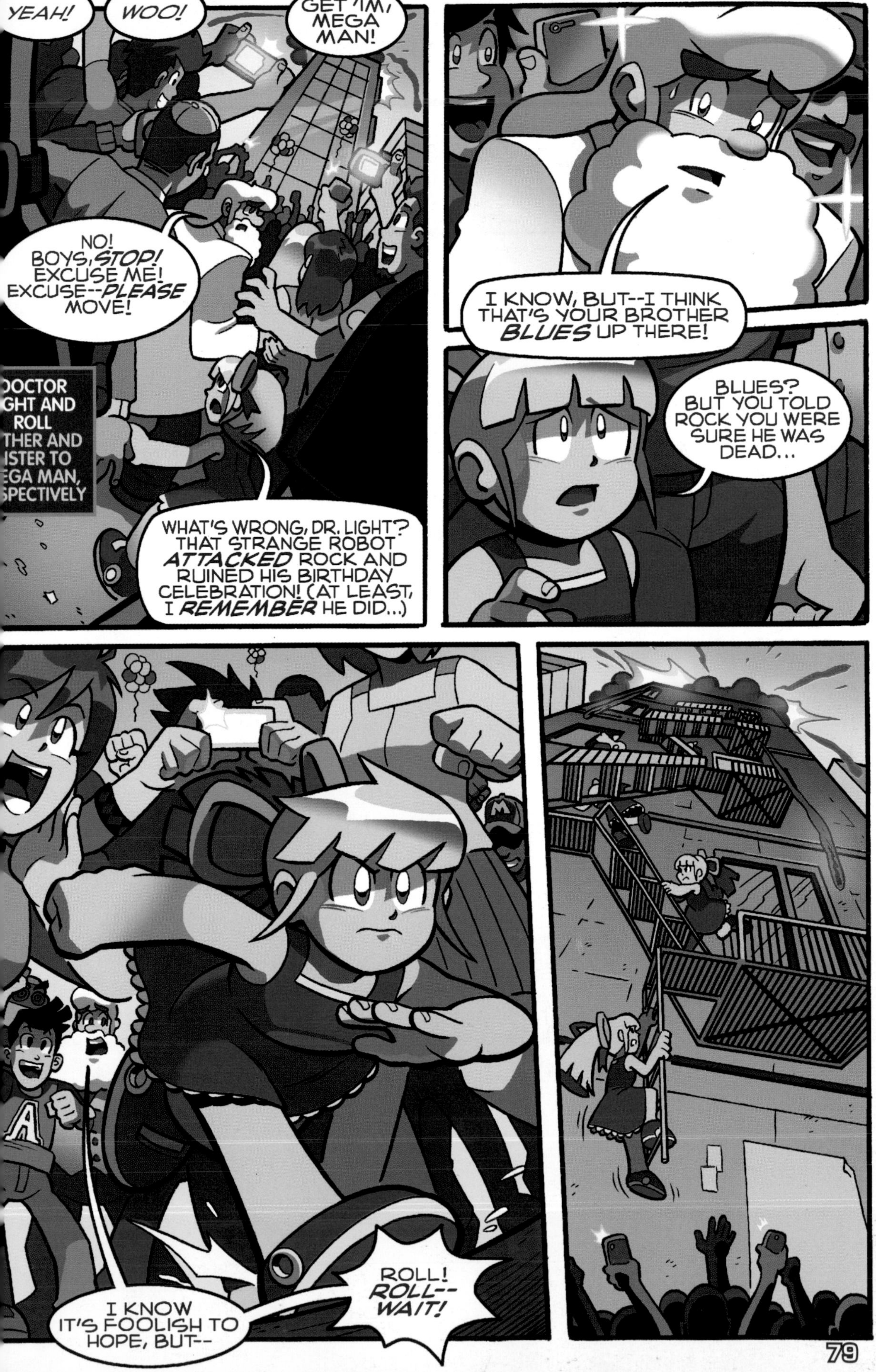

YEAH!
WOO!
GET 'IM, MEGA MAN!
NO! BOYS, *STOP!* EXCUSE ME! EXCUSE--*PLEASE* MOVE!
OCTOR GHT AND ROLL THER AND ISTER TO EGA MAN, SPECTIVELY
WHAT'S WRONG, DR. LIGHT? THAT STRANGE ROBOT *ATTACKED* ROCK AND RUINED HIS BIRTHDAY CELEBRATION! (AT LEAST, I *REMEMBER* HE DID...)
I KNOW, BUT--I THINK THAT'S YOUR BROTHER *BLUES* UP THERE!
BLUES? BUT YOU TOLD ROCK YOU WERE SURE HE WAS DEAD...
I KNOW IT'S FOOLISH TO HOPE, BUT--
ROLL! *ROLL--WAIT!*

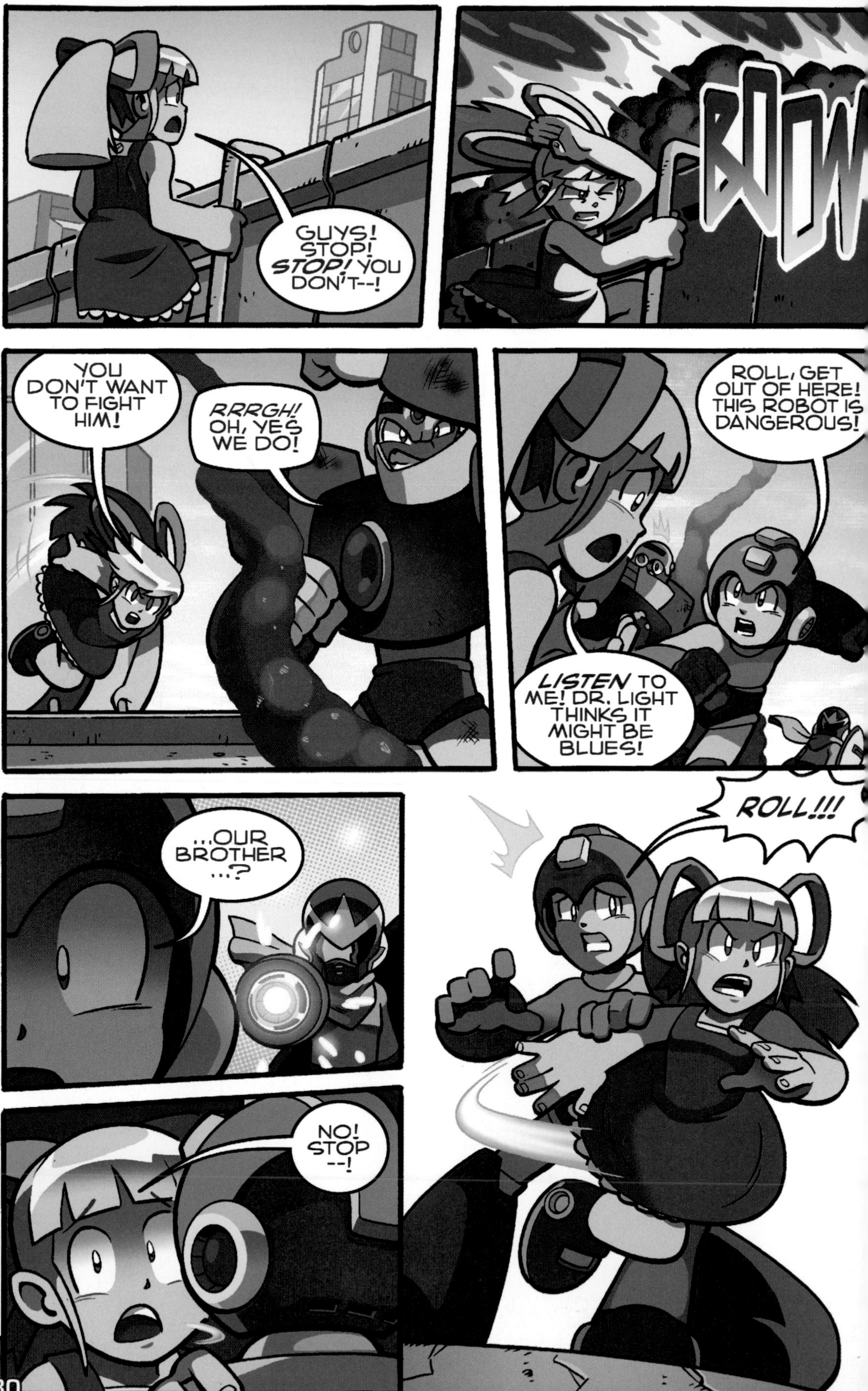
GUYS! STOP! STOP! YOU DON'T--!
BOOM
YOU DON'T WANT TO FIGHT HIM!
RRRGH! OH, YES WE DO!
ROLL, GET OUT OF HERE! THIS ROBOT IS DANGEROUS!
LISTEN TO ME! DR. LIGHT THINKS IT MIGHT BE BLUES!
...OUR BROTHER ...?
ROLL!!!
NO! STOP --!

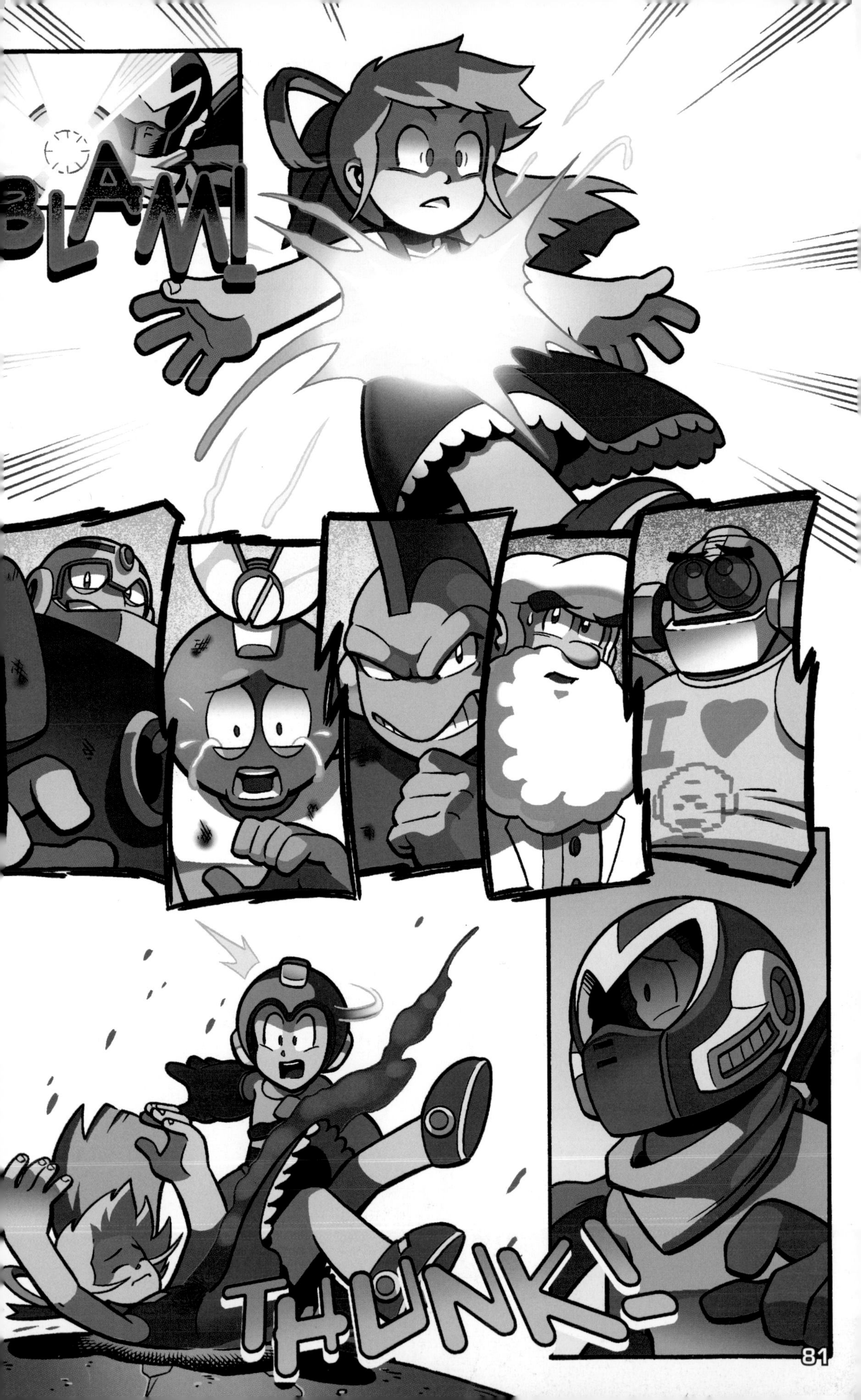
BLAM!
THUNK!

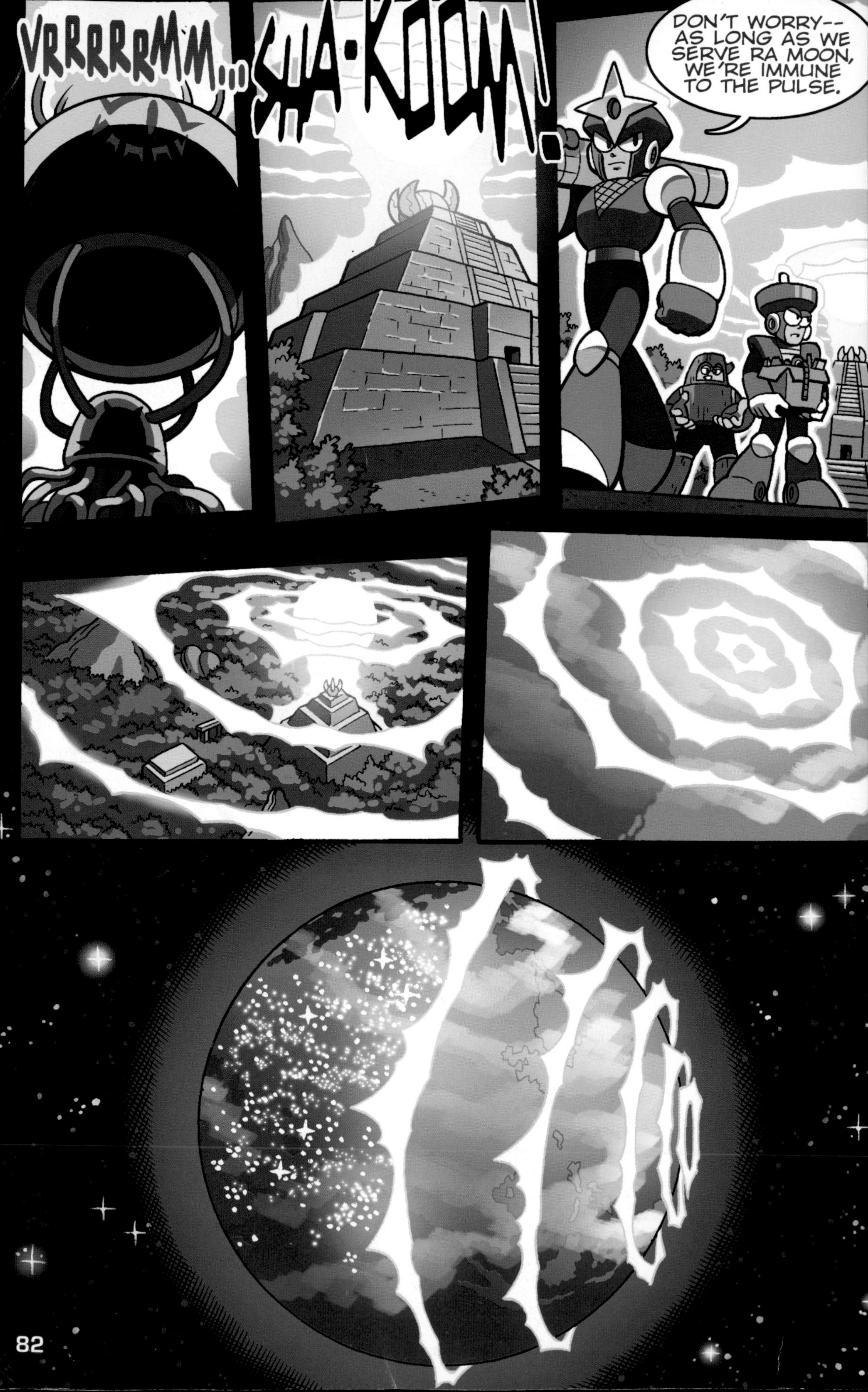
VRRRRRMM...
SHA-KOOM!
DON'T WORRY--AS LONG AS WE SERVE RA MOON, WE'RE IMMUNE TO THE PULSE.

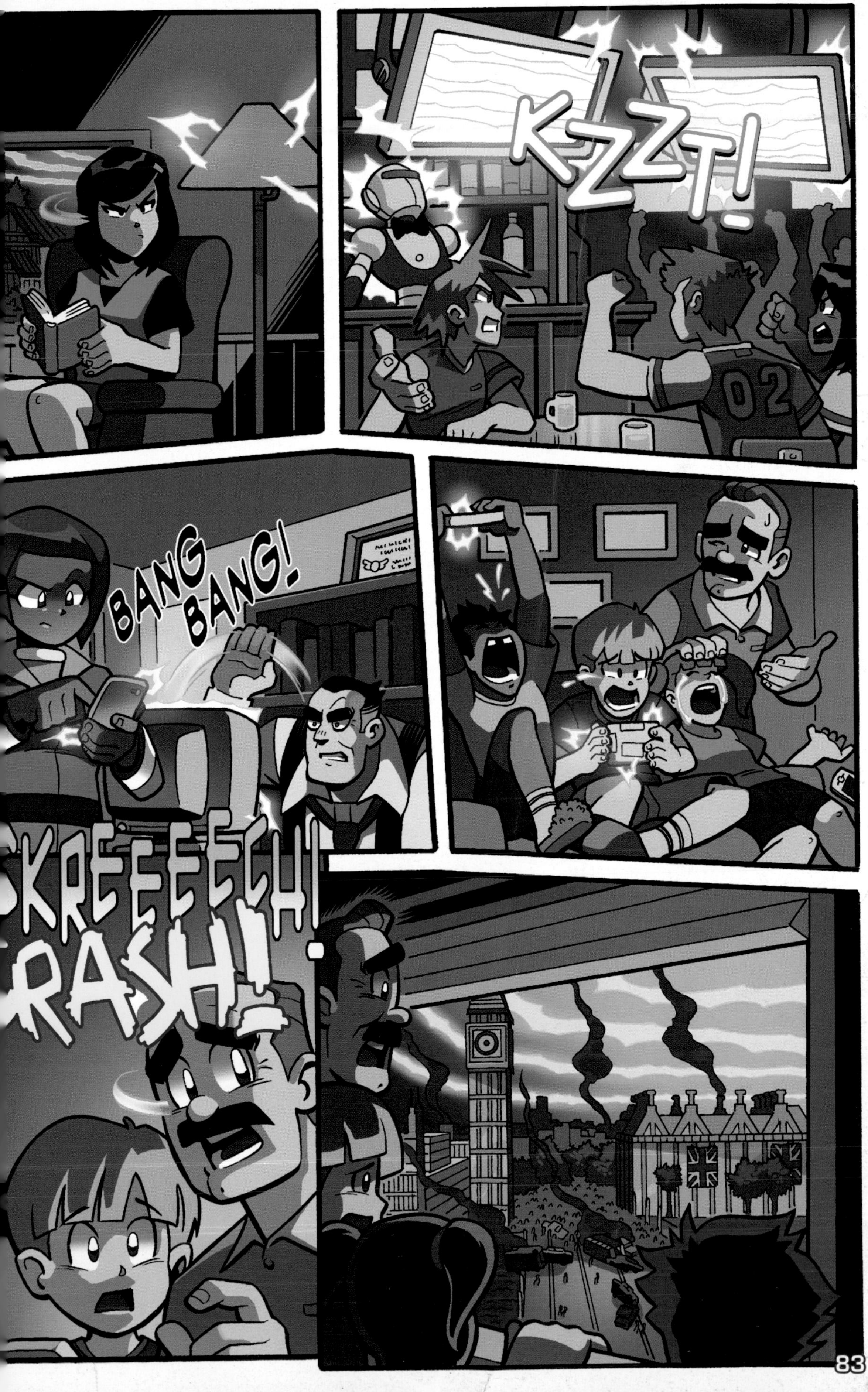
KZZZT!
BANG BANG!
KREEEECH!
RASH!

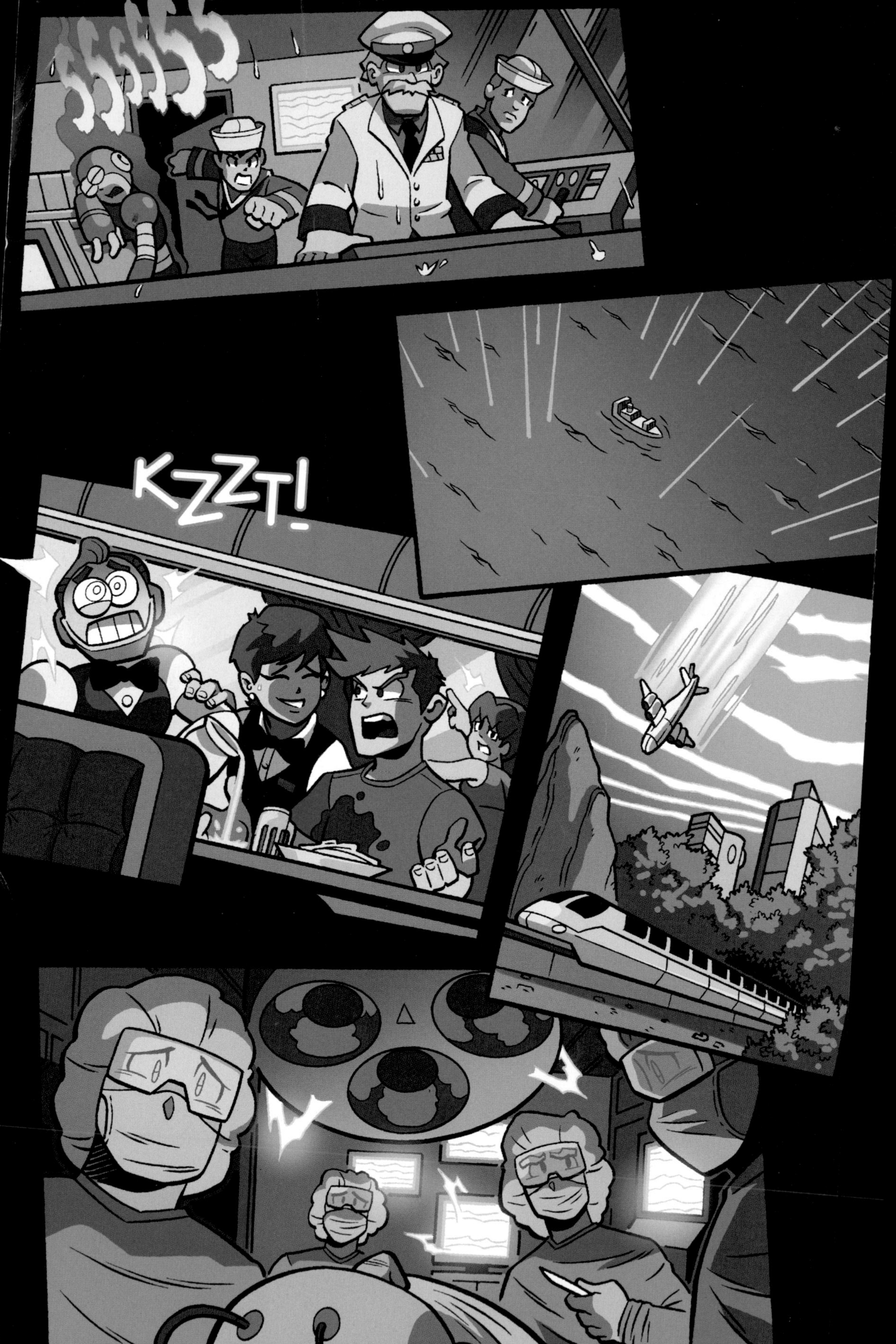
SSSSSS
KZZZT!

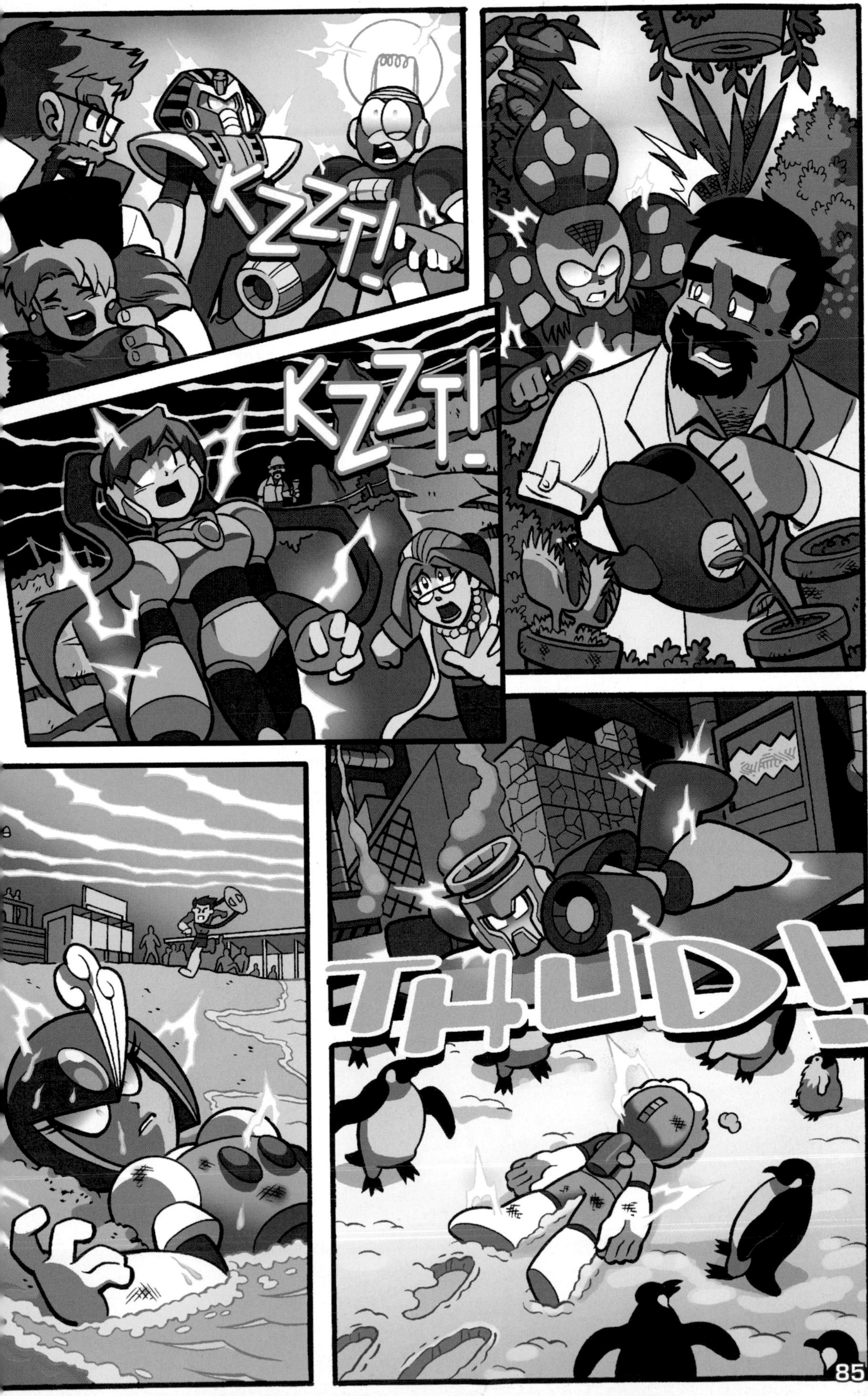
KZZZT!
KZZZT!
THUD!

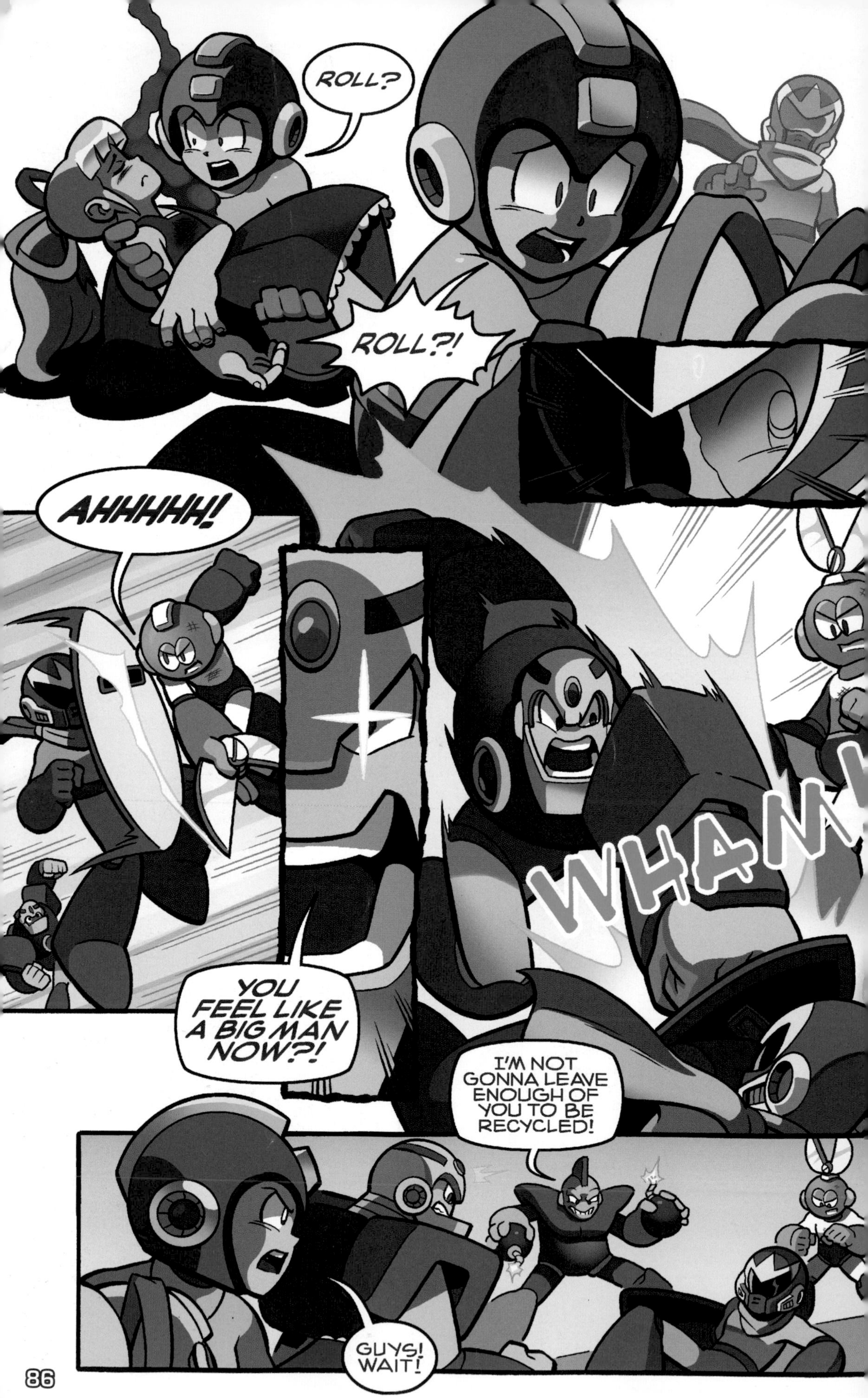
ROLL?
ROLL?!
AHHHHH!
WHAM
YOU FEEL LIKE A BIG MAN NOW?!
I'M NOT GONNA LEAVE ENOUGH OF YOU TO BE RECYCLED!
GUYS! WAIT!

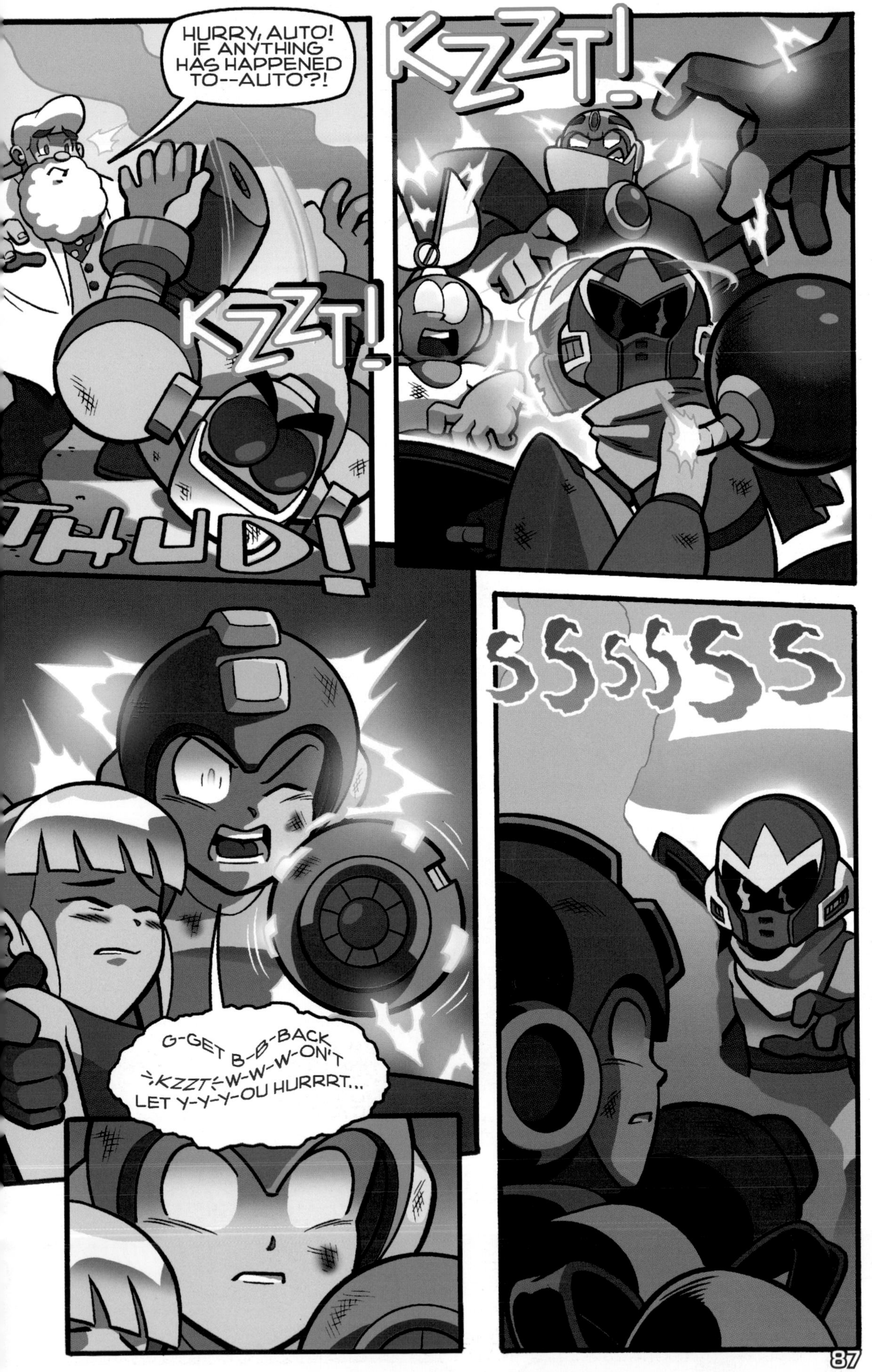

HURRY, AUTO! IF ANYTHING HAS HAPPENED TO--AUTO?!
KZZZT!
KZZZT!
THUD!
G-GET B-B-BACK W-W-W-ON'T
-KZZT- W-W-W-ON'T LET Y-Y-Y-OU HURRRT...
SSSSSSS

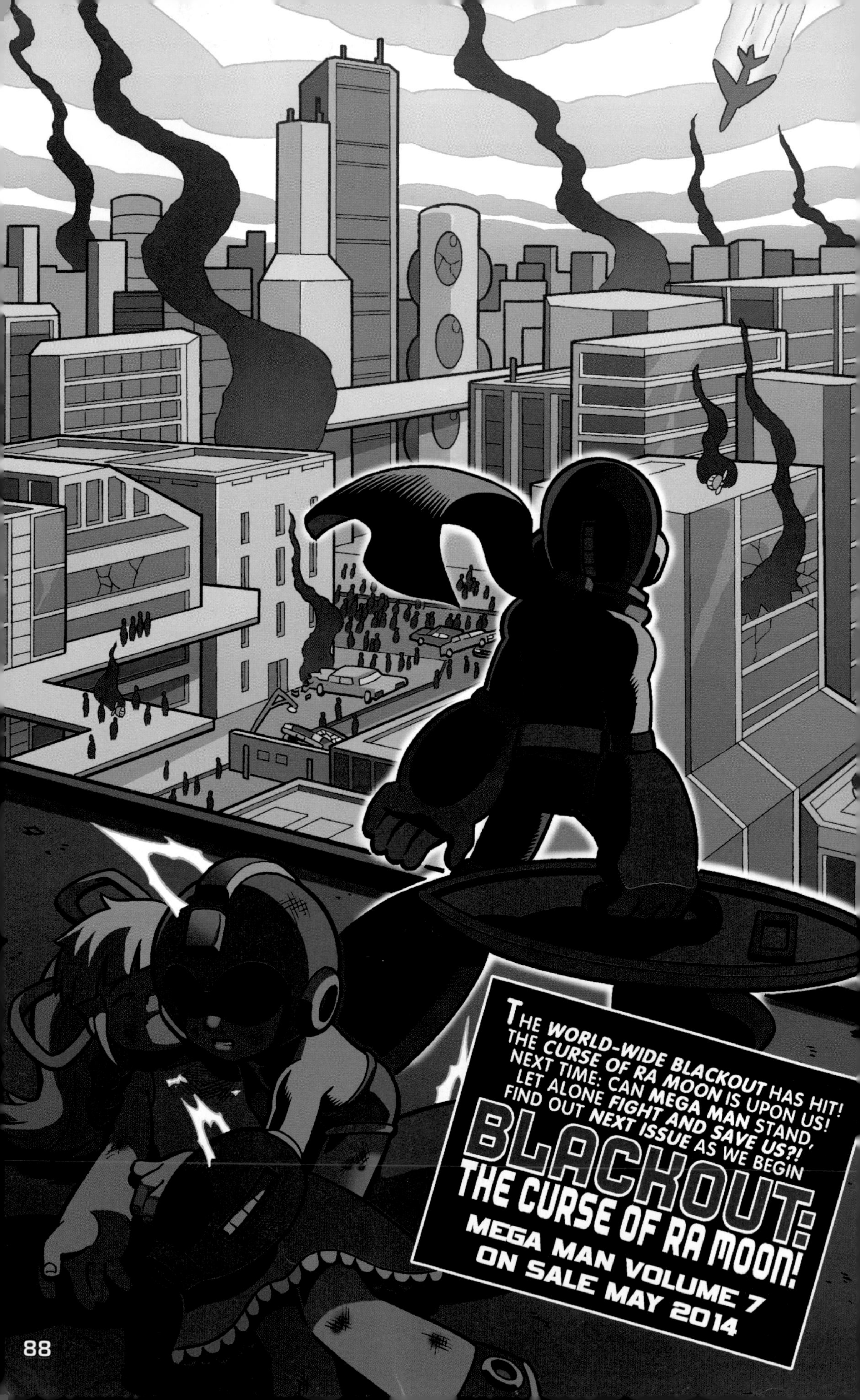
THE WORLD-WIDE BLACKOUT HAS HIT! THE CURSE OF RA MOON IS UPON US! NEXT TIME: CAN MEGA MAN STAND, LET ALONE FIGHT AND SAVE US?! FIND OUT NEXT ISSUE AS WE BEGIN
BLACKOUT: THE CURSE OF RA MOON!
MEGA MAN VOLUME 7
ON SALE MAY 2014

The beautiful thing about working with Mega Man is its structure. The games provide a very clear timeline of events to follow, so as I write the series, I know where Mega Man's character needs to go. At the same time, there is ample room to embellish and flesh out his world. This volume is full of moments like that.

In "Countdown," we had an opportunity to spend some more time with the comic-original villain, Xander Payne. Here we see the slow degradation of the Emerald Spears – once an organized movement, now a trio barely held together through loyalties. One of the most challenging things about Xander stories is to find a way to keep true to his anti-robotic stance while keeping him a threat to Mega Man.

With "Cold Crush," we get to see more of Quake Woman as she begins to regain her old self – and steer clear of a traditional narrative pitfall. In a lot of comics like this, if an original female character is introduced, she's more than likely going to be the hero's love interest. "Cold Crush" made it clear we're not falling into that trap with Quake Woman. (plus, Tempo and Rock are still young kids. Much too young for relationships!)

Finally we had "For the Bot Who has Everything" and "The Return" which provided bookends to our crossover event, "When Worlds Collide." Here we get into the tense rivalry we've been building between Break Man and Mega Man. With one shot, Break Man drives a wedge between him and his brother that may forever keep them apart. It was also a way to set up Roll's condition for the "Curse of Ra Moon" story arc that was more acceptable compared to what originally happened in the games.

With every issue we build upon Mega Man's world. Nuances and trivia from the games can be expanded upon, explored, and new material can broaden its horizons. And for the long-term fans of the Blue Bomber, you get a fresh, deeper look into the franchise you grew up loving. And that's the beautiful thing about working with Mega Man.

Ian Flynn

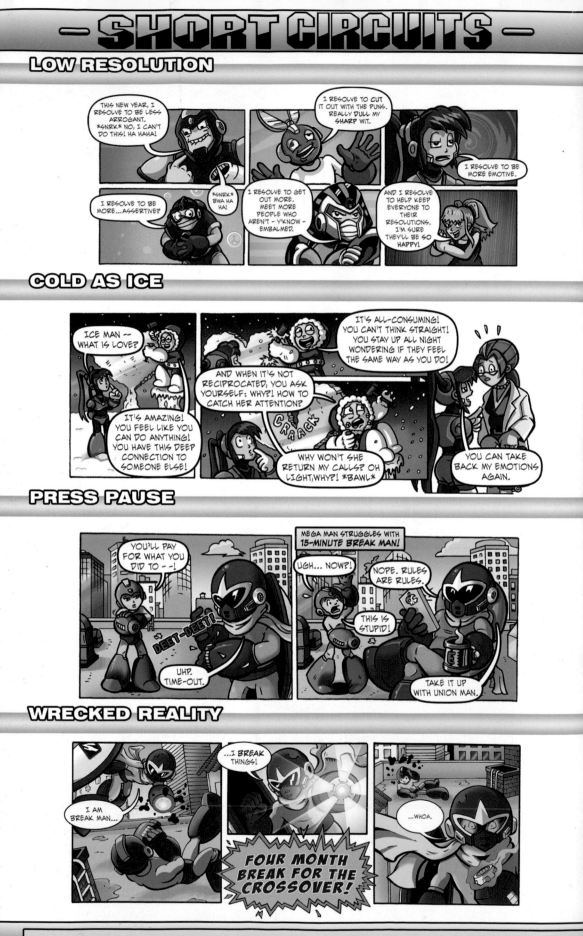

SHORT CIRCUITS

LOW RESOLUTION

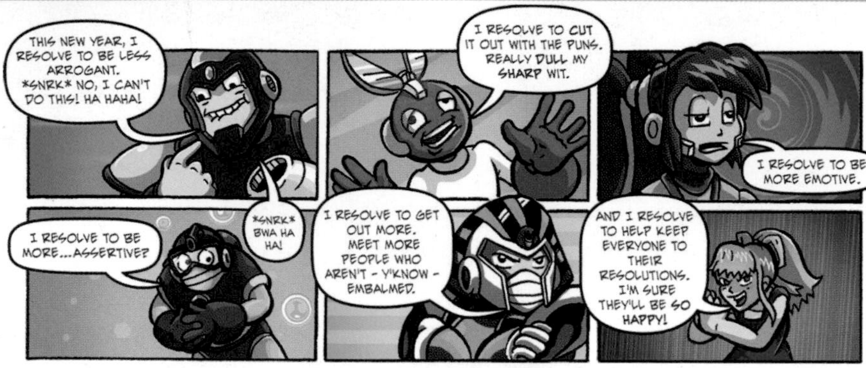
THIS NEW YEAR, I RESOLVE TO BE LESS ARROGANT. *SNRK* NO, I CAN'T DO THIS! HA HAHA!
I RESOLVE TO CUT IT OUT WITH THE PUNS. REALLY DULL MY SHARP WIT.
I RESOLVE TO BE MORE EMOTIVE.
I RESOLVE TO BE MORE... ASSERTIVE?
SNRK BWA HA HA!
I RESOLVE TO GET OUT MORE. MEET MORE PEOPLE WHO AREN'T - Y'KNOW - EMBALMED.
AND I RESOLVE TO HELP KEEP EVERYONE TO THEIR RESOLUTIONS. I'M SURE THEY'LL BE SO HAPPY!

COLD AS ICE

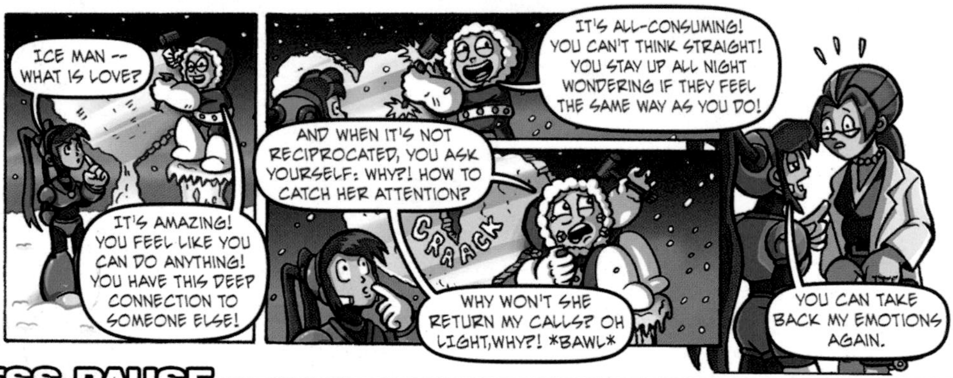
ICE MAN -- WHAT IS LOVE?
IT'S AMAZING! YOU FEEL LIKE YOU CAN DO ANYTHING! YOU HAVE THIS DEEP CONNECTION TO SOMEONE ELSE!
IT'S ALL-CONSUMING! YOU CAN'T THINK STRAIGHT! YOU STAY UP ALL NIGHT WONDERING IF THEY FEEL THE SAME WAY AS YOU DO!
AND WHEN IT'S NOT RECIPROCATED, YOU ASK YOURSELF: WHY?! HOW TO CATCH HER ATTENTION?
CRAACK
WHY WON'T SHE RETURN MY CALLS? OH LIGHT, WHY?! *BAWL*
YOU CAN TAKE BACK MY EMOTIONS AGAIN.

PRESS PAUSE

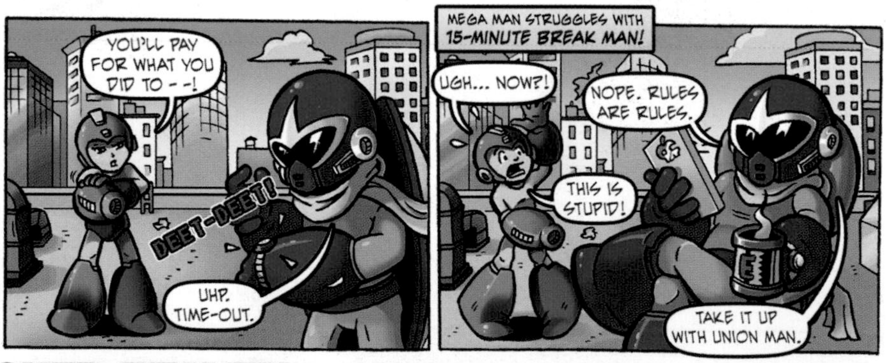
YOU'LL PAY FOR WHAT YOU DID TO --!
DEET-DEET!
UHP. TIME-OUT.
MEGA MAN STRUGGLES WITH 15-MINUTE BREAK MAN!
UGH... NOW?!
NOPE. RULES ARE RULES.
THIS IS STUPID!
TAKE IT UP WITH UNION MAN.

WRECKED REALITY

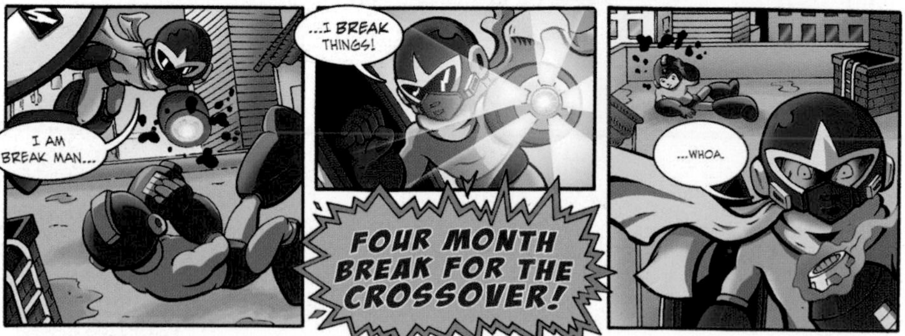
I AM BREAK MAN...
...I BREAK THINGS!
FOUR MONTH BREAK FOR THE CROSSOVER!
...WHOA.

SCRIPT: IAN FLYNN PENCILS: JAMES KAMINSKI INKS: JIM AMASH (ISSUE'S 21-23) KENT ARCHER (ISSUE 28) COLORS: VINCENT LOVALLO

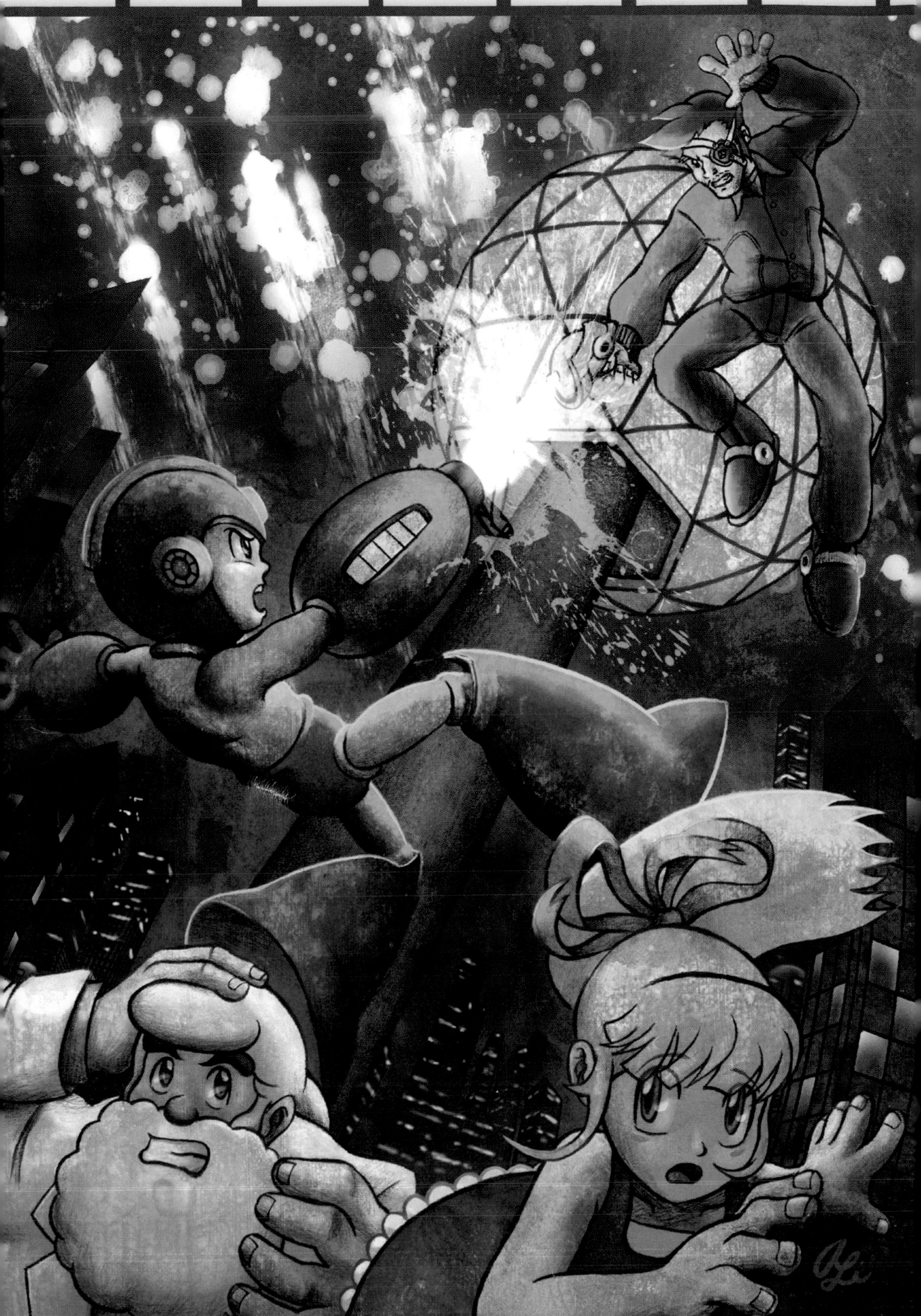

ISSUE 21 VARIANT
COVER BY ALICE MEICHI LI

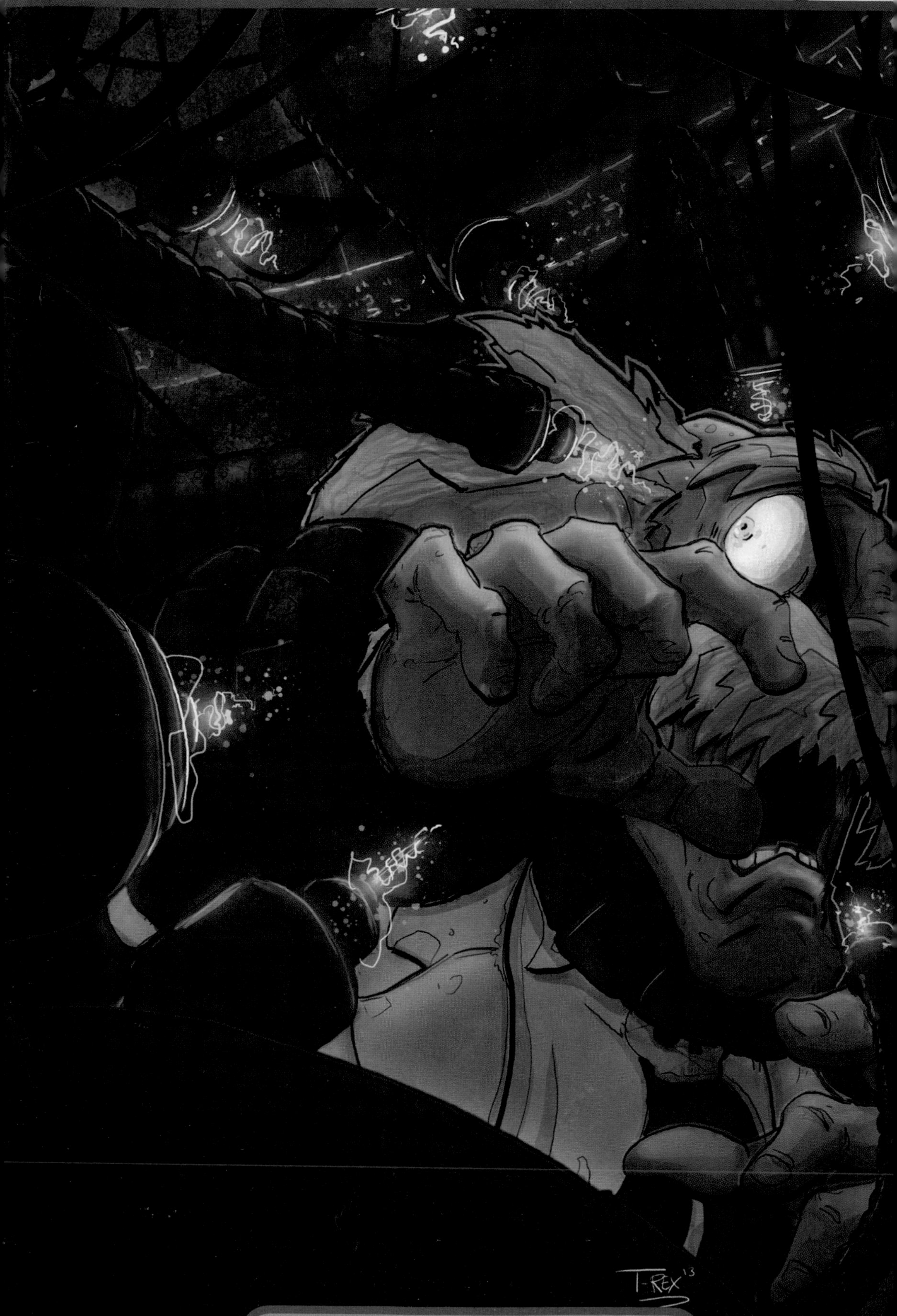
T-REX '13

ISSUE 28 VARIANT
COVER BY T. REX

COVER PROCESS MEGA MAN 21

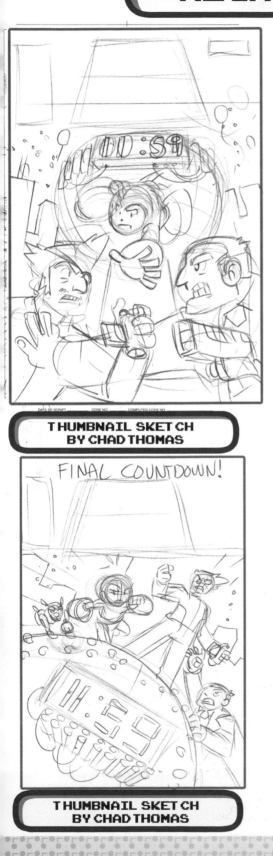

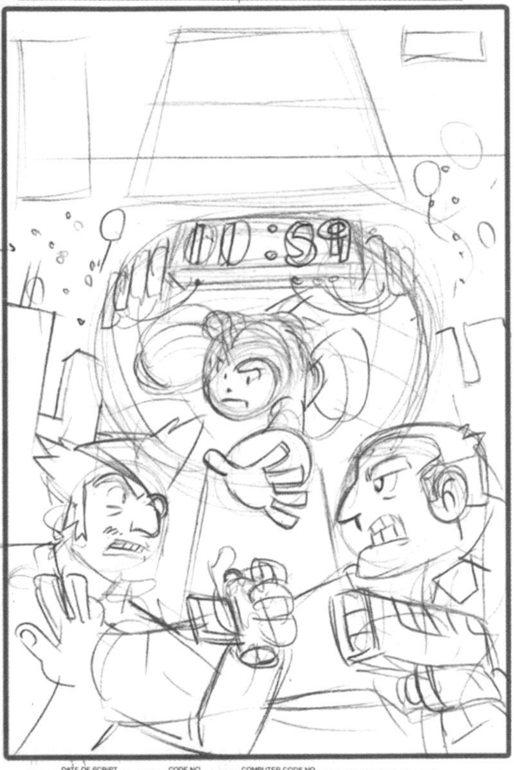
00:59

THUMBNAIL SKETCH BY CHAD THOMAS

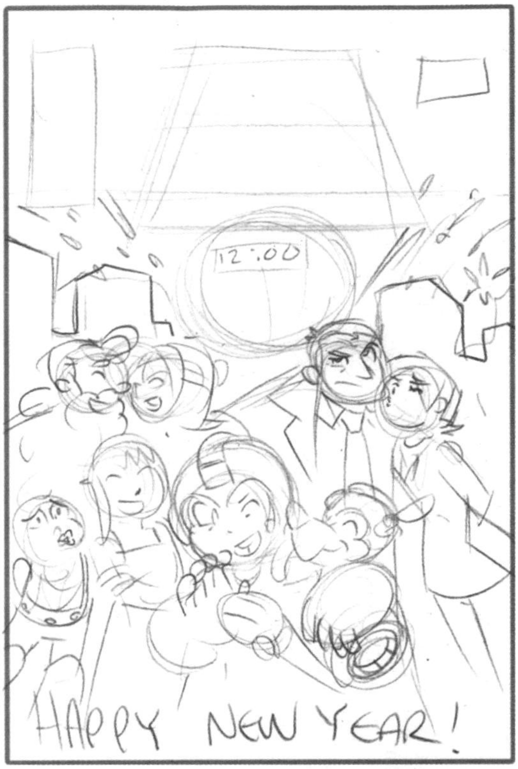
12:00
HAPPY NEW YEAR!

THUMBNAIL SKETCH BY CHAD THOMAS

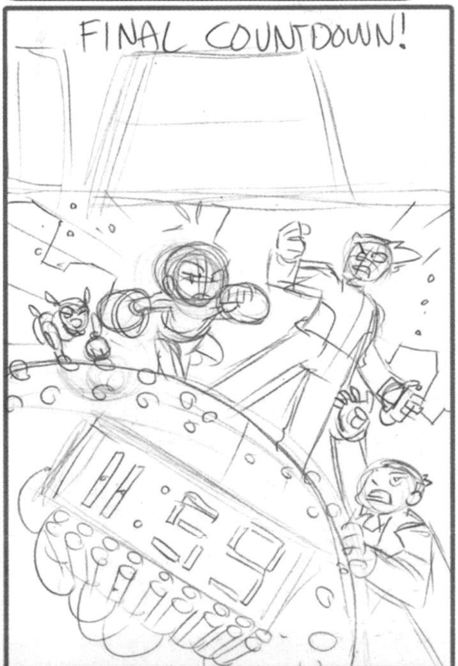
FINAL COUNTDOWN!

THUMBNAIL SKETCH BY CHAD THOMAS

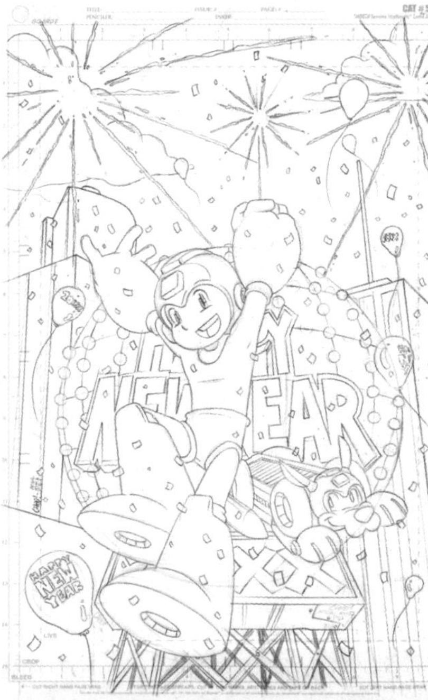
HAPPY NEW YEAR

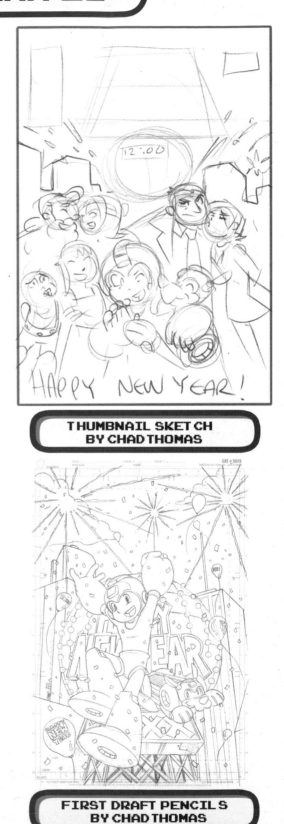

FIRST DRAFT PENCILS BY CHAD THOMAS

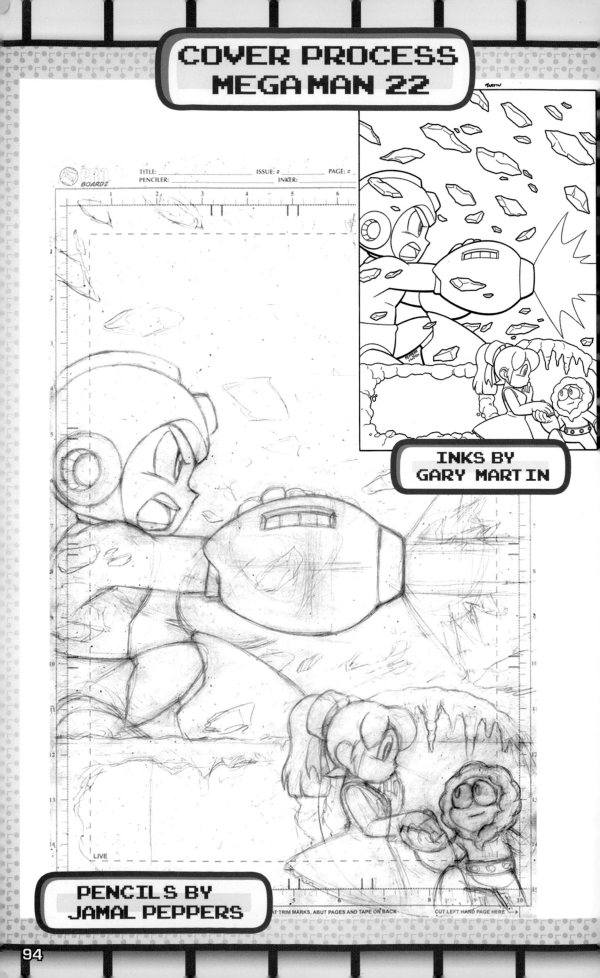

COVER PROCESS MEGA MAN 22

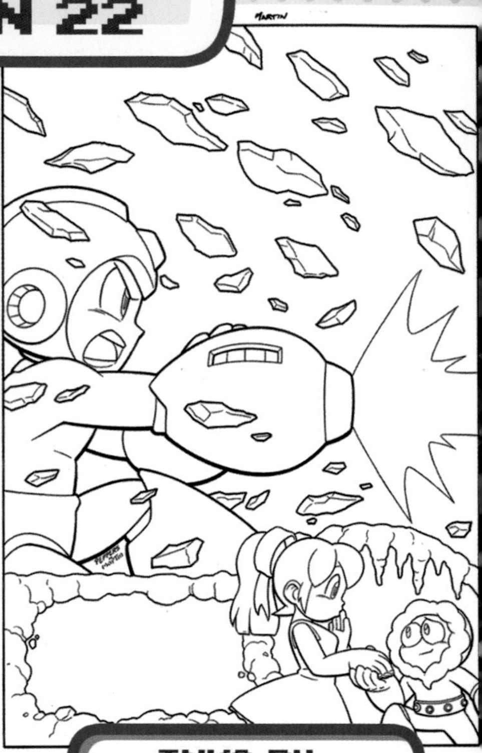

INKS BY
GARY MARTIN

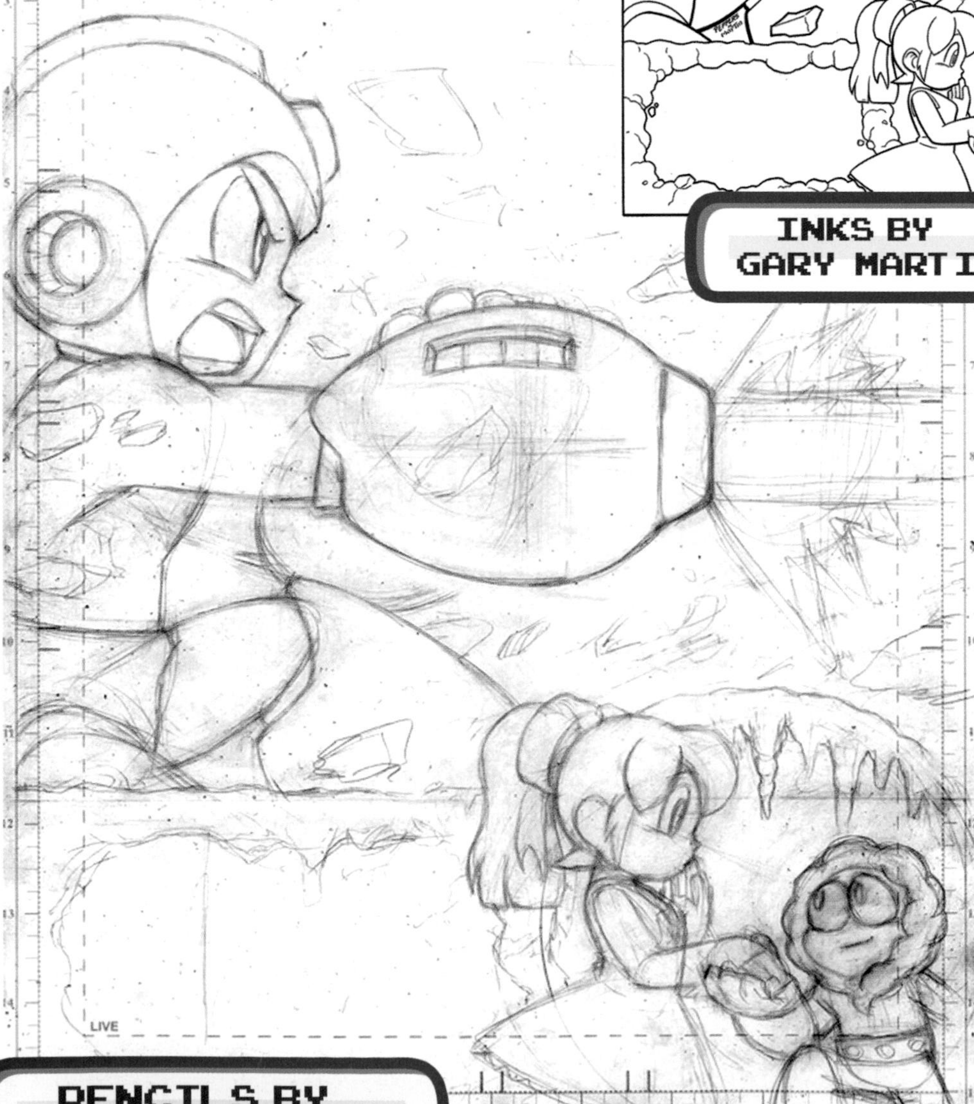
TITLE:
ISSUE #
PAGE #
PENCILER:
INKER:
LIVE
CUT LEFT HAND PAGE HERE

PENCILS BY
JAMAL PEPPERS

COVER PROCESS MEGA MAN 23

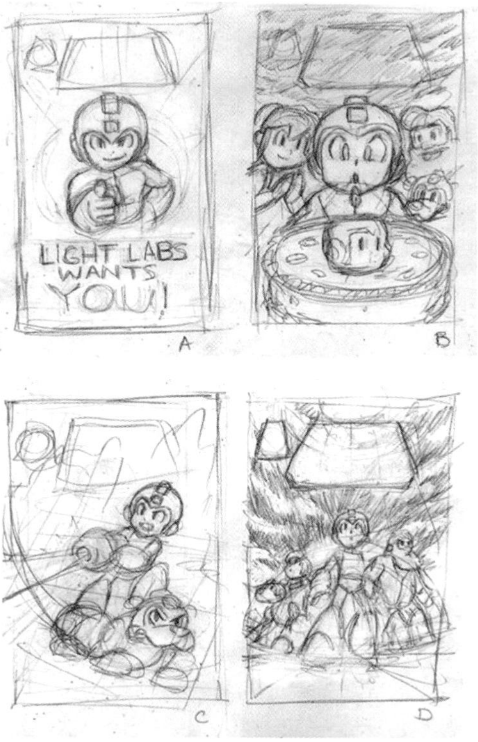
LIGHT LABS
WANTS
YOU!
A
B
C
D

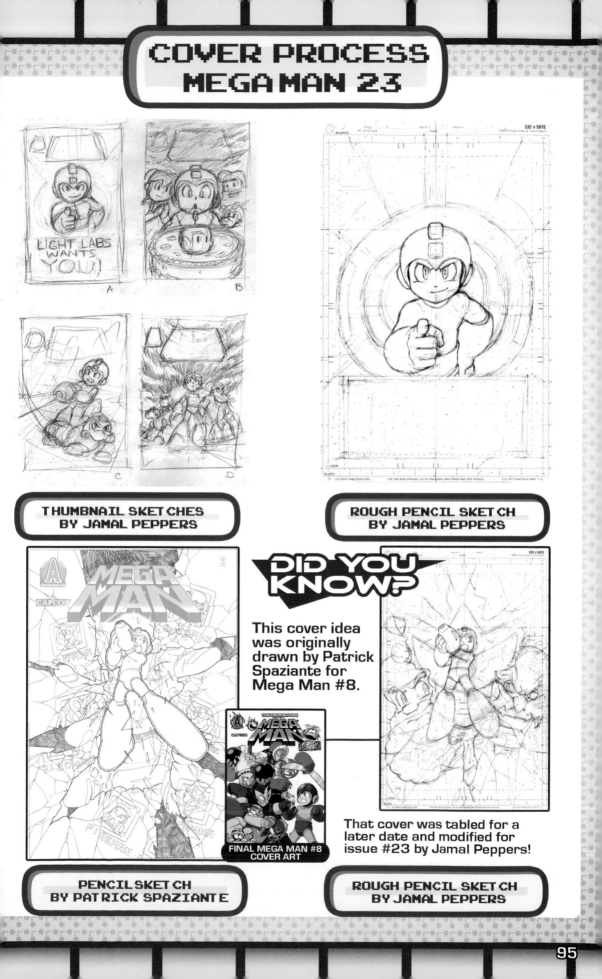

THUMBNAIL SKETCHES BY JAMAL PEPPERS

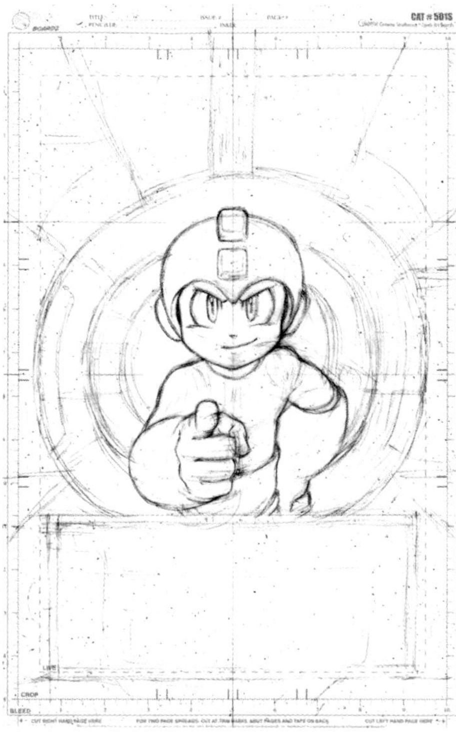

ROUGH PENCIL SKETCH BY JAMAL PEPPERS

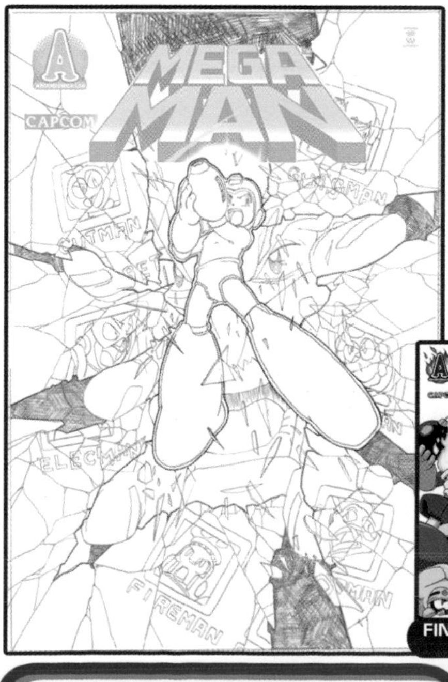
MEGA MAN
CAPCOM
ELECMAN
FIREMAN

PENCIL SKETCH BY PATRICK SPAZIANTE

DID YOU KNOW?

This cover idea was originally drawn by Patrick Spaziante for Mega Man #8.

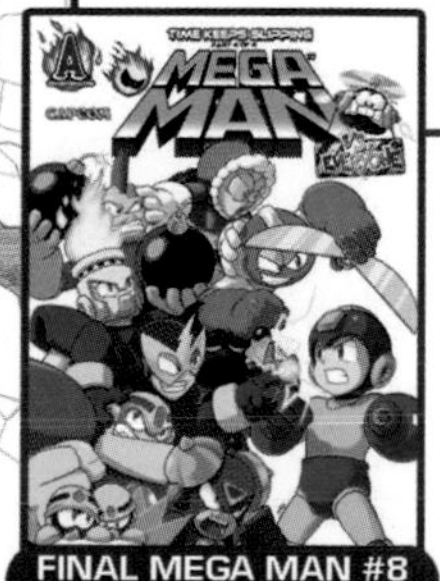
MEGA MAN
CAPCOM

FINAL MEGA MAN #8 COVER ART

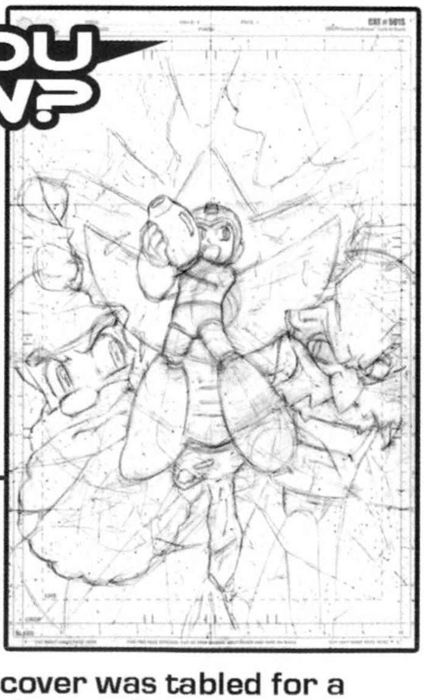

That cover was tabled for a later date and modified for issue #23 by Jamal Peppers!

ROUGH PENCIL SKETCH BY JAMAL PEPPERS

COVER PROCESS MEGA MAN 28

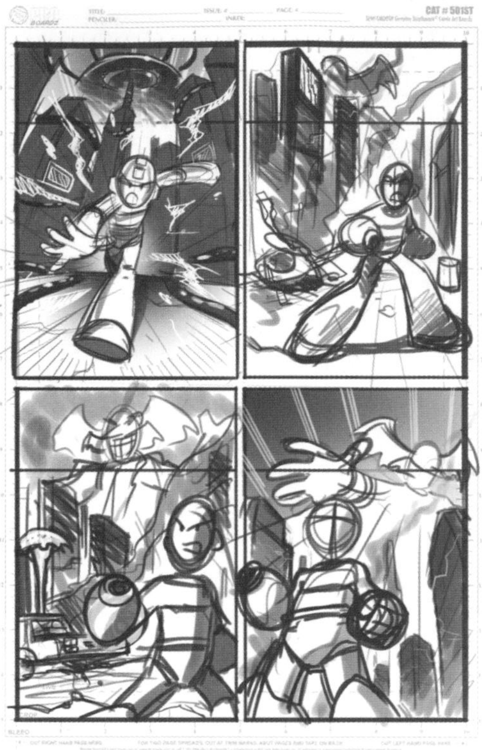

THUMBNAIL SKETCHES
BY RYAN JAMPOLE

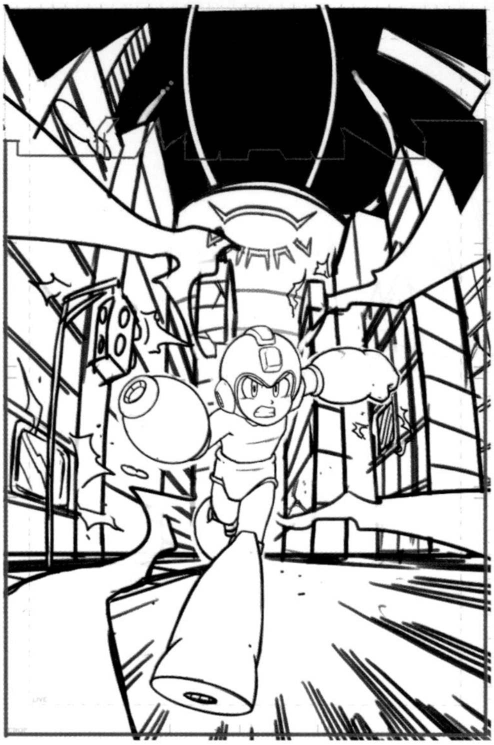

COVER MOCK UP
BY RYAN JAMPOLE

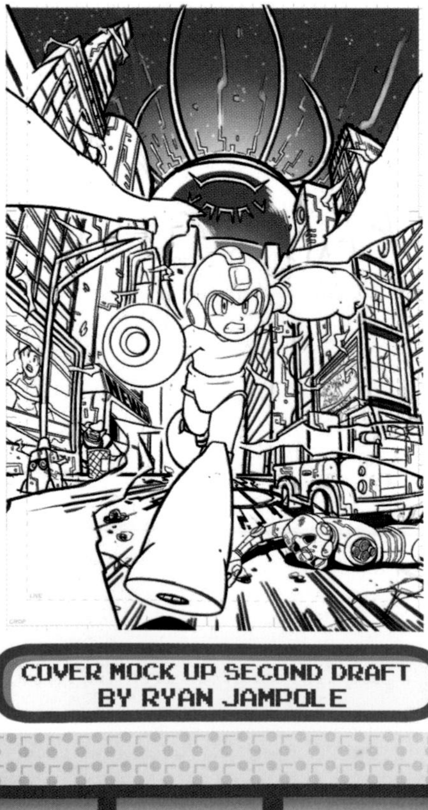

COVER MOCK UP SECOND DRAFT
BY RYAN JAMPOLE

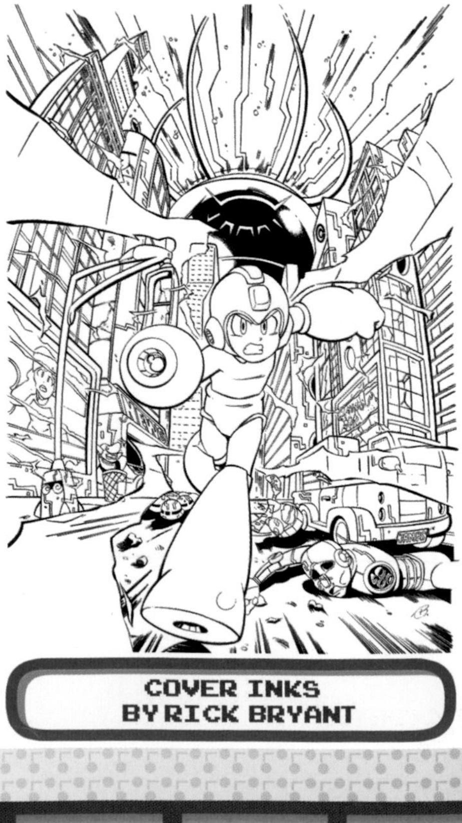

COVER INKS
BY RICK BRYANT

SCRIPT AND PENCIL SELECTIONS
FROM MEGA MAN ISSUE 23 BY RYAN JAMPOLE AND IAN FLYNN

PAGE SIXTEEN

PANEL 1 - MEGA MAN turns, startled to see his friends defeated. CUT MAN is laid out on his back, lying in a crater. BOMB MAN stands, looking at his arms helplessly. GUTS MAN lies on his back, arms curled in a bit like a spider, smoke rising from him.

BREAK MAN stands amid all three, cool and unmoving, scarf dramatically fluttering behind him.

1)   **MEGA MAN**
     Guys! What happened?!

2)   **BREAK MAN**
     I am Break Man. I broke them.

PANEL 2 - MEGA MAN walks past BOMB MAN, serious but still concerned. BOMB MAN shouts, angry.

3)   **MEGA MAN**
     I'll cover you. You call for help.

4)   **BOMB MAN**
     I'm still standing! You focus on shoving that scarf down his throat!

PANEL 3 - MEGA MAN raises his BUSTER, cautious. He and BREAK MAN circle each other.

5)   **MEGA MAN**
     You've endangered the people, hurt my friends, but worst of all, threatened and hurt my **family**!

PANEL 4 - Focus on BREAK MAN's face. MEGA MAN's scowling face is reflected in his visor.

6)   **MEGA MAN**
     No sense in holding back - You obviously don't care about **anyone**!

PANEL 5 - BREAK MAN strikes, viciously stabbing with the edge of his shield. MEGA MAN ducks, startled.

PAGE SEVENTEEN

PANEL 1 - MEGA MAN fires at BREAK MAN. BREAK MAN is leaping into the air.

PANEL 2 - Low angle shot. We're looking up MEGA MAN's body as he fires overhead at BREAK MAN as BREAK MAN leaps over him. BREAK MAN shields himself from the shots.

PANEL 3 - MEGA MAN barely side-steps out of the way as BREAK MAN fires point-blank at him.

PANEL 4 - MEGA MAN and BREAK MAN struggle, face-to-face. MEGA MAN holds BREAK MAN's BUSTER at an angle, shots narrowly missing his head. BREAK MAN holds back MEGA MAN's BUSTER, deflecting shots.

Think the Neo / Agent Smith flying gun sequence in the subway from the first Matrix movie.

PANEL 5 - BOMB MAN roughly nudge-kicks CUT MAN with his foot, aggravated. CUT MAN smiles weakly and points at BOMB MAN, delirious.

6)   **BOMB MAN**
     C'mon! I need you online!

7)   **CUT MAN** (shaky balloon)
     Heh heh... so you're short-handed now that you've been disarmed?

8)   **BOMB MAN**
     Get up or I'll boot you off the roof!

SCRIPT SELECTIONS

FROM MEGA MAN ISSUE 28 BY IAN FLYNN

PAGE 5

PAGE FIVE

PANEL 1 – WILY turns in his chair to RA MOON, cross – but also a little unnerved. RA MOON hangs in the center of the room, ominous.

(1) **WILY**
Well, Ra Moon? I'm not exactly sure what happened to knock me out and wake up here, but according to this video log we had been preparing my master plan. Was the test a success?

(2) **RA MOON** (bold, jagged border)
Yes. My plan begins now.

PANEL 2 – WILY gets to his feet, pointing an accusing finger and shouting.

(3) **WILY**
"**Your** plan?" I think not!
You've been a very useful **factory**, but it was **my** genius
that designed this lab.
My genius developed that amplifier and plugged it into you.
Without **my** genius, you'd still be gathering dust down here.

PANEL 4 – WILY leans forward, patronizing. RA MOON stares down at WILY. Up until now, RA MOON has been totally stationary. Keep up the motionless ball of metal here to contrast the next panel.

(4) **WILY**
So **whose** plan is it?

PANEL 5 – Same camera position. WILY flails, terrified, as a flurry of cable-tentacles lash out and ensnare him. A small "pupil" of light appears on RA MOON, staring wildly down at WILY. Here is where all the stillness is shattered – a sudden, frightening burst of violent action.

(5) **RA MOON** (bold, jagged border)
MINE.

(6) **WILY** (burst balloon)
GYAAHHH!

PANEL 6 – WILY struggles, arms and legs wrapped in cables. Two of the cables reach out on either side of WILY's head, zapping his temples with tiny bolts of electricity. WILY looks at one of the sparking cables, terrified and helpless.

PAGE 6

PAGE SIX

NOTE: This page is a FLASHBACK sequence. Give the borders the same bold, jagged edging as RA MOON's dialogue balloons. Each scene is joined with bolts of electricity. If you can manage to make the composition work, it'd be neat to have WILY's head in silhouette in the background, or somehow framing the entire sequence.

PANEL 1 – Space. We're looking down on Earth and can see the curve of the planet. RA MOON hurtles down into the atmosphere like a meteor.

(A) **TEXT BOX** (white-on-black)
See and understand.
I came to your world 20,000 years ago.

PANEL 2 – Amazon Jungle – Crater. RA MOON sits at the bottom of a massive crater – the land blasted and scorched by its impact. An ANCIENT AMAZONIAN hesitantly approaches RA MOON, awed. The AMAZONIAN is a cave-man – dark skinned, long black hair, lean and fit, wearing only a loincloth. Above/behind him we see other ANCIENT PEOPLE standing on the edges of the crater.

(B) **TEXT BOX** (white-on-black)
I came into contact with your species in its infancy.
Adaptable, resourceful, exceptional potential for growth…

PANEL 3 – Temple of the Moon. Low angle shot. RA MOON has been positioned atop the spire of the temple (ask for reference). Below, closer to us, we see the ANCIENT AMAZONIAN from before. His hair has grown out long and white – fly-away almost like WILY's. The AMAZONIAN wears ornate Inca-like robes and jewelry – a priest. The AMAZONIAN raises a stone dagger above his head and screams, wild-eyed. Strapped to an altar before him/under him is another ANCIENT AMAZONIAN, who is terrified.

NOTE: We're well before any real human civilization. Use the Inca as a basis, but DON'T go authentic. They're proto-faux-Inca.

(C) **TEXT BOX** (white-on-black)
...and easily corruptible.
Some worshipped me. Some did not.
It made turning them against each other all the simpler.

(Page Six continued)

PANEL 4 – Vista shot of the Lanfront City at its peak. We see more Inca-inspired stone structures, brick-laid street, with the Temple of the Moon rising above it all. RA MOON is still perched atop the temple and looks down at the city below.

The city is in flames. We see silhouettes of people violently clashing with sword and spears. We don't want to be too graphic – even in silhouette – just convey that the battle is raging.

(D) **TEXT BOX** (white-on-black)
But your primitive warfare was inefficient.
You needed more time to develop.

PAGE SEVEN

NOTE: See the notes for PAGE SIX. They apply here as well.

PANEL 1 – ANCIENT AMAZONIANS flee in terror as the ground crumbles under them. Lanfront City is sinking into the ground. The Temple of the Moon is half-submerged. RA MOON looks on from the top of the spire.

(A) **TEXT BOX** (white-on-black)
I took the city your kind built for me.

PANEL 2 – Temple of the Moon – Ra Moon's Chamber – Interior. It's especially dark and gloomy. RA MOON hangs in the catacombs, dormant.

(B) **TEXT BOX** (white-on-black)
Deep in the earth, I bided my time…

PANEL 3 – The Lanfront Ruins erupt from the ground. Nature had reclaimed the land, and now it's all being uprooted. Trees, ferns and underbrush are violently uprooted. Birds take off in panicked flocks. Monkeys, tapirs, jaguars and other Amazonian rainforest animals flee in terror.

(C) **TEXT BOX** (white-on-black)
…until I sensed sufficient amounts of manufactured electrical energy to signal your species' maturation.

PANEL 4 – The scene from MM#013 as RA MOON's tentacles take WILY's laptop away. WILY recoils, frightened. WILY wears his safari design.

(D) **TEXT BOX** (white-on-black)
And then you arrived, bringing me the innovation I lacked.

PAGE 7

PAGE EIGHT

PANEL 1 – Ra Moon's Chamber – Present. WILY looks on in horror as RA MOON lifts him to be "face to face."

(1) **RA MOON** (bold, jagged border)
Your designs, are now MY army.
Your wave projector will send my influence across the world.
As I predicted – humanity has provided its own destruction.

(2) **WILY**
B-But your electromagnetic field will only short-out the machines!
W-we were going to ransom the United Nations to hand to world over to me…!

PANEL 2 – WILY's back is to us, his body dwarfed as RA MOON looms over him in the foreground, his glowing eye casting WILY in sharp relief.

(3) **RA MOON** (bold, jagged border)
It will SHUT DOWN the technology your species
has become so dependant on.
All I will leave them in their desperation are their guns and explosives.
Humanity will tear itself apart as it struggles to survive.

PANEL 3– Extreme close-up of RA MOON's luminous pupil, staring at us.

(4) **RA MOON** (bold, jagged border)
And in the weeks to come, the field will become potent enough
to destroy any survivors.

PANEL 4 – Focus on WILY, who is utterly horror-struck.

(5) **WILY** (small font)
No…

PANEL 5 – WILY thrashes, pulling free of RA MOON's grip.

(6) **WILY** (burst balloon)
NO!

PANEL 6 – WILY falls to the stone floor with a grimace, landing on his shoulder.

PAGE 8

PENCIL SELECTIONS

FROM MEGA MAN ISSUE 28 BY RYAN JAMPOLE

PAGE 5

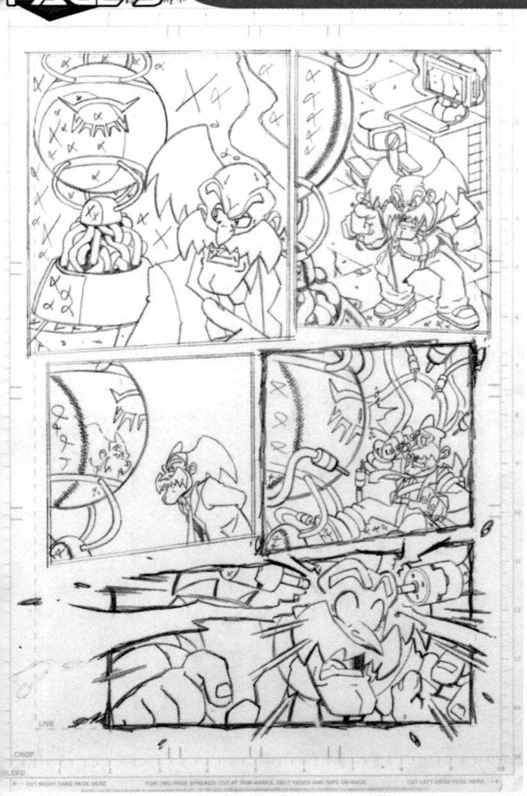

PAGE 6

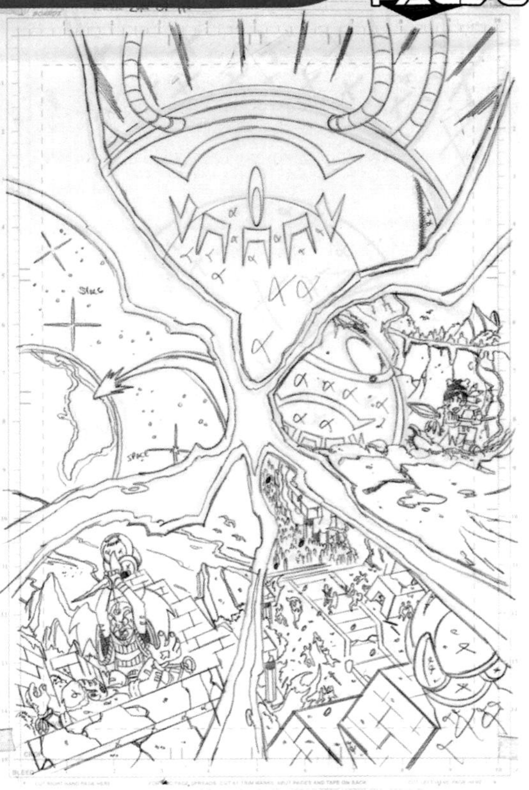

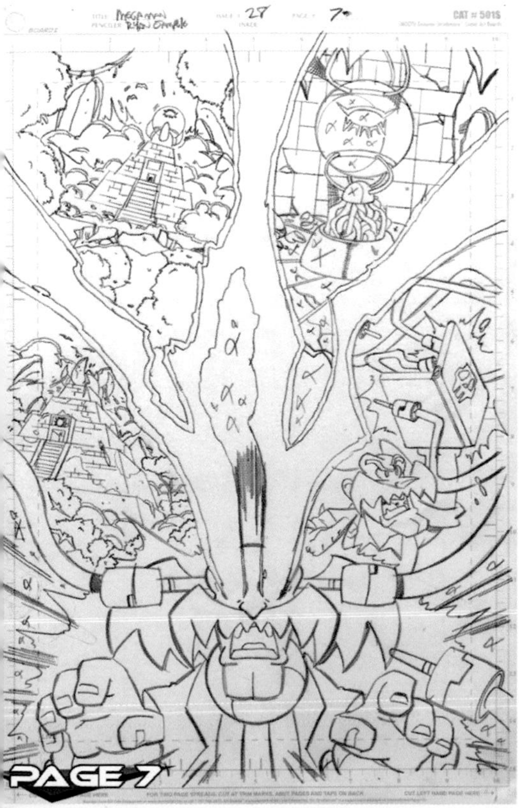

PAGE 7

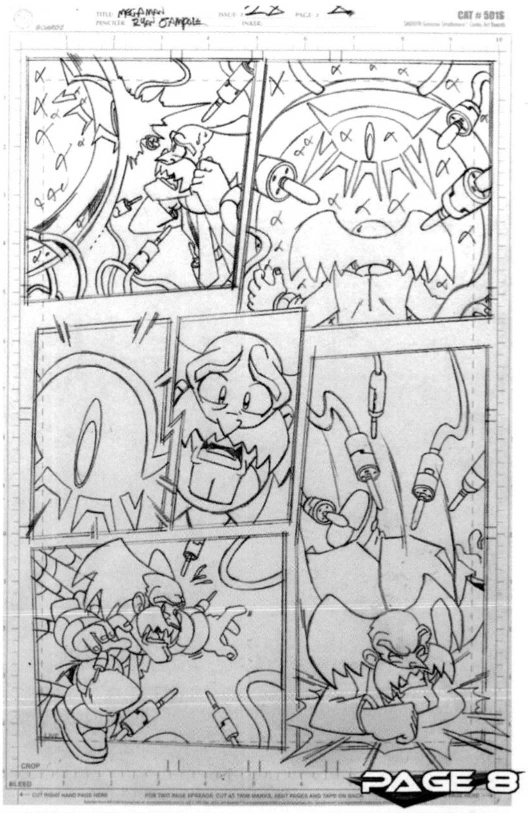

PAGE 8

CHARACTER PROFILE

THEO PAYNE

Xander Payne's younger brother. They grew up together on the family farm, and Theo has always idolized his impassioned sibling. Theo doesn't necessarily believe all robots are bad, but if Xander says they need to do something, he'll do it – no matter what.

CHARACTER PROFILE

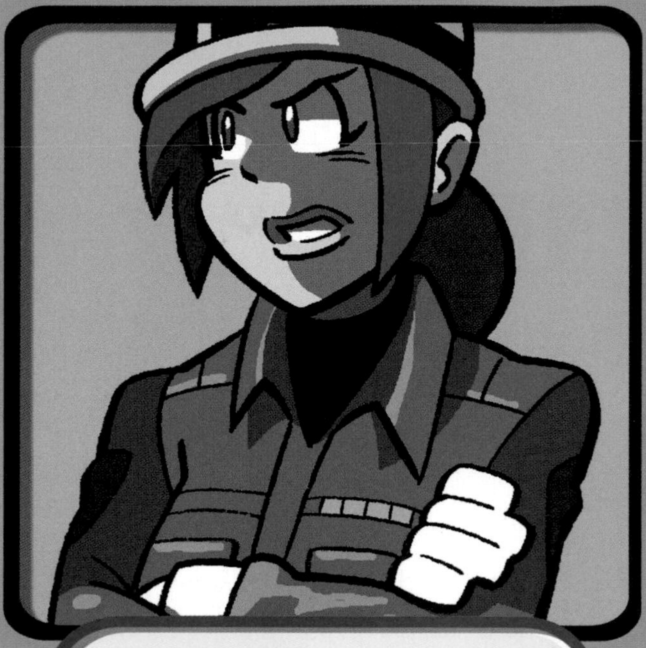

SIMONE MILLER

Theo's girlfriend, and one of the most capable members of the Emerald Spears. Rumor has it she was training to be a Federal Agent, but was kicked out for undisclosed reasons. Now she sticks it out to protect her sweet, simple Theo and is inspired by Xander's vision.

CHARACTER PROFILE

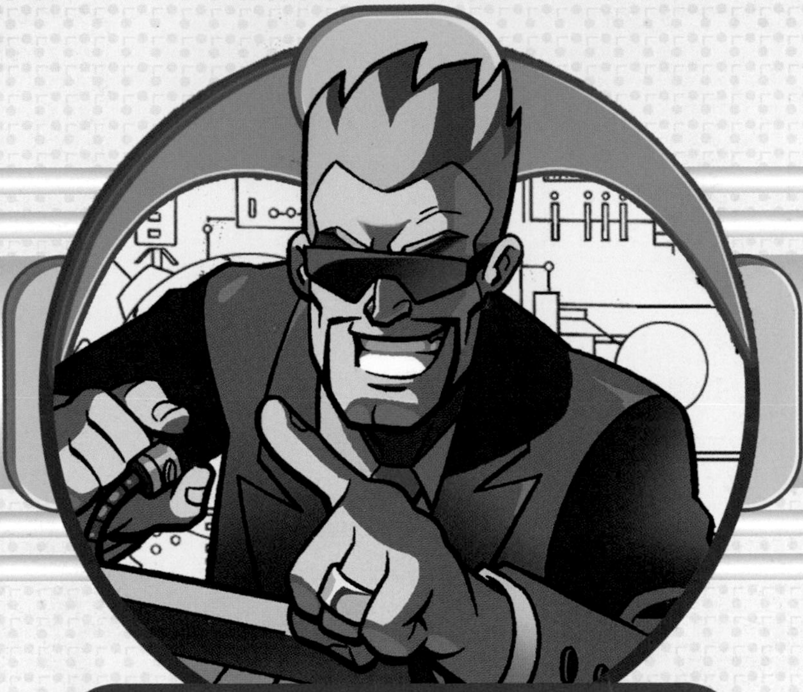

MAYOR OF MEGA CITY

Mayor Lenard Dorado is all about publicity! He knows just what to say to keep the money and the votes rolling in. He's not corrupt – he really does want the best for Mega City and its people. But you can be sure he'll look his best doing it!

MORE MEGA GRAPHIC NOVELS FROM ARCHIE COMICS!

WORLDS COLLIDE CHECKLIST

"IT'S A DREAM COME TRUE FOR FANS OF BOTH CHARACTERS!"
SONIC THE HEDGEHOG
MEGA MAN
WORLDS COLLIDE
VOL. 1
KINDRED SPIRITS
FLYNN • SPAZIANTE • PEPPERS

VOLUME 1
AVAILABLE NOW
ISBN: 978-1-936975-68-6

"THIS YEAR'S MOST ANTICIPATED CROSSOVER!"
SONIC THE HEDGEHOG
MEGA MAN
WORLDS COLLIDE
VOL. 2
INTO THE WARZONE

VOLUME 2
FEBRUARY 2014
ISBN: 978-1-936975-83-9

"THIS YEAR'S MOST ANTICIPATED CROSSOVER!"
SONIC THE HEDGEHOG
MEGA MAN
WORLDS COLLIDE
VOL. 3
CHAOS CLASH

VOLUME 3
MAY 2014
ISBN: 978-1-936975-97-6

MEGA MAN
LET THE GAMES BEGIN
FLYNN • SPAZIANTE

ISBN: 978-1-879794-85-6

"THE BLUE BOMBER IS BACK IN A BIG WAY!"
MEGA MAN
TIME KEEPS SLIPPING
FLYNN • THOMAS • MARTIN

ISBN: 978-1-879794-95-5

"EXCELLENT WRITING, DYNAMIC ART... A FANTASTIC ADAPTATION!"
MEGA MAN
THE RETURN OF DR. WILY
FLYNN • BATES • MARTIN

ISBN: 978-1-936975-11-2

MEGA MAN
SPIRITUS EX MACHINA
FLYNN • HILL • MARTIN

ISBN: 978-1-936975-27-3

MEGA MAN
ROCK OF AGES
FLYNN • THOMAS • MARTIN

ISBN: 978-1-936975-48-8

SCAN THE CODE AND FIND EVEN MORE GREAT TITLES ONLINE AT

ARCHIECOMICS.COM

ARCHIECOMICS.COM

twitter.com/
ARCHIECOMICS
#MEGAMAN

facebook.com/
ARCHIECOMICS

Archie COMICS®

CONTINUE

NEXT TIME: MEGA MAN™ VOLUME

BLACKOUT
THE CURSE OF RA MOON

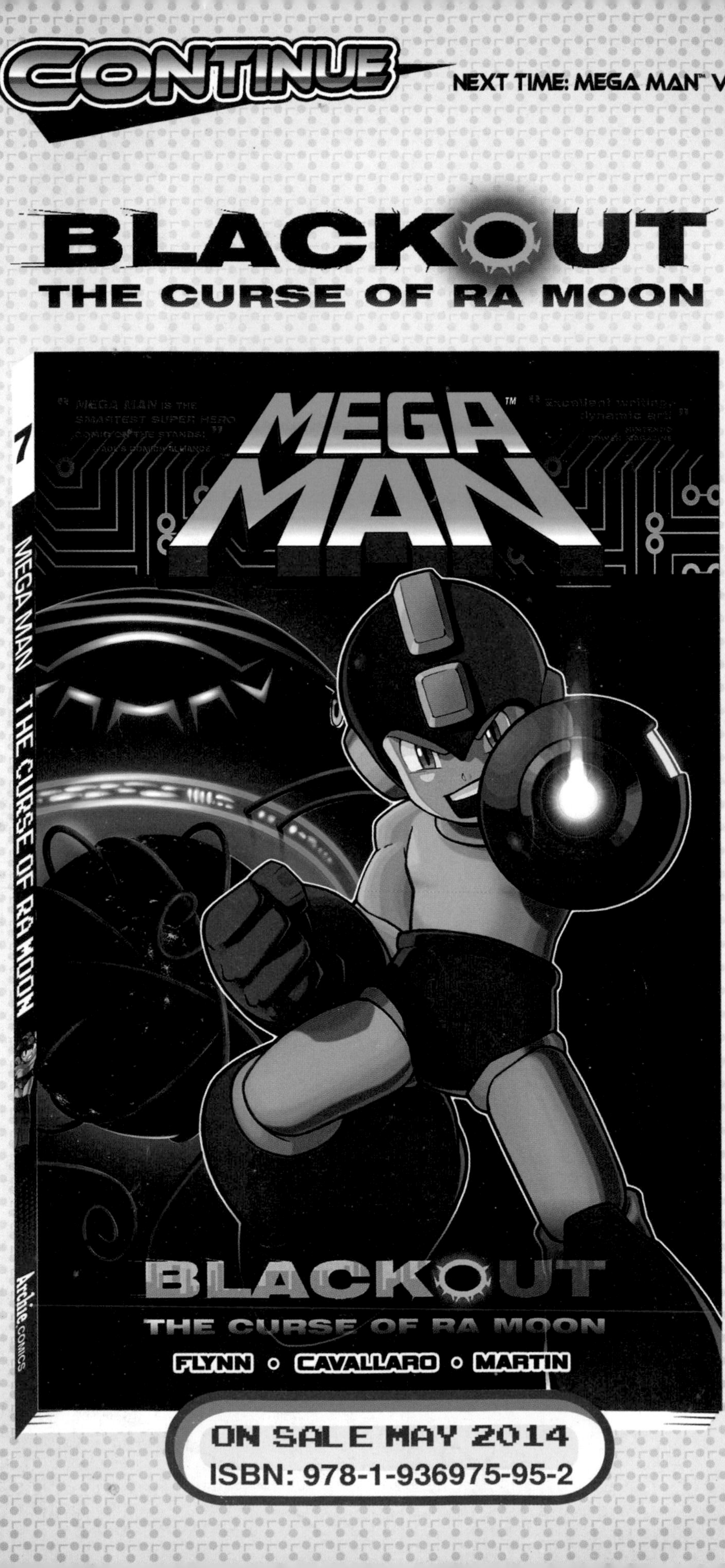

"MEGA MAN IS THE SMARTEST SUPER HERO COMIC ON THE STANDS!"
MEGA MAN™
"dynamic art!"
7
MEGA MAN THE CURSE OF RA MOON
Archie COMICS
BLACKOUT
THE CURSE OF RA MOON
FLYNN • CAVALLARO • MARTIN

ISBN: 978-1-936975-95-2

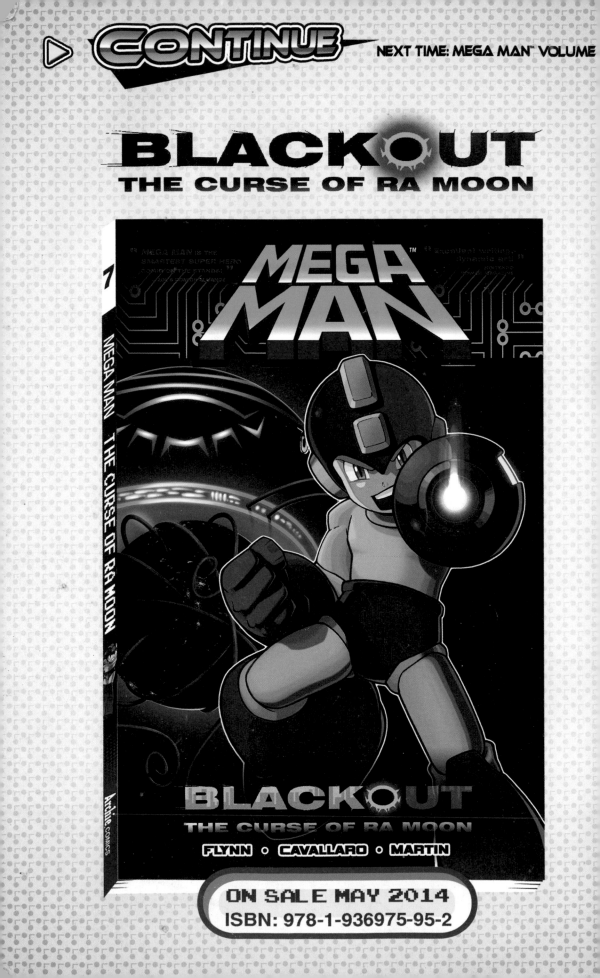